PENGUIN BC
SMALL REMI

Shashi Deshpande is the author of five n _____ _mall Remedies, including *That Long Silence* which won the Sahitya Akademi Award. Her publications include five collections of short stories, four books for children and two short crime novels. Her works have been translated into various European and Indian languages.

Shashi Deshpande is married and has two sons. She lives in Bangalore with her husand Dr D.H. Deshpande.

Also in Penguin by Shashi Deshpande

The Binding Vine
The Dark Holds No Terrors
The Intrusion and Other Stories
A Matter of Time
That Long Silence
The Narayanpur Incident *(Puffin)*

Small Remedies

Shashi Deshpande

PENGUIN BOOKS

Penguin Books India (P) Ltd., 11 Community Centre, Panchsheel Park, New Delhi 110 017, India
Penguin Books Ltd., 27 Wrights Lane, London W8 5TZ, UK
Penguin Putnam Inc., 375 Hudson Street, New York, NY 10014, USA
Penguin Books Australia Ltd., Ringwood, Victoria, Australia
Penguin Books Canada Ltd., 10 Alcorn Avenue, Suite 300, Toronto, Ontario M4V 3B2, Canada
Penguin Books (NZ) Ltd., Cnr Rosedale & Airborne Roads, Albany, Auckland, New Zealand

First published in Viking by Penguin Books India 2000
Published in Penguin Books 2001

Copyright © Shashi Deshpande 2000

This is a work of fiction. Names, characters, places and incidents are either the product of the author's imagination or are used fictitiously, and any resemblance to any actual person, living or dead, events, or locales is entirely coincidental.

All rights reserved

10 9 8 7 6 5 4 3 2 1

Typeset in Sabon by Digital Technologies and Printing Solutions, New Delhi

Made and printed in India by Swapna Printing Works (P) Ltd.

This book is sold subject to the condition that it shall not, by way of trade or otherwise, be lent, resold, hired out, or otherwise circulated without the publisher's prior written consent in any form of binding or cover other than that in which it is published and without a similar condition including this condition being imposed on the subsequent purchaser and without limiting the rights under copyright reserved above, no part of this publication may be reproduced, stored in or introduced into a retrieval system, or transmitted in any form or by any means (electronic, mechanical, photocopying, recording or otherwise), without the prior written permission of both the copyright owner and the above-mentioned publisher of this book.

Acknowledgements

The epigraph has been taken from P. Lal's *The Golden Womb of the Sun* (Rig Vedic songs in a new transcreation). I am very grateful to Prof. Lal who, generous as always, has kindly allowed me to use the lines.

The Vishnu-stotra on p.80 comes from Poile Sengupta's play *Keats Was a Tuber*. I thank her for letting me use the verse in translation and for sharing with me the story of how she got the lines from a speech of Prof. Radhakrishnan, then the President of India, who himself heard the lines being chanted by a devotee in a temple.

Acknowledgements

Father of the earth,
        protect us;
Father of the sky,
        protect us;
Father of the great and shining waters,
        protect us,
— *To which God shall we offer our worship?*

Rig Veda, Màndala X, Song 121

Prologue

This is Som's story. Or rather, Joe's story as related to us by Som. To me, the two men, narrator and object, are equally part of the story; to remember it is to think of both of them. Looking back now, from this point of time, it is clear to me that the story was not so much told to us, as offered to us by Som. It was his tribute to Joe.

At that time, only a few months after Joe's death, we needed to bring him back amongst us, to fill the empty space of his absence with memories, to conjure up the man, recreate him through words. Already by then, the fog of bereavement had lifted a little, our wounds were gradually healing. It was possible to think of Joe, to speak of him, without pain or melancholy, with laughter and amusement even. And yet, we were close enough to the time of his living for our memories to be fresh and fluid, not set as yet into a rigid shape. So that the story we heard came out alive, with the stamp of truth on it.

It was to be Joe's farewell party. After thirty years of association with the hospital and college, after having been a teacher to generations of students, Joe was clearly to have not just one farewell party, but many. This one, however, was to be the most special one, hosted by his own 'unit' of students and assistants, 'a party to end all parties', 'the mother and father of all farewell parties'—these, obviously, not Som's own words, but hyperboles used by the students themselves as they made their plans. Plans, which indeed culminated in the longest party on record, beginning in the early afternoon with a movie and ending late night after dinner, with drinks—cocktails, Som said, once again, we could see, quoting—squeezed in between. It was, in effect, a two-session binge, so that those on duty in the afternoon could join it in the evening and, of course, the other way round as well. While a few lucky ones, like Som, whose off day it was, were part of the whole celebration.

They had arranged for a Western movie, for Joe's special benefit. He loved the genre, or so it was rumoured. A rumour that was, however, given the lie by his innocent remark: 'Why didn't anyone tell me about these things earlier, eh?'

'What movie was it?' Tony's question, Tony's curiosity surfacing, as it always did. Som, a lover of Hindi movies, fumbled for the title of the movie, gave up and went on to talk of Joe's treat to the students during the interval: ice-cream cones, which were rare and an unusual luxury then. Joe personally carried the cones around to each one of them, so inspired by the movie that he pointed the cones at them before handing them over, saying 'Bang bang' with a big grin. Som imitated Joe's gesture as he spoke these words himself, and we could see Joe's high spirits resurrected in him.

Finally, there was dinner at the Savoy. For many of them, it was their first time in such a place.

'Don't ask how much that cost, either. Between the drinks and the dinner, I was broke for the next two months. But it was worth it. Course after course after course.' Som would have gone on, trying to remember the dishes, reciting the list, if we hadn't stopped him.

And then it was over.

'We came out of the restaurant,' Som said and paused. On the brink, we guessed, of the punch line of his story. In the silence of that pause, I could see them standing on the pavement outside the restaurant, the sea breeze blowing on their hot, flushed faces, the excitement slowly fading, the racing pulses reluctantly slowing down to a normal regular throb. All of them still united by the companionship of the last

2

few hours, unwilling to move, to part, to end the evening, the celebration.

'And then Joe said . . .'

Som got up at this point, hiking up his trousers, leaning forward from the waist, looking from face to face, rubbing his hands together—he's a good actor, Som, he always was, and at that moment he was not just a man imitating Joe, but Joe himself.

'And then Joe said—*that was wonderful, absolutely wonderful. Shall we do this again tomorrow?*'

There must have been shouts of laughter from the students when Joe said this. Som waited for us to do the same, he seemed puzzled that the expected response was not coming, the beginnings of irritation showed on his face. But we were silent. Until then, it had come to us as a happy story, a story of people enjoying things together, enjoying being together, Joe at the centre of it, his lovableness radiating outwards, touching everyone, as it always did, even though we were listening to something that had happened long back. But suddenly, at that moment, we felt his presence among us. The silence was *our* tribute to him, it came out of the reminder of our loss.

In a moment, however, we began to laugh. Som relaxed, sat down and said, 'That's better, that's more like it. I was wondering what's wrong with you people.'

And then I spoke.

'*In the life of one man, never the same time returns.*'

I said this in my natural voice, not the declaiming one that puts quote marks round the words. So that, for a moment, they did not realize the words were not my own. Except Tony, of course. But in an instant the laughter ceased and amusement vanished from the room. My words were like a drop of black ink in a glass of clear water, staining it, darkening it. Suddenly the mood changed.

We were friends, the four of us there, Chandru, Som,

Tony—no, we were five of us, for Rekha was there too, already by then a part of Tony's life; I can see her looking anxiously at Tony, watching his reaction to the mention of a not-so-long dead father. Yes, we were friends, but it was not friendship that united us at that moment, it was something else. We were like strangers who come together in the face of a common disaster, the hijacked passengers of a plane, the group in a bus which has broken down in the middle of nowhere. Strangers coming together to confront a common enemy. It was my 'never' that took us to the edge of an abyss, a dark endless hole we found ourselves looking into fearfully. Yes, it was fear that invaded us then, consternation that replaced mirth. And it was I who had brought these things among us.

Tony took over then, completing the quote, racing through the words, joining them in one garbled tangle.

'*Onlythefoolfixedinhisfollythinkshecanturnthewheelwhich turnshim.*'

'T.S. Eliot,' he said. '*Murder in the Cathedral*'. His tone brisk, matter-of-fact, like a man dusting his hands. Then speaking to me, in a chiding tone, 'Show off!'

At which the hole disappeared and we moved back from the precipice, disaster staved off. Tony's rejoinder seemed such a natural response then, meaning no more than what we saw—Tony putting me in my place, Tony making sure he wasn't left behind in the game of quotes he and I often played. But now, looking back, I think: Tony knew what he was doing. He spoke at that moment, he said what he did, on purpose. He saw the abyss, he wanted to get away from it, he wanted to draw us back from that fearful emptiness.

When I think of this story—and I do so often—I remember not only Joe, but Som too, and his pleasure in reviving those moments of happiness. Now, for the first time, my own words come back to me, the line I quoted haunts me and I wonder: why did I say that line? What brought it into my mind then? A stray impulse? Some thought that connected to it, a thought I've now forgotten? A desire, like Tony said, to show off? Or was it none of these things, but something outside me, instead, that propelled me into saying that line, a force, a factor over which I had no control? A kind of nudge, a warning of the shadow waiting for us in the future?

The moment of knowledge. And I, the Eve, offering it to the three males there. Adam must have looked at Eve the way the three males looked at me at that moment. The apple of knowledge set against the illusion of Paradise. Who needs it? And why do you bring it to us?

I still have my copy of *Murder in the Cathedral* with me. My text in my final year of B.A. Heavily marked from the time I studied it. These lines too have been underlined, *v.imp.* scribbled beside them in the margin. I am sure I have written the meaning of the line, the implication of the words, their significance in the text, somewhere. But it's only now that I know what they mean, what the words really say. They say that each experience is single and unique. That it can never be repeated or replicated. It means that you can never get the same joy ever again, what's gone is lost forever. That Time moves on relentlessly and you have to go along with it.

The line tells me of the totality of loss, the irrevocability of it.

5

Part One

1

I wake up to the sound of voices. Emerging from the drifting mists of early morning sleep, I slowly become aware that these are children's voices. Singing. Young voices meeting in a slightly disharmonious whole. I can't make out the words of the song or even what language it is in; they are still too far away for me to be able to get anything more out of it than a periodic rise and fall of sound. I lie back and let the distant music wash over me. The voices come closer. Yes, it is a Hindi song, a patriotic song. I think of Leela's accounts of the 'prabhat pheris' of her youth: groups marching in the early morning, singing patriotic songs. But that was during the freedom struggle. Who's interested in these songs now?

The early morning silence confers a crystalline clarity on the sound. These are very young children—I can scarcely differentiate between the male and the female voices. I sit up— the window next to the bed is so low that I can look through it even while lying down. But the high wall of the compound obstructs my view. I can see nothing. There are only these queerly disembodied voices which are now moving away. When the last bit of the song turns the corner, I see a head moving across my vision, a person taller than the rest, the head moving with the swiftness of someone running. Then it disappears, as also the song. Silence flows back and with it the more mundane morning sounds: the tinkle of a cycle bell, someone clearing his throat, a man calling out something— milk, I imagine—the short bark of a dog. I think of the coincidence of my waking up on my first morning here to the sound of music. Is this a happy augury? But do I, can I, believe in things like happy auguries any more?

It has not been a good night. I woke up often, startled out of my sleep by something that evaded me on waking, yet left me with an unease that made it difficult to get back to sleep again. Some time—I didn't know what the time was, though there was the feeling of its being that heavy black time between midnight and pre-dawn—the uneasiness turned to a physical one. I needed the bathroom, my bladder was full. I felt reluctant to open the door and face the unknown territory outside. It was late when I got here last night. From the little I saw of the house, I knew there would be only one toilet in this house—the one I used last night, at the back of the house. I would have to traverse the entire length of the house to get to it.

Finally I had to get up. It seemed strange, unnerving almost, to find myself moving from room to room, each one exactly the same in the dark, so that I began to wonder whether I was going round in circles, coming back to the same point over and over again. All the doors were open. I could sense the presence of humans when I passed one. It was reassuring, like the sounds of a ticking clock I had left behind, which told me I was moving on. It seemed odd, the young couple leaving their bedroom door open when there was a stranger in the house. I had almost despaired of finding the bathroom—did I dare look for a switch, wake my hosts by switching on the lights?—when the ghostly light of a mirror on the wall told me I was in the corridor of the toilet block. The opening and closing of the bathroom door, the whoosh of the water flushing down the pan—all these sounds were magnified in the silent night, but on my return I heard the same steady breathing in the occupied bedroom. I had not woken them up. Already, on my return journey there was, thankfully, a feeling of familiarity; I knew the darkness, if not the rooms.

10

My room is now filled with the early morning light. It is possible to get out of bed, to move about the house without worrying about disruptive sounds. Nevertheless, I wait patiently in my room until, nearly half an hour later, she comes to see if I'm awake. To tell me tea will be ready in a few minutes. Will I join her or should she get my tea here to my room?

They are extremely conscious of my presence. I can see that they have altered the contours of their morning for me. I suspect the cups have been brought out in my honour; I notice the everyday mugs hanging from the shelf in the kitchen. The teapot, too, is patently unused. She handles it clumsily, she can't open the lid without fumbling. He takes his cup and with a murmured 'good morning' moves away. She and I are left to ourselves and to a rather stilted, uneasy conversation. She sits dutifully before me, yawning at irritatingly frequent intervals, rumpling her hair after each yawn, as if it helps to wake her up. Her face is flushed and slightly sulky, telling me she is not used to waking up so early, that she has made the effort for my sake.

He goes off to work in a while and she and I have the house to ourselves. It's a large house, nevertheless we keep blundering into each other and I have the sense of being a huge intrusive presence. During breakfast she speaks of her plans and asks me about mine. She's going to work late today, she'll be home in the morning so that she can help me to get to know the house and its routine. There's a cook who will come later to prepare lunch. Do I want to go to Savitribai's house before lunch or after?

I haven't thought of visiting her today, I don't have any definite plans about seeing her, but now it is impossible to say this.

'After lunch, maybe,' I reply.

She looks relieved. This fits into her plans. 'I'll take you there,' she says. 'I'll show you the way. You can walk back

11

home, it's not too far.'

Relieved to have got this out of the way, she relaxes and begins to flood me with questions. Practical things. Like, am I a vegetarian? They are, but if I want eggs . . . ? Is the room comfortable for me? What do I usually have for breakfast? Was the bed comfortable? Were there mosquitoes? Will I tell her if there's anything I need? There's a boiler for hot water in the bathroom, I need to switch it off when I have had my bath.

I am overwhelmed. After the isolation of the last few months, this makes me feel a little giddy. Interacting with humans seems to deprive me of air, it leaves me short of breath. Is this, my coming here, a mistake? But what better alternative did I have? This is a small town. I don't know if there are any hotels. Even if there are, a single female can't stay in one. And I'm likely to be here for some time. How much time? One month? Two months? And after that . . . ? I don't want to think of that. Yet the fact remains that I have to live here for some time. And that when I accepted their offer of hospitality, I hadn't thought of this, that I would become part of the life of two total strangers, live in such close contiguity with them. This is like my first few days in the hostel, when the thought of being with so many strangers was daunting, my loneliness emphasized by being in their midst.

Does Savitribai know I am here? she is going on. Do I want to ring her up before we go?

I can see she's looked up the number, she's ready to give it to me if I want to make the call. I think of this girl preparing for my arrival, getting things ready for me, and I wonder why she is taking so much trouble.

No, I tell her, I don't want to ring her up, we'll just go. I know Savitribai has been ill, that she hasn't fully recovered as yet. There's scarcely any chance that she will go out anywhere, is there?

She's ready to leave before I am. With her helmet on, her face takes on a martial air, it looks square and determined.

She's attentive to my comfort. Have I done this before, riding pillion on a scooter? She will try to go slow, she hopes I'll be okay.

On the way, she points out spots to me, accompanying this with a kind of tourist-guide patter. That's the bus stop nearest to the house. The rickshaw stand is over there. There are some shops here, but the real market is a little way off. Her bank is in the marketplace, she can always get me what I need. I mustn't hesitate to tell her. We move off the main road into a lane with small shops that open straight on to the road, and then to a bigger but quieter road. There are no shops now, only houses here, all fairly new houses. This is, obviously, a residential locality. We turn the corner and, 'this is the beginning of Savitribai's bungalow', she says. We go along the remnants of a wall till we get to an opening without a gate. Only the two posts are left. The house is at the end of a curved driveway, a large British era building. A bungalow with a tiled roof, an imposing portico in front and covered verandas along the sides.

She can come back to pick me up and take me home, she says. I can ring her up at her bank. Really, it's no trouble at all, she can always get away from her work for a few minutes.

I dissuade her, I promise I'll ask someone the way and watch her drive away. It's a relief to be free of her concern, yet when I see her receding back, I feel a little lost. Now that the scooter has moved away, leaving behind a silence, I can hear music. The door is open, but I don't see a bell. I can't just walk in. How do I get in? I should have rung up after all, I could have asked the girl to do it for me.

I am preparing to knock when a child runs into the portico. She sees me, stops, goes back in, and returns with a woman. The girl's mother, I guess, interrupted in her work, wiping her hands on her sari which the child is holding in a tight, accustomed grip. Like the child, the woman goes back in without a word. In a moment the music stops. Another

13

woman comes out and looks inquiringly at me. What language do I speak to her in?

'I've come from Bombay,' I begin hesitantly in Hindi.

The inquiring look vanishes. 'You're the writer, Doctor saheb's friend.' She is speaking in Marathi. 'Please come in and sit down. I'll tell Baiji you're here.'

She leads me right into the house. I'm too tense to look around me, I sit in the room she's left me in, my hand in my lap, listening to the murmur of voices from the next room. What did Chandru think he was doing, pushing me into this? Rehabilitating me? But this is a professional job, it's not for me. The voices stop and my guide comes out with a much older woman.

I remember Savitribai as a small-sized woman. Even from my child's perspective she had seemed petite. Age and illness have so shrunk her that she's a doll-sized woman now. She was also, in my eyes, a very beautiful woman, but my standards had not been very high. How many attractive women had there been in Neemgaon? The only women I'd known were the drab, badly dressed mothers of my friends. Naturally, Savitribai with her fair complexion, her gold-bordered sarees and pearls had stood out among the tired, shabby women I saw around me. Now I realize that she must indeed have been very attractive. Vestiges of that beauty remain. The skin is fine and delicate, even if it is crinkled like tissue paper. Her arms are still slim and firm, but the hands, with their branching of veins, seem incongruously large for those delicate arms. And her hair, that glossy, shining cap of hair I remember, is so sparse that the central parting has become a wide expanse. It is her eyes that have surrendered to age the most. The once dark sparkling eyes now have a frosty white veneer that speaks of cataracts.

Her disability proclaims itself in her shuffling walk and the arm hanging by her side, but once seated, she looks perfectly normal. I had expected that she would speak first of Chandru,

14

her doctor and my friend, the man who got me here. I thought she would speak of our past association, of my father who was her doctor in Neemgaon, of our being neighbours, I thought she would refer to Munni, that she would call me, as she used to, 'Munni's friend'. Why else, but because of our Neemgaon association, had she consented so readily to Chandru's suggestion that I write this book?

It doesn't happen this way. She's very businesslike. I'm here for a purpose, she recognizes that, and it is about that purpose that she wants to talk. She begins to cross-examine me, not on my credentials—she seems to accept that I am a writer—but on what I know about her. Have I read any articles about her? The interviews? She's got cuttings of most of them, she'll give me the lot. There's a book on her, have I read that? I shouldn't. The man who wrote it is an ignorant fool, he knows nothing about music, nothing about her music. She wants me to ignore that book.

Then she becomes practical. Do I have a tape recorder? If I haven't, I should get one. She wants me to listen to her when she is speaking, she hates being interrupted, being asked to repeat herself. It disturbs her when people, instead of listening to her, keep scribbling notes.

Tea arrives while she is speaking, brought out by the child's mother. The child is still hovering near her mother, but she stays outside the room, awed—or frightened?—by Savitribai, finger in mouth, eyes wide open, staring at us.

'Drink your tea.' She speaks to me as to a child. And remains silent until I pick up my tea and finish it. When I put down my cup she says abruptly, 'Call that girl.'

Girl? Which girl? Does she mean the woman who seated me here? Fortunately the woman comes in herself, saving me from the awkwardness of looking for her.

'I'm tired now,' the old woman says, speaking to neither of us. And turning to the woman, 'Tell her what time she is to come tomorrow.'

15

I wait until she returns after helping the old woman in. 'Can you come a little earlier tomorrow?' she asks me. 'She's at her best after her bath. She gets tired by this time of the day.'

We agree on the time. She's showing me out when two men enter. Very obviously twins. They look at me with identical expressions of surprise, gazing at me over their shoulders while they go to the corner behind the door to shed their slippers. Their movements, when they do this, are as synchronized as those of a pair of dancers.

'This is the writer from Bombay,' the woman tells them. 'She is going to write the book on Baiji.'

In perfect unison they smile, nod, fold their hands together in a respectful namaste.

The writer from Bombay. It's an identity so new, so strange, it feels like a disguise.

A writer.

'I haven't written anything,' I argue with Chandru when he suggests I take on the work of writing Savitribai's biography.

'You were working with *City Views*, weren't you? As Assistant Editor?' He pronounces the title as if it nails down my writer status.

'That was—*you* know what that was. Hamidbhai's hobby, really. Kind of amateur journalism. It doesn't really count.'

'But you did write, and some of those pieces you wrote were good. Everyone admired them. And don't forget, you also wrote Hamidbhai's biography.'

'Well, yes . . .'

'In fact, that's what made me think of you. I found my copy the other day and thought—why doesn't Madhu write this book on Savitribai? I gave the book to Yogi and Maya and they liked it a lot, yes, really they did.'

Chandru is determined I will do this thing. He has planned it, though he's trying to make me think he hasn't, that things happened by chance as he says they have. Impatience is showing on his face, in his voice; he wants to help, he is doing me a favour and damn it, I can't turn it down! At other times, this impatience would have turned to temper. But this is no longer possible for him. Now I'm a bereaved person, a bereaved *mother*. He has to be careful in dealing with me.

'If you could write that book, why not this one?'

'Chandru, that was—well, it was only a small booklet. This one has to be different.'

'Well, meet Yogi at least. Listen to him. After reading that book, both Maya and he are confident you can do the job.'

The book is on the table between us when I go to meet Yogi. It looks a bit pathetic—shabby and infinitely thin—on Yogi's brand new, large table. Everything is squeaky new here—the office, the furniture, his role as publisher, my role as writer. The photograph of Yogi and Maya on the table, taken on their honeymoon, proclaims his new husband status as well.

'I'm sorry Maya isn't here,' he says to me.

We are both uneasy, we're not comfortable with each other. We've scarcely met. Chandru's friendship with Som and me has not been able to embrace his wife and children, and his daughters are almost strangers to us. They have daunted me, since they grew up, with their smooth sophistication. These two now, Maya and Yogi, they're like one of those couples who feature in glossy magazines, they seem as distant to me as the pictures in those magazines. Nevertheless, I'm 'auntie' to Maya and I can see him fumbling with that, unsure about what to call me, wanting to keep this meeting on a professional level, not wholly at ease about doing it this way, either. And there's something more than social awkwardness. He's been warned by Maya, he's been told to keep off certain subjects. He's doing that, treading carefully through topics, as if he's walking on a minefield. There's this huge fact of what happened to Som and me, the fact of our son's death, lying between this young man and me. Even silence becomes a needle-prick reminder of my loss.

'Maya wanted to be here to finalize this with you, but she's held up, she should be back in a fortnight . . .'

He realizes he's said this twice before, his embarrassment shows. He takes hold of himself and moves on to the next thing.

'Will you have some tea?' he asks.

He rings a bell and tells the boy who appears, to bring the tea. It comes, not in shabby mugs, but in elegant china. There's a film of dust on the cups and saucers, they look like they've just been removed from the packing case. As he pours out the tea, concentrating on the clear stream, steadying it, I get a flash of insight into his mind. This is something he has dreamt of: being a publisher, receiving authors, having tea with them. But—am I the author they want? Will I be able to write the book that will launch them on this career? Chandru, I'm sure, has hustled them into this, I have an idea that he's financing the project as well. Nevertheless, the young man's doubts begin to reveal themselves.

'You've written this.' He pats the book between us. 'Papa—my father-in-law—' he corrects himself, 'says you knew Savitribai.'

'Years ago. And very briefly. She was our neighbour when we were in Neemgaon—but only for a year or two. I've never seen her after that.'

'I believe she was very pleased at the idea of your doing this book.'

'So Chandru says.'

'Maya and I are very excited about this.'

Savitribai should be a fascinating subject, don't I agree, he asks. And there's the long association with the family, Chandru's father being her doctor, now Chandru himself . . .

'It seems kind of right that this should be our first book.'

Yogi comes from a business family, I know it's business rather than sentiment that is the impetus for this book. He

18

reveals this himself, when he artlessly tells me about the survey Maya and he made before they embarked on the project.

'Fiction is dicey, poetry is out—nobody buys poetry—travel and cookbooks sell, but they're expensive to produce, you need photographs and all that. So we thought, why not biographies? They are always interesting and it's quite the trend now, isn't it?'

Yes, retired bureaucrats, politicians, film stars, acquitted murderers, policemen, businessmen—everyone is writing an autobiography or getting a biography written. But I don't say this and he goes on with his patter.

'Everyone likes to read about real people. And Savitribai's life has been so controversial, it can't not attract attention. And controversy. Her life is almost like a novel, from what I hear. An exciting novel.'

A novel? An exciting novel? Is that what they expect? Now I have to say something.

'You know I'm not a writer in that sense? Not a creative writer, I mean?'

He knows, he says. But that's not a problem, he assures me. Maya is there, she will help me, once I get the material. She'll be with me, we can work together, she and I . . .

'. . . and of course, the biggest advantage you have is that Savitribai knows you, which means she'll open up to you more than she will to anyone else.'

Now he gets down to practical matters. His pedigree shows; he's clear about details, and very businesslike. He speaks about the contract, about payments.

'You will have to go to Bhavanipur. You know she fell ill while she was there, and stayed on?'

I do. Chandru has told me that.

'Can you go and stay there for a while? You may have to, for a month or so at least.'

I'm ready to go. I have no problems. Yes, any time, I tell him.

19

Have I thought about a place to say, he asks me. He has, or rather, Chandru has. There's a patient of Chandru's in Bhavanipur and Chandru can write to him and ask him to fix me up some place, in his own home, maybe. Is that okay by me?

Anything. Anytime. Anywhere.

But before Chandru can hear from his patient—a patient's son, Chandru corrects me—I get a letter myself from Bhavanipur. From an unknown person. No, two of them, actually, for there are two signatures at the bottom. Hari and Lata. They've heard from Ravi Patil—Chandru's patient's son—that I am going to write Savitribai's biography and that I will be coming to Bhavanipur to meet her. They've also heard that I'm looking for a place to stay. Would I consider being their guest? They have a large house, with rooms to spare. I can be independent, I can have my privacy. And, of course, I'm free to ask Dr Dave to make inquiries about them from Ravi Patil.

I don't bother. I write back immediately, accepting the offer. It has the finality of signing a contract. And then I tell Som about it. I can see his relief. He's known about Chandru's plans, he's been hoping I would agree to do the book.

I don't want Som to see me off, but he does. Station platforms, specially in Bombay, are not places for speaking. In any case, Som and I have nothing to say. We've already spoken of the practicalities of my leaving home for a while. Now he waits patiently outside my window—a patience that is so alien to him, it arouses a faint pity in me—waiting for the train to leave. He's done all the things he should. He's got me some magazines to read, arranged my bag neatly under my berth, put a bottle of water on the table between the berths. There's nothing more to be done. There's no pretence of conversation between us, he stands outside silent and motionless. When the whistle goes, he looks at me. I have a feeling he wants to say something, but the train has begun moving, slowly, and it's too late. He stands still while people move around him, jostling, shoving, running.

In spite of being a slapdash kind of household, there's no chaos in it; only the disorder that comes from constant flux, the movement of life. Though their work timings keep them pinned down to some semblance of a routine, their lives have a sense of fluidity; they are always, it seems to me, on the brink of change, ready for it. The house is their ally in this, enabling them to live a nomadic existence within it. The bewilderment I had experienced on my first night's wandering within it was not just a middle-of-the-night-in-a-strange-house confusion. The house *is* strange. All the rooms—and there are many of them—are of the same shape, almost the same size, each one with shelves along the walls at shoulder height. The rooms are sparsely furnished and suitable for any purpose, which makes it possible to have all of them in use. The transistor, which she carries about with her when she's home, gives an indication of her movements and whereabouts, but his is a much more silent presence.

The fixed points in this house are the swing, an old style wooden one, with decorative brass studs on the wooden base, and the parrot's cage, both of which are in the front hall. She calls it a parrot—Popat-master, actually is her name for it—but I wonder whether it is, in fact, one. Are parrots so large? It does have green wings and a red beak, though the large feathers are as dishevelled as a girl's party dress at the end of a long evening She speaks to the bird as she would to a human, an inmate of the house. It speaks too. I was startled the first night to hear it suddenly breaking into words, the same words over and over again. 'He's home, he's home,' it says, using the plural for 'he', like someone speaking of a superior, or a woman of her husband. At other times it repeats the words 'go inside, go inside,' this time spoken in the intimate singular. (She has translated these words for me, the parrot's language, like hers, being Kannada.)

'Oh shut up you!' she calls out when it goes on and on, but it won't stop until she comes to it and ruffles its feathers. Sometimes it lets out a wordless frightened squawk. 'That's the cat,' she says and flies out swiftly. I hear her shouting 'shoo, shoo' loudly and angrily to the cat. I've seen it prowling round the house, tiptoeing almost, in a dainty, furtive kind of way, its back arched, tail up, in search, it would seem, of something. I see it walk away when she runs after it, tail still high, giving an impression now of offended dignity. Its going away has nothing to do with her, it's leaving on its own, don't think otherwise.

'Happy?' she comes back and asks the parrot, but it has lapsed into silence after her battle on its behalf, disowning, like the cat, the brief hostilities with an unseen enemy. This is a drama that's enacted every day, she and the parrot playing their role each time with the same frenzied energy, the cat with the same absolute disdain.

'My father-in-law,' she calls the parrot. At night when she has cleaned the cage, given it a bowl of water and thrown a cloth over the cage, she sighs. 'I can relax now that my father-in-law has gone to sleep.' The cat, of course, is the enemy. She calls it 'my mother-in-law'.

The house is her family home. This is obvious, not only from her familiarity with the house and everything in it, but her interaction with the neighbours. He lives like a guest, but that perhaps, is part of his reclusive nature. I scarcely see him, except on waking and during dinner at night. She has given up her attempts to wake up early for my sake. I make my own tea now, and a cup for him as well, once I realized he wakes up just a little after I do. He takes the cup from me and vanishes with a murmured 'thanks', going to the front hall with his tea, while I go to the side-room, as they call it, which overlooks the garden. In the evenings, I keep out of their way until she calls out to me, 'Dinner is ready, Kaku.' Yes, I'm Kaku. It doesn't mean anything, it's as meaningless an appellation as 'auntie', really. This is what I tell myself, yet each time she calls me 'Kaku', I am both startled and uneasy.

Sundays are different. This is my third Sunday here and I'm already familiar with its shape. They wake up much later than they do on other days. I've had my bath by the time they're up. Once up, she moves about swiftly, as if the longer sleeping hours have energized her. She makes tea for all of us and then settles down to the serious business of cleaning her scooter. I can see it is an important ritual for her. The house is rarely dusted, things lie where they are until, suddenly, with an exclamation of impatience, she attacks everything with a duster. But the scooter obviously is different. She collects the bucket, soap, mops and begins with gusto, making soft, hissing sounds from between her teeth while she works. Sometimes I imagine I can hear soothing murmurs, like a person addressing a pet being bathed. When it's done and the scooter is dry and shining, she gives it a pat, looking at it thoughtfully and affectionately, admiring, I can see, her own work. At which point he says, speaking from behind the paper, 'Why don't you do my bike now?'

'That! It needs to be dipped in the lake.'

A weekly exchange. And a signal as well, for at this point he laughs, folds the newspaper he's been reading and goes to the nearby Udipi restaurant to get us some breakfast. It comes in banana-leaf parcels which he unpacks and transfers into vessels. When he's set the table and the banana leaves, and string and plastic bags have been put away, it looks like a home-made breakfast, but sumptuous and with more variations than a made-at-home one. He has the same thing each Sunday—a masala dosa. She asks for something different each time, bitterly regrets her choice when it comes, and has a bit of his dosa, and something from what I've ordered.

After this, their day splays out into unexpected shapes. At

SHASHI DESHPANDE

least, I imagine it does, because they go out—they don't tell me where and I don't ask, either—and return at different times. Sometimes within an hour, sometimes late at night. She worries about leaving me alone. The cook has an off-day on Sundays, should she cook something for me, am I sure I can manage, should she ask the cook to cook something extra on Saturdays, do I know where the things are? So she goes on until he hustles her out. The sound of the motorbike recedes and the day is mine.

They have made room for me in their home and their lives with a generosity I cannot but admire. And also wonder at. Why are they taking so much trouble for a stranger? Nevertheless, it is a relief to be alone, not to have to keep up a front, not to have to respond to their overtures, their kindness.

Today is a grey monsoon day. It's drizzling, a rain that's so soft and fine that it scarcely percolates through the dense foliage of the large neem tree outside. An occasional drop comes through at irregular intervals, the drops combining to create a soft earth-meeting plop that joins the other rainy day sounds. The tree blocks out the light in this room even on sunny days. Today, the dim light has a greenish quality, there's a cavernous underwater feeling in the room.

I get myself another cup of tea and switch on the tape recorder.

24

2

I have had five meetings with Savitribai until now. I have not
addressed her directly so far, it's easy to avoid that, but I
think of her as Bai myself. To her household, she is Bai-ji or
Bai-saheb. Though I've begun to identify the others in this
household, I know only the child's name, as yet. 'Sunita,
Sunita,' I hear her mother calling from the back of the house.
The child has been warned not to disturb us. I see her flashing
past the door, pausing for a moment to peer at us, and
vanishing before she can be spotted by Bai. The two men, the
twins I saw on my first day, are accompanists: the tabla and
the harmonium player. They are part of the classes that are
conducted for students. There are not many of them. There's a
group of children—I've heard the chorus of voices repeating
the elementary vocal exercises—a young married woman, and
a very shy and silent boy who makes his presence felt only
when he sings. The young woman, nameless still to me, for Bai
calls her 'that girl', is the one who conducts these classes. It's
her voice I hear instructing the students, singing with them,
and sometimes it's her voice alone, as if she's doing her riaz.
Who is she? A paid companion, a student, or one of the
family? Whoever she is, she is the one who looks after all of
Bai's needs, moving swiftly in and out of the room, doing
things without being told. Which doesn't prevent the old
woman from grumbling, 'Where's that girl, why is she never
here when she's needed?'

The entire household is organized around Bai's needs, her
imperatives. Tea has to be brought to me within five minutes
of my arrival. And never just tea alone, there's always

something to eat. If there's a sweet, there's something spicy as well, to take away the sweet taste from my mouth before I drink my tea. 'Come on, eat something,' Bai urges me hospitably. She won't let me off, she watches me silently and intently until I have done justice to what's offered. 'Have your tea while it's hot,' she says. But once I'm done and the tray taken away, she becomes businesslike. She needs to have everything in order before we begin: her reading glasses, her glass of water, my tape recorder placed just right so that it's exactly between the two of us. She's obviously fascinated by this instrument, she sets great store by it. The first day she grilled me about it. Do I know how to use it? Do I have the right kind of cassette? 'Remember,' she warned me, 'I won't repeat myself. If you lose something, it's gone, you won't get it again.'

The first day, before we began, she told me, 'Say the date, the time, your name, and that you are interviewing me.' She was instructing me—this is how it's done, this is how you should do it. Self-consciously, feeling faintly foolish, I had done so. 'Now, play it back,' she said. And the two of us solemnly listened to my voice saying these things.

'All right, now you can begin.'

There was silence.

'Well, start,' she said impatiently. 'Where do you want me to begin? Ask me.'

'*I was born* . . .' Joe flashed through my mind, Joe giving me the book, telling me, '*David Copperfield*, one of the greatest books ever written. Read it.'

'Where do you want me to begin?' she repeated.

'With your childhood?' I am tentative, but it's enough for her.

'All right.'

And then, like a schoolgirl repeating her lessons, a child reciting a poem she's learnt by heart, she began, speaking carefully into the recorder, enunciating her words with careful precision.

'I was my parents' first child, a very pampered child. My father was the eldest of three brothers, so I was the first grandchild in the family. There were the daughters' children, of course, but they didn't count. They were not really our family. Everyone made a great fuss of me, not only my parents and grandparents, but my uncles, my aunts—all of them. By the time I was two, I had almost my own weight in gold ornaments. We were a very wealthy family. Lakshmi has made her home in this family—that's what they used to say about us.'

I realized on that first day that she didn't really need my questions. They were just a formality, a duty I had to perform, the cue to set her off on her almost rehearsed speech. She already knew what she was going to say. All these things have been related by her so often that the matter has gelled into a definite shape. There can be no alteration.

'It was my mother who showed me the beauty of music. She had a sweet voice. She sang the sort of songs women sang then, aarti songs, ritual songs, stotras. When she sang the Ramraksha, it became something quite different from what it was when the women just recited it; the music transformed it altogether. I loved listening to her when she sang it. I even picked up a few verses on my own. She heard me singing these one day and she was surprised. And so pleased. She began to teach me after that. She'd just had a baby so she had a little free time. I used to go to her in the afternoons and she would teach me. Just us, no instruments or anything.'

Playing the tape in my own room, I let it run on, scarcely listening to the words recorded on it until it reaches the point when Bai speaks of a family gathering during which her mother, excited about the child's talent, prodded her to sing. And the child, not shy at all, happy to perform, to let the others see how good she was. But before she could complete the song, in fact, very soon after she began, the grandmother said, 'That's enough, child. We don't need to hear any more.' So that the child had to stop.

There is a pause in the tape at this point and it runs silently, soundlessly, for a few moments. I think of her face when she told me this story, when she came to this point—a confused, resentful look. The child's resentment at being interrupted, at being told to stop doing something she is enjoying—this was what I saw on her face. I knew then, even as she spoke, that this was not part of her much rehearsed story. It had slipped out of some deep recess in her memory, taking her unawares, surprising her.

'It's a wonderful instrument,' I had told Hamidbhai, asking him to buy one for the office. 'Switch it on, sit back and let people talk. I can then write it out at my leisure.'

But now, confronted by the need to transcribe all this material, I find myself at a loss. How do I do it? There's the language, first of all. I have to convert Bai's Marathi into English, the language I'm going to write the book in. I have to translate, to find the right equivalents for her words, so that there is no distortion, no loss. It's going to make the job harder, the fact that Bai's language, like that of so many women of her generation, is explicit, disdaining euphemisms, and carelessly interspersed with casual abuses. I also need to filter out what's irrelevant, all the trivia the tapes are recording. And there are the silences, the pauses—like this one. They are part of her narration, part of my script, as much as the words are. How am I going to do this?

I switch off the tape and begin to write. I have to begin sometime, somewhere. First spell out the identity of the woman I'm going to write about, perhaps. This is the chalked line on which I will have to walk.

'*Savitribai Indorekar. Doyen of Hindustani music. Belonging to the Gwalior gharana . . .*'

Savitribai Indorekar. I lived next door to her and knew her

28

for months before I knew this name. In Neemgaon she was 'the singer woman', and there was something derogatory about the words, yes, I can see that now, about the way they said them. To my father, she was 'Savitribai'. But when he said the name, when he spoke of her, there was respect and admiration in his voice. To Babu, she was *that bai*', by which he meant 'that woman'—the words accompanied by a movement of the head which said 'the woman next door', as well.as indicated a kind of rude contempt for her.

To me, she was Munni's mother. I knew her as Munni's mother. When I came here, it was to meet Munni's mother. But she hasn't spoken of Munni, not once. She has not identified me, either, as Munni's friend, or as the daughter of my father, her doctor and her admirer. I find it strange. Has she forgotten? Does she not remember those days at all? Am I nothing more than an unknown woman who's come here to speak to her before writing her biography? And why haven't I declared my identity to her, either? Why haven't I said, *I'm Munni's friend Madhu. Remember me?*

It's too late now. I could have done it earlier, but now it's no longer possible.

'My name is Meenakshi.'

She introduces herself to me without any preamble. Needlessly as well, for I haven't asked her what her name is.

It is an important moment for me, one I have been looking forward to ever since I knew that a family was moving in next door. The two houses, built by two brothers, are in the same compound, only a low mehendi hedge separating the two. My father calls them the Dada-Bhau houses, a joke, I realize later, taking off from 'twin houses'. We live in the larger, the 'Dada house'. The smaller one has been empty as far as I can remember. Now, at last, it's going to be occupied. As an only child and practically a neighbourless one, I'm famished for company. I keep looking out over the hedge to see if there are any children in the family. Any girls, I wonder hopefully. Perhaps, who knows, a girl of my age. But it's almost impossible to identify who's family and who are the visitors. There are a number of people going in and out, but most of them, disappointingly, are men.

And then, suddenly, here is this girl speaking to me across the hedge, saying, 'My name is Meenakshi. What's yours?'

'Madhu.'

'Madhu.' She repeats it, considers it and gives me her verdict. 'But that's a boy's name!'

Her disapproval and her scorn make me view my own name with doubt.

'I don't like my name,' I say to my father. 'It's a boy's name.'

'It means "sweet". Why can't it be a girl's name?'

'I don't like it. Can I change it?'

'What would you like to be called?'

I haven't thought about this. Meenakshi? No, that's tricky, she won't like it, she may laugh at me, something tells me she will. While I'm considering the possibilities, he offers me 'Madhumalati'.

'Your mother wanted you to be named Madhumalati.'

He sounds helpful, but there's something in his eyes that makes me feel he's amused. At my mother? At me?

'Madhumalati? No, it's too long.'

'Good.'

Even if there's no smile on his face, I can feel one behind it, lurking in his eyes, in his voice, making it crinkly.

But I'm ready to present the girl with this name, however long it is, if she ridicules 'Madhu' once again. However, she's moved on to other things and I have other areas of my life to defend. Like my dresses—why do I wear such old-fashioned frocks? Why do I never button them? And why am I so scared of Babu? He's only a servant, isn't he?

This is how our companionship begins, it is the shape of

things to come. She has the upper hand, she can make me believe what she wants me to believe, she can make me do what she thinks I should. But she fails in one thing: she can't make me call her Meenakshi. I call her Munni, like everyone else does.

I get the name from my father, the evening after my first meeting with her. 'Oh, so you've met Munni,' he says.

'Munni?'

'The girl next door—Savitribai's daughter. Didn't she tell you her name?'

She did. 'My name is Meenakshi' she had said. And I have to wonder—if she's Munni, why does she call herself Meenakshi? And if she is Meenakshi, why does everyone call her Munni? Evenings, if she stays on late in our house, we hear a voice calling out to her—'Munni, Munni'. She pretends she hasn't heard, but Babu asks her rudely, 'Are you deaf? You're wanted at home. Go on now.'

Our meetings are almost always in our house. She never invites me to hers. I'm dying to go in, but she does not give me a chance. It's quite unlike the other homes around us. And it's not just that there are always people going in and out, a pile of footwear perpetually outside the door, and cycles—sometimes a tonga, once or twice even a car—waiting outside the gate. No, it's not just these things—it's the air of excitement that emanates from the house, the same feeling that I have when I'm sitting in the audience, waiting for the curtain to go up, hearing a snatch of music from behind it, the single boom of the tabla, the tinkling of the dancer's bells. There's a thickening in my throat then, a breathlessness. It's the same now. It's because of the music that flows out of the house, the strum of the tanpura, the beat of the tabla, the human voice singing. In the mornings it goes *aa aa aa aa* or *sa sa sa sa*—the voice stretching, rising, dipping. Voice controlling exercises, though I don't understand this then. It is in the evenings that the real proper music, as I consider it, begins, with the tanpura, the tabla and the singer coming together. It continues until late night. I know my father goes there at times, he tells me before he does, but I can't go with him. 'Not now, it's late,' he says. 'You have to go to sleep.' He also adds, 'You won't enjoy that music.'

I'm as fascinated by Munni as by her home. Unlike most of the children I know, Munni appears to be free of all restrictions. She can go out anytime, anywhere. There are no rules binding her, neither mealtimes, nor resting times. She can do what she likes. Even I, who am more free than most children—my father rarely tries to control or restrict me—have Babu's tyranny to contend with, but Munni's activities are wholly unmonitored. The only control that's visible is the voice calling her in the evenings if she's late. A male voice. This, again, is part of the oddity of Munni's life. Fathers never interfere in children's lives, as far as I know; it's always the mother. But for Munni . . .

'He's not my father,' Munni says angrily to me. 'My father is in Pune. He's not here.'

'Then who is he? I thought he's your father.'

'Chhut!' she says emphatically. 'You're an idiot.'

She seems to dislike this man. I can see her pretending she hasn't heard him when he calls her and when she does finally go out, she tries to ignore him, evading him when he tries to touch her. He's a kind man. I think so, anyway. He smiles at me, he never goes past without speaking to me, he often gives me sweets—lemon drops, we call them. He's good-looking, too. He's fair—which is considered an essential part of good looks—and dresses differently from most of the men in Neemgaon. A sparkling white churidar and kurta and a waistcoat with a tiny brocade border. I think he looks wonderful. I wish my father dressed that way, and I tell him so. He thinks it over seriously and then regretfully says he can't. 'Doctors' clothes get dirty very quickly. I'd have to change three times a day if I wore white.'

32

'He's not my father,' Munni has told me, yet each time her mother goes out, he is with her. She comes out first—I watch her with avid interest—then he follows, walking slowly, looking around. For Munni? Sometimes there's a car waiting for them. She gets into it briskly, and, when he lingers, I see her hand waving imperiously to him through the window, a slim arm wearing gold bangles.

Munni's mother is beautiful. I've never seen anyone like her. She's always elegantly dressed. She wears beautiful nine-yard saris with a narrow gold border, pearls round her neck and flowers that show off the glossy darkness of her hair. A very far cry from all the mothers I know—harried creatures in drab saris, forever in the kitchen, endlessly preoccupied with food and children. To me, motherless child, growing up in an all-male household, Munni's mother spells an enchanting femininity. I ask my father if my mother was beautiful. He hesitates, then says, 'Yes, to me.'

'Like Munni's mother?'

He laughs at that. 'No, no, no, not at all, not at all like Munni's mother. Quite different, quite, quite different.'

I wonder at his emphatic assertions, his laughter, but leave it at that. Perhaps he realizes that I have a crush on Munni's mother and is amused by it. Munni herself rarely speaks of her own mother. Unusual, because most children are forever quoting their mothers, going on and on about 'my mother said . . . ' Not Munni, though.

She speaks a great deal of her father, however. She tells me, often, and very distinctly, that he is in Pune. In Shukurwar Peth, she says, as if it is important for her to locate him exactly. He's a lawyer, she tells me, a very famous lawyer. He earns a lot of money, thousands and thousands of rupees.

I believe her, I'm as impressed as she intends me to be, but I'm still curious.

'Who's this man then?'

'He? He plays the tabla for my mother.'

33

I believe this too, because I've seen them at a performance my father once took me to. Yes, he was playing the tabla while her mother sang. I believe her, I know she's speaking the truth, but there are others who don't. Babu, for one.

She is in our house one evening, refusing to go home, insisting she will have dinner with me.

'Don't you have your own home to go to?' Babu asks her.

'No,' she says cheekily and I admire her. I'm scared of Babu, I don't dare to talk back to him.

'No, I don't have a home. I'll eat here and sleep here and stay here—what will you do?'

'I'll throw you out.'

'I'll tell Doctor-kaka. He'll be angry with you, he'll throw *you* out.'

It's true that Babu is held in check by my father. My father never seems to dominate, but I know, and so does Babu, that he is the final authority.

Munni has dinner with us, the two of us served by a silent, surly Babu. A little later we hear the voice calling out, 'Munni Munni'.

'There! You have to go now. Your father is calling you home.'

She turns on Babu with a savagery that is quite unlike her earlier teasing, bantering tone. 'He's not my father, my father is in Pune.'

Munni soon becomes my best friend. I have dropped most of the others, who were never friends like Munni is, anyway. She is the most exciting friend I've ever had. If she bewilders me with her swift changes of moods, if at times she dominates me and bosses me around, there's still something about her that I enjoy—something that gives an edge of excitement to my days. The girls in our neighbourhood, who have barely tolerated me until now—most of them are older (so is Munni, actually, but she ignores the difference and so do I)—suddenly become regular visitors to my home. I'm pleased and flattered

34

that they want my company, but I soon realize that it's Munni they've come to see, Munni they're really interested in. And not to play with, but to interrogate.

They pretend they don't know her name.

'I'm Meenakshi,' she proclaims.

'But I thought your name was Munni.'

'No, my name is Meenakshi.'

'Then why does everyone call you Munni?'

'I don't know. My name is Meenakshi.'

She's becoming stubborn now. I've seen this mood before, she won't budge. They sense this, and go on to other questions.

'If your name is Meenakshi, why does your father have a Muslim name?'

'My father doesn't have a Muslim name. My father's name is Sadashivrao.'

'No, it's not. It's Ghulam Ahmed.'

'My father is Sadashivrao, he's in Pune.'

'If your father is there, why does your mother live here in Neemgaon?'

'I don't know, I don't know, I don't know.'

I can't understand why the questions make Munni so angry. Children are often asked questions, why is she so upset about these? She looks like a cornered animal when she stops answering and says 'I don't know' over and over again.

I want to help her, but I don't know how. I stand a little away, making it clear that I'm not on the side of her tormentors. Once, after the questioners have gone, she turns on me fiercely, screaming at me for doing nothing, for saying nothing, for being there—as if it is I who am her enemy. And once she breaks down, shouting at the girls, 'My father is in Pune, you don't know him, if I tell him, he'll kill you, he'll kill all of you . . .'

The cruelty of children: making fun of the old and the crippled, throwing stones at mad women, torturing puppies,

35

turning on one of their own, on the most vulnerable, the weakest. Sharpening their knives, flexing their muscles, preparing themselves for the much more sophisticated, much more savage games of cruelty they will play as adults. Is this where they came from, those people who ran amok on the streets, hurting, maiming, killing? Planting bombs in buildings, buses and cars, killing the innocent and the young? People so ensconced in their cruelty that they are impervious to human grief.

3

Each morning, at the time of waking, for a brief while I have a feeling of being back in my father's house in Neemgaon. The illusion soon fades. It's not only the language which I hear that's different, it's the kind of people who go past. Here, it's retired men going for walks, women to get the milk, students rushing to school, to college. And there's the sound, even if it's muted at this time of the morning, of rickshaws, scooters and buses—something that was not part of Neemgaon when I lived there. It must have changed now, irrigation has brought greater prosperity to it, prosperity has made it more populated. Neemgaon was much more rural then, surrounded by villages, its only distinction being the TB sanatorium established by an American Mission. Which was what took my father there, but neither her stay in the sanatorium, nor being in Neemgaon, a place that was regarded as being health-restoring, helped my mother. She died just the same.

Bhavanipur is a larger town with well-established schools and colleges, even, recently, a university. There's a kind of self-consciousness about the place. You get the feeling that it's aware of its position as a centre of learning and culture, as a town famous for its writers and musicians. Bai's Guruji, Kashinath Buwa, settled down here, in the vicinity of the Bhavani temple, in the last years of his life. It became a kind of focus for the Gwalior gharana after that, students coming from all parts of India to learn music from Guruji. Bai was one of them. She too came here to become Guruji's student. Unlike the men, however, she did not stay in Guruji's establishment in the temple, but here, in Bhavanipur town. The house she lived in has long since been demolished. There's an ugly two-storied building in its place now, with uniform rows of rooms on the two floors, which are let out to students. You can see the underwear and wet towels hanging on the railings of the balcony. The house Bai lived in was ramshackle even then, I'm told. Just two rooms with an outside toilet shared by others. No electricity, of course. And water had to be drawn from the well. She had to travel by the local shuttle train to get to Guruji's place, with a two-mile walk through the fields at the end of it.

All this is part of Bai's history, an important part of it. I think of it now, I imagine her, a young woman who had lived the sheltered life of the daughter-in-law of an affluent Brahmin family, living this kind of life. A woman who'd been, both as a child and as a married girl, part of a large family, living in a strange town among total strangers. With the added burden of being a Hindu woman, a married Hindu woman, living with a Muslim partner, and, of course, the greater alienation that not knowing a language brings. I don't know if, in her years here, she learnt Kannada. If she did, there's no trace of it left now. She speaks to everyone in Marathi, uncaring of whether the other person understands the language or not. The cook doesn't—I hear the young woman repeating the instructions to her after Bai has spoken. The twins don't speak it, either, though perhaps they do understand the language. I've seen them nodding when Bai speaks to them in Marathi, smiling, uttering small interjections in their bad Hindi.

The Tower of Babel syndrome—I heard a pediatrician use the phrase to explain the late speaking of a child. I went to the dictionary then and from there to the Bible and read the story. That it was God who created many languages in order to bring about chaos—and this to stop men from building the tower that would reach heaven! Now, thinking of it, it occurs to me that if the Bible had been written in India, it would have been a different story. Look at the three of us here in the house—each one with a different language! Yet there's no chaos, because we've neatly sidestepped problems by speaking in one language—English. The language suits me. It avoids intimacy and familiarity and confers a formal politeness on our relationship. I imagine he prefers it this way, too. She, however, breaks away often from English and moves into Kannada or Hindi, mixing up the languages, which adds a kind of effervescent excitement to any conversation with her. She's the bravest of the three of us, venturing into unfamiliar territory, uncaring of the hazards. She tries her rudimentary Marathi on me, oblivious of her mistakes, of her confusion in genders. With him, she slips occasionally into Hindi—a faltering, searching-for-words-Hindi, that often ends in Kannada or English.

'I know all the words for love in Hindi,' she tells me. 'I learnt Hindi from the movies, mostly from the songs. Love, heart, pain—yes, I know so many words for those things. But you can't use them in everyday conversation,' she adds regretfully.

She is equally unfazed by her mistakes in English. 'Off the light' and 'on the light', she says. And, like a refrain, at the end of a recital of problems, small or big, 'What to do?'

'What to do indeed?' Hari gravely replies.

It's neither a reproof nor a correction; the smile on her face tells me that. Just as, when she sternly corrects his Kannada—she's teaching him the language, I hear the lessons going on at night—there's no sting in it for him. It's a game they're playing, a game they both enjoy. The language they speak, the words they use, are only the veneer for something else, for what they're really saying to each other. I've realized I'm sharing the house, not with a married couple, but with a pair of lovers. The air between them, when they're together, seems to crackle with excitement, their feelings hover, thick and almost palpable, about them. If there are no words of love between them, at least not in my presence, I can hear their love

39

in the way they speak, in their laughter when they're together in their room at night, in the silences that punctuate the conversation, when I know that it's their hands, their lips and their bodies that are speaking to each other.

The Lord got it all wrong. It's not different languages that bring about chaos, for you can dispense with words altogether. I think of Joe and Leela, his terrible Marathi, her English almost non-existent. Yet communication between them was perfect. But, of course, the best communication is always wordless, though Tony would certainly argue with that!

I have to stop thinking of them as 'he' and 'she'. I knew their names even before I came here, and now they have become more than a couple of signatures on a paper. I know that they have been married a little over a year, that she is the youngest of three daughters, that her father, who stays here with them (or rather, the other way round, since the house is his), is now in the US visiting his second daughter, and that the eldest lives in Bombay. I know a few things about him too, that he's a Delhi man, that he's lived and had most of his education there, that he was abroad for a time. He's an economist by qualification, but is working now on a development project in a group of villages nearby.

All this information comes to me through Lata, the facts not offered deliberately, but slipped casually into the conversation. I imagine this is how she embarks on any new relationship, handing out random slices of her life to the other person, wholly ignoring the spaces between them, explaining nothing. There are other things I learn about them: that she is restless, she can't stay in one place, one room, or even in the house for long. She goes out abruptly, often without a word, and comes back in a while, refreshed and invigorated. She needs to be constantly communicating with others, through words, through touch. As soon as she returns from work, I hear her speaking through her bedroom window to the two girls next door, her admirers I imagine, from the way they wait for her to return home. Hers is a pervasive presence. Even when she's not around; there are bits of her lying about—her radio, her bangles, her pins which she pulls out of her hair the moment she's home, releasing her hair with a sigh of sensuous pleasure. The mirror above the wash basin is dotted with her bindis, which she takes off before washing her face and then forgets to put on again. He is less visible, but I can sense his presence—or absence—through her. She seems somehow less vital when he's not at home, slightly shadowy.

These things come to me from my role as a spectator. They are conscious of my presence, of my observation. I know this for I see her acting for my benefit, her actions and responses just a little louder, a little more emphasized, than they would have been without my presence. Whereas, he seems to avoid my gaze, ducking like a camera-shy person. When she is louder than usual, adding more flourishes and colours to her behaviour, I see that he becomes aware of what she is doing, I have a sense of his throwing a protective mantle around her, guarding her from my possibly critical look. I could reassure him if I wanted to, I could tell him I'm no critic, only a spectator.

I seem to have gone back to the role I took on when I went to live with Leela and Joe after my father's death. It was not only the knowledge that I was merely passing through, that I would be going to the hostel in a month; it was the unreality of the situation I found myself in which alienated me from my surroundings. My father dead, Babu gone, I knew not where, the home that had been mine ever since I could remember, no longer there—these things made me suddenly a stranger to my own life. As if I had been moved sideways, away from my place. My own life had ceased to exist and I could only watch, from a distance, others living out their lives.

Which was how I looked at the strange family I had been so abruptly thrust into. I can see them even today, the way I saw them then, one particular picture engraved on my memory. The family at the breakfast table, Paula speaking exclusively to Joe, ignoring the others, Joe himself eating his toast and spearing his omelette with his usual swift efficiency, nodding meanwhile at Paula's comments, Tony, blank-faced, concentrating on his plate, Phillo rushing in and out with more toast, cups of tea . . .

Leela is there too, keeping her distance from the others, her chair a little askew, a little away from the table, a cup of tea and her usual loaf of 'pav' before her, her glasses perched on her nose, steadily reading the Marathi newspaper. Not speaking a word, making herself almost invisible, but conscious of me, waiting for me to finish, getting up only when I am done, knowing that I need her protective presence here. Leela, my only connection to the world after my father's death, the person who brought me back into this world, to a normal life. Paula played a role in my resurrection too, for Paula's hatred and anger did as much to jerk me out of my sorrow as Leela's love and care did.

And now it is Hari who converts me from an outsider and an observer into something else. Not a participant, not part of their lives, no, not that. But a connection is established between us and I can no longer remain a total stranger.

This is the first evening we are on our own, Hari and I. Lata has gone out to check the accounts in her father's shop—a bookshop that sells mostly textbooks to students. There is a manager, but during her father's absence, she does the accounts once a month. Lata has told me this in the morning, now Hari repeats it as we have our tea together. He's very consciously trying to play the role of host, a role that Lata has passed on to him for the evening. He's extremely conscientious about it, not letting me clear or wash up after tea. I watch him work, notice the efficiency with which he washes and dries, which tells me he's used to working in the kitchen, that he's comfortable with these chores.

I say this aloud and he replies, 'I've lived on my own since I was seventeen. I'm not a bad cook, either.' He smiles, a rare thing with him. 'Actually, I'm planning to cook something today. I'm sick of the cook's stuff. There are all these leftovers, but . . . Do you mind?'

'I? Why should I? Would you like me to make something?'

'No, no. I can manage. Let's put all this stuff in the fridge first.'

He gets the vegetables out at the same time and we sit at the dining table working together. As we string and peel and chop, he tells me who he is and why I am here. And in a moment, everything changes.

It was he who wrote me the letter when he heard that I was coming to Bhavanipur. He knew my name, he had heard of me—oh, very long back—from his mother. She had spoken of me as 'Babymavshi's Madhu'. He smiles as he says this, whether at the name, or at the memory of something that his mother said or did then, I don't know.

'Your mother is . . .?'

'Was. She died many years back. My mother was Narmada's daughter.'

I look blank at that. He goes on with a touch of impatience, wondering at my ignorance, thinking, perhaps, that I *should* know.

'Your mother's sister Narmada.'

My mother's sister Narmada? But I can't make any connections through my mother, I have to go to Leela. So then it becomes Leela's sister Narmada. This makes more sense to me.

'You're Narmada's grandson?'

'That's right.'

His grandmother, Narmada, spoke often of her sister Leela. (He keeps speaking of her as Sindhu, which confuses me until I remember that Leela's name before marriage had been Sindhu.) Narmada was the sister next to Leela, and like in all large families, where there are always special alliances between siblings, Narmada and Leela had formed a pair. They were very close as girls, but with Leela's marriage and her going to Bombay, they lost touch. Nevertheless, Narmada followed the course of her sister's life with great interest. An interest which she passed on to her daughter, Hari's mother, who was fascinated by this unusual aunt, the rebel in a wholly conventional, tradition-bound family.

'She used to see her aunt's name in the papers once in a while and she always cut the item out and saved the cutting. That's how I came to know about her. And you too—for somehow my mother had got the information about you as well.'

I know next-to-nothing about my mother's family. Even during the short course of my mother's married life, she had had no contact with them. With her death, as far as my father was concerned, they did not exist. He never spoke of them, except once, when we were listening to a Lata Mangeshkar song beginning, 'Ganga Yamuna.'

'Your aunts,' my father said.

He spoke seriously, without a smile, and I truly thought the song was about my aunts. I said this to Leela later and she laughed.

'You do have aunts called Ganga and Yamuna,' she said. 'And Godavari and Narmada as well.'

Named after the rivers, all six of them, Leela being Sindhu and my mother, Kaveri (though, inevitably, she became Baby.) We pool our information now, and I am surprised by the paucity of Hari's knowledge, which is almost as meagre as mine. In fact I am a little better off than he is. I can tell him a few facts about the sisters. Yamu, the beauty of the family, who, it was felt, was destined for a great marriage. With her looks, how could it be otherwise? And when she was married into a 'royal family'—to the ruler of one of those states no bigger than a large town—the family exulted and gloried in the connection. But with Independence, he lost everything, considered himself above an ordinary job and squandered what little money was left. Yamu and her family sank into middle-class insignificance after that.

Gangu, slow, placid and good-natured, had a baby every year. Sixteen children were born to her, the reports went, though only three lived. And Goda, the short, dark one, the despair of the family—who'll marry such a dark girl?—was married off to a landlord, a widower with three children. The landlord entered politics and later became a minister, so that Goda was elevated, despite her dark complexion, into becoming the pride of the family.

Leela told me these things about her sisters. I pass on the information to Hari, though I say nothing about Narmada, I am silent about Leela's description of her—'very bossy and wanting to dominate everyone, Namu was'. I can't say this. She's Hari's grandmother, after all.

But Hari is not interested in any of these people, not even in his grandmother. It is Leela he wants to talk about. Leela and my mother—the two rebels of the family, both the sisters disowned by the family. Leela became, she told me this herself, her rare laughter breaking out as she spoke, a figure little girls were threatened with when they were disobedient or troublesome.

'Do you want to become a Sindhu?'

The black sheep of the family. A widow who remarried. And, what was worse, infinitely worse, married a *Christian* man. These were the things the family spoke of. Leela's other activities did not matter to them, none of her achievements registered. Her years of teaching, her role in the trade unions, her work among the factory workers—these were blanked out, they did not exist.

At first, I think it is Leela the communist Hari is interested in, that perhaps he is, or was, one himself. A Naxalite sympathizer, maybe? But he disclaims this. 'I believed in it,' he says, speaking of Communism. 'What thinking person wouldn't! But I was disillusioned with our local brand, with the kind of leaders we have here. So wholly political, so little concerned with the ideology.'

It was Leela's role during the Emergency that caught his attention, he tells me. Her involvement with the striking railway workers, with their families. Of course, all this came out only after the Emergency had been lifted. But even in the Emergency days, there was the grapevine on which Leela's name travelled.

'I heard about her and suddenly realized who she was. I felt good about it. Having someone in the family who was part of the resistance to the Emergency—I thought it was wonderful!'

He's smiling, his rare smile, one that makes him a very attractive young man, not a dour, sombre one. And I wonder whether his father being a bureaucrat in Delhi at the time—and therefore part of the establishment Leela was fighting against—has anything to do with this enthusiasm for Leela's role. He is eager, all lit up, wanting to know about how it was at that time, how it was for Leela. While I, racking my brains, trying to remember something, can only think of Leela saying sternly to me when I'm visiting her in prison, when, scared to death, I've passed on the letter I've been instructed to give her, 'Don't do this again. Tell them I don't want you involved.'

Waiting for me to speak, he switches on the mixer to grind the spices and my stumbling attempts to speak are, fortunately, smothered by its demonic sound. He's standing by it, hand on lid, waiting for me to go on as soon as he

46

switches it off. When he does, the silence is as deafening as the earlier sound.

Lata walks into this silence, sniffs, takes a deep breath and 'Hari!' she exclaims. 'Something smells good—you're cooking!' Then she looks at our faces and says to me, 'He's told you.'

'Why didn't you speak of this earlier? Why didn't you mention this in your letter?' I'd asked Hari.

'I thought . . . such a distant connection . . . maybe it would seem pushy . . .'

His voice trailed away and I left it at that.

She says it now, what he had left unsaid. 'I wanted him to talk to you about it, but he felt it was not the right time, he thought you wouldn't be interested in such things now . . .'

Not the right time. So they know about it, they know about Adit. How did I imagine they wouldn't?

I go to bed hoping to dream of Adit, of his living, breathing presence, but there's nothing. In my sleep I seem to inhabit just dark blank spaces. A frightening emptiness. So that I wake up with relief to the solid substantiality of the objects in this room—familiar now and no longer disorienting. Sometimes I think I would even welcome those dreams of horror that came to me night after night following my father's death. Nightmares out of which I woke up sweating, shivering and terrified. But Leela was there then, Leela who drove out the demons and brought me back into a sane, waking world.

There are neither dreams nor demons now, nevertheless I wake up battered and bruised. The day lies ahead and I have to get through it, to go through the motions of living. A cup of tea, a bath, and a thin new skin forms over the wound. Until the night, when the skin is ripped off again, the blood flows and the wound gapes red and angry once more.

How long can I go on living this way?

Tony asks me this very question, it's what he's come here to say, though he pretends Rekha and he are just passing through.

I was fifteen when I met Tony. Cocooned in the shock of my father's death, I scarcely noticed him at first. Until the day he came upon me in Paula's room when I was changing into my nightdress. He stood and stared at me for a moment, then lunged at me, his hands grabbing at my body, trying, perhaps, to touch my breasts.

'It was not my fault,' Tony said later, when we could laugh at the incident, at ourselves. 'Blame my hormones that kept me in a state of constant lust, leching after females. Any female. All females. And there you were in my own house, half undressed—even if you were such a skinny thing, I couldn't help myself. It was like it happened in spite of me.'

Yes, he was as surprised as I was. We stared at each other for a moment. And then I hit out at him, wildly, a blow that astonished me as much as it did him.

'Damn it if she didn't get at me with a boxer's punch—like Mohammed Ali almost,' Tony told Rekha, recounting this incident when he first introduced me to her. 'I never expected it. There she was, this meek mild Hindu girl who never spoke above a whisper—she went on *pss pss* even with Leela. And then that fist coming in my face! I could hear the birds singing—I swear, just like in the comics.'

We stood in shocked silence after that until Paula entered, staring at us suspiciously. Tony smiled at me then and walked out of the room as if nothing had happened. The beginning of our relationship, a relationship which has brought him here to Bhavanipur.

Tony's arrival, a total surprise, is, as always, like the entry of royalty in a Shakespearean play. A kind of fanfare accompanied him even when he travelled in his old Fiat. Now, in his Contessa, with a driver in front and Rekha by his side, it becomes an authentic royal procession. His voice, calling out to me, speaking to Rekha, to the driver, arouses the whole street. I can see scores of curious faces at windows and doors watching us, while he hugs me and walks to the house, his arm still about me.

'We were on our way to Goa, we thought we'd break our journey overnight here, spend a few hours with you . . .'

'I know you always fly to Goa, I know you're here to see me. It's okay, Tony, you don't have to pretend.'

'What do you expect me to do when we don't hear from you? Not one letter since you left Bombay! I thought the best thing was to come here myself and see what you're up to.'

His tone is rough and angry, it takes us back to our usual intimacy, bypassing the strangeness of the last few months. I don't want to respond to this, to get into any kind of confrontation with him, not right away, not at all if I can help it. Rekha comes in now, greeting me as Tony had done, with a hug. I take them both inside, show Rekha the bathroom and go in to make tea for them. When I return, they've both had a wash.

'Sit.' Rekha takes me by the hand and makes me sit by her. 'Are you angry we're here?'

'Angry! My God, Rekha!'

'It was my doing. Tony was uneasy, he was very anxious to see you, so was I. Finally we decided we'd just come.' She encircles my wrist with her thumb and finger and exclaims, 'Look at this! You've lost even more weight.'

'Yes, look at her. What have you done to yourself, Madhu?'

Tony's finger makes dents in my cheeks, taps my collarbone.

'You remember, Tony, the day we first met? Leela took me home and you were the first person I met there. She told you who I was and then do you know what you said, do you remember what was the first thing you said to me?'

He shakes his head, waits for me to tell him.

'You said—*my mother died*. And I asked you—*how did she*

49

die? And you said—*she just died.* I thought it was funny, the way you said it—*she just died.*'

'Yes, I remember now. You looked such a sad, peaky little thing, I thought, her father's dead, poor kid, let me tell her my mother died too.'

'And now? What have you come to say to me this time? What comfort have you come to offer me, Tony?'

'Nothing. There's nothing I can say, I know that, Madhu. I wanted to see you, that's all. Can't you accept that? Just relax, girl.'

Yes, why am I so grouchy, so fierce with Tony—Tony, for God's sake! What am I guarding so fiercely from everyone? My pain? My grief?

Tony, as always, fills the house with his presence, and is so soon so much at home, that when Lata returns from the bank, it's he who welcomes her, like a host. And when, a little later, Hari comes home, again it's Tony who goes forward to introduce himself. A very odd introduction. 'I'm Leela's stepson,' he says.

Which is what prompts Hari, I imagine, into making the rejoinder, 'And I'm Leela's sister's grandson.'

The simplest, the best way, I imagine, of mapping relationships. Using one person as the centre, everything radiating from there, all the lines connecting to this centre. Yes, blood ties, even if they're more complex, more difficult with their conflicting demands to cope with, are so much easier to explain. For Tony and me, to put our relationship into words, has always been next to impossible.

'My sister,' Tony says sometimes, introducing me to strangers. And we can see the doubtful faces, the puzzled looks. It's not just the complete lack of resemblance—which becomes irrelevant, in any case, after a certain age—it's our names, so distinctive of our backgrounds, of our communities. Madhu Saptarishi and Anthony Gonsalves.

'Rakhi sister?' a smart Alec asked once. And was mystified

50

by the horrified looks Tony and I exchanged. By our almost simultaneous reaction, as if we'd rehearsed it: 'Rakhi brother and sister! No indeed!'

Our prompt and simultaneous response, the way both our minds flew at once to Emma and Mr Knightley, should have revealed the real tie between us. But this is impossible for an outsider to understand. When we speak Marathi, our lack of connection becomes even more loud. Tony never misses a chance to thank Leela for teaching him Marathi. Which, in a sense, she did, because, with her English being what it was, he had no choice but to speak to her in Marathi. Her contribution, however, ends there. She has nothing to do with the kind of language he speaks.

'If it hadn't been for Leela, I'd have ended my life speaking gutter Marathi,' Tony declares. Leela and I always laughed at this, for it presumed that what he had was a much better version of Marathi. Which is true to a small extent, but the language is still odd, and to a purist, certainly queer. His use of the singular 'tu', for example, the tone of rough intimacy that this immediately establishes, works with friends, colleagues, subordinates, young people. But when he speaks this way to older persons, it arouses both curiosity and offence. Tony is, fortunately for himself, oblivious to both.·

Here, in Hari and Lata's house, we don't need to explain anything. Our relationship is clear: we share Leela and Joe. Two people who are Tony's parents definitely—a father and stepmother—but also, equally and surely mine, even if they're no more than an aunt and her husband. When we speak of these two, Tony and I enter a different world, a world of our youth and yes, the cliched adjunct, our innocence. A lost world, which we inhabit for a while when we bring out our memories.

There's nothing mournful about these memories. The sadness, if there is any, is shelved for the moment and we speak only of joyful moments. Family stories never get stale,

51

they're brought out at each meeting, enjoyed and laughed over as if they've never been recounted, never been heard before. Our stories too emerge as if we've never spoken of them earlier. Generally, Tony and I are like a pair of doubles players in this. Now, he's doing it alone, gamely running all over the court, playing his usual shots. 'Remember? Remember?' he asks me, inviting me to join the game. Fortunately for him, Hari and Lata are a couple of enraptured listeners, Lata, specially, sitting with her chin propped in her hands, eyes fixed unwaveringly on Tony.

Tony is speaking of Joe's *'Think of the Brontes'*, a catchphrase he brought out when we complained too much, 'whined' as Joe put it, moaning about our lot.

'Think of the Brontes,' Joe would say. And finally, one day, Leela asked him curiously, 'Who are these Brontes, Joe? Friends of yours? How is it I've never met them?'

'Leela thought Bronte was a Maharashtrian name—like Kale or Gore, you know. And then she wondered why we were laughing. Remember, Madhu, how bewildered she was? She just couldn't understand why we were laughing. The more confused she got, the more we laughed.'

'Remember, Madhu, remember?' Tony goes on. But while he speaks, it's Tony himself I'm thinking of, of his stubborn affection that has brought him here to the house of two strangers.

Strangers is the wrong word, nobody can be a stranger for long with Tony—or Rekha, either. Intimacy comes swiftly and naturally with both of them and it's been arranged that the two of them are not going to a hotel, they're going to spend the night here.

'If you don't mind the inconvenience?' Lata asks hesitantly.

Lata is dazzled, by their personalities as well as the aura of success Tony carries around him. She's heard his name, though she doesn't exactly remember in what connection—Hari is the one who identifies him with the name of his advertising agency—but she knows he's a celebrity. Learning now that Rekha is one in her own right, hearing about the art gallery she's recently established, Lata's awe increases.

A little later, Lata takes Rekha to the room she's got ready for her and Tony. Hari roars away on his motorbike—to the market, I presume—and Tony and I are left alone. I feel myself tensing, wondering what he will say, willing him not to speak. He smiles, gauging my apprehension, and says, 'I met Som before I came here.'

He pauses for me to say something, to ask, perhaps, 'How is he?' But I don't need to. I have only to look into the mirror to know how he is, I only need to look into myself to know what he's feeling.

'Madhu . . .' Tony begins, ready to go on to something else, when I stop him with a firm 'Don't. Tony, don't. Just leave it alone.'

'You won't let me speak, you don't say anything yourself . . .'

'What's there to say?'

Yes, it's true. There is nothing. There are no words for a void, no words for emptiness.

We stare at each other in silence for a moment before he capitulates. 'Okay, I give up!'

I can hear sounds from the kitchen which speak of Lata starting dinner. 'I must go and help her.'

'Relax, Rekha is there. She'll enjoy taking over their kitchen. Listen, she's already invaded the puja room.'

We can hear her clear voice chanting '*Shantakaram* . . .' There's nothing hesitant or apologetic about Rekha's religion. It's loud and clear.

'Nice couple,' Tony says and it's a signal—he's not going to speak of all those things he's come here to say to me. Nevertheless, throughout the evening, whether he's speaking to Lata or Hari or to all of us generally, I can feel him tugging at me, trying to pull me into the circle of companionship Rekha and he have created with this young couple, struggling to get me out of the lonely world he knows I've been inhabiting since Adit's death. But after a while, in response, perhaps, to a signal from Rekha, one of those invisible-to-others signals that couples exchange, he stops. Rekha takes over the conversation, moves it on to Bhavanipur, to Bai, and then to Hari's work. It's a project dealing with the rehabilitation of devdasi women, a subject which both Tony and Rekha find so absorbing that I can relax for the first time.

'Stop worrying about me, Tony,' I tell him when they're ready to leave the next morning.

'How can I? You're asking for the impossible.'

I know he will never give up, but right now, understanding my feelings, he speaks only of the book.

'How's it going?'

'I don't know, I have absolutely no idea what I'm going to do. I really can't imagine why Chandru thought I could write this book.'

'Oh come on, you know you can. You're literate, you can use the dictionary, you have the thesaurus—with these assets you can write a novel, let alone a biography. They all do it these days, don't you know? Didn't you hear the Latest Literary Phenomenon say the other day in an interview—"Oh, my novel just happened!" Go ahead, don't doubt yourself.'

'If I do, I know where to go for reassurance.'

'I'll come again,' he tells me when leaving.

'What for? Don't, Tony, don't bother.'

'What do you mean—don't bother? Of course I'm coming. You can't keep me away. If only I could help, if I had some idea of what to say to make you feel better . . .'

'Don't say anything.'

'What else am I doing but that? But it isn't right. I must say something. Like my grandmother would have said, if I'd had one, that is . .' The way he brings out this corny old joke of his, half-heartedly, a little abashed, tells me how desperate he is to reach me. 'As my grandmother would have said, just keep going.'

'But what for, Tony? There's nothing left. What should I keep going for?'

There's too much honesty in our relationship for him to say anything more than 'Because there's no choice, Madhu. That's what it's all about in the end—we keep going.'

Both Rekha and he hug me again when leaving. I am so unused to physical contact that I can feel myself drawing back, my body going rigid. I find the odour of humans strange and disturbing, as if I've been cursed like Ashvatthama, cast out of the human circle. Such a dreadful curse, I realize that now.

When they've gone, I think of my question to Tony—why should I go on? I didn't need to ask Tony that, I have the answer myself. I have to go on because I must find an explanation for what happened. I have to know why my seventeen-year-old son had to die such a horrible death, I must see whether I can make any sense of this freakish thing that happened to us, turning our lives, Som's and mine, into this arid desert.

'I'll be back,' Tony has promised me and I know he will. He won't let go, he'll hold on, he'll be with me until he's sure I'm all right. 'Damn it,' I can hear him saying to Rekha, 'Damn it, I'm going to see that Madhu is okay, I'm going to bring her out of this. I can't let her go on like this!' I can see him, no, not brooding over me, he's not a brooder, but suddenly remembering me, thinking of my problem, deciding he has to come here, do something about me . . .

I sometimes think Tony got his idea of being a brother from the movies. Brothers in movies are always there when their sisters need them, they turn up at the right times, they agonize over their sisters' sufferings . . .

I'm being unfair to Tony. What's between us is real. And anyway, Tony was a brother already when I met him. He was Paula's brother. He still is. Always there for her as he is for me.

Always there. I think of the early Tony, the boy I met when I first became a part of Joe's home. A blank-faced boy, giving away nothing of his feelings. Seemingly emotionless. And elusive. Slippery. Slithery, Tony corrects me when I use this word about him. Hard to catch. Giving us only a glimpse of his back, disappearing round the corner, slipping out of the door.

Where did he go?

'I'd gone to see some friends,' he would say when he was questioned—by Phillo, generally. Joe knew little about his movements and Leela never interfered. 'I'd gone to meet a friend.'

Which was not true. Tony told me later about how the boys harassed him, how they made fun of him. His name came in very handy for this. 'Anthony Gonsalves—Jesus, what a name to give a chap!'

But how was Joe to know—or Tony's mother, actually, for it was she who named him—what the name would stand for later? Leela asked him this question when he complained. As a matter of fact, the movie came much later, it came out when Tony was an adolescent—the worst time for him, no doubt. The movie became a hit, Amitabh Bachchan already by then a cult figure, and the song a rage. And so there it was, the song being played all over the place, sung by everyone. *My name is Anthony Gonsalves . . .* Naturally the boys sang it the moment Tony was seen—coming to the line *Exxx—cu—se me, please* when he was passing by, the words followed by hoots of laughter.

I didn't know this then, nor did Leela. Tony kept his troubles to himself. He spoke of it later. 'I used to sneak out hoping no one would see me. Sometimes, in desperation, I thought I would change my name. When you married Som, my first thought was: Madhu Saptarshi—such a dignified name. Nobody, I thought, but nobody, can make fun of that name! I envied you. How I hated my own name! And then one day I thought—damn it, it's *my* name. They're not going to take my name away from me.'

Was that the moment of change for Tony? Is that the point at which the vague, awkward boy became a person sure of himself? Did he stop his purposeless rambling at that moment and turn on to a new path? No more dodging, no more slithering. Or did it happen later, when Paula left home, leaving Tony to become the only child at home, all at once the son of the family? Or was the point of change even later, when Tony met Rekha and the fickle, one-girl-friend-a-week young man became Mr Steady, steadfast in his emotional attachment to Rekha, faithful in spite of being in the midst of all those young beauties who modelled for his ads? When did he become the Tony I now know?

4

'It's like a Monday,' Lata says, when going to work the day after Tony has left. 'The Sunday fun is over.'

For me too, there was a kind of wrench when I saw the car moving away, a moment of loss and desolation. But there was relief as well. I was free from the responsibility of coping with Tony's distress, his distress on my behalf, his angry helplessness at being unable to do anything for me.

Being with Bai is more restful. I mean no more to her than an audience, a pair of ears listening to her, registering her words. I'm beginning to appreciate this position of anonymity she has pushed me into by ignoring our Neemgaon connection. By making a stranger of me, she's unburdened us of our past. We're meeting on fresh territory, with no luggage to clutter up the space we're inhabiting. This is an entirely new relationship. In this avatar, as the writer of her biography, I'm very welcome in her home.

I walk into the house now without any hesitation, shed my chappals on top of the untidy heap of footwear outside the door and go straight into the 'interview room'—the anteroom to her bedroom. I occupy my chair, which has already taken on the contours of familiarity, shaping itself obediently to my body as soon as I sit down. I put my recorder on the table before me. My table. The other table, next to Bai's chair, is Bai's.

My chair. *My* table. So quickly do we stake out our territories wherever we go. But the calendars piled on the wall opposite me, calendars left there year after year, make me conscious of the presence of time, they seems to mock this pretence of ownership.

I am now a familiar part of Bai's household. I know all of them, though I scarcely meet anyone. The twins, the accompanists, sometimes pass me on the road when I'm coming here. They go past on their moped, speeding, their scanty hair flying behind them in a comet tail effect. I can see from their gleeful faces that they enjoy the speed. They look like figures in a cartoon; I can almost see a balloon over their heads with a WHEEEE written within it. They wave cheerfully to me when they see me, but when we meet in the house they scarcely take any note of me, they are subdued, as if they have put away their exuberance along with their chappals on entering the house. I don't speak to them, either. I have learnt and accepted the rule of this household—that all conversation has to be with Bai. Bai is very particular about this, she gets agitated when she hears me speaking to anyone but her. 'What was she saying? What were you asking her? Ask me whatever you want to know. That girl doesn't know anything. You don't need to talk to her.'

That girl. But she's no girl, she's a woman over thirty, I imagine. Her name is Hasina. I was surprised when I heard the name. I'd never thought her to be a Muslim. Her bare forehead, without any kumkum, if I'd thought of it at all, had meant widowhood. It's her perfect Marathi that misled me.

Hasina is Bai's student, as well as her companion. She's also the person who takes on the students who come to Bai. Officially, they're all Bai's students, but it is Hasina who takes the classes. Bai is nowhere in the picture, except when it's Abhay's class. For some reason—is it because Abhay is the one serious student, the talented and promising one?—Bai retains control over this class which is held in the room next to the one Bai and I are in. The door is left open so that she can hear what's going on. It seems to me that she's wholly engrossed in talking to me, that she isn't listening to the music, but she suddenly stops speaking to call out, 'What's wrong? Why have you stopped?'

As soon as the music ceases, the complaints begin, complaints that encompass all sorts of things: the tanpura is not properly tuned, the note is wrongly placed, the raaga is the wrong one for the time of the day. Abhay and the accompanists rarely get any of this criticism, most of it is for Hasina.

I never know what this does to Hasina. I can hear the music, but I cannot see her, I can't see any of them, they remain invisible. One day, however, after Bai's constant griping, the music stops.

'What is it?' Bai calls out. 'Why have you stopped? It's not yet time. The boy must get his full hour.'

There is no reply. The silence continues.

'Go and bring that girl here,' Bai tells me. 'I want to talk to her.'

Reluctantly I go out. There are no accompanists that day, only Hasina and Abhay. Abhay is putting his tanpura away, he stands it up carefully in the corner and goes past me without a word. Hasina, her back to me, is looking out of the window. I call out her name. She turns round in a sort of slow motion.

Hers is a nondescript face, only her sharply outlined eyebrows and large eyes saving it from total insignificance. But she always gives me a feeling of being in the shadows, her face looking out at the world from behind a *jaali* window. Now, when she looks at me, for the first time I see it unshaded and clear. I had expected tears, grief. Instead there's a savage anger. We stare at each other for a moment, then she goes past me. I go back to Bai and tell her I can't find Hasina.

Bai's anger is spent. She smiles and says, as if explaining her anger, 'That girl still has a lot to learn.'

I've heard Hasina doing her riaz, I've heard her singing with Abhay during her lessons. Her voice is lighter than Bai's, without its resonance. But it is a true voice and when she moves up and down the scales, there's no jerk, her voice rises and plummets without any sense of strain. Yet Bai says she is no good.

This nasty, tyrannical creature is Bai too. Is this woman going to be part of my book?

Tony is wrong. It's not the writing of the book that worries me—not as yet, anyway. That problem lies ahead, that anxiety will begin only after I start on the actual writing. What's troubling me now is the material that Bai is offering me. She is not good with words. She rarely gets the right words and she's not careful with them, either. Precision is not her strong point, though there's no paucity of words, she's fluent enough. In fact, sometimes she's too garrulous and I have to grope my way through the density of words to get at her meaning. At times, she leaves blanks, her equivalent of 'you know' or 'like, you know' that some people use when they can't find a word. And she forgets, very often she forgets words, names, connections.

Chandru has warned me about this, about the 'residual deficits' her stroke has left her with, affecting her language and her memory. The stroke was a minor one and she's recovered from it very well. It's only when she stands or walks that there's a glimpse of what it has done to her. Nevertheless, there are sudden shifts in time, jumps and leaps from one occasion to another, which confuse me. And just when I think her memory has deserted her, that it is hopeless expecting her to remember things clearly, she goes into endless detail about something from the past. She speaks about her married home, for example, in great detail. She builds it like a palace of many rooms and staircases, latticed windows, courtyards with ponds and palm trees, she inhabits it with a throng of people—men, women, children and servants. When I listen to her, I have a sense of *deja vu*. I've heard this before, but where?

Or have I read about it somewhere?

If I've forgotten where I got this information from, Bai has forgotten nothing. She tells me even the names of the servants, the driver and the priest who came to do the daily puja. She speaks to me of her first music teacher. I was only a child then, she says. But when was this? In her father's house? And yet, wasn't it her father who thundered at her mother when the mother, giving in to the child's insistence, sent her to learn music? An innocent little group, Bai tells me, of little girls from a few families living in the neighbourhood. But the father was furious. 'Do you want your daughter to be one of *those* women?' he asked his wife. That was the end of those music lessons. So, how did she get a music teacher finally?

Very casually she mentions a stepmother—my second mother, she calls her. But there is no mention of her mother's death. Surely, a mother's death is a momentous event in a child's life? If it doesn't register as significant at the time, doesn't it become so later? I'm surprised that Bai bypasses this death entirely.

Of her father, however, the man who had no sympathy with her love of music, she speaks a great deal. She tells me she was his favourite, that she was much petted by him. She proudly speaks of how the whole family had to be careful not to displease or anger her, because her father wouldn't stand for it. And he was the head of the family, what he said or did mattered to everyone.

'I fell down once,' she tells me, 'and had a deep cut on my forehead. It bled so much that the blood ran into my eyes, I couldn't see anything, I thought I'd gone blind. I wouldn't let anyone come near me either, I screamed when they tried. It was only my father who could soothe me, he washed my face, he took me to the doctor . . .'

Now I remember, now it comes back to me where I heard about Bai's married home, where I got a description of it. It is the way she speaks about her father that reminds me of it. Munni described this same house, her father's house, in almost exactly the same words Bai uses, words that conjured up a picture of a rich home, a loving father and she, Munni, the centre of the household, the beloved of the entire family, waited on hand and foot by everyone in the family. Yes, it is Munni that Bai reminds me of, Munni, who like her mother, used words to create a glorious world she had left behind when she came to Neemgaon and manipulated me into believing all that she told me.

Munni makes me believe she's in Neemgaon on a brief visit. She really belongs to Pune, she says, her home is there, her father's home, that is. She'll be going back there very soon. She seems to carry a map of Pune inside her head, she traces her way over it when she talks, as if making sure it's still there, ensuring that she's forgotten nothing. She speaks of it in endless, tedious detail: the streets, the shops, the temples, the gardens, the theatres.

'We went to Tulsibag, there's a shop there and then we went to Laxmi Road . . .'

When she talks, it is as if she is recreating that world, going back into it, traversing the streets, blinking at the bright lights, jostling in the shops, ringing the temple bells. She makes it so real that when I visit Pune, years later, I have a sense of familiarity about roads and places I'm seeing for the first time in my life.

Munni despises Neemgaon. There's nothing here, she says, her entire face a sneer. And I, who have never thought about it at all, now begin to look at our town, its untarred roads and few shops with a freshly critical eye. Nevertheless, in spite of her contempt for Neemgaon, Munni seems to know all about it, about the people in it, within a very short time, much more than I, who have lived all my life here, do. She tells me stories about people, always with many salacious details about their lives.

This girl's father is a drunkard,—do I know that? He gets drunk every night, he beats her mother with his belt, even with his chappals sometimes. Do I know that?

That girl's mother—she's so fat, she has to piss standing. Can I believe that? Imagine it, she says, with a splutter of laughter so infectious that I join in too, imagine standing and pissing!

This girl wets her bed every night, yes, she's nearly twelve, but still she pisses in her bed.

This one's sister ran off with a boy and got married. Do I know that they did *it*—yes, *it*—even before they were married?

It? I don't dare to ask what this *it* is, but my ignorance obviously shows, for she tells me, 'It's something all married people do. They take off their clothes and do *it*. How come you don't know this, stupid?'

There are stories about her own life too. She's been kidnapped and brought here to Neemgaon. 'Do you think I'd have come here otherwise?' she asks me. 'My father would never have let me go.'

'Why doesn't he come here and take you back then?'

'Because if my father comes here, *he* will kill my mother.'

The 'he' she speaks of with such emphasis is the kidnapper, the man who plays the tabla. Ghulam saab his name is, I've heard them call him that. The kind man who smiles at me, pats me on the cheek, gives me sweets—he's the kidnapper? I like him, I like everything about him, except his habit of calling me 'Baby'. Baby? But that's my mother's name, he's confusing me with her. I tell him so and he laughs and says, 'All right, I'll call you Madhu.' And he does, scrupulous and careful about doing it.

Yes, a gentle, kind man. But Munni says he's cruel. She speaks of starvation, of being tied up and beaten. She shows me a scar on her arm. It looks like a mosquito bite to me. She's offended when I say so, she squeezes it to make it bleed. Nothing happens. She covers it up swiftly and says, 'Don't tell anyone. If he knows I've told you, he'll whip me.'

Yet, when I see the two of them together, Munni and her kidnapper, he seems affectionate and loving. It's Munni who turns her back on him, Munni who ignores him and he who looks hurt and sad.

'You don't know,' Munni says to me, contemptuous of my ignorance, 'you don't know anything. He's different outside the house. When there are people around he pretends. But at home . . .'

She leaves her sentence incomplete. There's a sinister quality to the silence and my blood runs cold. I think of Munni being tied up, being beaten and whipped. But can he do such things? It's hard for me to imagine him, whip in hand, standing over Munni, it's impossible to think of him with a cruel look on his face. His voice when he calls out to Munni, his face when he looks at her—there's no cruelty anywhere. On the contrary, it's Munni's mother who rarely speaks to Munni and when she does her voice is sharp, like a knife. I saw her slap Munni once, I've heard her scolding her. Yet Munni insists it's the man who is her enemy.

'You don't know,' she says, 'you don't know him, you don't know how clever he is, how he can pretend.'

I stare hard at him when we meet, so hard that he asks me, 'What is it, Madhu? Have I got two noses suddenly? Or . . .' he rubs his hand over his face, clowning, I know, 'maybe I've got four eyes, huh?'

I can't join in the game, I can't pretend, I can't tell him why I'm staring, either. I'm wondering—are all the stories Munni tells me true? Is he such a bad man? Is it possible for people to hide things so well, for them to pretend to be what they are not? This seems worse to me than the cruelty itself. Cruelty, I think, should have an evil face. Like the villains in a Hindi movie who proclaim their evil nature in their looks, their clothes, their mannerisms, their talk, their harsh mocking laughter. If they don't reveal it openly, how will we know? How can we guard ourselves against them? I want to ask my father about this, but Munni has made me promise not to speak to anyone.

'If you do . . .' She leaves the threat incomplete so that I don't know whether it is she who will be threatened by my speaking out, or I who am being threatened by her. In any case, it is sufficient to gag me, to seal my lips. Yet I am constantly wondering about the mystery of Ghulam saab. Is he Munni's stepfather? I ask her. That would make some sense. (Though wicked stepfathers are, as yet, beyond my ken—they're waiting for me in the future, when Joe will give me *David Copperfield* to read. Right now, I've only heard of wicked stepmothers.)

'Is he your stepfather?'

'Chhut!' Munni says angrily. 'He's nobody of mine.'

It is difficult to believe Munni, but not impossible, because she is Munni and she is my friend and yes, I'm always on Munni's side. It's the safest place to be. As long as I'm with her, I'm guiltless of all those terrible things others are doing—like getting drunk and being beaten and taking off their clothes and doing 'it'. I'm smug and pleased when Munni tells me about these things. I don't do them, we don't do these things, Munni and I.

Babu dislikes Munni. He tries to discourage me from playing with her, he tries to prevent her from coming home. He's as harsh to her as it's possible to be, but he knows—and Munni does, too—that he can't go beyond a point. My father won't like it. Not only is she a neighbour and my friend, she's also Savitribai's daughter. My father admires Savitribai. When he comes back after listening to her, he says, 'Wah! What a woman! What a voice!'

No, Babu can't speak openly against Munni or oppose her

visits to our home. She knows it and she takes full advantage of it.

But after the birthday present episode, even my father becomes a little dubious about my association with Munni.

'My birthday is coming,' Munni tells me. 'Next week. You have to give me a present.'

She even tells me, orders me rather, what I should give her. 'A pair of earrings. We'll go and buy it ourselves. Your father said we could go. He said not to trouble him.'

I agree. I take the money from the first drawer of my father's table—'your father said you can take the money', Munni had said. She takes me to the jeweller's shop on the main market road. The shop is on a level above the street, three steps leading up to it. The small space is crowded now with four customers, there's no room for us there. We stand on the street, waiting for him to be free. If I stand on tiptoe, I can look into the glass-fronted counter facing the street. Munni, who is taller, is peering at it avidly, muttering, almost to herself, 'I like that one, the one with the red star and hanging pearls.'

Finally, even she gets tired of waiting. How long are those people going to take? They're buying some silverware. The items come out, they are weighed, the jeweller jots down figures on a piece of paper, the stuff is put away, brought back again . . . it goes on and on.

Munni, shuffling impatiently, calls out to the jeweller. 'Sonar-kaka, aho, Sonar-kaka.'

At last he sees us. 'What do you want?'

'She wants to buy earrings.'

I'm astonished by the statement. *I* want to buy earrings? Munni pinches me, preventing me from correcting her statement.

The jeweller now takes in our presence. I see recognition dawn on his face when he looks at me.

'You're the doctorsaheb's daughter.'

I nod.

'And you want to buy earrings?'

I nod again.

'Do you have the money?'

I open my hand and show him the notes I've taken out of my father's table drawer.

Quick as a flash he leans over and takes the money out of my hand. Before I can open my mouth, he puts it away and says, 'Come back with your father. He'll buy you whatever you want. Tell him I have your money.'

'But—but . . .' Munni, who has, surprisingly, been silent until now, is ready to argue. He turns away from us, repeating, 'Come back with your father'. He goes back to his customers who have been staring at us, he ignores us so completely that we have no choice but to walk away. Nevertheless, a prickling sensation down my back tells me they are staring at us, they are talking about us. For the first time I have a sense of wrongdoing. I'm filled with shame. And fear. He'll tell my father. What will my father do?

That night, my father talks to me about it. Yes, I say, we were going to buy earrings for Munni. The money? I got it from the drawer. Munni told me he had said I could.

'Why didn't you tell me? Why didn't you ask me for the money?'

'Munni said not to.'

'I see.'

Then he asks me, do I really want to buy Munni a gift? A pair of earrings?

'Yes.'

'All right, then. We'll get them for her.'

He gets the earrings. He opens the box and shows me the pair he has chosen, but he won't let me give them to her. 'I'll do that myself,' he says. And gets me some sweets to give her instead on her birthday.

He goes to Munni's house in the evening. I know he's given her the earrings, because he returns without the box. But

Munni never speaks of them. I never see her wearing them, either. And, the drawer where my father keeps his money is now locked.

'Your mother gave it to you, didn't she?' Babu says with a cruel pleasure when Munni comes home next. Munni's hand goes to her cheek, as if reminded of a blow. Then she makes a face at him and says, 'All lies. Who told you?' But about the earrings she says nothing.

That evening—or is it some days later?—it begins raining. She runs out into the rain.

'Come on, come out, come here,' she says to me.

But I can't. This is one of my father's few restrictions. I'm not allowed to play in the water, I can't go out in the rain. I watch Munni dancing in the rain, envying her and yet, for some reason, disturbed by the sight of her. There is nothing pretty or girlish about her dance. Her movements are gauche, almost savage. She looks ungainly, terrible, her hair plastered to her scalp, her clothes clinging to her skinny body, her face fierce and somehow angry.

'Come on,' she keeps calling out to me, 'come on out here. It's such fun.'

I want to join her, but I know Babu is inside, waiting, daring me to go out. And so I stand at the door watching her. In a while I go in, tired of a game I have no part in. When I come out a little later, she's no longer there.

Lata tells me a story about the twins, Bai's accompanists— Hasina's accompanist's rather—the 'tabla-master' and 'peti-master', as they're known locally. The two, Lata says, have never been seen apart. They got married on the same day and lived after that in the same house with their wives and children. When one of the wives died, the brothers stayed on together with the surviving wife and their joint brood of children. And nobody knew exactly who the father of a particular child was, not even—this is the climax of Lata's story—the children themselves. One of the girls was in Lata's class in school. When she had to enter her father's name in a form, she wrote it sometimes as Shivshankar, sometimes as Bhavanishankar. And, it was said, she countered the teacher's objection with 'What difference does it make?'

'Hari doesn't believe my story,' Lata says. 'He thinks I'm making it up. He doesn't actually say that, but he gives me a look—like this you know . . .'

She apes Hari's look of polite disbelief to perfection.

'But it's true, I swear it is.'

Her hand goes to her throat to strengthen her oath, a mannerism that, I imagine, has stayed over from her childhood.

I believe her. I've seen the twins together, I know how they give me the feeling of being one undivided self. I've seen one of them put on his glasses when the other begins reading, I've seen one twin tidy his hair when the other's hair is disordered. It's as if they're constantly looking into a mirror, seeing their reflections before them. I think of Adit's question, Adit who admired his cousins Rohan and Sanjay, twins too, but with their individualities clearly marked out, unlike these two. Nevertheless, Adit, fascinated by their twin-ness, asked me, 'Mama, why don't I have another me?'

Yes, why didn't he? It has occurred to me often since then: why didn't he?

The twins are the town's main link with Bai. None of her students have anything to do with her. I've seen the twins with her, though, sitting respectfully before her, nodding their heads in perfect synchronization, saying 'Hunh, hunh' together. These are, however, rare occasions. What does surprise me is that there is so little curiosity in the town about Bai. This was not how it was in Neemgaon. The town was buzzing with talk about her, about her activities and her visitors. Of course, Bai was a young woman then, young and beautiful. Now she's old, and interest in a woman who's neither young nor beautiful is obviously minimal. An old woman becomes almost invisible, people scarcely notice her. Bai, however, is not just any ordinary woman, she's a celebrity. I suppose some journalists did come when she fell ill in Bhavanipur. Now she's a part of the town, her presence accepted, even, maybe, forgotten. The house, deep within its grounds, a little away from the town, is like an isolated castle. There are no visitors. The only regular visitor is the owner of this house, Ravi Patil, Chandru's patient's son. The bungalow, which had housed the District Collector, had fallen into disuse and was bought by him. But his mother refused to move out of their ancestral home and so it lay vacant, until the time Bai fell ill during a visit to Bhavanipur, and, deciding to stay on here, needed a home. Ravi, one of her admirers, then offered her this bungalow. It is Lata who told me this. I hear much of the man Ravi Patil from her—he's an old family friend, she says—but I've seen him only once. A small-sized, boyish looking man, he scarcely gives me the feeling of being the local magnate and legend, which, I hear, he is. Having given up a successful career in the United States to return home when his father died, he's now started an industrial unit a few miles from Bhavanipur.

There are three ways of approaching Bai's house and I've tried all of them. There's the main approach, along the road and through the non-existent front gate, the route Lata had taken on the first day. There's another, the shortest route, which involves entering from the back of the house and going past a disused well and the dilapidated remains of a row of rooms, which were once the servants' quarters. The tiles have fallen off the roof, leaving the rooms open to the skies, but the doors are still secured by locks.

There's a third way, the one I now regularly take, stepping over the sagging barbed wire and going through the mango grove to the right of the house. Here, the undergrowth has been cleaned by whoever it was had gathered the mango crop at the end of summer. The grass is growing back, but even as it grows, it carries the impress of my feet, and I can see the faint outline of the path I followed the previous day. I walk carefully in my own steps and each day the path becomes more clear, more distinct. The mango grove is a silent place, resting, it seems, after the turbulence of its fruiting. Sometimes there are sudden startling sounds in the trees, squirrels, mostly, that run swiftly along the branches, only the glimpse of a bushy wagging tail, of shining eyes among the leaves, giving a hint of their presence.

Today, as I wait for Bai to come out, I can hear a jumble of sounds from the music room. Hasina's voice first, then the harmonium and the tanpura, Abhay's voice finally joining in. Abhay is at the fledgling stage, with a faint shadow of an incipient beard, a nose that's too large for his face and an Adam's apple bobbing up and down in his throat, marking the scale of his nervousness. But his voice, a deep and mature voice, seems to have vaulted over the awkwardness of adolescence and landed squarely into manhood. Something about the boy troubles me. I find myself unwilling to meet him, even to look at him. Fortunately, his shyness makes him avoid me, sparing me the discomfort of having to do it myself. Listening to his disembodied voice is peaceful, it's as soothing as the *kroo kroo* of the pigeons on the window ledge outside.

Abhay's voice ceases, Hasina resumes. Once again, the tabla joins her. I can hear a voice speaking out the beats—*dha dhin dhin dha*, hands clapping in time to the beat. Hasina suddenly changes course and moves into a tarana. The harmonium gets into it, I hear Hasina laughing even as she goes on with the syllables—*tana dir tom tani.* A male voice begins to laugh too and stops suddenly as if the person is frightened by his own temerity. Only just in time, for Bai now calls out from her room, 'Hasina, Hasina, where are you?' There is sudden silence and Hasina goes past me into Bai's room, her face sombre and shaded as usual, not a trace of gaiety or mischief visible on it. There are murmurs in Bai's room. Hasina comes out in a while with a pile of books in her hands—no, they're photograph albums—which she leaves on the table before me.

'You can go,' Bai tells Hasina when she has seated her. 'And tell that woman to send the tea hot—it's never properly hot. I can't drink lukewarm tea, you know that. All right, go, go, they're waiting for you. And no more fooling. I heard you, don't think I didn't.'

'You can put your machine away,' she says to me. 'I want to show you these pictures today.'

This is a guided tour of her career, of its highlights, its great moments, her performances all over the world, her awards, the accolades she has received. She is so familiar with these albums that she never falters in her instructions, nor is she ever wrong. 'Go on, a few pages ahead,' she says. 'That was in Geneva. It was the first time I went abroad, I never knew it would be so cold. I'd taken my shawl and sweater, but my feet . . . I was wearing men's socks that evening, thick woollen socks, under my Benaras sari.'

This was in Delhi. This was Gwalior—it was a great occasion for me. This is the Maharaja—he was the one who invited me. This is in Calcutta.

I go on turning the pages and she goes on enumerating the occasions, the places. She tries to remember what she sang that day. There are pictures with prime ministers and ministers, with the president, with other singers, dancers and writers. Her success and her achievements are here in these pages. This information is already with me, I have it in the articles about her, in the interviews with her. But now it comes to me in her own words. And to watch her face while she speaks, to see the animation that transforms it, to listen to the liveliness in her voice, makes it a different thing altogether. Her pride in these things, her childlike pleasure in her proximity to the great, her glee in her awards, in her travels abroad, is amazing. Very clearly, the years have not dulled the glitter of all this for her. She's reached the top, but the wonder, the surprise of having got there, hasn't left her. The naivety of it is touching. There's something a little sad about it as well. Surely, after a certain age, these things should not matter so much? Surely, when you've achieved so much, you should be above parading these triumphs?

There's a single picture that has fallen out of one of the albums. I pick it up. It's Bai as a young woman, her arms, almost bare in the very short sleeves of the time, as slender as a girl's, her sleek, well-oiled hair drawn straight back from her face. There's nothing posed about this picture, she's been caught unawares by the camera, her eyes staring into it, startled, defensive, vulnerable.

'What's that?' she asks me. 'Show it to me, give it here.' When I give it into her hands, she looks at it for a moment, says, 'Hmm.' After a pause, she gives it back to me. 'Put it back. Somewhere. I don't know where it came from. Hasina will know, she'll put it back. I want to show you my picture with Pundit Nehru. It's in that album, that red one. Yes, open it.'

While I turn the pages according to her directions, she tells me the story of that evening. Punditji was to attend her performance, she says. But a little before the programme was to begin, she received a message saying that he was a little tired and unwell. He would not be able to stay very long, so could she begin with whatever was her best? A raaga, maybe, that wouldn't take more than half an hour?

But Punditji stayed on after that first raaga. He stayed till the end. And when it was over, he posed with her for pictures.

'He gave me the rose from his buttonhole. I'm holding it in my hand in the picture, yes, there it is. See?'

She's as pleased as a child showing off her treasures to an adult. I look at the pictures—Bai and Punditji in one. And in

74

another, she and her entire group with Punditji. Ghulam Saab is here, I recognize him immediately. Yes, this is the man who lived next door to us, the same man, a little more fleshy perhaps, a little less hair maybe, but still handsome. Elegant in his churidar and brocade-edged jacket. I notice something else too. He's the only one in the picture looking neither at the camera, nor at Punditji, but at Bai.

So she hasn't been able to wipe him out of her life entirely. He was part of her career, of her profession, her success and her achievements. She couldn't do away with that.

But Munni . . . ?

Munni's likeness to her father strikes me when I see his picture. I didn't notice it earlier, perhaps because she tried hard, I realize it now, to cover it up, deliberately cultivating a bedraggled ragamuffin look, far removed from his tidy elegance. Or her mother's delicate beauty, either. I remember her drawing her hand over her hair, roughing it, dishevelling it, I see her standing before the mirror, making a face at herself, distorting her features. At the age when girls are so conscious of their looks, when they long so ardently for beauty, Munni treated her own natural good looks with lofty disdain. She resembled her mother more than her father, but her eyes, her light grey eyes, cat's eyes, as they were called, unmistakably linked her to the man she so strenuously disclaimed as father.

'Look, she's got cat's eyes,' I remember the girls exclaiming.

'Chhut!' Munni would say emphatically, denying the fact that stared her in the face when she looked into the mirror. But the eyes gave away the relationship she hated.

It was the eyes I noticed when I saw her in a bus in Bombay. She was occupying almost the entire seat. I let myself down gingerly into the little space she had left.

'Can you move just a bit?' I was forced to ask when I found

it impossible to seat myself properly.

She turned to me then, gave me a look and quickly turned away, making a slight movement that allowed me an inch more of space. That glance was enough; I knew this was Munni. The eyes stood out like a familiar landmark in a wholly changed landscape. She looked like any other middle-class Bombay housewife, more overweight than most, perhaps, the rolls of fat around her middle pushing her blouse up, forcing her to tie her petticoat in the proximity of her navel. Her hair, short and only just greying, was gathered at the nape of her neck by a clip, there was a bunch of keys at her waist and a plastic bag at her feet. The disguise was almost complete—except for the eyes that let her down.

'You're Munni,' I said abruptly, startled into recognition.

She looked at me, I could swear there was recognition there, before the face became blank and inscrutable.

'My name is Shailaja—Shailaja Joshi.'

The name was uttered slowly, clearly, her hand going to her mangalsutra as she spoke. Was it a habitual gesture? Or was she reassuring herself that she was indeed that Shailaja Joshi the black beads had transformed her into? A slight tremor in the hand seemed like a quiver of doubt. Am I Shailaja Joshi? Or Meenakshi Indorekar? Or Munni?

She went back to staring steadfastly out of the window after that, a determined ignoring of me and my question. She made it impossible for me to say, 'I'm Madhu, Munni—your neighbour, Madhu. Remember me?'

I knew she had recognized me, but she wouldn't admit it. When my stop arrived, I got up. My sari was caught between her back and the seat. I tugged at it. She felt the tug, and still not looking at me, she made a small movement that released it. I was waiting near the door when the conductor rang the bell. At the 'ting' she looked back, making sure perhaps that I was indeed getting off, or, wanting to look at me once again. I looked back at the same moment. Our eyes met—she was taken aback, she hadn't expected to be caught. So exactly did she look when she said to the girls, 'My name is not Munni, my name is Meenakshi.' Fighting with her back to the wall for the identity she wanted to have, the one she claimed finally, successfully denying her old one. Shailaja Joshi—a long way from Munni, daughter of Savitribai and Ghulam Saab.

Years later, reading *The First Circle*, when I came to the horrifying interrogation of the diplomat Innokenty, I found it chilling, terrifying, the almost wholly dehumanized interrogators repeating their questions over and over again, each time in the same order, in identical words:

What is your name?

Your patronymic?

Which year were you born?

And so on and on, over and over again, an endless repetition of the same questions put in the same order. It reminded me of something, something I could not figure out at the time. The evening after I met Munni, I made the connection when the questioning the girls subjected Munni to came back to me.

What's your name?

What's your father's name?

Where is your father?

Who's the man who lives with your mother?

And, like Innokenty's questions to his interrogators, Munni's answers too were ignored by her tormentors. Her replies—my father is in Pune, my father is a lawyer, my name is Meenakshi—were brushed aside as if they were of no consequence. Then there were the comments:

Look, she's wearing new clothes. That's for Id, isn't it?

Ayya, she's stinking of meat. Did you eat biryani?

Munni, however, never wavered in her defiance, in her stubborn adherence to her own truth, her bravado concealing, I think of it now, her terror, her distress and her grief.

It occurs to me that like her daughter, Bai too is into denial. There's no Munni in her life, no illegitimate child, no abandoned husband, no lover. In showing me her album, she's presenting me with her own illusion of her life. A life of success and achievement. Nothing lacking; no unreconciled child, no dead daughter.

Her obduracy tempts me to say to her bluntly, 'I'm Munni's friend, your daughter's friend'. It makes me want to put a knife to her skin, to see her jump. Often Bai reminds me of Munni herself, flaunting a secret, tantalizing me with hints, refusing to go on, saying, 'No, I won't tell you.' And I think—Bai knows what she's doing, she's mocking me, she's daring me to speak of Munni; it's the mischievousness, the provocative brattishness of the old. Even more often I wonder: what kind of a woman are you, denying your own child? Only the lowest, the meanest kind of creature could do such a thing.

5

It seems strange to me, one of the ironies of life, that I should be spending so much time engaging with words. Having lived in a house with two rather taciturn men—Babu almost a miser with his words, my father prepared to use them only when necessary, not otherwise—I was never a girl to set much store by speech. But after that there was Joe, Joe who led me into the magic of language and words, Joe who was so fascinated by these things himself. He's the only man I know who quoted prose as others do poetry, Dickens, specially. 'On the rampage and off the rampage. That's life, Pip!' he would say with a resigned shrug when one of us was in a temper. And often, when people were trying to pack themselves into his car, a Fiat, waving his arms in a large generous gesture, he would say, 'Oceans of room, my dear Copperfield, oceans of room.'

And there was Tony, subdued it seems, as long as his father was alive, keeping his reading and his pleasure in it to himself, but, after Joe's death, taking over, as it were, from his father, indulging himself in quoting poetry. With marriage, I came into contact with Som's father, a Sanskrit teacher who quoted Sanskrit as easily and fluently as Joe and his Dickens. It was so much a part of their family life, so deeply ingrained a habit of his, that the others scarcely noticed it. Nor did they care whether he was quoting from the *Gita*, the *Upanishads* or Kalidasa. His sing-song chanting was only a background to their daily life. But I often listened, caught by the magnificence of the language when it was chanted, so different from the tongue-twisting pain it was when I studied the texts in school and college. Som's father, pleased by my interest, would recite the shloka once again, slowly this time, tell me where it was from, what it meant—ever the school teacher, ready to explain, to instruct.

When I heard him recite the Vishnu-stotra, at first it was just a sonorous wonderful-sounding chant. But when he repeated the shloka for my benefit and told me the meaning, delighting, I could see, in the richness of the imagery, it was the tongue-in-cheekness of it that fascinated me.

What can I offer you, my Lord,
Whose house is studded with jewels
and whose consort is Lakshmi,
the giver of wealth?

Where is it from? I asked him.

Unusually for him, he didn't know. 'I suppose it was composed by a devotee,' he tendered a guess.

Of course, all prayers are composed by humans, they don't spring out of nowhere, wondrous myths notwithstanding. This one too. A devotee speaking to a resplendent god in a tone, a voice that, even if personal, seemed full of awe. Yet, I sensed reproach in the praise, an almost Leela-like touch of censoriousness. It was in this same way that Leela spoke about the mill owners. 'They have so much'. Yes, that was how this prayer was. 'You have all this. Now, what do you expect from me?'

The stotra came back to my mind after Adit's birth, when I could have said, in a parody of it, 'What can you give me, my Lord, I who have everything?'

Yes, I had it all, I knew I had it all. But would I, could I have uttered those words? Prickles of superstitious fears would have precluded me from saying them, would have stopped my mouth.

Don't say that. Touch wood, quickly. Cross your fingers.

As if we believe that there is, in truth, someone up there—or wherever that mythical being we dignify with capital letters lives—listening to us. Ready to strike us down when we get too cocky. Waiting to trip us up for our bravado. Nemesis. The Lord with his chakra spinning on his finger, prepared to send it towards us, to slice off our heads.

And so the Ganeshas in niches, the decorated thresholds, the mango leaf *torans*, the Oms, the Swastikas, the charms and amulets—all to keep disaster at bay, to stave off the nemesis of a jealous god.

It doesn't help; nothing does. It's always a losing battle. Such small remedies, these, to counter the terrible disease of being human, of being mortal and vulnerable. Like concocting a poultice on the kitchen fire to fight a raging gangrene. The only remedy is to believe that tragedies, disasters and sorrows are part of the scheme—if it can be called that. To understand that it's a package deal: you get the happiness, you've got to accept the sorrow and the pain as well. You can't get one and escape the other. But what's new about this thought? We all know the philosophy of duality—life and death, day and night, sorrow and happiness. It sounds good, it sounds *right* and when we speak of it, we nod our heads and agree that this is the truth of life. But when we're in the process of living, when the going is good, can we really make ourselves believe this? Will we concede, even to ourselves, that the sinister other of happiness is waiting for us round the corner? Basking in the bliss of family life, would I have let myself think: *this is not forever, this happiness is ephemeral, it is illusory*? No, I could not. How could I when, at that moment of experience, the happiness was so real, so substantial?

All this is futile thinking. You can never erase the past. The pictures remain, they return, over and over again, tantalizing me, tormenting me. I see Adit doing his Suryanamaskar along with Som, the two of them in identical white shorts and T-shirts, Adit looking at his father, carefully following his actions, imitating him to the smallest detail, repeating his words, and often getting them wrong. Lapsing for a moment from his solemnity when his own name comes into the prayer:

Om Adityaya namaha. Grinning at me then in uncontrollable delight, giving Som a quick fearful look. And at Som's mock-stern frown, putting his tongue out in self-reproach, going back to the namaskars, on to the next prayer, *Om Savitre namaha.*

Som walking into the sea with Adit sitting on his shoulders, my heart in my mouth as the water comes up to Som's waist, to his chest, his shoulders, touching Adit now. And then Adit running back to me, his face blazing, his small body quivering with excitement, tugging at me, saying, 'Mama, you come, you come also,' holding my hand as if reassuring me, imagining that the fear he has sensed in me, in my voice as I called out to the two of them, is for myself. Giving up finally and running back to Som, who's standing at the edge of the waves, his arms spread out for Adit to run into. Adit's tiny figure, which covers the whole landscape for me, running into his father's arms . . .

Sepia, forever the colour of innocence to me now.

Both Leela and Joe are disappointed with my refusal to go on with my studies after graduation. Leela speaks wistfully of her own lack of education, of how she had to struggle to complete her matriculation, how she hoped I would study more. Joe has his own dreams for me, he speaks often and openly of them. He wants me to do my M.A. in English Literature, to go abroad after that—Oxford, maybe? (oh, the ambitions of Joe!)—and come back home to teach. At Xavier's, his old college. Nowhere else, mind you! My graduation present from him is a beautiful volume of Shakespeare's collected works. This is the beginning, he hopes, of a career in which I will be teaching these plays to students.

But I have one good reason not to go on. My father's money is over. There was not much in any case; how much could a doctor in a place like Neemgaon earn? Leela had given me an

account of what there was after my father's death. You are not
dependent on anyone, she reminded me. It's your own money,
she said. Now I have come to the end of it.

Joe is eager to support my studies. 'Look upon it as a loan,'
he says. 'Pay me back when you start earning.'

But I am determined. I will start working, I will earn my
own money, become independent. It seems a godsend when
Joe's friend, Hamid Merchant, offers me a job with his
magazine *City Views*. It's only temporary, he says, only until
his editor Feroz returns from leave. Feroz is going for an
operation, he'll be back in three months. Can you help out?
Hamidbhai asks me. You don't mind?

Don't mind? I'm delighted. And when it turns out that Feroz
won't return—Feroz is nearly sixty, his son in Canada wants
his parents to go and live with him—my pleasure is complete.
The job is now mine, Hamidbhai tells me. Joe is not happy, I
hear him arguing with Hamidbhai, but Leela is reconciled. She
can understand my desire to earn money, to be independent
financially.

City Views is a very small magazine, run on subscriptions by
Hamdibhai for a group that calls itself the Bombay
Aficionados. Tony and I find the phrase excruciatingly funny.
Even after we look up the meaning in the dictionary, it doesn't
cease to amuse us. 'The Bombay Aficionado' we mouth at
each other, carefully pronouncing the word *aficionado* when
Hamidbhai rings up or visits Joe.

All this changes when I begin working for the magazine. I
don't allow Tony any levity, I refuse to join in his jokes. The
aficionados pay to run the magazine, they pay my salary!
Unfortunately, they want to write in the magazine as well.
Which is why, every month I have a heap of articles before me,
badly written, rambling and irrelevant, with very little of
Bombay in them. The magazine is supposed to be about
Bombay, its history, its buildings, its development, its eminent
people. But the articles are, most of the time, about the writers

themselves, their families, their feelings. My job is to choose from the pile and edit—which really means rewrite—the ones chosen. In spite of this drudgery, I enjoy my work immensely. I'm amazed by how comfortable I am with this work, at how soon I've made myself at home in it. I'm easy with the language—which I really learnt only since coming to Bombay, attracted to it by Joe's enthusiasm. I have to thank you, I tell Joe. But he disowns his share in my English. It's Dickens, he says, and Thackerey and the Brontes and all those others whom I need to thank. He smiles as he says this and I know I'm forgiven for letting go of his dreams, for taking up this job.

There are three of us working for *City Views*: Dalvi, the most senior, who's in charge of everything but the editorial, Venkat, the dogsbody, who does everything from typing to going to the press and mailing the letters. And I.

From the first day it's clear that Dalvi hates me. I'm an interloper. My sudden entry, the importance I get from the moment I'm in—he puts these things down to nepotism. He doesn't dare to criticize Hamidbhai, he is deferential, almost obsequious in his presence. And so, when he complains about my undeserved status, he never refers openly to Hamidbhai. He speaks of Joe, instead, as if it is Joe who's got me this job. 'It helps to be someone's niece,' he says. There's a kind of emphasis on 'niece' which puts it in inverted commas, marking out the peculiar relationship between Joe and me. He and I are the only two Marathi-speaking people there, but he refuses to speak to me in Marathi. That would mean admitting to some kind of a bond between us. He criticizes whatever I do, however I do it, he never ceases to compare my work, my ideas and my language with Feroz's. And though he has no authority over me, or the editorial functioning, he's been here so long that he knows he can get away with what he's doing.

He works out his hostility in other ways too. He comes to my table to berate me, his face angry, his tone sarcastic, but his eyes and his hands say other things. The eyes dart over my face, drop down to my body, they linger over my breasts, his hands brush lightly, and seemingly by accident, but I know with deliberate intent, against my body, my face. When he comes close to me, in what seems like intense anger, the short distance between us crackles with his desire, his lust. Venkat knows what is happening, he sees what Dalvi is doing, but he doesn't dare speak. His job matters to him. I already know he's the only earning member of his family. If he stays with *City Views* long enough, he hopes Hamidbhai will give him a better job, in one of his companies, as secretary perhaps. And so Venkat is silent. Dalvi turns the office into a battle zone: the two hard-working males working for a living, their families dependent on the money they earn, against one pampered female who's here to pass her time. I know I'm not the dilettante Dalvi implies I am. I'm a fairly ignorant amateur, but I intend to learn everything. And learn fast.

Most of the time I can ignore Dalvi and his vicious behaviour. I am enjoying myself too much to worry about such things. I have everything I want: work I enjoy, an income of my own, a room to live in.

This is something I've been very worried about. Where will I go when I leave the hostel? I am sure I won't live in Joe's home, not permanently, anyway. Paula is no longer there, she has gone to live with her aunt in London, but she exerts her influence over Joe, over his home, even from there. Leela has offered me her Maruti Chawl home. Of the two rooms, one is an office for her various activities; I can have the other. But there's no privacy there. And I want something of my own. Hamidbhai, sensing my need, offers me this room, part of the two large flats which house both his home and the office of *City Views*. A long corridor separates this room from the office, a swing door from Hamidbhai's own living space. A tiny bathroom, the size of a toilet in trains, and another little space in the corridor, which becomes my kitchen, complete my new home. To me it's heaven. Lying on my narrow bed on the

SHASHI DESHPANDE

divan in my almost bare cell-like room, I have a sense of
absolute freedom, of soaring in space. Even the
monsoon-beaten grey dingy walls of the next building, the
only view I have from my window, can't quench my joy, my
sense of having grown wings. I'm happier than I have been for
years. Dalvi's harassment can't take this away from me.

And Dalvi, to do him justice, has his good days as well, days
when he leaves me alone. Dalvi is our map expert. Each
month, he brings out a map of a particular area of Bombay.
He does it with painstaking care, working out the fine details
with the skill of a miniature artist, so absorbed in his task that
each time Hamidbhai has to remind him to put in the dots,
crosses and numbers that locate the landmarks.

'Look at that, Saheb! If you hadn't reminded me, I would
have completely forgotten. What kind of a head have I got!'

In spite of the enthusiasm with which he speaks to
Hamidbhai, he does this part of the work reluctantly,
unwilling, it appears, to mar his masterpiece. The good
humour continues until the map is complete and, carefully
placed between sheets of paper, goes into the drawer that
stores all his maps. Hamidbhai has promised him an
exhibition some time, one the Bombay Aficionados are
planning, in which Dalvi's maps will be the highlight. Each
time a map goes into the drawer, Dalvi speaks of this
possibility, with a pretence of self-deprecation—'I don't know
why Saheb wants to do this, my maps are not worth it.' Then
its over and he's back to nasty looks and malicious remarks.

But Dalvi's harassment (harassment? I never gave it as much
importance as the word implies) is a fleabite, nothing as
weighed against the other things: my pride in my work,
Hamidbhai's praise, letters from subscribers, phone calls from
Hamidbhai's fellow-aficionados, Joe's pride in me.
Nevertheless, Dalvi's role in my life is talked about,
commented on.

'Good day or bad day?'

It's the first question Tony asks when he visits me. Tony is a regular visitor to my room. I don't know how it began, but it became a habit for him to come every Saturday. At some time, Chandru and Som join us and soon my room becomes their regular weekend haunt. I'm surprised at the regularity of their visits. All three of them have comfortable homes of their own, why do they come here? Not for me, I'm sure of that. Tony, of course, is a brother. And both Som and Chandru have their own romances going. Chandru is already engaged to Satee, though it seems from their conversation that he has other girls as well. Nothing serious, he claims, and they laugh. Som is in the midst of a tumultuous romance with Neelam, his classmate, the gorgeous, sensuous, whimsical Neelam, who has a long string of boyfriends, of whom Som is one.

In a while, the reason why they come to my room becomes a non-issue. Their visits have become an established regular practice all of us look forward to. I cook meals for us in the narrow passage with its tiny counter and doll-sized sink. I learned to cook out of sheer necessity. Leela's cooking and Phillo's vegetarian attempts are usually total disasters. I began in Leela's room, but was constrained by her severely limited stores, by the kerosene stove that produces either a devouring flame which chars everything within minutes, or a reluctant one that makes boiling even a cup of water a painfully tedious process. Here, in my own room, I buy what I want, I experiment, I learn to combine diverse ingredients into something that transcends all of them. I have a hugely appreciative trio enjoying my efforts, but it's not for them that I'm doing this. It's for myself, my own pleasure.

Ketaki, the only friend left over from my college days, finds my association with these three young men exciting. Looking out from the safe dull haven (as she sees it) of her own family life, her assured future of marriage to Atul, a man she's known all her life, she envies me my freedom, my Bohemian lifestyle, as she imagines it to be. She sees romance, not friendship, in our meetings. She's sure there's 'something' going on, she doesn't believe me when I tell her that my pleasure in their company is, in fact, because there's nothing.

The truth is I'm comfortable with men, I've grown up among men—my father, Babu and the Kakas, my father's friends. I understand men. It's the women I find harder to understand. At times, like when Ketaki's mother speaks to me, I think I need someone to translate the language for me. There seems to be some disjointedness between her words and what she means.

Our companionship flowers in that room. Tony and I are, of course, already friends, but Chandru and Som, whom I've known as Joe's students and Tony's friends, were strangers to begin with. Now it's different. There's something magical about everything here—the food, the smells, the conversation, the laughter. And there are the drinks that Chandru almost imperceptibly introduces into our evenings. I'm a little uneasy about it. I've already asked Hamidbhai's permission for their visits. 'It's okay,' he says. 'Have fun,' he says. 'Enjoy yourselves.'

But drinks? I don't tell him about it. The bottles are smuggled in and out, the glasses washed and hidden away, though I know Hamdibhai never enters my room. Yet he seems to know all that's going on. He never says anything, but I sense his knowledge. In fact, he sees more than there is.

'I hope I'll be the first to know the good news,' he says once.

Good news? I don't know what he means. Later, when I tell him about Som, that Som and I are engaged, he grins. 'So,' he says, 'am I the first to know, after all?'

Two years after our marriage, Adit is born.

A child's birth is a rebirth for a woman, it's like becoming part of the world once again. The first time you emerge through someone else's pain and blood; this time, it's your own. The pain of your body opening, on the point, you think, of splitting apart, as if a divine Krishna is standing somewhere nearby, giving Nature the signal by splitting a blade of grass. The stretching that goes on and on, the pain maddening you until you think—I want to die, I want to be out of this. And then, at the moment when it seems impossible, when death seems the only recourse, the miracle happens, the pinhole opening becomes a head-sized aperture. And from death you return to life, not just the new life you've produced, but your own life, renewed, given back to you.

Does this happen to everyone? Does every child bring such radiance into a parent's life? How is it I never noticed it until it happened to me? Have I been blind? Or, am I specially privileged, enjoying something rare, something unique? Looking at the baby in his cradle, I am dazed by my own happiness. When he smiles at me, when he holds out his arms to me, or so I imagine, I feel burdened by my joy, my whole body heavy and sluggish with it, gorged, like my breasts are with milk. I haven't put on much weight—they all remark on it, they seem to think it unnatural that I haven't gone flabby and fleshy—but when I walk, I am conscious of the weight of my body, I feel the imprint of my feet on the ground.

What can you give me, my Lord, I, who have everything?

But happiness is enclosed in a glass case, so fragile that it seems it can shatter at a touch of the fears that surround it. The baby is so small, so frail, so vulnerable—how can I, how will I keep it safe? The little opening in the skull terrifies me. And the wispy neck that threatens to snap at a touch. How could Nature be so stupid as to allow these things? I'm in a cold sweat each time someone picks up the baby, I can't bear to see my mother-in-law do it, she holds him so casually, surely she'll drop him, his head is drooping backwards, can't she see that . . .?

It's a friend of mine who gives me, as a gift on Adit's birth, a book called *Small Remedies*. Full of 'tips', as it claims, about dealing with a baby's minor problems. Motherless, knowing nothing about babies and mothering, unwilling nonetheless to entrust my baby to anyone else, I turn to the book with relief, I clutch at it as if it's a life-jacket. It becomes my Bible. Diarrhoea, colds, a stuffy nose, colic, teething, weaning—it gives me answers to all these things. They laugh at my dependence on the book, Chandru, Tony, Rekha—all of them think it's amusing bringing up a child by a book. Even Leela finds it funny. 'Get out the book,' she says in a kind of mock resignation the moment Adit sneezes or whimpers. Som names it '*The Kadha Pustak*'—the 'get out the book' book. It's so much read, so often opened, that within a few months it's falling to pieces. But it has served its purpose. Adit has outgrown the problems it contains. I need to look elsewhere.

I am surrounded by doctors but it's Rajani—Leela's niece, Sunanda's daughter—the pediatrician, who's my ally, my Guru, my God. I am constantly ringing her up about Adit. Som disapproves. 'She's a busy woman, Madhu,' he says. 'You shouldn't bother her over trifles.' But Rajani doesn't mind; at least, she never gives me the impression of minding. But even she, I know, doesn't really understand. She's all right about the tangible enemies—the colds, the fever, the teething—but she will laugh, I know, if I speak to her about the other fears that seem to me to hover over Adit.

My father would have understood. He knew about these enemies, he had his own weapons against them. I was one of those children forever falling and hurting myself, my knees and elbows perpetually stained red with Mercurochrome, always bandaged. It was after I'd fallen at least half-a-dozen times in the bathroom that my father told me about the invisible 'they', who, he said, are always waiting to trip you up, to make you fall and hurt yourself. You have to fool them, he said.

My father was not a whimsical man, he said this with the utmost seriousness. And I believed him utterly. 'This is what you have to do,' he told me. 'Pretend you're going somewhere else—like this.'

And he strolled nonchalantly towards the door, lips puckered in a soundless whistle. And then suddenly, veering round, he moved towards the bathroom.

'You've got to do it quickly, before they realize where you are,' he said. 'That's the way to fool them.'

I followed his instructions to the letter—the whistle, the casual walk, the sudden change of direction. It seemed to work. I had fewer falls, for long periods no falls at all.

But the invisible foes are not so easily fooled. They're always waiting for you, biding their time to catch you off-guard. When I go to Bombay to see my father in the hospital, he is still conscious, he sees me, but he can't talk. Yet his eyes hold a smile, his lips are puckered as if he's whistling, his hand with the tube rises slowly and falls in a gesture of helplessness. And I remember then our game of fooling those invisible enemies, I know what he's saying, I know what he's trying to tell me: *They got me after all, they always do.*

6

The human mind goes beyond the possible, the capacity to believe vaults over the physical world and its laws. And therefore it is that we hope for miracles, we pray for the impossible to happen, for the dying not to die, for the dead to return. It never happens, it has never happened yet. Nevertheless, we go on hoping, we believe, we pray. And we dream.

For the first time in months, I wake up from a dream, a peaceful and quiet dream, like a routine day when everything happens as it should, nothing unexpected or disturbing marring the course of it. Adit was part of it—I didn't see him, he was not bodily present, but I knew he was there, inhabiting the world I was in. Som was part of it too, though invisible like Adit, the three of us together in a vast landscape of tranquillity. For a moment, for a minute fraction of a moment after waking, I clasp that dream in my arms. Then it slithers away from my grasp and I am left with nothing; only the reality of my life here without Som and Adit. Alone in a strange house. But no longer among strangers. It would be churlish of me to say that, unfair to Lata if I were to do so.

Lata no longer allows me to be a stranger. I come upon her sobbing one day. I want to back out of the room, but she makes no attempt to hide her grief from me, she shows so little discomfort at my presence that it does not seem an intrusion. And her grief is so large, so genuine, that it would be unkind of me to walk away from it. I sit with her until she recovers. Finally, it's over. She wipes her sodden face with her dupatta, blows her nose, rubs her swollen eyes with both her hands and says to me, 'It's so stupid to cry, isn't it, Kaku? But once I start it seems I can never stop.'

She does not tell me the reason for her tears, nor do I ask. The grief is real, that's all that matters. And she has allowed me to share it, she hasn't kept me out.

I'm family. Lata's behaviour to me spells this out. It is as if Hari's revelation to me has made me family overnight. She's shocked when Hari, after either not addressing me at all, or occasionally calling me 'Ma'am'—which slips out, I think, in spite of him, shocking her and taking him unawares—begins to call me 'Madhu'.

'You can't call her that,' she remonstrates with him.

I guess she means it's disrespectful. Considering my age, perhaps? And our relationship—which is what? She figures it out: since Hari's grandmother and my mother were sisters, Hari's mother and I are first cousins. Therefore, I am Hari's aunt.

'You can call her Madhu-mavshi,' she says with a grin.

'By which logic you shouldn't be calling her Kaku. She's scarcely your father's brother's wife, is she?'

'That's different.'

It's true it's not the same. It doesn't matter what she calls me, the distance between us has dissolved. Her certainty about this makes it impossible for me to ignore it, either. All the guest frills have been put away. We drink our tea out of the everyday mugs, tea which is poured directly from the long-handled steel vessel, the teapot having been restored to the cupboard, to its usual place. And when the cook takes leave, because her daughter has had a baby, I'm allowed to cook the afternoon meal. There are days when Lata comes home to join me at lunch. She's enjoying the food, she says. It's a long time since I ate this kind of food, she says appreciatively. Both Hari and I love good food, but we're lazy, at least I am, she says. And he comes home too tired to bother

93

about anything. And so, we eat whatever the cook feeds us with.

It is during these mealtime conversations that she makes giant leaps into intimacy. She's bored with her job at the bank, she tells me. It's tedious, dull, repetitive. She longs to get away. She's lived in this house, in this town, Bhavanipur, all her life. 'Imagine that, Kaku! Just imagine it!' She wants to get away. Her sisters keep inviting her—to Bombay for a visit, to California for a holiday. And there are Hari's parents—his father and stepmother—who would love to have her spend some time in Pune . . .

'But it's not the same, is it, Kaku?'

She can't clearly explain what it is she wants. I glimpse vague dreams of freedom, of being able to move about, going to unknown places, of not being tied down to anything.

'But I can't give up my job, we need the money.'

Hari's project, she tells me, is for two years. They don't know what will happen after that. He could be without a job for a while. So . . .

This naivety seems endearing to me, the naivety that makes her unaware of the fact, or makes her ignore it perhaps, that the burden of earning the money should be Hari's, not hers. That she does not have to take on the responsibility of being the wage earner of the family.

But there was Leela, part of a generation even before mine. She always supported herself. When her first husband, Vasant, died, she took up a job and educated her brothers-in-law. Even after marrying Joe, a doctor with a fairly good income, she continued to live on her own money. And after Joe died, she moved back into her Maruti Chawl home the very next day, the place where she began her married life at the age of fifteen.

But Leela was an unusual woman, ahead not only of her generation, but the next one as well; I'm realizing this only now. I've never thought of her as anything but Leela—Leela, who took me into her home and was always with me after that. But here, in this home, I'm beginning to see her as something else. This new image of Leela comes to me through Hari. When Hari and I speak about her, between his questions and my answers, she takes on the stature of a heroine.

To Lata, Leela is no more than the link between us. I am the object, as far as she is concerned. But to Hari, I am the medium through whom he hopes to see something of Leela. I can see that he has constructed an epic figure of Leela, taking what came to him from his mother and grandmother and building on it.

'If I were you,' he says to me, 'I'd write about Leela, not Savitribai.'

I've begun to understand that Hari has no great regard for Bai. It's not only that he's not interested in music—I'm almost wholly tone-deaf, he says—he looks askance at Bai's life, he thinks of it as a self-indulgent one. There's a touch of the puritan in him. No, it's not really puritanism, it's more a disapproving criticism of a life that doesn't look beyond one's own self. In a way, he's like Leela herself, though without her transparency, her openness. I remember her comment after watching Bimal Roy's *Devdas*, my treat to the family when I got my first salary. 'Why that dreary weepy film?' Tony had groaned, but for a girl my age, an anguished, tragic Dilip Kumar was irresistible. I could see Tony was bored, Joe charmed, as he always was by anything unusual, taking pleasure in my happiness. But Leela, who almost never saw a movie (*Kismet* was the last one she had seen, she said and Tony was awed; that's nearly prehistoric, he said) watched this one with the same concentration, the same earnestness, with which she did everything in her life. She was silent for a long time after we came out. I thought that the hero's dying of TB had brought back memories of her husband Vasant who had died of the same disease and my mother, her sister, who died of it too. I was regretting my choice of the movie, when she broke her silence. But from her words, it was clear that she hadn't been brooding over her dead husband or sister at all. No, she'd been thinking of something quite different.

'Now, I know,' she said, as if she had solved a puzzle. 'Now I know why that poor man drank so much. He had nothing to do, he didn't have any work at all. I'm serious, what are you all laughing at,' she asked us severely, unable to understand our amusement—only Leela could have made this statement! 'If an intelligent man like him remains idle, what else can he do but take to drink?'

And here's Hari, her sister's grandson, who, I'm sure, thinks the same way. Who imagines perhaps that Bai's life lacks the usefulness, the purposefulness he thinks every life should have. I don't know, maybe I'm imagining the disapproval.

Whatever it is, he's grown up, I can see, with this idea of Leela's life as being an exceptional one, of Leela as an extraordinary woman. He asks me questions about her participation in the '42 Quit India movement. Is it true there was a price on her head? Is it true that, while underground, she was responsible for many daring deeds? And that, while she had narrow escapes, she was never caught, but came out only after an amnesty was declared? He heard that she was opposed to satyagraha, that she believed in direct action. Is that true? And did she resign from the Communist Party because they didn't select her as a candidate for Parliamentary elections and chose a much younger person instead?

He seems surprised by my uncertain, halting answers, by how little I can tell him about these things. Did she resign from the party because of Tibet? he asks. Did she? I try to think. She said something about it, I can remember that, about how it hurt. But, no, she was still a member of the party when I went to Bombay. Was it the Chinese invasion then? That seems more likely, she was angry then, furious at the party's response to it. Wasn't it after this that she became a part of the Socialist group? I'm not entirely sure. But certainly, her leaving the party had nothing to do with not being selected as a candidate for the Parliamentary elections. She'd been a Corporator, she was one when I went to Bombay, but I remember how disillusioned she was about being able to do anything from within the system. It's much better to work from outside it, she said to me once. You are more free, less fettered.

There are a few bits of information I can give him though, things she spoke to me about. Like the fact that, yes, she had been opposed to the Gandhian methods of ahimsa and satyagraha. I thought there was something ridiculous about letting oneself be beaten up, she said. It goes against the grain of human nature, she thought, to submit that way. A blow for a blow—that's how we're made, that's natural. She told me this, adding, 'I was young then, my blood was hot. When your blood is boiling, you can't think clearly, you can't see straight.' But she'd changed, she said. She was not happy about some of the things she'd done at that time, she told me. She regretted it, she said. Deeply. 'That year of my life, I sometimes wish I could erase it, make it never have happened.'

I tell Hari that she spoke to me of this when she was, in fact, taking part in a movement that had adopted the Gandhian method of satyagraha. The all-women anti-price rise movement that snowballed into something much more. She was one of the leaders of that movement. But he's read about this, the information is not new to him, and he brushes it aside almost brusquely.

I can see that he's disappointed with the little I can tell him. How can I have lived so long with her and yet know so little about her? But the Leela I knew was not the public Leela. Even when I visited her in her Maruti Chawl home, when I stayed there occasionally with her, her public life remained in the background, she never involved me in it. I know only my Leela, an ordinary woman who, when I took her out on a rare visit to Juhu, ate her bhelpuri with as much gusto as Adit, and said, 'What fun that was!' Who sternly admonished Adit when he wouldn't eat all that was on his plate, 'Eat it up now—lick it up chatta matta. You shouldn't waste even a grain.'

I may not know when Leela officially became a member of the Communist Party, but I can tell Hari where the beginnings were. Leela has often told me how she dislikes her natal family regarding itself as something special. 'We Inamdars'—she heard the expression all the time and she wondered: what made them special? What had they done, except hold on to the lands which they had inherited, lands they had done nothing to deserve? And there is her story of the bangle woman who came every month to equip the females of the family with glass bangles.

'We had to wear our oldest saris when she fitted us with the bangles and after we'd finished we had to have a bath—because she'd touched us. Such a smiling, loving woman. I can still remember how gently she held our hands in hers, how softly she pushed the bangles up so that she wouldn't hurt us. But she was unclean because of her caste. And yet, when she'd finished putting the bangles on us, we had to touch her feet, do a namaskar. Crazy!'

This was when, I imagine, Leela moved away from caste and disowned it. It meant nothing to her, which is why she alone in the family accepted my parents' marriage, rejoiced with them and invited them to stay with her in Maruti Chawl, while my father looked about for a place to take his bride to.

I don't think Hari is interested in this Leela, in these personal matters. In fact, though he has stopped calling her Sindhu and now calls her Leela, as I do, we still seem to be speaking of two different women. His Leela is the public figure; my Leela is the woman who made me a part of her life after my father's death and brought me out of the terrifying emptiness I faced when he died. It was because of Leela that I never felt an orphan. Both her families took me in. Vasant's brother Raghunath and his wife Sunanda adopted me immediately as a niece. To Rajani—Raghunath and Sunanda's daughter—I became a sister right away. And if I was kept out of Joe's family by Paula's relentless hostility, I still forged a relationship with each of them, separately. Even Phillo, who'd been inimical at first—another Hindu stranger invading their family—thawed when she realized I'd lost both my parents. An orphan herself, one who'd been brought up in an orphanage, she developed a fellow feeling for me and took me under her wing. But her compassion was wasted. I had Joe and Leela with me; how could I feel orphaned?

Leela and Joe. To me Leela is, above all, part of that wonderful companionship, that beautiful relationship. I would like to tell Hari about the miracle of their meeting, Leela living in the crowded chawls among the cotton mills, Joe in his Bandra flat. The two brought together by that deadly rod, the TB bacillus. Leela, motivated perhaps by the guilt that came from my mother's death—she always felt that my mother got the disease in Maruti Chawl, where she stayed for a few days after her runaway marriage—worked among women who ignored their symptoms until it was too late. She sent them to Joe's clinic, the one he had specially established for TB patients. I'd like to share with Hari my wonder at the strangeness of Joe, a widower with two children, falling madly in love with this woman, a widow, who wore, as Phillo said, 'ayah saris'—cotton saris from the mills her husband had worked in, saris she was loyal to until the mills themselves closed down. A woman who could speak no English and knew nothing of literature or music, the two great forces in Joe's life, in addition to medicine. A woman who had, as Joe often said, 'no sense of humour at all.' Joe himself spoke impeccable English—like an Englishman, according to Phillo. And quoted from his favourite writers at the drop of a hat. 'Alas, poor Yorick!' he is supposed to have exclaimed to some bewildered students during a postmortem class. Actually, he's the only man I've known who used the word 'alas' in his conversation—not as a witticism, or as a quaint exclamation, but matter-of-factly.

I wonder sometimes whether Joe turned to Leela, living in the midst of the teeming life of a Bombay chawl, a life rampant with emotions and drama, as a reaction to his failed marriage, his disappointment in his exquisite Rita, who, at the end of her life, isolated herself from everyone and everything, playing to herself in an empty room, the scales falling coldly into emptiness, into space.

No, to think this way is to wrong Joe, to wrong both Leela and Joe and the emotion that held them together, the love that transformed not only their lives, but mine as well. And Tony's. But this love story is one I can't speak of to this solemn, rather priggish young man. It will not reach him. I have a feeling his ears are as little tuned to it as they are to Bai's music.

Am I wronging him by thinking this way? Is he not part of a love story as well? Lata and he—two persons from entirely different backgrounds, different languages, different ideas—what else is it but love that holds them together?

When Munni narrated the stories of the movies she saw, all of which centred round love, it was only a word to me. Unwilling, as ever, to admit my ignorance to Munni, I nodded sagely when she spoke of it to me, as knowingly as I did when she spoke of the mysterious 'it'. But neither of these meant anything to me then. Later, when my friend Ketaki, addicted to the romantic mush of pulp fiction, brought the word back into my life, I was no longer a stranger to the word or to the idea. I had already located it, on a point between the two extremes of Munni's 'filmi' love and the 'it' which, though at the other end of the spectrum, was somehow related to it. And then Adit was born and I understood something more: why it is that we give this single emotion so much significance, so much space in our lives. It is in this love that new life has its source, it is here that family life begins.

One of the favourite games of the girls during my childhood

was playing 'house house', in which the 'mother' settles down with her little pots and pans to cook, the 'children' go to school or self-consciously play, and the 'father' goes out to work. When he comes home, he sits, legs crossed, calling out loudly to the children or the mother. (Being father is the easiest really, but no one wants to be father. There is no excitement in it. The girls reject the role, the older boys scorn these games and even the little ones have to be coerced or bribed into becoming 'father').

I find this a very boring game. I can't relate to it, because I've never seen this pattern, I've never been a part of it. My father gives me no orders, he does not yell at me. He and I are equals in a way. Babu is the domestic authority—he cooks and cleans, but he is no mother. He is surly, his sternness never redeemed, as far as I can remember, by a single moment of softness or tenderness. I know nothing of mothers, anyway, because not only am I motherless, my mother is not even an absence, a tabula rasa on which I can write what I want. The only picture of hers we have at home shows her as a girl, with two thick plaits, holding a trophy in her hands—scarcely a mother figure. The only story I have heard about her is the one told to me by my father when I was in bed with a temperature. He was trying to cover his anxiety—I know he is always very anxious when I am not well—but in his nervousness, he dropped the thermometer which shattered into tiny bits. Collecting the tiny slivers of glass, he told me about my mother who once broke a thermometer. Deliberately. She threw it on the ground, he said with a small smile, because she was angry that her temperature wouldn't go down. While my father tried to pick up the shining globules of mercury, I thought of his story, of the girl flinging the thermometer away in a childish tantrum. This girl my mother? Scarcely a mother figure.

Babu, harsh though he is, is the one who has to teach me about being a girl. 'Don't run out in your petticoat,' he warns me. 'You must come home before dark,' he tells me. 'If those

101

boys talk to you, ignore them,' he says when I'm a little older. It is Babu who persuades my father to engage an old woman as a servant after I've officially grown up. She has nothing to do but to wash my clothes, fold them, and be there whenever I'm home. Following me about. Which enrages me, but she persists. And I know it's no good appealing to my father. Babu's word, in many matters, is the final law.

Children are so totally incurious. I know so little, almost nothing about Babu—where he came from or whether he had a family. I only guess that my father and Babu have known each other for a long time. My father calls him 'Baburao' when he's in a good mood. And even if Babu does not smile, I still know he's pleased when my father does that. After my father's death Babu disappears. He accompanies me to Bombay, he's there in the hospital, I see him, standing by himself, rarely speaking to anyone. I see him in Leela's house when they bring the body home, no, I don't *see* anyone, but I'm conscious of his presence, I hear him grunt when he bends down to pick the body up from the floor. I never see him after this, never again.

After that, there's only Leela and Joe. I enter their home holding on to Leela's sari, as it were, but I never become part of the family. This is not a proper family, nor the kind of family the girls evoked in their 'house house' game, either. Joe and Leela are a couple, but they are not father and mother. Paula draws a line around Joe and herself, she ignores Leela completely. For her, it's as if Leela does not exist. Leela responds by making herself invisible—she scarcely speaks in Paula's presence. Perhaps Paula would have liked to include Tony in her circle, but Tony, vacant-faced, elusive, keeps slipping away, he doesn't seem to want to belong.

I can never be part of this set-up, I have no place in it, not even as an outsider. Paula, zealous sentinel, bars my way. But I slowly forge relationships with Tony, with Phillo, outside the family and independent of it. After Paula leaves Bombay and goes to London to her aunt's house, for a visit it is said, Tony becomes my brother. Properly. He decides to regularize our relationship, he tells Leela he wants me to do the *bhau-bij aarti* for him. And suddenly, overnight, we become brother and sister.

Simulate family life and it becomes real. Except for the mother-child relationship, where there is a visible physical connection, all the others are built on faith, anyway.

It's only when I marry Som that I get into a real family. For the first time I see a model family laid out before me, like a model house, correct to the last brick, to the last tile on the roof. They remind me of a school primer, setting out relationships and roles. Things reduced to the simplest basics, because there are not enough words as yet to deal with complexities.

This is Baba. He is the father. He goes out to work.

This is Aai. She is the mother. She looks after the home and the children.

This is Dada, the oldest brother. He helps his father.

This is Akka, the oldest sister.

And so on. Each one playing out her or his allotted role to perfection. The dignified father. The nurturing mother. The serious, responsible oldest brother. The eldest sister, a surrogate mother to the youngest two. Even Som and Nisha, the two youngest, though they retained their names, not losing them like the others did, to their role names—Dada, Akka, Tai—they too confirmed to the stereotypes to some extent: Nisha, the youngest girl, the rebel, the boldest, the prettiest. And Som, the younger brother, jovial and happy-go-lucky.

It is not surprising that Som's family is bewildered by the 'bride's party' in our wedding. Som's immediate family knows about Leela and Joe, but as for the others ...

I am like any other bride in my Benaras sari, green bangles and silver toe rings. But there's Tony—who is he? Acting like a host, distributing the *akshada* just before the ceremony, urging everyone during lunch to 'eat more', 'eat slowly', speaking a queer Marathi that does not include the plural 'you', so that he talks to everyone, old and young, in the same way—who is he? And Phillo in her best and shiniest dress which is too tight over her stomach, clutching the huge handbag—Joe's last Christmas present to her—sitting in the front row like an honoured guest and wearing her shoes even when she enters the mandap—who is she? And Hamidbhai, in spite of his English suit, unmistakably a Muslim, and Joe, so intimate with me and yet so clearly not-a-Hindu—they are all mysteries to the guests.

Only Sunanda and Raghunath make sense. Sunanda in her nine-yard traditional sari and Raghunath in his dhoti, kurta and black cap are a script the others can understand, one that they can read. Yet, in a way, they are a puzzle too. How are they related to the bride? If they're performing the *kanyadaan*, they have to be close relations of the bride. But what exactly are they? They're her Kaka and Kaki, Som's mother says. Distant cousins of her father's. It's better than explaining that they're the bride's aunt's first husband's family. However, they seem to know what to do, their behaviour and actions are correct, just what they should be, so that the ceremonies go through without any hiccups. Sunanda, specially, wearing all her traditional jewels and at her winsome best, charms everyone. No one else seems to do things right. Phillo kisses Som after the ceremony—yes, actually kisses him! And Joe kisses me—this is worse, everyone is horrified.

And there's Leela. After the ceremony, when Som and I start on our round of namaskars to the elders, we have to go in search of Leela. Instead of being right there in front, witnessing everything with avid interest, she's at the back, disassociated from all the bustle around her, deeply absorbed in some thought. I know that expression of hers, I'm not surprised when she says to me the moment we approach, Som and I, as if continuing a conversation, 'Aga, Madhu, we quite forgot to write to your Kaka about your wedding.'

I begin to laugh then, at the idea of Leela agonizing over the fact that she has forgotten to inform my father's brother, the man who has not thought of me for the last ten years, about my wedding. Laughter that increases at the look of dismay on her face—Leela's emotions are always larger than life-size, there's too little room on her face for them—and the offended look (what's so funny, eh?) that replaces the dismay. They are shocked, I hear this later. Som's family is horrified that at a time when I should be sentimental, emotional, sobbing perhaps, in my aunt's arms, I am laughing hysterically.

I am immediately taken into the heart of Som's family, I am one of them right away—I am told family secrets, shown everyone's jewellery, consulted about names for babies to be born, invaded by large groups without any notice. Relationships swirl about me in long endless tapes that bind everyone in a confused, inextricable tangle. I've never seen anything like this, I enjoy it, I tell Leela all about it, and she listens to me with the air of an anthropologist hearing about the customs of a new tribe.

But it's with Adit's birth that I really become a part of it, a full member of the society. Suddenly everyone matters to me; they're Adit's grandparents, his uncles and aunts, his cousins. But above all, I learn the magic of that small circle, the basic unit of family life—father, mother and child. The beginning of the world, the Gangotri of humanity. Now, at long last, I'm playing the game of *'house house'*, I'm playing the mother's role. I think of the girls of my childhood who, as part of their role as mothers, stretched out their legs after they finished 'cooking', uttering little 'oh oh's' of weariness, aping, I imagine, their own mothers. I don't know this fatigue. I'm tireless, full of energy, I can go on and on, shopping, cooking, cleaning. Pictures of the three of us are all over the house—Adit, Som and I, Adit and Som, Adit and I, Adit alone. The albums are crammed with pictures of Adit with his grandparents, uncles and aunts, cousins, friends. It's as if I know that this happiness is a bubble that can burst any time, that I have therefore to capture it, put it on record.

I put away all the pictures before I came here. Som is now living in a vacuum. A house where there are no records of the past, no mute witnesses to it. Just blankness.

'We can't turn our backs on the past.'

I heard Hari arguing with what is, for him, an unusual passion, with a friend who had just returned from Hampi. Hampi, that symbol of devastating ruin, of the wanton destruction of grandeur and glory.

'I couldn't bear to see it,' the friend said. 'And there were busloads of schoolchildren being brought to see it. I'm sure they were told it was part of their history lessons. It frightened me. Do they need to see this hatred and destruction? Should they see what is done in the name of religion?'

We need to know our history. We can't turn our backs on it. We have to know the truth. And what is the truth about the end of the Vijayanagar empire? It wasn't only religion, was it? There were political imperatives. There's human nature. The necessity of war. Historical inevitability. And of course, the empire itself—like all empires—was built on so much exploitation, that this end was inevitable.

Hari's words. Hari, being Hari, had to speak about exploitation. But it's his words—we can't turn our backs on our past—that I really heard, that I wanted to argue with.

No, Hari, you're wrong, we don't learn from history, we never do. Look at our story—the same mistakes over and over again. The same stupidity, the same cruelty. The truth is, we don't want to learn from our past. History can offer us nothing. That it teaches us something is a lie invented for God-knows-what-reason. The truth is, we want to forget. Which is why we have cultivated a vast collective amnesia. In

106

our individual lives too. We remember the wrongs done to us, but we forget our sins, we dye them with the colour of innocence, of good intentions. To remember is to make living impossible. And therefore it is that Som and I prefer to be apart. To see Som is to remember. In his face, in his eyes, I see my own grief, my guilt, my anger. In his silence I hear my own questions that ricochet off the soft walls of my mind, leaving sharp points of piercing pain. We're like the twins, mirror images reflecting each other's physical selves, each other's souls.

No, better to be apart, better to forget, better to be like Bai. I've been looking at the fact of Bai's silence about Munni, turning it around, seeing sometimes a disease-induced amnesia, at other times a deliberate cruel forgetting. But perhaps it's neither, maybe it's just indifference that has made forgetting possible. Indifference is, after all, the best armour you can wear.

If I don't care, I can't be hurt.

7

I've been hearing the sounds all day, so monotonous that they've become a soothing background to my day: the soft thud of the pickaxe against hard earth, each thud followed by a grunt and then by shovelling, scraping noises, all these sounds punctuated by predictable lengths of silence. It's a wizened old man who's doing the digging in the garden. I saw him in the afternoon fast asleep under the neem tree, his turban folded into a pillow under his head. Now I can hear Lata, just back from work, talking to him. And his guttural interruptions—not arguing, but somehow contentious. Finally silence. I get back to work.

When I come out a little later after a wash, I find Lata still in the garden. She's sitting, a brooding look on her face. She doesn't take in my presence until I am before her.

'Planting something?'

'God knows what I'm doing. Look at it, Kaku. Where do I begin?'

It's an odd kind of garden, not at the front of the house, nor at the back, but on one side of it. At some time it must have been a well tended garden. There are still vestiges of carefully laid out beds in the chaotic growth of weeds and straggly tomato plants, with pea-sized tomatoes hanging from the branches. A guava tree, a lone and flourishing survivor, is actually a source of trouble for Lata. There's a constant battle between her and the schoolchildren who pluck the fruit as they pass, fruit that are still small and hard. 'They won't let them ripen,' she grumbles. 'They leave nothing for my poor Popat-master.' Right now, the pride of the garden is the parijaat tree, at the moment at its flowering best. The scent drifts to me when I go out and I remark to Lata on its wonderful fragrance.

'Can you believe Kaku, that this was once a wonderful garden? We had two rows of mallige bushes. In summer we had so many flowers, it was a job plucking them. My mother used to make me do it. And then she gave the flowers away to our neighbours. It made me furious!'

Now, however, she thinks of it with nostalgia. The house was redolent with the perfume of the flowers, she tells me. Sometimes, she says, she imagines she can still get a whiff of it.

She doesn't say why it was neglected and allowed to reach this stage of desolation. Lack of water? A melancholy looking well in a corner, its mouth boarded up, declaring its defunct status, seems to hint at it.

'Each year I decide I'll do something about it. My sisters make fun of me. Whenever they come home, they ask me—when are you beginning? God knows why I never seem to get beyond this digging.' She waves her hand at the small patch the old man has dug up.

'What I really want to do is to get rid of this.' She gets up and kicks the stump she's been sitting on. 'But the old man says he can't do it alone. I tell him to get someone else. And he says yes, yes, I'll do it, I'll come tomorrow, the day after, but he never does. So it goes on year after year.'

I ask her about the tree—a large tree, it seems, from the circumference of the stump. She gives me a quick look and says it was a jackfruit tree. I can see she doesn't want to talk about it, so I drop the subject. But she goes back to it herself after dinner.

We have an early dinner. Hari has gone to Delhi—he has his six-monthly meeting with the project sponsors. He's going on to Pune from there to see his father. She's missing him, though oddly she's more often at home these days, as if it is Hari's presence that gives her the freedom to move about, to be restless. The days have altered their shape to accommodate his absence, but the gap remains. And as always, without a male in the house, we're more relaxed, there's a greater sense of ease. Strange that Hari, the most undemanding of men, should yet make his male constraints felt on the household routine. Now we decide to make do with a scrap meal, and serving ourselves, we take our plates to the side room, from where we can look out to the neem tree and the garden beyond it.

After we've finished eating and have cleared up, she suddenly asks me, 'Do you believe in omens, Kaku?'

She's released her hair from its confining band, as she does the moment she returns home. Now, while she talks, her hands go up to her hair, over and over again, twisting it into a knot at the nape of her neck. Her hair is too soft and fine to stay up, it comes down each time and she knots it again, coiling it, patting it to make sure the knot stays. There's something about these pats, impatient, angry dabs, like a tired mother patting her child to sleep. It's like she's saying—stay up damn you, stay up damn you, damn you, damn you. All the emotions she's keeping out of her voice and her face are there in that gesture.

'Do you believe in omens, Kaku? My mother did.'

This is her preamble to the story of the jackfruit tree's destruction, something she has obviously been brooding over ever since I asked her about it. I know this is not one of those bits of information she flings at me so casually, that there's something about this story that stirs up her emotions. This is almost the first time that she is speaking of her mother. Her father comes into the conversation often, he is still part of her life, but her mother has been an absence until now.

'My grandfather planted the tree when he built this house. It was unusual, not many jackfruit trees around here, have you noticed, Kaku? And it grew very fast, so they say. I know it was huge, it was enormous, you can't imagine its size. And the fruit was simply wonderful, as sweet as honey. Many people

110

don't like it—they say the sweetness is too cloying, the smell is too strong. My sisters didn't like it, nor did my mother. But my father and I loved it. I was even ready to pluck the pods from the cut fruit—you know how sticky and black your hands get doing that. But I didn't mind. I used to smear oil over my hands and do it with great enthusiasm.'

And then the tree began to harbour bats. Her mother considered it a bad omen.

'My mother saw omens everywhere. Her whole life was ruled by these things—good omens and bad omens, good days and bad days. She consulted the almanac for everything—not only for things like weddings and pujas, but for journeys, for making purchases, for exams and sending in application forms.'

And to her the bats were a bad omen. One of them got into the house one day.

'It was just quietly hanging there in the back corridor, Kaku,' Lata says to me. 'If we'd left it alone, I guess it would have gone away on its own. But my mother wouldn't. She had to disturb it. Naturally it got confused and flew all over the place, even in her face. She got hysterical, she went absolutely crazy. The tree had to come down, she said. She wouldn't listen to reason, she just wouldn't hear anything anyone said.'

She threatened to starve herself, Lata says to me, the amazement and fear the girl must have felt coming back to her face.

'She said she would stop eating until the tree was chopped down. And she would have done it, she was capable of it. So my father agreed.'

I am still not clear where she's heading, but the distress is surfacing, breaking through the control.

'I was at school when the men came to chop it down. By the time I returned home, they had completed the job. All the branches, that is. The trunk was still there. They finished that the next day. The branches covered every bit of our garden, it

111

took them an entire day to cart away the wood and the debris. When it was done and the place clear—you can't imagine, Kaku, how bare it seemed—my mother said, *Thank God it's gone. Now I can stop worrying.* I can still remember her saying that. She was never a very happy person, but that day she looked happy. Smiling and happy. Within a month she was dead. She killed herself.'

She pauses. I am silent to. I can't think of what to say, I don't know what she is really trying to tell me. Whatever it is I expected when she began this story, it was certainly not this.

'It's no use trying to avoid things, isn't it, Kaku? If it's going to happen, it will. You can't change that.'

Later at night when I'm trying to get to sleep, struggling like every night against the fear of getting into the dark realm of unconsciousness, Lata's words come back to me. If it's going to happen, it will, she says. Does this mean that the future is already there, that it exists, that you have no choice but to go along the path on which these things are waiting for you? Is this what she means?

But that is never how the future appears to us, is it, as something that is already there, as an existing entity? We don't see it as so definite, so clear; it's always hazy and unreal. And invariably, better than the present. I remember the astrologer in Maruti Chawl who lived two doors away from Leela's rooms. With a voice so loud that she could be heard all along the corridor. Telling all those who came to her with their load of despair and questions: you/your son will get a job soon, your daughter will get married soon, your wife/husband will get back to normal health soon. All will be well. Everything soon, nothing but hope waiting ahead. This is the future we want to know, this is the future we believe is ours, lurking round the corner. *All will be well.* But instead . . .

Yes, instead there is this great unknown waiting for us, a hostile stranger uncaring of our desires, our hopes and dreams, wholly unconnected to them. No, this is not true, either. There is nothing *waiting* for us. The future is *with* us, it is within us, it walks along with us. We move together, inextricably entwined, like a pair of Siamese twins. This time we are now going through, Som and I, it was with us, with Som and me, from the beginning, it was part of us, part of what we were.

Does this mean that, like Lata says, we can't change things? To agree with Lata lets Som and me off the hook. No need then for us to torment ourselves, to lie awake at nights agonizing over our guilt, to flay ourselves with the question—was it my fault? He would have died anyway. Whatever we did, his death was inevitable. But this is not true either, I can't believe in this. However comforting the thought is, it is false. Adit's death need not have happened. And anyway, what kind of comfort is that, what kind of solace is that, thinking—*he would have died anyway?* If guilt disappears, grief still remains. And the pain of being alive, of living the rest of my life without my son, of living on when he is dead. Hopelesness, childlessness, emptiness—none of these change their colours because guilt has gone.

No, there's no comfort, no comfort anywhere. I knew it from the beginning, so that when they came and spoke to me of Time and its healing, of Som and his need for me, of our need to think of what we had had and not of what we had lost, I turned my back on them. Nothing can help. The day when our son died changed us forever. The bomb that killed him defined us for all time, shaped us into different beings. Each moment of our lives is now imbued with the fact of his death, with the fact of how he died.

I'm alone in the house. There was a phone call for Lata from Hari and his parents, asking her to join them for the weekend. She was reluctant to go.

SHASHI DESHPANDE

'I'm not very comfortable there, Kaku,' she said. 'Oh, it's not that they're not good to me, even Hari's stepmother is nice, but—it's—they're too posh, if you know what I mean. I feel like a village girl when I'm with them.'

She uses the Kannada words for 'village girl', with a smile that puts them into inverted commas, as if she's parodying the way the movies use the word, with nuances of virginal, girlish innocence.

'And their home is so spotless, I'm always scared I'll drop something and make a mess. And you know, Kaku, the funny thing is, I always do! I never spill things here, I'm not clumsy, but there I'm forever doing stupid things like that.'

When she finally left, it was not this that weighed on her mind as much as her uneasiness at leaving me alone. I could see that she felt it was an abandonment of her duties as hostess. I had to work hard at reassuring her: I'll be all right, I don't mind being alone, no, really, I don't . . .

I was not being polite. It is a relief to be on my own; solitude is a luxury I'd almost forgotten. There's a sense of ease, of cramped limbs suddenly finding room to move and stretch. I walk about the empty house, for no reason but to savour the freedom, to enjoy the sense of space. Unlike my first night's bewildered wandering, when I was totally adrift, this time I find myself seeing each room as a different entity, each with its own personality. Like two people communicating directly, meeting for the first time without the friends who introduced them to each other, the house and I seem to be forging a new relationship.

The whole house has been left open to me, including their bedroom. That room has never been closed to me even when they're at home, it's I who have been chary of intruding, of violating their privacy. But it's an innocent room, bare of any traces of a passionate relationship between the couple. In fact, there's very little of Hari in this room, as little as there is in the rest of the house. Nothing, except for his books and the

114

photograph of his mother, Kishori, Narmada's daughter. A long-faced woman, with slightly protuberant eyes and full lips parted in a smile—a grudgingly yielded smile, it seems to me. Yielded, I guess, to the son who was taking the picture. The eyes, though, are melancholy. A mood, perhaps. Or maybe it is I who am imagining things, seeing a melancholy that is not there.

It suddenly strikes me that there's no picture of Lata's mother anywhere in the house, not in Lata's room, nor in her father's, either. Mistress of the house, dead wife and mother—I wonder why she's been wiped out of here. Boarded up, like the well outside.

But Lata is all over the house. Even when she's away, she makes her presence felt. The parrot has been speechless since she left, like it is when Lata throws the cover over its cage at night. There have been no squawks of fear either, the cat too keeping away, finding no reason perhaps, to prowl, to indulge in the teasing, provoking game it plays with Lata. When I ruffle the parrot's feathers, like Lata does, it gives me a hooded look, a muffled croak, that seem to say—don't disturb me, I want to sleep. Last evening, I saw the girls next door sitting astride the wall, as they always do, their skirts riding high up their skinny thighs, a wistful, expectant look telling me they were waiting for Lata. I was prepared to tell them she'd gone out of town, but the moment they saw me, they jumped off on their side of the wall. I had no desire to talk to them, but their avoidance of me gave me a pang, I felt a prickle of uneasiness. I thought of our home, with Adit's friends forever rushing in and out, of the pakodas and bhajias I fried for them, of the boys who stayed the night. And the room in the morning, smelling of small boys, erupting into life the moment I woke them up.

'You can work in peace,' Lata said to me when leaving. But I can't. I don't want even to look at the pile of transcribed pages on my table, pages I have yet to read, to sort out and put in order. I'm tired of Bai, I've been cooped up for too long in too small a space with her. She's getting on my nerves, I tell myself. But I know there's something more to my reluctance to go back to Bai's life. I can no longer ignore the empty spaces on those pages, the blanks, the absence of Munni. Why haven't I spoken of Munni to her? Why don't I speak now? Why don't I ask: why did you abandon your daughter when you left home? And when she came back to you, why did you send her away again? Do you know she's dead? Do you know how she died? Does she come to you in the night crying out for justice, for your love? And do you turn your face to the wall and weep in despair over the loss of your daughter?

It's too late now to say anything, too late to speak of Munni. We've gone so far ahead on the path of being two strangers meeting for the first time, it is almost impossible to go back to the knowledge of our earlier connection. Yet Munni remains, as stubborn as she was in her life, blocking me, refusing to let me go past her.

If she's doing this to me, what does she do to her mother? The Munni I knew would never let go, she would haunt her mother, claim her right (like she claimed her father's house in Pune), cry out for justice, rage against the obliteration of her life, of her entire existence, by her mother. Forgiveness had no place in Munni's thinking. She chuckled in delight as she recounted the villain's end in a movie—the bloodier the better, she thought. 'Very good!' she would say triumphantly. 'Serves him right,' she would mutter vengefully. The one movie we saw together, I remember her clapping vigorously when, at the climax, the hero dealt punishing blows to the villain. Almost as loud in her applause as the crowd in the cheapest seats below us.

Did she learn, as we all do soon enough, that it's only in movies and books that the sinner is punished, the order set right and justice done? Did Munni accept the fact that this rarely, almost never, happens in real life, where punishments and rewards are strewn about with scant regard for justice?

Paula—I remember thinking with longing of the idea of her suffering, of her dying in agony. If I'd known any incantations or spells, I'd have used them against her. As it was, I could only pray, mumble over and over again, to some power that I hoped existed and was listening to me—please punish her, please, please punish her.

But look at Paula now: a woman who has everything, well, almost everything she wanted. A rich and adoring husband, even if he's an aging one. An Australian husband, which gives her what she always wanted—a life abroad, even if it's in Australia, not in England, which she claimed as her home. She has, in a small way, a reputation as a pianist. She's part of an elite artistic crowd, she holidays in Europe. And when she comes here, which happens more and more rarely now, she's treated like royalty by Rekha and Tony, who look after her, entertain her and run around in circles trying to please her.

But Paula has no children. Perhaps this is the punishment my curses have brought down on her. Childlessness. Since ancient times the worst curse humans could think of for their enemies. And yet, is it a punishment at all for Paula, self-centred and selfish as she is? And if it is indeed a punishment, what about me? What have I done to deserve it? Is a curse a boomerang, coming back to its originator, still loaded with the same lethal quality?

I never meet Paula, I have no desire to meet her. We never speak of her, Tony and I, she has no place in our relationship. Our relationship, which began with excluding her, continues on that same foundation of exclusion. Now, when Paula comes on one of her visits, I stay away from Tony. He never invites me, either. But I saw her once, at a play Tony and Rekha had brought her to. I was there too, I watched her from a distance, taking in with pleasure the changes in her. The promise of beauty she'd once had, had vanished. Her face was sharp and bleak, the nose prominent, the chin almost pointed.

A little witch-like. In another decade, I thought with pleasure, children will be frightened by her, they will run away from her, a few years later they will run after her. I noticed too, that in spite of her sophisticated dress and demeanour, she had a confused and bewildered look on her face.

Do I still hate Paula? No, I exorcized that ghost of hatred the day I spoke to Leela about her. Leela and I had never spoken of her, either. Even when I told Leela that I wanted to go to the hostel right away, she'd asked no questions. She may have guessed, but she didn't ask, nor did I speak of Paula. In those last days of Leela's life, however, when we spent much time together, I told her about Paula. Of what happened between us, of what she did to me.

Leela is recovering from the surgery, she is doing fairly well. The bad days are still ahead of us. Both of us are women who've lived and are still living among doctors. We know, therefore, what's waiting for her. The knowledge makes this time only more precious and we recognize the value of it. I spend as much time with Leela as possible, I'm with her all afternoon, until it's time for Adit to return from school. It's she who keeps a sharp eye on the time. 'Off you go,' she says. 'It's 3.30, you should be home before the child returns.'

It's during one of these afternoons that I tell Leela about Paula, about Paula's hatred of me.

It begins the very day Joe and Leela take me home, the very moment she sets her eyes on me. We've been staying in Leela's rooms in Maruti Chawl until then, it was there Leela brought my father's dead body, it was from there that he was taken for cremation. I assume that we will continue to live there, Leela and I. I don't take it in, enveloped in my own misery as I am, that Leela is married to Joe, that her home is with him, that she is staying here only for my sake. I have no idea either, that Leela is nervous about my stay in that chawl, that she worries

118

that I, a small-town girl, am as vulnerable as my mother, that I am not armoured with the immunity I need to live in this place which is a breeding ground for the TB bacillus. Now Joe takes the decision. He want us to go back home—yes, he calls it my home as well. I'm going to live in the hostel, it's already been arranged, but the hostel opens only when college does. More than a month before that happens. So we go to Joe's home in Bandra, Leela and I.

Paula makes her hatred of me obvious the moment we meet. We have to share a room, she and I, and I can feel the anger in her when I go into the room. She pushes my clothes off the chair, from the bed—wherever I've placed them. She walks all over them in her shoes as if she can't see them. I see her footprints on my dress, on my petticoat, my towel when I pick them up. She never touches them, or any of my belongings, with her hands, nor does she ever speak to me directly. Except at night.

I wake up at night with a vague feeling that someone is talking to me. I open my eyes. It's Paula, her face close to mine, so close that I can't see her whole face, only bits of it, her eyes, mainly, gleaming in the dark. 'Wake up,' she's saying. 'Don't sleep. How dare you sleep when I'm talking to you! Wake up, wake up, you.'

She doesn't stop until I open my eyes and look at her, look her in the face, her angel face framed in the two wings of her sleek, shining hair, distorted by anger, almost unrecognizable. She begins her tirade then, strings of abuses. She calls me a beggar, a disgusting pauper, a savage, a stinking bit of filth. The word 'Hindu' is added to every abuse, as if the prefix adds to the offensiveness. She uses words I've never heard before—my English is not up to much, certainly not up to words like *whore, bitch, cheap tart*; these epithets are for Leela.

I begin to dread the night, I'm terrified of the dark hours when this monster visits me. I can't react, I'm frozen into

119

immobility, pinned to my place by her eyes, struck dumb by the hatred that blazes out of them. I feel suffocated by her rage and her hatred which fill the room, dazed by the onslaught of cruelty she unleashes on me. I can't close my eyes, for the moment I do, her elbow jabs painfully into my chest—she never touches me with her hand. 'Get up, wake up, open your eyes and listen to me,' she says, until I am forced to open my eyes, to look at her face. Anything to stop the pain of her elbow hurting my body.

Leela listens in silence while I tell her all this. And then I go on to what I have learnt to call (to myself, for I have never spoken of this to anyone else) 'the war of the turds'. The first day when I go to the bathroom and see the mess, I think it's an oversight, she's forgotten to flush. It doesn't horrify me too much, I'm a doctor's daughter, taught from the beginning to regard these functions as natural. But it happens again the next day. And yet again the day after. And the day after that. I know now it's deliberate. I try to wake up early, beat her to it, but whatever time I wake up, she's been there before me. It gets worse. One day the mess is spread carefully all over the seat. I feel sick; it's not just the sight and the smell, it's the thought of her doing this, taking enormous care, I can see, to make it as disgusting as possible. I clean it up nevertheless, have a bath and come back. She's in bed, but I know she's awake. I know she's heard me having a bath, I can see her eyes shining in the dark, malicious, triumphant.

I stop using her bathroom after that day. I use Phillo's bathroom instead, the one at the back of the flat. It's after this that I speak to Leela and tell her I want to go to the hostel.

When I come to the end, Leela, who has been silent so far, startles me by beginning to laugh.

'Your aunt has no sense of humour at all, Madhu,' Joe used to say in a resigned tone, when his jokes failed to amuse her, when they left her flat. And now, lying in bed after a major surgery that's removed one breast, she begins to laugh. Girlish laughter. I can imagine her laughing this way with her sisters.

Finally she wipes her eyes and tells me what it is that has amused her.

'My poor Joe,' she says. 'I was remembering him saying—it's good for the girls to be together. I'm glad Paula will have Madhu's company. Oh, my poor stupid Joe.'

And then, speaking more seriously, she goes on, 'I'm glad you didn't tell me any of this then. Who knows, I might have been tempted to tell Joe about it. And you know how he was about Paula!'

I tell Leela nothing, except that I'd like to move into the hostel right away. She too says nothing, she asks me nothing. She warns me, however, that it may not be easy, that they may have to bend the rules a little. But I'll try, she tells me. It's Joe who demurs, who's unhappy when Leela gets special permission for me to move in before college reopens.

The hostel is empty when Leela takes me there. Our voices echo when we speak, they bounce back at us. For the first time, Leela looks a little nervous. She's reluctant to leave me and go, she stays with me as long as possible, she takes me to the Assistant Superintendent before she leaves.

'She'll be all right, don't worry,' the young woman says. She talks a lot, she's eager to be friendly. 'I'll keep an eye on her, I'll visit her room often.'

She keeps her word, but after answering her preliminary inquiries—where am I from? Who is Leela?—I have nothing to say. It's a strain for me to be with her, to become what she would like me to be—a protégé whom she can patronize. Discouraged, she leaves me alone. I don't mind. The silence, the solitude, the vacuum in which I'm living don't bother me much. It's only when the others start returning, their voices rising in spirals from the lift well as they call out to one another, the voices greeting old roommates and classmates snaking through the corridors, that my own loneliness hits me.

I'm never deserted, though. Leela comes almost every day,

121

Joe visits me whenever he has time, he takes me out for a drive, for a meal, Sunanda invites me home for lunch on Sundays. It seems to me that they are all trying to comfort me with food. Even Leela, so little food-oriented, comes with batata wadas in a greasy parcel, laddoos one of 'her women' has made, specially for me, she says, and chivda and chaklis, just made, hot and crisp.

'Your brother is here,' the watchman comes and announces once. My brother? I go down to find Tony waiting in the lounge, blank-faced as usual, hands in pockets.

'Leela couldn't come. So I said I would.'

He takes me out to tea, and orders a big meal. I'm impressed that he isn't worried about how much it costs (he doesn't tell me that Joe has financed him). I'm also amazed by the amount he eats. We don't speak much. He concentrates on his food and I don't really have much to say. Besides, I'm too busy watching the amount of food that goes into his skinny frame. When he drops me at the hostel, we've scarcely exchanged a dozen sentences, but something has happened. We've connected.

If there was Paula, there was Tony as well. Two sides of the same coin. When I saw Paula at the play, there was, I remember, a cold feeling in the pit of my stomach, as if my fear of her, my hatred, had gripped me again. But her face—I stared at her and then I saw her as a human being, not the monster of my childhood. An unhappy human being who lacked something, so that she had those frequent breakdowns that had frightened Joe and devastated him. As I watched that ravaged face with the peculiar blankness that disturbed people have, my fears dissolved, my hatred seemed a weapon I no longer needed.

I am not a liberal. I believe that evil should be punished, that wrongdoers should get their deserts. I believe that we are responsible for our actions, that there are no excuses we can shelter behind. After Adit's death, I've felt something savage in me that craves for a rough, rude justice. An eye for an eye. But whose eye do I exact in revenge? Which one human in the faceless mob can I hold responsible? And what do you do when the masks of evil are taken off and you see instead the faces of vulnerable human beings?

8

The days are getting a shape, each moment labelled for a purpose, no moment without one, most of them centering round the body, as if the body is now all that there is. Even grief is finding its place in this tightly knitted scheme, no longer obtruding into places it does not belong to. Yet, at the end of each day, I am left with a zero. I long sometimes for something to fill the emptiness, even a surge of adrenaline, perhaps, that will send anger racing through my body. But nothing happens. Even Som's letter, the second since I came here, glides off the surface, leaving me untouched.

In any case, it is not a letter to arouse any emotions at all. It's like one of those model letters we had in our English composition text, a letter belonging to the category of 'a letter from a husband to his absent wife'.

He's all right, he writes, he hopes I'm all right. It's been raining, though not too much this year. The family is well. He's sending me a cheque. I should let him know if I need more money.

That's all.

If Som's letter is odourless and colourless, Maya's, which comes at the same time, gives off the sour smell of doubt. On the face of it, it's a cheerful letter. She hears I'm working hard, she's sure the work is progressing well, both Yogi and she are dying to read some of it. When will that be? I should let them know. And soon. They want to keep to their schedule, they are sure I won't disappoint them. And so it goes on.

But in spite of the breezy, confident tone, I can sense a host of questions behind her words. Can I do it? Can I give them what they want? Why am I taking so long? Can I write the book at all? Will it be what they want—a book that will be much reviewed, much talked about—or will it be a dud?

Can I write this book?

I've realized that there are three books here. Firstly, there's Bai's book, the book Bai wants to be written, in which she is the heroine, the spotlight shining on her and her alone. No dark corners anywhere in this book, all the shadows kept out of sight, backstage.

Then there's Maya and Yogi's book. A controversial one. Trendy. Politically correct, with a feminist slant. A book that will sell.

And there's my book, the one I'm still looking for. It's evading me, not giving me a hold anywhere. But today, for the first time, I think I got a glimpse of it.

Bai is sleeping, Hasina tells me when I get there. She asks me to wait, she'll be up in a while, she says. Bai has been wanting to talk to me today, she says. I mustn't go away. And then, most unusually for her, instead of going away and leaving me alone, she lingers, moving about the room, picking up things, tidying up, ostensibly. I guess she wants to say something, but she doesn't know how or where to begin.

It is I who open the conversation, asking her about Bai and her routine. Hasina replies in monosyllables, she gives me a feeling of being distracted, scarcely hearing what I'm saying. Suddenly she seems to come to a decision and moves towards me. At that moment, we hear Bai's voice, coughing, calling Hasina. She stares blankly at me—something in her eyes startles me—and then she is gone without a word.

'What were you talking to Hasina about?' Bai asks me the moment Hasina goes out of the room.

'We were talking about you. I was asking her . . .'

'If there's anything you want to know about me, you ask me. I can tell you whatever you want to know. I may be old

125

and sick, but I'm not an idiot. And I'm not dead yet, you know.'

She seems agitated. I remain silent, let her go on, work it out of herself.

'The only thing is, I forget. Sometimes I can't remember the stupidest thing—like who came to see me yesterday. And I forget names. But I can still tell you things about myself, remember that.'

I continue to remain silent.

'Well, go on,' she says impatiently. 'Ask me what it is you wanted to know.'

'Nothing really. I was asking her about your daily routine.'

'What use is it knowing these things? What does it matter what time I wake up, or drink my tea, or eat my food, or how often I go to the toilet . . .'

I have to smile. 'I wasn't asking about those things. I wanted a general idea of your day.'

'Rubbish! What kind of a life do I have now? One day is like another. The only thing that mattered to me, the only thing that mattered about me, was my music. And that's over for me now. I'll never sing again—not even a "sa". I never thought this would happen to me, I thought I would go on until I died. And then it was over—just like that!' She makes a clicking sound between her finger and thumb.

For the first time she seems uncaring of whether the recorder is off or on, for the first time I regret I haven't switched it on as yet. I do so now; she doesn't notice it, though generally she's very observant.

'They tell me I made a mistake, that I didn't do enough recordings, in the early years specially.'

It's a fact that there are very few records of her early years.

'But the truth is I was scared. Nervous. What if I made a mistake? It would be there forever. And what if it was one of

126

those days when everything comes out flat and lifeless? That too would remain forever. People who heard me would think—so *this* is how Savitribai sings. And the time—I couldn't bear to think that there was a time limit, that I would have to stop at exactly that moment. That they would say to me just when I was getting into it—that's it. No more time.'

I think of the child to whom an adult had said, 'That's enough now, child.'

'How can you sing like that, with a watch held out before you?'

She pauses, waves a hand deprecatingly and goes on, 'It's too late now. My Guruji didn't make any records either, he never went into a studio. But what difference does that make? He's still a great musician, the greatest. Those few recordings they made of his are enough to show the world what he was. And for me and for all those who heard him at his best, it's all here.' She taps her head, her chest. 'It's like there's a gramophone inside me, I can play it any time I want, I can hear him again if I want to.'

She is silent for a moment, tired I think, by the vehemence of her speech. Engrossed in some memories that have been revived. Then she says, announces rather, 'I want to speak of my Guruji today.'

Her relationship with her Guruji is already a legend. There is no music lover, no Savitribai admirer, who hasn't heard the story of her search for a teacher. Her determination, after she heard Pundit Kashinath Buwa, that he had to be the one. Her persistence in seeking him out, the long wait before he finally agreed to take her on as a pupil. These are all the much-told, much-dramatized incidents of her life.

But now I hear it from her, I hear it in her own voice and for the first time I feel a stirring in me, an excitement, something that tells me: this is it.

She first heard Kashinath Buwa during a Ganapati festival in Pune. He sang, as he did every year, in the house of a wealthy music-lover, one of his devoted admirers who'd become a friend. It was an all-night performance. Bai could attend it only because it was at the home of a family friend. Even then, she could not have gone alone. She was with a group of women, for whom it meant no more than an occasion to go out, a break from the tedium of their daily routine, their humdrum lives. But for Bai, it was something else.

When she went there, she had no idea what was waiting for her. She had heard his name, she knew of his reputation, but that was all. After that night, she knew she would never be the same again. She'd had a glimpse of something she had been waiting for all these years, she'd seen the world that she wanted to be a part of, a world which she knew had to be hers.

'I kept hearing his music in my ears. I've always been able to do that, you know. Once I've listened to something, I can hear it again, from the beginning to the end, without any change.'

After this, she could not bear the thought of going back to her pathetic (so she seemed to her now) music teacher, to hearing her teacher sing. But the teacher was of some use to her. She made it possible for Bai to attend some of the performances arranged in private houses. Without her, she couldn't have gone anywhere. Often, they had to sit in another room, away from the room in which the performer and the male audience were sitting.

'I didn't mind. It was better than not going, much better than not being able to hear any music at all. I was so desperate, I was willing to disguise myself as a man and go for a public performance.'

But her aim was to meet Pundit Kashinath. She waited patiently for a year. When she went to Bombay for a family function, she met him. She doesn't remember what she said. 'I was too frightened, I think I didn't say anything at all. Only my Guruji could make me nervous like that. I've never been frightened of anyone else.'

But she remembers he was very dismissive. To him, she was just another young woman from a well-to-do family, trying to get some excitement into her life by associating with music, with artistes.

A year or two later, she went to live in Bombay. She started her lessons with someone, but it was only a stopgap arrangement for her, she knew that Kashinath Buwa was the man she wanted as her Guru. She went to him now almost every other day, trying to persuade him, but he was unrelenting.

She never gave up. She approached him through various people, but the answer was always the same—'No!' Despair finally set in when he fell ill and she heard he was close to death. But he recovered and then it was said that he was leaving Bombay, going back to his home town, Bhavanipur. He wanted to live the rest of his life near the Bhavani temple.

She decided to take a final chance. If he says 'no' this time, I will never ask him again, she told herself. But she had to try once more, a final and desperate assault.

When she tells me all this, I am aware of the gaps in her story, I know that she is following the one straight line of her pursuit of her Guruji, bypassing everything else. I have to fill in these blanks myself. So I presume that when she first heard Guruji sing, she was a married woman, that the first time she went to Bombay and met him, she was still living in her married home. I also guess that when she says she went to live in Bombay, that was the time she'd burnt her boats, she had left her husband and home and was living with Ghulam Saab. But these things are not mentioned. To Bai, these things have no place in the story of her life as a musician. Though I've avoided questioning her about anything until now—the time for questions has yet to come—there is one thing I do ask her: why was her Guruji so determined not to take her on?

She answers my question without any hesitation, surprised I

think, by my stupidity. How is it that I don't know the answer to this one?

Because, she says, he thought music was no profession for a respectably married woman. Because he, a traditional man, did not want to encourage her to step out of her traditional role. Oh, if she wanted to take up music as a hobby, it was fine. But for that, there were others who could teach her. He was not the man for it.

So you see, she says, it became a curse, my being a Brahmin woman. My belonging to a respectable family.

Why then did he still refuse her when she had already abandoned her home, her status? I don't ask her this question. Sometime I will and the answer, hopefully, will come.

She goes on then to her meeting with Guruji in Bhavanipur. This time nothing is held back. It happened over half a century back, but she speaks to me as if it happened only yesterday. More than fifty years have passed, and she has forgotten nothing.

They (yes, she says 'we' now, not specifying, however, who the other person is) get off at Bhavanipur early in the morning. It is a very small station—the usual row of rooms on a short length of covered platform, with open stretches on either side. She notices a group which alights with them, some of whom are carrying bulky cloth-covered instruments. Tanpuras. They must be musicians. Yes, it's Guruji's group, she sees him get off, he's the last to descend from the compartment. They are obviously returning from a programme. Her heart leaps in joy and hope. Maybe this is an omen, a good omen? Maybe she will succeed in breaking through his rejection this time?

She doesn't want to approach him here, travel-stained and weary as she is, her voice hoarse and froggy after a night on the train. But when she notices the group is not walking out of the station, she lingers too. They are obviously waiting for a vehicle; one of the group goes out and returns shaking his head. They are all speaking Kannada, a language she cannot understand. But she can sense the atmosphere of ease and good fellowship among them, the slightly elevated state that speaks of their returning from a successful performance.

They prepare to wait. Guruji goes to the raised platform around a tree, one of the men follows him and sits by him. He opens the cover of his instrument and touches the strings tentatively, as if making sure it's all right. There's the whistle of the departing train, then it's gone, leaving behind a silence in which the chirping of the birds comes loud and clear. And the drone of the tanpura as the man tries it out. Guruji, listening, his head cocked at an angle, absentmindedly takes a cup of tea that's brought to him, his attention focussed on the instrument, on its tuning. After he's finished his tea, he clears his throat and gives a note to the tanpura player, as if they're starting a performance. The entire group has gathered around Guruji now, all of them with their cups of tea, each one as intent as Guruji is on the man's effort to get the right note. Suddenly it's there, he's got it—they smile at one another.

Bai smiles as she comes to this point, I see their smiles in hers. Guruji begins to hum. The man with the tanpura hesitates, looks at Guruji, then goes on with greater confidence, properly accompanying him now as Guruji embarks on a full throated *a-a-a*.

It's a Todi that he's begun.

She's never heard a Todi sung like the one he sang that day, neither before nor since. She's not the only one to be affected by it. The sleepers curled into their rough woollen blankets stir, sit up and listen, the railway staff come out of the rooms, the porters squat and stay there unmoving. Even the tongawalas come to the palings out of curiosity and continue to stand there, their whips hanging from their hands, unmindful of the snorting, restless horses. When a goods train steams in noisily, Guruji stops, and when it's gone, he picks up on the exact note on which he'd left off. A man struts on to the platform, ready obviously to announce the arrival of the car. But he's drawn into the music too and sits on a bench listening.

When it's over, it's like a spell has been lifted. People begin to stir, to move, they seem to start breathing once again. Other sounds, held in abeyance until now, flow back. She goes straight to Guruji; he shows no surprise on seeing her. She says nothing either, just touches his feet and moves away.

That evening, she goes to his house. She tells him she's not leaving Bhavanipur until he takes her on as a student. She's going to sit here, outside his house, without food or drink, until he agrees. She'll continue to sit here until he relents.

'Learnt the old man's tricks, eh?' Guruji says and laughs.

The reference to Gandhiji passes her by, but she observes his laugh, his good humour. For the first time, she is hopeful. 'Come tomorrow,' he says. 'I need to think.' And she knows he will take her.

He doesn't give in totally, he lays down his own conditions. She will live in Bhavanipur town, nearly ten miles from the temple and his home. She will come thrice a week in the afternoons. She has to unlearn all that she has learnt so far, this goes without saying. He may have to start with the basics. He tells her they will have the official ganda-tying ceremony on Dasara day.

She agrees to everything. She regrets only the fact that she can't live near the temple like his other students, the male pupils. They, being on the spot, can listen to him doing his *riaz*, they have the benefit of the classes he suddenly decides to take on the spur of the moment, hours which are, she hears with envy, much more rewarding, illuminating sometimes, than the scheduled classes. She is miserable when she hears of the impromptu performance—a jugalbandi—that takes place when one of Guruji's friends, himself a great singer, visits him.

But Guruji is firm. She can't stay in his house with the male students. She's a woman, a Brahmin woman, a married

132

woman—Bai repeats this twice. Have I shown surprise or incredulity that she feels the need to repeat this statement?

And so she lives in Bhavanipur, travelling each day by train, the shuttle service that moves between Bhavanipur and the next town, halting at the temple station only for a moment. And then she has to walk two miles from the station to Guruji's house.

'They were the best years of my life,' she says to me. 'Life was simple. Just one room to live in, nothing to think of or worry about except my class with Guruji. The days I didn't go for my class, I spent in absorbing what he had taught me, I did my *riaz* for nearly ten to twelve hours a day. Can you believe it!'

'I was such a fool,' she says a little later. 'When I began with Guruji, I thought I would master the Todi I heard him singing that day. But even after seven years with him, I felt I had got no nearer to it. When I said this to Guruji, you know what he told me? He said—*that Todi was mine. You can never get that. You have to create your own, it will come through your life, your experiences, your joys and sorrows.* That was the kind of man my Guruji was, that was his wisdom. No one else could have given me that understanding.'

In this story I see the artist, the woman in search of her genius, of her destiny. But the artist was born of the woman. First there was the woman and then the artist. Is it possible to cut the umbilical cord, to sever the connection between the two? Did Bai manage to do this?

To me, Bai was Munni's mother. She was different, certainly, from other mothers—I never saw her do the mundane things other mothers did, I never saw her behave the way the other mothers did. Nevertheless, her identity was, for me, connected to Munni. That she was something else, something more, was brought home to me the day I saw her on

stage. It occurs to me, as I remember this, that I was privileged
to see one of her very early performances. I was there that day
only because Babu was away and my father couldn't leave me
alone at home.

It was a great occasion for Neemgaon—the inauguration of
the new radio station in the town. There was a buzz of
excitement and children stood and watched as the shamiana
went up and the red jute matting was laid on the ground. The
Minister was coming from Delhi, famous musicians from all
over the country would be there. Invitations to the function
were much prized. My father was there, not only as the town's
most popular doctor, but also because he was the Station
Director's friend. And Bai was to sing on this occasion, to
share the stage with the great Bismilla himself.

At that time, her Guruji had been dead for some years. Bai
had begun her professional career, but she was still a very long
way from the heights she would reach in the next decade. This
was an important event for her, her being invited here was a
kind of landmark in her career.

I can't remember much of that evening, neither Bismilla's
music, nor Bai's. Ghulam Saab comes back to me though, I can
remember him smiling at me from his place on the dais. And
my pride and pleasure at being so distinguished by someone
important enough to be up there. I kept my eyes steadily on
him, I remember, hoping he would smile again, single me out
for recognition. But his eyes, once the music began, were on
the singer. I can see his hands resting on the tabla in an
absolute stillness. And then, pushing up his sleeves, making
tiny flexing movements of his hands, the hands finally coming
down with deliberation on his instruments. The first deep
resounding boom, the fingers flying as if they'd taken wings,
the steady beat, the two of them smiling at each other. I
remember all this. I remember looking at the singer too,
admiring her beauty.

And this glamorous creature on the stage, the centre of

attention, was Munni's mother! But why was Munni not there to hear her mother sing, to enjoy her glory? I thought of it when I met her the next day, and asked her the question.

'I hate music,' she said. 'I simply hate it.'

But she loved film songs, I knew that. She sang them often, she had a sweet light voice. My father heard her singing a Lata-Mukesh duet one day—*mai bhanwra tu hai phool, yeh din mat bhool* . . .

'Wah!' he said. 'That's wonderful! You're Savitribai's daughter after all! Listen to that voice!'

She had stopped singing as soon as he came into the room. 'Go on, let me hear the whole song.'

But she wouldn't. Her lips came together in a tight, determined line, daring any music to emerge. My father kept on at her, asking her to sing for him. She had a septic finger, she came every day to my father to have it dressed. 'I want my payment,' he said each time. 'One song per treatment.'

But her mouth was sealed.

Yet she took part in the school concert. She was part of the orchestra, playing the jaltarang, which gave her the place of honour, in the centre of the semicircle of players, the only one to be facing the audience. She was serious, intent on the dainty water-filled china bowls before her, tapping them with the little stick, producing tinkly sounds out of them. Most of the parents were present on the day, specially the parents of children who had a role in the concert. Even my father had taken time off to see me dance; it was a folk dance, a fisherman's dance. I looked out for him and yes, there he was, raising his hand to draw my attention. Knowing he was there, I leapt about energetically, putting all my heart into the dance, enjoying myself much more because I knew he was watching and enjoying my performance.

But Bai was not there to watch Munni play the jaltarang. After the concert was over, Munni walked home with my father and me. It was one of those rare times when Munni seemed to be in peaceful accord with everyone. My father, relaxed and in a good mood too, was humming to himself. We dropped Munni at her gate. She looked at us, then ran quickly in.

'Poor child,' my father said.

Poor child? Munni? I looked at him, but he said no more. Swinging on my father's arm, euphoric after my stage performance, what did I care what he meant?

These are the festival months. In Bombay, you know which festival it is from the stuff sold in the markets, on pavements and handcarts—there always are fruits, flowers and vegetables appropriate to each festival. Here, in Bhavanipur, the festivals proclaim themselves through the activities of the women, their silk saris, and the little girls whom I see walking about, holding their long *zari* skirts up, conscious of their own importance in this dress. And of course, there's the smell of the festive food which wafts out from the houses.

I'm surprised that Lata is not part of these things. Not only is there no sign of any of the festivals at home, she does not associate with the neighbours' celebrations either. I wonder whether, like so many wives do, she's taken on Hari's radical views. But no, she says that she had enough of these things as a child. Her mother earnestly observed every little feast, every puja.

'When I was a kid I found it exciting, specially the dressing-up part of it. You know, wearing my silk *lehengas*, flowers in my hair and all that,' she tells me. 'Then I got bored with the whole thing. Last night they'd invited me next door—it was a *mangala-gowri puja*. But . . .' She shrugs, makes a face. 'They went on all night. They made such a racket. Did they disturb you, Kaku? Actually, they'd asked you too, but I knew you wouldn't want to go, I was sure you wouldn't be interested.'

136

No, I wouldn't. Not now. But when, in the first year after my marriage, Som's mother had made me perform this puja, a combined one, along with Nisha and a niece who'd been married for less than five years too, I'd been fascinated by the whole thing—the all-night revelry of the women, the songs, the husband's name-taking ritual peppered with jokes, some of them bordering on the obscene. And there were the games they played, the *'phugdis'*, which even the older women took part in. Agile and skilful in spite of their age and size, each pair, hands linked, twirled in eye-blinking speed, hair coming loose and flying behind them, breasts bouncing, feet thumping. The ribald jokes the women made and laughed at until the tears poured from their eyes were equally astonishing. The women were a revelation to me. There was something uncontrolled about them, a kind of wildness, a volatility, an energy, as if these, finally, were their real selves, breaking through the masks of Aais, Maamis, Kaakis and Maais that they wore through their lives.

Women without men, I realized then, are totally different creatures.

And it's true. There's Lata—her openness, her swooping dives into intimacy when we're by ourselves, become something different, more guarded, when Hari is with us. At such times, it's as if a thin, opaque sheet has fallen between us, creating the sense of a barrier. No wonder women need to be on their own at times, away from men and children. Brought up by a father, I never felt the strangeness, the otherness of men myself, nor did I feel the need to be part of a female group, but, of course, I had Leela and Ketaki. And earlier there had been Munni. It was Munni, actually, who first introduced me to the exciting world of female friendship.

Living in such close proximity, with only a low hedge separating our homes, it was inevitable that Munni and I become friends. Yet it never was a friendship between equals. She was not only older than me, she took the lead, and from the moment of our meeting, set the tone and the pace of our friendship. If propinquity was the starting point of our association, there were other things which held us together as well. My fascination for her beautiful mother, her unusual home, her bewilderingly unexpected changes of mood, the stories she told me—these things were also part of it. As for her, I think she needed me as an audience, a person before whom she could enact the drama of her life, with herself as the poor, victimized heroine.

There was something else which, looking back now from this point of time, I see as the real uniting factor between us: both Munni and I were outsiders. In the conventional society of Neemgaon, where each family had its place marked out for it according to religion, caste, money, family background, etc., our families, Munni's and mine, were difficult to place, not conforming to the norms. In a sense, neither of us belonged. Munni's family, with her singer mother, absent father and another man—a Muslim—sharing the home, was of course, radically, shockingly different. But my father, with his unorthodox ways, was an oddity in Neemgaon as well. It was not just his being a widower and bringing up his daughter on his own, with only a male servant at home; it was not merely that, while the world fasted and feasted, observed festivals and pujas, we did nothing. There was more to it. My father never concealed the fact that he drank—he 'took', as they called it. I was used to seeing him in the company of a friend, or on his own, with a glass before him, a cigarette in his hands. To me, it was normal, it never seemed wrong. On the contrary, the smell of the cigarette, the aroma of the drink, spelt security to me. In the town, however, there must have been talk about my father's drinking habit. I don't think it mattered to my father, anyway. He was a self-sufficient man, going his own way, uncaring of everyone, except me.

But my father was accepted and his peculiarities and foibles were overlooked, because he was a doctor, and a very trusted and popular doctor at that. And, of course, being a man, he could get away with much. He could live the way he wanted, without open censure or disapproval. It was not so with Munni's mother. As Savitribai Indorekar the singer-woman, some oddities in her behaviour were permitted, possibly tolerated, but it didn't take away the aura of disapproval, or the curiosity, either. Which was why, perhaps, very few local people were allowed entry into that home. Most of those who visited it were people from the music world, or music lovers; social visitors were extremely rare. Even I, Munni's friend, entered Munni's home scarcely a handful of times. There was only one occasion, I remember, when Munni took me into her mother's room. I have never forgotten this, because it was the first time I saw a dressing table. I remember Munni looking into the mirror, and then quickly away, as if annoyed by what she saw there.

Our friendship, Munni's and mine, was brief. How long—two years? A little more? Whatever the duration, it left its mark on me. I never forgot Munni or our times together. Our association ended abruptly. I always thought it ceased when Bai moved away from Neemgaon, but looking back, I think it ended before that, when Munni spoke to me about my father and his mistress. I didn't know the word then, nor did she use it. 'He goes to a woman' was how she put it.

'Do you know he goes to a woman at night?' she asked me and then went on to spell out in graphic detail why he went to her and the things he did. I was horrified, I felt sick. It was not the fact of his having a mistress—which, at that age, didn't mean anything to me. It was beyond my capacity to understand the implications of that. It was the way she put it, the context of absurd vulgarity into which she placed it, making my father both ridiculous and disgusting, that upset me. My father doing those disgusting things! And with a woman—a strange woman! The two of them removing all their clothes and . . .

139

SHASHI DESHPANDE

Was this another one of her stories, stories she told to frighten and shock me? Like the time she had me believe, no, like the time she *made* me believe that there was an intruder in the house. There were only the two of us at home that evening. Babu had gone out somewhere. Suddenly she switched off the light. 'Sssh,' she said. 'There's someone trying to get in.'

Obediently I stayed silent, my bladder almost bursting with the tension and fear while we listened to the odd, stealthy sounds that came to us from the dark. 'He's coming,' she whispered. 'He's in the next room now.'

Suddenly there was the sound of the door banging, the light was switched on and there was Babu. Sheer relief made me burst into tears.

'Go away,' Babu said angrily to Munni, when he learnt why I was crying. 'Go home. Frightening the child like that!' he exclaimed in disgust.

No, this was not the same kind of story, I knew that. She wasn't trying to scare me this time. And I didn't want Babu coming in and helping me out of this, I didn't want him to hear this story she was telling me. I would deal with this myself, I would fight Munni on my own.

'Chhut!' I retorted immediately, using her own enormously emphatic exclamation of denial. 'He doesn't do such things, no, never, never, never.'

'Ask anyone, everyone knows. Ask Babu.'

Of course I wouldn't ask anyone, I wouldn't speak to anyone about it. Did I believe her? Deep down, I think I did, so that years later when Leela told me my father had left some money for a 'friend', I knew at once that this was his mistress. Doubt and disbelief had no place in my relationship with Munni. And, except for that one great fiction she created about her own parentage, there was truth in most of the things she told me. Her lies, I think now, were not dispersed, but concentrated in this one area of her own life.

But at the time I rejected Munni's information. I didn't want

140

to hear any more, I didn't want to talk to her. I stopped speaking to her after that. When she came home, I asked Babu to tell her to go away, which he did with enormous pleasure. I heard his voice, cruel and gloating, turning her away and I cringed. But I couldn't, I wouldn't speak to her. Saying such horrible things about my father! In a while, she stopped coming. It is possible that there was a gap between this and their going away from Neemgaon. I don't remember. I only remember the locked door and the absence of music next door. And then, the cry of the watchman, the barking of dogs, the croaking of frogs, the ceaseless racket of the cicadas—all these coming back at night, as if the music had held the sounds at bay. All these things are there in my memory, unconnected however, to any other event. I make the connection only now, only now I think—I turned my back on Munni, I let Babu drive her away.

Have I done the same with Ketaki?

If Munni and I chose each other, each for her own reasons, it was Ketaki who sought me out as a friend—I never understood why. A sophisticated Bombay girl from a well-to-do family, a girl who came to college in a chauffeur-driven car, she could have had her pick of friends. Instead, she took pains to become my friend, awkward, small-town girl though I was. Astonishingly, she seemed to admire me, she played the Ananda to my Buddha; to her I was the epitome of intelligence, sense and wisdom. And when later I revealed that I had my reckless moments, when I turned my back on sense, like the time I flung myself into the sea, knowing nothing of swimming, just because she dared me to, she admired me all the more.

On our very first meeting, she rushed into intimate revelations. She told me she was already engaged, a family arrangement, she said. He was her father's friend's son, she said. As soon as he completed his engineering, they would get married. She was not sure she liked the idea. He was so dull!

They'd spent a whole evening together without his trying even to hold her hand! Really!

I soon realized that Ketaki was a romantic. She dreamt of a passionate lover who would sweep her off her feet, make violent, savage love to her—like the heroes of the romantic books she read. (And wholly unlike her polite, well-behaved Atul, who wouldn't even kiss her until they were married.) She offered me these books to read, but I, who had by then climbed on to Joe's hobby horse of Dickens, found them insipid. I gave her *Our Mutual Friend*. To me the most passionate love story was in there, the one between Eugene Wrayburn and Lizzie Hexam. She returned it to me the next day, confessing she couldn't read it. So dull, she said.

Ketaki's generosity took me into her family, it made me one of them. A large household, a joint family of two brothers, it absorbed me with ease. It was seeing Ketaki's family that made me realize how odd my own background was. Ketaki and her cousins hugged and fought, they wept easily and threw tantrums. I, who had grown up among two men, men who never valued childhood so that I became an adult early, found this behaviour strange. After our graduation, we no longer met every day. She enrolled for her M.A.—to pass the time, she said, until her wedding—while I joined *City Views*. She visited me often in my little room, she loved it, she envied me my freedom. As her own wedding approached, she became a little wild, she spent money recklessly, foolishly. She came to my room only to change and go out, she wouldn't tell me where, she asked me to back her up in her lies that she was with me when she wasn't. She rang me up at all times of the day, going on and on. I listened, tapping my pencil on the paper, doodling, wanting her to stop, conscious of Dalvi's basilisk eyes on me.

'Let's get sozzled,' she said one evening. That's the word she used—sozzled. We opened a bottle of wine—Phillo's sister's home-made wine. After just a glass, she lay on the bed, kicking up her legs, humming a tune. And suddenly she fell asleep, her mouth a little open, her arm crushed awkwardly under her body. I removed it and she turned over and lay on her back, small snores escaping her in her sleep.

'You'll stay at least a week with me before the wedding,' she said to me. But it was time for *City Views* to come out and I could go to her only the day before the wedding. The mehendi ceremony was going on and she seemed cool and composed, except that she wouldn't let me out of her sight. On her wedding day, she showed no signs of nervousness or agitation. She took a long time to dress up, taking enormous care about every little detail, carefully getting every pleat of her sari, every single hair adjusted to perfection. And when it was done, she sent everyone out except me and sat staring at herself in the mirror, a long, thoughtful look. I watched her in silence. I knew something was going on within her, I was conscious that she was sharing the moment with me. I think now of Ketaki's generosity in sharing this experience with me. During the reception, she was another creature altogether—gay, vivacious, chatting with Atul in the intervals between guests. But her usually gesturing, fluttering hands lay still on her lap, palms upwards, showing off the baroque flourishes of the mehendi.

'Promise me,' she said when we were parting, 'promise me we'll always be friends.'

We were, we did meet, she never held back, pushing everything, all the clutter of her crowded life—her husband, her duties as a daughter-in-law, her babies and later, her own business—aside, clearing a space in which we could meet. I remember my own grudging reluctance to find time for her after Adit's birth, I think of how it was she who came home each time, bringing her girls with her, leaving them to play by themselves, while she joined me in my baby worship.

Adit's death changed everything. Ketaki seems to belong to a life that's so distant that I can't relate to it any more. She kept coming, she rang up almost every day, but I didn't want to talk to her, I had no desire to meet her.

Ketaki is a great one for remembering.

'Remember,' she would say, 'remember the time when you jumped into the sea? Remember the time when those two men were after us? Remember the time I got drunk?'

She might do the same thing now if we meet. Remember, she might say, remember all the things we did together? Remember our problems with our children, remember how we complained about them to each other? Remember the dreams we dreamt for our children, remember our hopes for them?

Remember? she will ask me. Remember?

Yes, I do, I remember everything. That is my problem. I remember everything, I have forgotten nothing. I remember, above all, my delusion about motherhood: a small centre, a vast exclusion—I thought this was love.

9

Hamidbhai is immensely pleased with me. *City Views* has moved on, it has got beyond the few subscriptions with which it began. It's now being sold on news-stands, the circulation has doubled, no, more than doubled.

'This is your doing, Madhu,' Hamidbhai says.

I accept the credit, the praise, I don't pretend to be modest. I know it's I who have done it. *City Views* has changed its contents, its image, its reputation, because of me. I've levered it out of the small elite group of Bombay aficionados (Tony and I still grin at the phrase, the humour attached to it seems never to fade), taken it to ordinary people to whom Bombay is important as well. We invite stories, poems, articles, photographs on Bombay from people. We call for memories of the city, of events that took place in it. I even search out Marathi poems and articles, translating them myself with pleasure. We give prizes for the best poem, the best photograph, the best article. Through Leela's connections with the mills, through my own knowledge of Maruti Chawl and the people living in it, I bring in the world of Bombay factories, the mills, the workers who come from all over the country and live together in chawls. The film world, which Hamidbhai's group has such contempt for, enters *City Views* too, as another bit of Bombay, another colourful, chaotic world teeming with brave hopefuls.

And then I get pregnant and decide to give up my job. Hamidbhai is aghast, he tries hard to dissuade me. Take some time off, he says. When you come back, we'll get extra help, we'll get a typist so that Venkat can take on more, you can work shorter hours, I'll give you an extra room . . .

Hamidbhai tries all the baits he can offer, but I am adamant. I'm going to be there for my child all the time, I will not give my child a measured amount of time, only a part of my life.

Hamidbhai gives in, he accepts my resignation, he says no more. He's ill by then, it's cancer, but he doesn't tell me about it. He dies within six months of Adit's birth. I'm full of grief for the death of a good man, a good friend. There's guilt too. But no regrets. No, I regret nothing. Motherhood absorbs all of me, I've nothing left for anyone, for anything.

This sense of isolation is something I haven't anticipated. All the mothers and babies I've seen—in Som's family, in Ketaki's home—are the centre of a crowd, surrounded by others—mothers, aunts, friends, servants. For me too, there's always someone at first. Som's mother stays with us for three months, his sisters are forever visiting, Sunanda and Leela drop in often. But as far as I'm concerned, there's only Adit and me in this new world I've entered. The others are mere shadows. Som is part of our world, but he's on the periphery.

In any case, Som has very little time. He has given up his hospital teaching job, he has started his own consulting practice and he's on the move all day, going from nursing homes to hospitals. In the evenings, he sits in his own consulting rooms, waiting for patients to come to him. He doesn't have to wait too long, his appointment book is gradually filling up. Som is lucky, he's entered the right speciality at the right time. There are more and more men with the wrong food habits and high-stress jobs who come to Som, men with increasing blood pressure, palpitations, anxiety about heart attacks, actual heart attacks.

But all this is yet to come. Right now, he's running around, worried, wanting to make money. I want it soon, he says. I want good money, he says. For us, for our son, he says. But there's more to it. For the first time, on a day when he returns home early—there have been no patients at all that day—he confesses to me his resentment at having had to take Chandru's patronage all his life. Our trip abroad, our flat, our car, Som's consulting room—these have been possible only because of Chandru's generosity. But it goes back even further, to their days in school and college, when Chandru was there to help Som, son of a schoolteacher, with his gifts—books, a cricket bat, a picnic Som would have opted out of because it cost too much. They are friends, they've been friends since they were infants, and Chandru thinks nothing of the things he does for Som; nor, I have imagined, does Som. But now Som tells me he wants to be on equal terms with Chandru some day, he wants to stop feeling small, always on the taking side.

There's no obvious change in their relationship. Chandru and he still meet once a week, they have long sessions of intimate conversations, interspersed with their usual arguments and quarrels. They meet in our house—Som won't go to Chandru's house, where Satee's brooding silence creates an air of tension. I leave their dinner on the table and go to bed, reading, until it's time for Adit's last feed. Then I switch off the light and lie in the dark listening to their voices, to the clink of glasses, the tinkle of spoons on plates. It's soothing, peaceful. I fall asleep at some point and wake up when Som comes to bed.

'I had to drive Chandru home. *Saala*,' he says, 'he's drinking too much. I'm going to stop drinking, I don't want Adit to see me drinking.'

Yes, Adit is part of all Som's plans too. He's a fond, indulgent father. But I—I'm—what's the right word? I'm—yes, I'm besotted. That's it, I'm besotted.

So many things happen in this time. Joe has a heart attack, but it's a minor one and he soon goes back to working at his old pace. None of us say anything, but I can see the shadows on Leela's face, the tension in Tony. Leela gets involved in the anti-price-rise campaign. I learn this, it shames me now when I think of it, from the papers. She's in the thick of it, her room in Maruti Chawl becomes a kind of headquarters. She's there almost all day, going home only at night. I'm with her one day when she gets a call from Joe; they ring each other up a number of times in the day. And her face, when she speaks, when she listens, is like a young girl's speaking to her lover. Leela is arrested twice and let off. Tony gets engaged to Rekha, he brings her home. I have a party for the engaged couple, Joe and Leela are there, we are all together. 'This is wonderful,' Joe says, 'wonderful to be with all of you.' He has a happier relationship with Tony, I can see he likes Rekha.

But all these happenings come to me through the thick haze of motherhood I've surrounded myself with. The first thing that penetrates is Joe's death. I leave Adit for the first time to be with Leela and Tony in the hospital. 'Go,' Som tells me. 'Don't worry about Adit.'

I go, but how can I not think about Adit? It's not worry, it's an actual pain I can feel inside me. Nevertheless, I'm there the two days until Joe's death. We're together, Tony, Leela and I. No, Leela is not with us, she has withdrawn to some place where she is alone, or with Joe perhaps, with Joe who's fighting for his life. It's just Tony and me in that small room, where time has no meaning. The lights are on all day, but the shadows of the night have gathered and settled on the faces of people, faces darkened by anxiety and fear. Each one dreading the moment when the white-clad messenger approaches; whose name will it be, whose turn is it now?

'Dr Joseph Gonsalvez?'

The nurse tentatively offers this name to us, it's not an announcement, it's more like a question. But we know instantly that Joe is dead. Tony begins to sob then, suddenly, loudly and awkwardly, like a growing boy jolted out of his adult self back into childhood. Leela comes back from where she's been—Joe has let her go—and both of us move instinctively towards Tony, to shield him from the others in the room. But we can't shield them from the sounds of his grief. Fear spreads through the room in ripples, all of them knowing that they're just a hair's breadth away from this moment themselves, each one thinking: is it my turn next?

I bring Leela home to stay with me for a while. She's very peaceful, there are no outward expressions of grief. She spends her time with Adit. She's not a baby-worshipper, she never was; she doesn't coo over him, use baby talk or caress him. But she sits by him, looking at him with a kind of wondering awe. There's a serenity about her when the two of them are together. It comforts me, it pleases me.

Something has gone out of Leela, though—a passion, a force, a fire. A bit of it reappears when the railway strike begins, when the workers are arrested and their families thrown out of their homes. I have to go home, she tells me. There's going to be trouble. I have work to do. And she's right. Indira Gandhi declares an Emergency.

For long—and I'm even more ashamed of this—I don't know that Leela is part of the struggle against it. I know, vaguely that something is going on, something she doesn't want me to know anything about. But it's only when Tony tells me she's going to be arrested, that her name is on the list—an anonymous phone call has given him this information—it's only now that I wake up.

'Tell her to go into hiding,' Tony pleads with me. 'I've tried, but she won't listen to me. You're the only one she may listen to. She's too old, too frail to stand jail life. I've been hearing stories of how they treat political prisoners. I'm frightened for Leela, Madhu.'

I know it's no use, but I speak to Leela. 'Going underground again?' she asks me with a smile. 'No, Madhu, I'm too old for that.'

She's in prison for nearly a year. I visit her—the visits are always arranged by others, anonymous calls and notes tell me

149

when to go—but each time my heart is in my mouth. Will I be marked by my connection with her? Once someone gives me a note to pass on to her. I do so, my heart pounding so loud I'm sure the warders can hear it. She takes it from me with a rapidity, a skill, that tells me she's done this before. She also gauges my fears. 'Don't do this again,' she says. 'Tell them I don't want you involved.'

When she's released, I bring her home. She's a frail shadow of her old self, she's not fit to be on her own. I tell her so. I'm happy to have her with me, I enjoy seeing her with Adit, seeing Adit drawing her into his games, his conversation.

Adit, Adit—all my happiness, all my moments of joy centre round him. As he grows, my world enlarges, it includes all those who matter to him—his cousins, Nisha's twin sons, his nursery friends, his teachers. He enjoys family gatherings immensely. The family gets together for festivals and occasions in Som's Dada's home—the parents are now living with him, their older son. I never miss a single occasion. For Adit's sake I'm always present, even if Som can't come.

But fear is always lurking under the surface of happiness, the undertow waiting to suck me in. Now that Adit is no longer a frail vulnerable baby but a healthy child, I can relax about him. Then new fears get hold of me. What if something happens to Som and me? What if we both die leaving him alone? I've always been a strong girl, a healthy woman. Now I become a hypochondriac. I have a headache and it's a brain tumour, or meningitis, my jaw feels stiff and I have tetanus.

'This comes of living with doctors,' Leela says in exasperation, when I weep in her presence one day over my persistent cough. It's TB, I'm sure I've got TB. My mother died of it, now I will.

'For God's sake, Madhu, it's not inherited,' Som tells me for the nth time. But living in Bombay, it's always a possibility. How can he dismiss it so easily?

Ketaki has a lump in her breast, she rings me up in panic.

150

I'm with her when they do the biopsy, again when the report comes. It's benign. She breaks down and sobs, so do I. Atul laughs at her, at both of us. He doesn't understand. I'm crying as much for myself as in relief about Ketaki. What if this happens to me? What will I do? I feel my breasts like a passionate lover each time I undress. Is there something here? Is this a lump?

Selfishness has entered me, but it's only when I'm afraid for myself the time I visit Leela in prison, the day I pass her the note, that I become conscious of it. Leela's stern 'Don't do this again' pierces through my armour of self-deception; she's looked into me, she's seen my cowardice, my real fear. What about Adit if something happens to me? What about Adit if something happens to Som, to both of us?

Som is doing his bit, he's earning well now, there's enough money to send Adit to a good school, to buy him all he wants, to take him out on holidays. It's for me to make sure there's someone to look after Adit in case both of us die. I begin my search. Whom can I entrust him to? Som's sister Akka? She'll do it gladly, but she's rough, a little stupid and also dominating. She won't understand Adit. Nisha? Adit is very happy in their house, her sons are his companions. But Nisha is a busy professional, she's brisk and sharp even with her own boys. She can't give Adit the softness and warmth he needs.

For the first time I wish I had a sister. I've had Leela, my mother's sister, I know how easy and natural this relationship is. With Leela in my life, I've never felt the lack of a mother. I see Akka with Nisha's sons, I've seen the difference in her behaviour with Adit, her brother's son. Yes, a sister's child is different, something special. Why don't I have a sister?

Tony and Rekha—of course, they're my best bet. They have no children. (I've gone so far in selfishness that this fact gives me satisfaction, if not pleasure.) They love Adit, both of them do, I know that, I'm sure of it. As for Adit, Tony is his favourite uncle. And there's Rekha—Adit is comfortable with

SHASHI DESHPANDE

her, he responds to her generosity and warmth. Yes, Tony and Rekha it will have to be.

I speak to Tony about it one day, shamefaced, trying to be casual, making it out to be a matter I've only just thought of.

'Are you crazy?' Tony is aghast. 'Such morbid thoughts—what's wrong with you, Madhu?'

'These things happen. Look at me, both my parents dead before I was fifteen.'

'But why should it happen to Adit? *To lose one parent may be regarded as a misfortune, to lose both . . .*'

My glare stops him. Is this the time for quoting games! And Oscar Wilde whom, Tony knows very well, I hate.

'Sorry, sorry. Consider that unsaid—unquoted, rather. What I wanted to say is—why should it happen to Som and you? Go to the statisticians—go to Nisha—she'll tell you what the chances of that happening are!'

'I don't care about statistics. I don't want Adit to go through what I did.'

Each time my father goes out, he tells me where he's going, he tells me when he'll be back. When I start reading, he leaves notes for me, saying 'Back soon.' As long as I see his messages, I'm fine. They're the points on which I chart my day. Then he dies, he goes away without a word and I'm left with nothing. An abyss.

'What's wrong with you?' my teacher in college asks me. 'You don't attend classes, you don't do your work. You came here with a good record. What's wrong? Are you not well? I'd like to meet your parents. Where's your father?'

'Dead.'

Maybe he's hard of hearing, maybe I've spoken too softly, mumbled, been indistinct; he hears it as 'Delhi'.

'Delhi? All right. Ask him to meet me when he returns.'

I feel a little better at the thought of my father being in

152

Delhi. A negligent, careless, absent father away in Delhi is better than a dead one.

'I don't want Adit to go through what I did,' I repeat to Tony.

'You had Leela and Joe.'

'Exactly!' I'm triumphant. 'That's why I want Adit to have Rekha and you.'

He senses my earnestness, my obduracy.

'Okay, baba, okay, relax. If Som and you pop off, Rekha and I will take on the brat, we'll look after him, we won't beat him, we won't send him out to work labelling bottles in factories. Happy?'

Happy? How can I be happy, how can I relax, when the fears continue to hover about me, changing shapes but always there, continually haunting me? I'm constantly thinking of safeguards, plans for Adit's safety, for his happiness.

The one contingency I never think of is that Som and I will outlive Adit. That Adit will die before us is the one eventuality I'm totally unprepared for.

Why am I thinking of these things? I have come here to forget, to get away from memories, to distance myself from Som, the one person who can connect me to those terrible days, to the horror of our son's death. Here, I'm safe. With Hari and Lata, I'm Madhu, I'm Kaku; in Bai's house, I'm the woman who's going to write a book on Savitribai Indorekar. Nowhere am I *Aditya-chi-Aai*, Aditya's mother, the identity I've had, the identity I've drowned myself in for nearly eighteen years.

I long sometimes for the tabula rasa of amnesia. Everything wiped out. A slate of virginal blankness. Starting, like a baby, with nothing. (But maybe a baby carries memories of the dark months in its watery home, a load of memories of earlier lifetimes—how do we know?) But this is not possible. The writing can never be wholly erased. The impressions remain, faint scorings that can be deciphered by those who know what was there earlier.

And yet, there's Bai, Bai who never speaks of her daughter Munni, the daughter she neglected for the sake of her career. Munni, my friend for such a brief while, and who died, by a strange coincidence, like my son, on the same day, victims, both of them, of the same madness, of the same violence. I think of it sometimes, the two of them in the same bus, on the same seat, perhaps side by side, like Munni and I were seated once, unaware of the past link between them, not knowing that they would be linked once again in death.

If I think of Munni so often, can Bai have forgotten her? Is it possible to forget? Never, not unless it is the disease that has conferred the boon of forgetfulness on her. The cells that stored memories of Munni dead, the memories lost, consigned to oblivion.

But something tells me this is not the truth. I've been here, with Bai, long enough to know that. Bai's forgetting, I think, is deliberate. She has drawn a line through Munni's and Ghulam saab's names and erased them from her life. This is something she did long back, when she turned to respectability, when she began her journey to success and fame. Perhaps she thought that to attain these things, this denial of her lover and daughter was necessary. I imagine that the denial also made it possible for her to live with herself.

Whatever the reason, however successfully she has managed to turn her back on her past and her child, I have to wonder: what happens to her in the dark hours of the night? What happens when she wakes up in the middle of the night, that terrible time when you hear the voices of your dead, when they come back to torment you with the wrongs you did them and confront you with your guilt—what happens to Bai then? Does she not face the stark truth at that time, the truth that confronts me every moment of my life—the futility of life without children?

In the months since Adit's death, my mind has been ceaselessly exercising on the treadmill of this one thought: how does one live with the knowledge of a child's death? It is our children who reconcile us to the passing of time, to our aging, to our irrelevance, our mortality. Without them the world makes no sense, without them we have no place in it. How then does one live without them? Can Bai give me the clue to this? Has she found the secret?

Part Two

10

It was my sense of guilt that made it impossible for me to refuse when Hamidbhai's nephews asked me to write a book on him. I had deserted Hamidbhai in his time of need—this was the way I saw it for a while after his death. And therefore, I thought, I owed him something. The family gave me the material, everything that they thought I needed. All I had to do was to put it together and make it readable. I am amazed now at the brashness that made me take the job on. Guilt apart, what else did I have, what did I know about writing a biography? I didn't have a clue. But I began with no qualms, no doubts, except about finding the time to write.

I worked on it in the afternoons, sitting at the dining table, papers spread all over it, my ears cocked to catch the slightest sound from the bedroom where Adit was sleeping. Adit was less than a year old then, but he was a good baby. He rarely disturbed me, he slept through the afternoon, so that I had two hours at a stretch to work in. The book, to my surprise and pride, was ready in three months; they gave me twenty-five copies when it came out. Som proudly distributed most of them to family and friends. The few copies that were left, I put away in a place where I couldn't see them. For some reason, I didn't like looking at the book, I didn't like being reminded of it. It embarrassed me.

It was just a booklet, really. What I wrote didn't come to more than thirty pages. The family padded it out with photographs and tributes from friends and colleagues—as if Hamidbhai, after death, needed these references. Even Dalvi had contributed his bit, a piece that began 'Hamidbhai Sir was not a man, he was a god . . .' I read this with a sense of utter disgust and then put the book away from me firmly.

But this wasn't the only reason why I disliked the book. What I had written was part of it as well. I knew it was flawed, I had no doubts that I'd botched it up. I'd written all the facts about Hamidbhai—his nationalist father, his saintly mother, his business acumen, his philanthropy, his patriotism, his simple life, etc., etc. Yes, all this was there. But Hamidbhai himself was nowhere in the book, he had eluded me. The truth was that I hadn't really known him at all, except as Joe's friend. Hamidbhai uncle, who became plain Hamidbhai—not 'sir' which he hated—when I started working with him. Even when I went to work for him and, in a sense, shared his home—for my room was separated from his living space only by a long corridor that ended in a swing door—his personal life remained invisible. Each day he came to the office, on the dot of eleven in the morning. We had a meeting then, Hamidbhai and the three of us who worked for *City Views*, while we drank tea out of his exquisite china—tea and Marie biscuits. And then he disappeared until the next day. It was the same kind of fleeting appearance that he made in my book. But Hamidbhai's absence was not the only thing that was wrong about the book; I was not in the book, either. I'd kept myself carefully, scrupulously out of it, making myself the invisible narrator. There was not even a 'dear reader' kind of reminder of my existence anywhere.

But making myself invisible, merging into the background, had become second nature to me after my father's death. Living, even for that brief while, in Joe's house, I became a very careful and circumspect girl, not letting any part of my life spill over into Leela and Joe's life, into that house. Paula's hatred and fury reminded me each moment that I was an intruder. I knew I had to stay out of sight, I had to remain unnoticed, not for myself alone, but for Leela's sake as well.

Working for *City Views* did away with my desire for

obscurity. It gave me enormous pleasure to see my name on the paper, to see my name associated with what I had written. When, after a few months, Hamidbhai gave me the title of Assistant Editor, I could never have enough of seeing my name with that description before it. My delight in the two words was boundless.

But this was in my working life. In my personal life, I was still effacing myself. The three young men who visited me scarcely noticed me. They came to get a few hours of respite, both from work and their homes, they came to be together, to talk to one another, to be in an excitingly unfamiliar milieu. I was only the audience, the listener. The absent Neelam, Som's flame, and Chandru's Satee, were more present in the room than I was.

Or so I imagined.

But this idea of myself as being invisible exploded when I grasped the fact that Som, who'd only recently been jilted by Neelam, was pursuing me. Suddenly I was a woman, a desired woman, a desirable woman, the woman Som wanted. Som's attention marked me out, underlining my presence, italicizing my femaleness. Som, giving weight to each word I spoke, to my silence, to my anger, my smiles, put me squarely in the limelight and made it impossible for me to go back to the shadows.

Now I know that it is impossible for a young woman to be unnoticed. Nature won't allow it, it doesn't suit her purpose. A young woman ready for mating, a young woman bearing a child—yes, this too—cry out to be seen, to be taken note of. I remember the time Som and I went to a South Indian restaurant to eat a *thali* meal, something for which I had a sudden uncontrollable urge. I was seven months pregnant then, and so large that it was not possible for me to squeeze through the narrow space between the long communal table and the benches provided for the customers. All the customers there were men—it was a place where single men, or men

161

staying away from their families, came for a meal. The men, those who were sitting at the table we chose, seeing my plight, got up and without a word moved the table so that I could get in. I remember the awe and the pleasure that came to me from the men. Their attention put a circle round my fertile femininity.

Now I know that of course they were all aware of me as a woman—not Dalvi alone, but Chandru and Som and Venkat and yes, Hamidbhai too. (Everyone, except Tony, who had, as he said to Rekha, 'successfully sublimated' his lust by becoming my brother.) Invisibility comes to a woman when she's old, but then, at that point, being ignored no longer seems such a desirable thing. On the contrary, it becomes a humiliation. You can stand in a public place for hours and remain unnoticed.

It's becoming increasingly clear to me that I cannot keep myself out of this book of Bai's, that I cannot be the invisible narrator. The child who knew Bai, the girl who knew Munni, the woman who is constantly aware of Bai's blanketing of Munni's name—they are part of the book, they will be part of Bai's story; it cannot be avoided. And the words will be mine. There is no way I can disown responsibility for them, as I tried to do in Hamidbhai's book. It's not possible to pass the buck on to someone else, to any other source; we no longer have the scapegoat of a muse or god to help us out, either. Yes, the words that present Bai to the world will be mine, I need to acknowledge that before I begin to write.

Yet, how do you capture a person in words?

Tony will argue that it can be done. Tony believes in the power of words. Both Tony and I are Joe's disciples. Not only did Joe lead us to books, he aroused our curiosity about words. 'Go to the dictionary,' Joe said, when we were puzzled by a word, when we had doubts about its meaning. Both of us got dictionaries as gifts from him. Tony read his as if it was a work of fiction, he pursued the meanings of words through

time and space ('Do you know bezique comes from
baazigar?'), he puzzled over oddities ('If disgruntled is
dissatisfied, how come gruntled is not satisfied?'), he rejoiced
in rarities.

It's amazing, I say to him often, that he should have gone
into a profession where words are stripped of their meanings,
where they are used to confuse, manipulate and dazzle. He
denies it. I never do that, he says. To him the word is indeed
God. And so, when I was doing the Saraswati puja at home
during Navaratri, induced to do this by Adit who had seen it at
his uncle's house, after much thought I kept the Oxford
Dictionary on the table as the symbol of Saraswati. Som
laughed at me, but Tony was delighted. Approving. 'You
couldn't have chosen anything better,' he said to me.

'*God called the dry land earth and the gathering of the
waters he called the sea.*'

Which shows, Tony said to me, after quoting this line, that
naming things is part of the act of creation. Without words
there can be no ideas, no emotions. We need words, not only
to speak, but to live out our lives as well. Wordless, we are
blank. Vacant.

Tony lying with his head on Rekha's lap, Tony completely
at peace, while Rekha's caressing fingers pass gently through
his hair, both of them wordless—what, no emotions here,
Tony? But I don't ask this question, I don't use this moment as
an argument against him. It would not be fair.

What about dance then, I ask him instead. What about
mime? Paintings?

Ah, paintings! Remember Van Gogh's statement?
Remember what he said? The painter's lips are sealed.

Nevertheless, each painting does speak, doesn't it?

Tony is not impressed. All these, according to him, are
inferior forms of communication. Vague, unclear, often
ambiguous. They don't have the precision, the accuracy of
words.

SHASHI DESHPANDE

Words precise, accurate and unambiguous? I have to laugh.

So we argue, Tony and I. But Tony is immovable. If his faith in words remains intact, despite working in a profession in which words are so often alienated from their sense and images and icons are taking over, how can I hope to make any dent in it? In any case, he says to me, I am a prejudiced woman.

I accept that. Growing up with two reticent men, I never felt that words were needed for a relationship. I saw it for the first time in Ketaki, I see it now in Lata, both of whom use words to construct a relationship, each word a brick that goes into the building of it. But *what* these words are does not matter; they are only the material. So too in Bai's profession. I've been listening to music, not only hers, but others' as well. And it's being brought home to me how insignificant words are to singers. They treasure their storehouse of texts—their '*cheez*'; Bai boasts of the large number of song-texts given to her by her Guruji. But when I listen to them singing these texts, I know the words really mean nothing. All of them speak of love and longing, of meeting and parting, but the singer's emotions are not connected to these words at all. Their emotions come out of their own selves, out of their moods, they work them out through the combinations of swaras, through the chosen raaga. The raaga gathers momentum, not because the story is reaching its climax, but because the singer is now in total control and getting close to the heart of the particular emotion she is trying to convey through the raaga.

No, words are not important to Bai. The words she uses belong to others, they are clay for her to mould.

And I have to work on her life, to sculpt her with words.

I have the basic information about her now—her birth, her parents, her marriage, her early music lessons, her years with her Guruji, her rise to fame and success. I know the context I

164

have to put her into: she is the last of the musicians of the great classical style, one of a handful of purists, the doyen of all Hindustani vocalists today, indeed of all musicians. She has made no concessions to change, to innovation, to the demands of contemporary audiences. Her repertoire has not gone beyond what was given to her by her Guruji. She is very clear that there is no need for her to go beyond it, no need either to improvise or to innovate. She considers innovations to be cheap gimmicks.

If I am to write a straight, chronological narrative of her life, this is enough. It will be like my book on Hamidbhai, only bigger, because I have much more material. Bai's life has been more eventful than Hamidbhai's was, it already is a longer life. If history is, as I read somewhere, the arranging of events in a temporal sequence, this book, Bai's history, is easy to write. I have only to put events in a sequential order, as if Time is the only connecting factor. A straight line on which Bai has been steadily moving, a deliberate progress through events.

But I can't do this. No one can. We don't live our lives this way, we don't see our lives this way. We see our lives through memory and memories are fractured, fragmented, almost always cutting across time. I remember the little servant girl I had, to whom everything in a film that was not part of a straightforward chronological narration was 'swapna'—a dream. Memories, flashback, voice-overs, songs, dances—all these were 'swapna' to her. She felt cheated by any movie which had none of these things. It was not the same without them, she said; it was dull, boring. Who wants to watch this, she would say. Truly, dreams are the stuff of life, the hidden truth that lies beneath the hard reality. Invention, creation, is sometimes the greater, possibly the best part, of reality. Even to write our own stories, we need to invent. Like fiction writers, like historians, the teller of her own story needs to construct a plausible narrative. How else do you connect but by imagining? You can't change events; events are immovable, rooted, like those road rollers that stayed for months at one spot in Neemgaon. But you can change the way you look at events. I think of the dancers on the stage who were transformed into totally different beings with the changing colours that the light shed on them. It seemed like magic to us children, an unseen power creating this enchantment, evoking 'ooohs' and 'aaahs' of pure delight from us. We never knew about the hands that worked this magic, swiftly moving different coloured paper over the lights.

I can take over Bai's life and make what I want of it through my words. I can trap her into an image I create, seal her into an identity I make for her. The power of the writer is the power of the creator. Yes, I can do much. I can make Bai the rebel who rejected the conventions of her times. The feminist who lived her life on her terms. The great artist who struggled and sacrificed everything in the cause of her art. The woman who gave up everything—a comfortable home, a husband and a family—for love.

'Don't be afraid of bringing out the truth'—Maya and Yogi's words. Yes, we want the truth. But what are the truths we seek? Battered children, rape, incest, adultery, the gruesome actions of perverted minds—these are what we want. This is the age of voyeurs, what we want is to look through the keyhole of the bedroom, of the toilet, to catch humans at their worst, their most undignified, their meanest levels. And this, we call the truth.

What is the truth about Bai? Why did she leave her home, and that, with a Muslim lover? A step so great that even today it would require enormous courage. The stuff even movies still hesitate to take on. Was it truly love? Or a way out of a situation she could no longer endure? Did she use the man for her own ends? Or was she seduced by him?

Bai is holding on resolutely to her own idea of her life. She is refusing to relinquish control, to let me have anything more than what she has decided I can have. She denies the sacrifice the articles about her invariably speak of, she minimizes the struggle, she sidesteps it. Even the problems she is supposed to have had with other artistes are never spoken of. As far as she is concerned, the story of her life does not need anyone else. She sees herself as someone unique, she refuses to be set even in the context of other singers. The spotlight has to be on her and her alone; she is still, I sometimes think, inhabiting the I-ME-MYSELF world of a child. Whatever it is, the way she offers her life to me, it is a bland story, as bland as the ghee-dal-rice meal she ate as a child, something she often refers to now with nostalgia.

In all this, there is a curious innocence about her. She is as unaware of trendy feminism as she is of political correctness. She speaks of herself as a Brahmin in a way that assumes her superiority on this account alone. (It reminds me of the 'we Inamdars are superior' slogan of Leela's family). She also rejects the safe ledge of the woman artist to stand on. From that platform, if only she knew it, she can do no wrong. Abandoning her husband, her lover, her daughter—all these can be justified; indeed, they will be applauded. This is the story Maya and Yogi want. Victim stories are out of fashion, heroines are in. Heroinism—a word which falls oddly on my unaccustomed ears, a word devoid now of its earlier attributes of passivity and beauty—is the word of the day.

But Bai is unaware of this. She clings fiercely instead to her respectability, the respectability she claimed in her second birth as a singer, when, after a gap of two years, she reappeared in public view, wearing at that first public performance the mangalsutra of the married woman, instead of the pearls she had worn until then. A respectably married woman. Both Ghulam Saab, her lover, and Munni, her daughter, no longer part of her life.

It's becoming increasingly clear to me that the book I'm going to write will have no relation to the hagiography Bai expects, or to the book Yogi and Maya want. If I don't know as yet what kind of a book it will be, I know this: Munni will have a place in it. I've been stalking Bai since I came here, waiting for her to mention Munni, waiting to see Munni in her eyes, in her face, in her silences, in the nuances of her words. So far she has revealed nothing. And yet a child cannot be anything but important. The desire for a child, the anguish of childlessness—these have been a part of humankind since ancient times. Both the *Ramayana* and the *Mahabharata* begin with the tormented desire for children. From the beginning, the child has been the single most important factor of human life. And why not? A child is a beginning, a renewal, a continuation, an assertion of immortality.

And Bai stands away from this. But perhaps it is through her music that she is reaching out to immortality, it is by putting her life on record that she hopes to live on, it is through this book that she hopes to satisfy her longing for eternal life. Watching Lata scatter her belongings through the house, like scattering bits of herself, I've thought—women leave their impress on quotidian life much more than men do, to make up perhaps, for the blanking out that is a woman's destiny after her death. Nothing left, often no picture, not even a name. Except—I now recall—the Sati stones. Stones engraved with the names of those women who died satis. An example to other women, perhaps; or was it a kind of bribe? Deny the possibility of life without a man, and your name lives forever. What a terrible price to pay for immortality—to be burnt alive!

If Bai wants to live through this book, I can give her the immortality she desires. Yet there is a price she will have to pay: the daughter she denies, the daughter whose existence she has obliterated (so successfully, that I have seen only one mention of her in a Marathi magazine, and that, only a sentence), this daughter will be part of her life again. Why, when she had the courage to walk out on her marriage and family, is she so frightened of revealing the existence of her child? She gave that child the name 'Indorekar'—the name she adopted as a singer (from her mother's home town Indore)—not compromising either her maiden name or her married one. Meenakshi Indorekar. Marking her out as *her* child alone, not the child of her marriage, not the child of her lover. This surely is a statement I cannot ignore?

But Munni hankered for the name her mother had left behind, she yearned for the conventional life Bai had found so stultifying.

Whatever it was between them, mother and daughter, Munni's death should have changed things. Death disarms you, you can't fight any more, you have to lay down your arms. This has not happened with Bai. Her hostility continues. What else does her silence indicate but this? She is still the same Bai I saw as a child, walking on without a backward look at the child hovering in the shadows, the child who was waiting, it seems to me now, for a word from her mother, a glance. Any kind of recognition of her presence. A recognition which she is still being denied.

If Bai does not open her mouth, I have to find my reasons for her rejection of her daughter. Find? No, I have to invent reasons. Fiction, then, it seems, is inevitable.

Perhaps biographies should be written only after the subjects are dead—when you can safely appropriate the person's life and make what you want of it. There's a kind of cruelty, a treachery, in writing of a living person when the person's life is still fluid, inchoate and incomplete. It's like taking control of that life, giving it a direction and a shape that defies the very possessor of that life. When I bring Munni back into Bai's life, when I try to explain her rejection of her daughter, I will be saying: *this* is how it was. *This* is why it happened. Whereas, the truth is that we don't always know why we do things. There aren't always clear-cut reasons for actions, rarely such definite motives which we can pinpoint.

Yet, to leave Ghulam Saab and Munni out of Bai's life

entirely or to give them minor roles, to put them in the footnotes, is to throw a cloak over one of Bai's myriad selves. There are so many selves in us which are called forth by other human beings, selves which are dependent on others for their existence. I know how I changed because of Leela and Joe, how Adit made me into a person I could scarcely recognize myself, how, living with Som, some of the fine dust of his careless generosity, his ease with people, was sprinkled on me as well. Sometimes I wonder whether there is, in fact, a pristine self in us, which will be revealed only when we are totally isolated from others. Or, whether, without others, we are nothing. A blank slate.

But for all of us, there's a self inside which we recognize as our real selves. For Munni, the self that she saw as her own lay in the future, it was towards that self that she moved with deliberation, it was that self I met in the bus—an ordinary looking woman with an ordinary family life and a name so ordinary that it covers pages in the telephone directory. When I think of the real me, it is the child I see, running out after a bath in her petticoat and knickers, eager to go out, unheeding of Babu's angry shouts. Unhampered. Unburdened. Free.

Now, after all these sessions with Bai, I know that Bai looks back at the young woman training under her Guruji, the young woman living in one room and travelling between it and Guruji's home, as her truest self. Free for the first time in years, living the life she wanted, steady in the pursuit of her goal, pure of purpose.

I have to negotiate my way between this woman and the cruel mother of my memory. Between this woman and the dazzlingly beautiful singer with her lover, whom she kept purposefully in the background.

11

There are ellipses in all stories, even in the narratives of our own lives. There is so much I don't know about my past, so little that I know about my parents. I do know, however, that they met when my father was visiting a friend in Belgaum. My mother was there at the time, taking part in an inter-school athletic meet. She injured her foot during the final event and was taken by her teacher to a doctor she knew. The doctor who was my father's friend, was then invited to the prize-giving ceremony that evening and my father, who was on a holiday, tagged along as well. And there he saw this tall girl, limping up to the dais over and over again to receive her prizes. I like to think of them exchanging looks, knowing that it was a fateful moment. But this is only a surmise. I know nothing of how they met and continued to meet. Perhaps, using the excuse of her injured foot, she stayed on for some more time, and that was the beginning. My mother was just a little over sixteen then.

They got married as soon as she was eighteen. There was, of course, enormous opposition to the marriage from her family. Not only was my father much older—nearly fifteen years older than her—he was not a Brahmin. Nevertheless, they got married. A year later she had a child and in a few months she was dead. It was TB, galloping TB as they called it then, which killed her within six months. This is the brief story of my parent's marriage, of their relationship. Or rather, this is all that I know of it.

My mother remained a blank space through my childhood. She is that even today. I see my father in myself when I look in

the mirror, I saw him in Adit, in the line of his jaw, his ears
with their large lobes, in his gravity and the smile that
suddenly transformed that gravity. My dead mother surely
is—was—there in him, and in me as well, but I can't identify
her in us because I never saw her. That I know so little about
my mother is natural. But my ignorance about my father, my
sole parent for fifteen years, surprises me now. Though, to
think of it, it shouldn't be so surprising, after all. Children are
incurious creatures; a parent is only a parent, there's no more
to the person than that. And I had no sibling to share my
information with later, which is why my knowledge remains
incomplete. For long, I did not even know that my father's
first name was Eknath. There was nobody who called him by
that name. He was Doctor or Doctorsaheb to most people; to
his friends, he was Majorsaheb—the rank with which he left
after his brief stint in the army. I knew that he came from
Gwalior, that he did his medical studies in Bombay, that he
joined the army and was with it for a year or two. He left when
the war ended. He came to Neemgaon because of the TB
sanatorium; when his wife died, he continued to live in
Neemgaon.

Some of these things I learnt from Leela. And it was Leela
who told me the most astonishing fact about him—that he had
been married earlier, before he met my mother. My mother
was his second wife. His first marriage had been as brief as his
second one, that wife dying in childbirth. The child also died.
For some reason, this knowledge was hard to assimilate, more
difficult to accept than the fact of his having a mistress. Munni
had thrust this information on me, as a weapon during a
quarrel between us. Leela spoke of it too after my father's
death, when she told me that there was a woman, a 'friend' she
called her, to whom he had left some money. I knew then that
this was the mistress Munni had spoken of, the woman whose
existence I had so angrily denied without understanding what
having a mistress really meant. By the time Leela spoke to me

172

SMALL REMEDIES

of it, I knew what a mistress was. Nevertheless, the knowledge of my father having had one did not hurt; it didn't seem wrong. It was his having had a wife before he met my mother, it was the child he had had before me—these were the things that disturbed me. I couldn't connect these things to the man I knew.

My father was not really a family man. My own recollection of him gives me the picture of a man not really cut out for conventional family life. There seemed to me to be some kind of incongruity in his having married twice. The one single factor that marked his identity, the factor that stamped him, was his being a doctor. This was the main thing about him. Our lives in Neemgaon, our place in society were shaped by the fact of his being a doctor. It set him apart and distinguished him from the others. His looks—he was tall, slim and with an erect bearing—did that as well. And there was the motorcycle he used for his rounds, which gave him a dashing air few men of his age had. None of the fathers I knew could be compared to him. When he smoked—and he was always smoking—there was an elegance about him. The way he held his cigarette, tapped it on the back of his hand before lighting it, the way he held it casually in his mouth while he worked—all this gave him the debonair air of a hero in the early Hindi movies. The dark glasses he invariably wore out-of-doors completed the picture.

The smell of his cigarettes permeated my early life. Our home was always full of the fumes of tobacco. He had a bath every evening after his day's work was done, he sluiced himself with cold water on the stone floor of the bathroom and then changed his clothes. But the odour of his cigarettes clung to him still. It was never an unpleasant smell to me. On the contrary, it meant his presence, it meant he was around, it meant security to me. Even today, when I get a whiff of his cigarettes (and it's odd that none of the men in my life smoke), I am overcome by nostalgia. I am back in my childhood home,

173

my father is at home. And then the illusion disappears and I suffer all over again the pain of the knowledge of my father's death.

When I saw my father for the last time, in hospital, I did not associate his condition, his impending death, which was visible even to me, with his smoking. Just as, earlier, it had never occurred to me that his constant cough or his occasional bouts of breathlessness had anything to do with the cigarettes he incessantly smoked. Later—possibly this was Ketaki's influence—I wondered whether the smoking was part of his grief over my mother's death. Whether, knowing the possible fatal results, he still went on smoking, to his certain end. I no longer believe in this theory, in the death wish which was part of Ketaki's idea of love. Even if the cigarette packs of those days did not carry a caution, surely he as a doctor knew the lethal consequences of smoking? And if he did, would he not also know the details of the terrible process of such a dying? Who, for God's sake, would choose a death as painful as that? In his last days, before he went to Bombay for his surgery, I saw him dying each moment. Each breath he drew was like a painful rebirth.

In any case, there was never any hint of despair or tragedy in my father, or in his life. He was a matter-of-fact person and our home was a cheerful one, even Babu's dourness could not cast a gloom over it. There was a picture of my mother on the wall in his room, but I don't think it held any special tragic significance for him. It was part of the furniture in our house.

Yet, he was a lonely man, I know that now. He had his friends, not many of them, but they were staunch and one or the other visited us every day, so that there was always someone with him at night, the two of them chatting, listening to the radio, having a drink together. There was also his mistress, but that, I imagine, was a purely physical thing, though, remembering now that he left her almost as much money as he left for me, I hope there was affection too. But he

174

was, undoubtedly, a lonely man. As a child, while I lay in bed and listened to him chatting with his friends, security and comfort came to me along with the smell of the cigarettes, the aroma of the drinks. Today, when I think of it, the smell of his loneliness comes to me as well.

I knew none of these things when we were together. It was enough for me to have him home with me. We were always comfortable and easy with one another. The space between us was not crowded with demands, doubts, assertions or questions. There was enough air for us to breathe easily. Ours was a relationship built, not on information, but on trust.

Munni tried to dislodge me from this paradise by offering me the knowledge of my father's mistress. But I thrust this knowledge away from me. It had no place in our life together. Child though I was, I had the wisdom to know that you don't need to know everything about a person.

I want to believe that Bai's was a love story, I want to think that she left her husband and home with another man out of love. I imagine I can see that love in the picture of the two of them taken during a performance, a picture I found in one of the albums. There they are, she and Ghulam Saab, looking at each other, smiling, each conscious, it seems, only of the other. But I know this is not how it was. I've seen this kind of thing too often not to know that their smiles are not the shared feelings of lovers, but a moment of rapport between singer and accompanist, the ecstasy almost that they attain when they reach their destination, the moment of 'sam' together.

Yet, I like to think that love was part of this exchange too. I find myself on the same side as Ketaki and Munni, both of whom, I realize now, were searching for love—Munni in the movies and Ketaki in her books and magazines. I don't scorn that search, the faith that it exists somewhere, this perfect love. I want to see this fantasy in Bai's life, to know that it was an unconquerable emotion that brought her and Ghulam Saab together. I would like to write about their love, a love that transcended all barriers, I would be glad to make Bai the heroine of a passionate, beautiful story. It is possible. What else but love could make a woman of her class, a married woman, take on a lover and leave her home with him? For some reason, possibly because I've seen the two of them together, she always a little ahead of him, she always the focus of attention, I see her as the one to take the initiative, the first to speak of her feelings to him. And he, only then, speaking of his own feelings, telling her he reciprocated her love.

And yet there's the other Bai I see as well, a calculating, ambitious woman, using the man for her own ends, abandoning him finally when her need for him is over. Was this how it was? True, Bai is a worldly woman, but when she sings, she transcends her own worldliness. Why not then in love as well? She had a child by the man before she left her husband's home. What else but passion could have led to the conceiving of a child? But let me not forget that she abandoned that child when she left home with her lover. I'm suddenly halted by the thought. She left her baby, scarcely a year old, behind. Could a woman who did that be capable of great love?

Why not? Isn't this itself a sign of her love for the man? When a couple is very much in love, when they are wrapped up in each other, they have less to give their children.

All these are only theories. I have to push my way out of them and get to the woman herself. The complex, complicated human being who comes to me through her words. It's with words that she builds a huge cutout of an artist, a musician, barring my view of the human being behind it. There are times when she falters and then, like seeing the eyes of a burqa-cloaked woman through the eye-slits, I get a sudden glimpse of a human being behind that shield. It's this darkness

176

that interests and tantalizes me; I know it's in this darkness that the woman I want resides. Her silences about her personal life, about her life with her husband, with her lover, her muteness about the hardships she suffered as a woman who flouted the rules of society—these are what link her to that woman.

Her control is absolute, magnificent. If it slips, it's so imperceptible that I have to be quick and sharp to catch her in it. Like, speaking of the time she was alone (a period of her life that's obscure, one I'm eager to hear about), she uses, to my amusement, the tabla as a metaphor for her loneliness. 'It was like singing without the tabla. Music without taal is meaningless.'

Does she realize that she's given something away here?

Ghulam Saab loved her, I've seen them together and I know that. But this is not enough material for me to create a love story. In any case, this is not a love story that ended on the note 'and they lived happily ever after'. For they did not—not ever after, anyway. He went back to his family some time after they left Neemgaon. Nor is their story the kind of tragedy Munni sobbed over in the movies. Bai moved on to fame and success.

And he? What happened to him? What went on between them at home? Bai carries that secret within herself, she will never reveal it. She has a right to her privacy, to protect her life from public gaze. But how do I write about her with this huge hole in the centre of her life? And why, if there was this great love at home, did Munni have to go looking for it so desperately in the movies?

I learned about love from Munni, that great lover of movies; she gets both the word and the idea of love from them. Munni sees all the movies that come to our two theatres in Neemgaon. As soon as the posters go up on the trees and lamp posts, her excitement begins. She stands, before the posters, gazing at them in rapt attention, her face taking on a glazed look, planning I know, to see the movie as soon as possible. Munni is one of those odd creatures, very rare among girls, who can see movies by herself. Girls invariably go in pairs, in groups, or with friends and families, but Munni prefers to be on her own. I see her once, returning home after watching a Dilip Kumar movie, tears pouring down her face, still caught up in the tragic plight of the lovers. She doesn't see me, not even when I shout out her name. It's only when I run up to her and touch her on her shoulder that she turns a startled look on me, a blind, unrecognizing look.

Munni tries hard to inveigle my father into letting me go with her. 'Please, Doctor Kaka, please, please let her come,' she pleads. 'I'll look after her, promise, God promise.' Once, in desperation she says, 'I'll pay for her.' At which my father laughs, but he does not relent. This is one more of the things about which my father is firm: I am not allowed to go into a confined, crowded theatre. It's part of my father's fears for me, fears linked to the cod liver oil I swallow all the years of my childhood. Rarely, twice a year maybe, he takes me to a movie himself. He buys balcony seats for us and we sit in isolated splendour, high above the whistling, groundnut-eating crowd below, distanced, it transpires, even from what is happening on the screen, because we don't feel the emotions—either the tragedy or the humour—the way Munni does. Munni laughs so much when relating the comic scenes to me that she can scarcely speak coherently, but when I watch the movie myself, it doesn't seem all that funny, after all. Maybe it's being down there among the crowds that brings the drama close.

Munni sits in the women's section. It's almost like being in purdah, in spite of the fact that the thick musty curtains hang uselessly on either side. Little boys who've been brought into this enclosure by mothers and sisters, since these tickets are cheaper, are ashamed to be seen there. As soon as the hall is dark, they vault over the low barrier that encloses the women and join the males, leaving the women in the 'zenana'—all of them as responsive as Munni is to what's happening on the screen. I see them wiping their eyes when they come out, sobbing over the heroine's death, over the hero's despair, giggling over the antics of Johnny Walker.

Each time Munni sees a movie, she tells me the entire story. We have long sessions during which she narrates the story to me. It's always, I gather, about love. '*Prem*' she calls it. He—the hero, that is—loves the heroine and she loves him, but everyone else is the enemy. Fathers, stepmothers, stepsisters, proper full-time villains—all of them are constantly conspiring to prevent the lovers from coming together. There's a kind of magic about this '*prem*', or so it seems to me from listening to Munni's stories. She, the heroine that is, hears him calling her when she is fast asleep, even though he's in a distant town. Her voice, crying out his name when she's in trouble with the villain or when she's ill, reaches him though he's in a place that is miles and miles away. She comes to him after her death—he doesn't know she's dead—she holds out her hands to him and leads him into the mists, into death really, so that finally they're together.

On occasions, Munni interrupts her narration to sing a song, at the exact point at which it is sung in the movies. At times she dances, like the heroine must have done, hands on hips, giving coy looks out of the corners of her eyes, coquettishly tossing her head, whirling around, her skirts flying about her in a circle. This is wonderful entertainment for me. And education as well, though I don't realize it then. I'm learning about love.

Love is an adult emotion.

Joe's words. He was speaking to Tony—I can't remember

the occasion on which he said it, but I know it was a reproving comment. Made, I imagine, on one of Tony's frequent changes of girl-friends. Joe's voice sharp when he said this, loaded with the sarcasm he reserved for his son.

Love is an adult emotion.

Joe thinking, maybe, of his own feelings for Rita, Tony's mother, when he said this. The dainty beautiful Rita whom he married when they were both very young. A marriage that never worked, Rita gradually, imperceptibly drifting away from him, staying less and less with him in Bombay, more in London with her mother and sister. Her death, only the final decree of divorce, the marriage having ended much earlier, even before Paula was born.

Or was Joe thinking more positively when he said this, thinking of his feelings for Leela? When I met them, I had no idea that I was seeing that thing Munni spoke· of so much. *Prem.* Love. They were just Leela and Joe, two middle-aged people. But they were lovers. I learnt this later, I gradually absorbed the wonder of their love. Joe was an ardent lover, he waited fifteen years to marry Leela, he waited patiently until she agreed to marry him. Joe married Leela in spite of Paula—I never cease to marvel at that. Paula vehemently opposed their marriage, she hated and despised Leela, she never accepted her. And yet Joe, who could never bear to displease Paula, married Leela. Leela's reluctance to marry Joe was only because of Paula. Her own family, her dead husband Vasant's family that is, were all for it. It was Paula and her feelings that kept Leela from giving in to Joe's importunities. She gave in finally, because—and she told me this herself—she didn't think it was right to deprive Joe and herself of happiness 'because of a spoilt brat'.

After Leela's death, I found a packet of letters among her possessions. Letters written by Joe in those fifteen years they were apart. I gave them to Tony—they were Joe's after all. But no, Tony said, they were meant for Leela and therefore I had a better right to them.

Finally we read them together. We had to, before we could decide what we were to do with them. Short letters in very simple words, since Leela's English couldn't have coped with more and Joe knew no Marathi. Each word was loaded with love—and with passion. Yes, there was that too, it was clearly there. We couldn't go on, it was impossible, we burnt the letters. It seemed the right thing to do.

Love is an adult emotion, Joe said to his son. And added, 'Some of us never grow up, some of us never reach adulthood.'

I saw the questions on Tony's stricken face then. 'Never be an adult? How shall I know it then? How shall I recognize love when I see it?'

But Tony did, when he met his Rekha—Rekha who shines benevolently like the autumn moon over his life. I rejoice for him, I rejoice that he proved his father wrong. I think Tony and I, after seeing Leela and Joe together, knew the difference between the true feeling and its false shadow, the glittering image that Ketaki and Munni pursued. I knew that what the movies showed, what the books wrote about, was not the real thing, but tinsel, fairy gold.

'Your aunt, Madhu,' Joe would say of Leela, 'your aunt has no sense of humour at all.'

'Your aunt, Madhu,' he would tell me, 'your aunt is the only woman who can look dignified sitting in a chair even with her feet inches off the ground.'

Romantic words? Words of love? Ketaki would have laughed herself sick if I'd told her this. But I knew, oh yes, I knew. And so when Som came to me after his break-up with Neelam, showing none of the emotional frenzy that he'd exhibited in his affair with Neelam, when he made me understand that he wanted to marry me, I knew this was the real thing. And therefore, when Som said, 'I want you to be my wife, I want to live my life with you, I want us to have children,' I was certain of his feelings, I had no doubts at all.

And I was right. It was real, it was good. After marriage, passion entered my life as well. It was in my little room in Hamidbhai's flat, our home now, Som's and mine after our marriage, it was on that narrow bed that I discovered what passion was. Fireworks and big bangs, the world turning cartwheels, giving me unexpected glimpses of beauty and light.

'Come on, come on,' Som says, while I prepare for bed, going through my last-things-at-night chores. 'Come to bed, Madhu, come to me.'

The bed is so narrow I can only throw myself on him, I feel him, moist-tipped and aroused under me. My delight in him, in what he is doing to me, our delight in each other, the laughter and conversation we indulge in while we're making love, his hands moving all the while, teasingly, tantalizingly over my body—this is passion. It's love too.

None of this is unexpected. If I've received ideas of love from others, my own mind and body have sent me messages that have told me about this physical love. No, none of this is unexpected. I'm not only happy, I'm a little complacent too. I'm an adult, mature, in full control of my feelings. All those tears, the agony, the distress, the turmoil that I hear about are not for me.

I don't know that this is still waiting for me in the future, that my testing time is still to come. I have no idea that I will meet it soon, the emotion which will denude me, strip me of my skin and make me open to pain. Make me wholly vulnerable.

Motherless child that I am, motherhood is an unknown world to me. The mothers I see in my childhood are drab creatures, forever working, forever scolding their children; certainly they're not the women to arouse a sense of deprivation in me. 'Poor child,' they say sometimes, absentmindedly, when I visit their homes. 'Poor child,' they say and I know they're referring to my not having a mother. But my father is enough for me; I don't want anything more. For obvious reasons that I now understand, mothers don't figure very much in Munni's stories. This, in spite of the importance of mothers in most movies. It's the stepmother, that enemy of lovers, who figures in her stories. I get some images of motherhood in the movies I see myself, through the songs that speak of '*maa ka pyar*'. But real life shows me something entirely different. Munni's mother who ignored her daughter; Ketaki's mother, stern, dictatorial and so partial to her sons; Sunanda, sweetly devious and manipulating; Som's mother, so demanding— none of them conform to the white-clad, sacrificing, sobbing mother of the movies.

Which is why I am wholly unprepared for what happens to me when I become a mother. Motherhood takes over my life, it makes me over into an entirely different person. The in-control-of-herself Madhu is lost, gone for ever. It's my baby's dependence that changes me; my place in the universe is marked out now. After the uncertainty, the indefiniteness of everything, of things whirling off, away from me, here is something a hundred per cent steadfast. Yes, that's it—steadfast. It is I who am providing the certainty, the central pole of a whirling universe for this small human being, and at the same time, it is he who is keeping me there, making me into this stable figure.

Even in the cradle, I can see his eyes moving in search of me. The moment he sees me, he smiles, his search is over, he has found what he wants. When he begins to crawl, he crawls to where I am, when he learns to stand, he holds my legs for support, and standing, rests his head on my lap, content, having reached his ultimate goal. His whimpers, his cries, die down the moment I pick him up, my touch is enough to soothe him, to make him happy.

His dependence fills me with delight, my power over him

183

awes me. I indulge him, enjoying my power to transform his
tears into smiles. I flaunt my feelings, there is no need to hide
them. It's not just legitimate, it's something to be proud of, this
mother love. It is never wrong, it can never do wrong—so we
say to one another, all of us mothers, the women I have
suddenly discovered to be those I feel closest to. Mother love is
one of the great wonders of this world, we tell one another.

And so I can justify my reluctance to leave my baby alone
even for a short while, I can justify my reluctance to leave him
with anyone else—this is mother love, this is what
motherhood is about. For a whole year I don't go anywhere
unless we can take him with us. But Som, in the interests of his
growing consulting practice, says we need to socialize, we
need to entertain doctors at home, we have to go out when
they invite us. And no, we can't take a baby along for a party.
And no, he can't go on his own, all the wives will be there, it
won't look good, it's not right for him to be without me. And
for God's sake, when we have people home for dinner, can't I
put the baby to sleep in time? What kind of conversation can
we have with a baby around?

He doesn't like his own son! I am aghast. We quarrel, fierce
quarrels that die down just as quickly; neither of us is capable
of carrying on a prolonged cold war.

When Adit is two, Som decides we can now leave him with
Nisha when we go out in the evenings. Adit enjoys his cousins,
the twins, and Nisha is willing to have him. I agree, but I want
to pick him up on our way back home. I can't sleep unless Adit
is at home, in his bed. It's nearly midnight when we get to
Nisha's house, and on one occasion, much after that. Nisha's
husband, who opens the door to us, makes his displeasure
clear and Nisha speaks to Som the next day: we have to leave
Adit with them overnight, or they can't have him.

I argue, but the next time we go out, Som drives straight
home, he becomes deaf and dumb, he pays no heed to my
protests. I go to bed in silent, sullen anger, I turn my back on

him, but he won't let me. He puts his arms around me, he nuzzles me, pulls the pins out of my hair, nibbles at my ears, my nose, my lips. Playfulness gives way to passion and he says, like he used to in our early days, 'Come to me, Madhu, come to me, my darling.' The smell of whisky on his breath, the cologne he uses after a bath, his chuckles of delight when I begin to respond to him—all these things arouse me and it's like being back on our narrow bed in that little room once again.

When I wake up, Som has already left to bring Adit home. Adit returns, pleased with himself, full of his evening with his cousins, still brimming over with the excitement of their activities. He's eager to repeat the experience, he keeps asking, 'When are you going out Mama, when will you go again?'

'I told you so,' Som says, but it hurts. I don't show the hurt, I'm learning to understand that this has to be concealed from everyone, I'm learning that it's no longer possible to flaunt my feelings as I could when Adit was an infant in his cradle. I'm beginning to understand that this desire to be with my son, my aversion to sharing him with anyone, is something most people will find odd. I know that Som certainly will be annoyed at my reluctance to leave Adit, that there will be endless arguments between us if I say this aloud and I will be made to feel I'm doing wrong. I become cunning now, devious, finding out different ways of avoiding going out with Som.

When Adit has typhoid, I'm distraught. My world turns dark. Som reassures me. Rajani, our pediatrician, tells me not to worry. 'What am I here for, Madhu? Leave it to me.'

But I can't. When he returns home from the hospital, I sleep on the floor in his room. And later, when on Som's insistence I go back to our room, I leave the door open. What if he wants me, what if he calls for me and I don't hear him?

'Damn you, damn you, damn you!' Som says in a cold fury, when I turn away from him at night. The intensity of his anger frightens me—it's so unlike him. I see something here that goes beyond the fact of my rejection. But I don't really want to know what Som is feeling, or why he's angry. That's the way men are, I tell myself; when it comes to sex, they're totally unreasonable. And I'm right, I'm justified, I have every right to do what I'm doing. I'm a mother, an anxious mother.

Adit's babyhood, his total dependence on me, is so brief it passes like a breath, a flash. Even as a toddler, I hear words, phrases and names from him I know nothing about, which tell me that he already has a world I can't follow him into. His school friends, his teachers, his cousins, neighbours—they enter his world and I want to share all of them with him. For some time he lets me into that world. I learn to drive, I take him and his friends, his cousins out—to the movies, to the beach, for picnics. When they come home, I'm there to feed them, to do things for them, I'm never impatient like other mothers, I'm happy to give them my time. 'Auntie,' they call out to me, 'Auntie'. And I'm happy, I'm doing this for Adit, I'm part of his life.

Then things change, he becomes evasive, he doesn't bring his friends home any more. 'Why, Adit?' I ask him. 'Why do you want to go to Sanju's house (or to Vinay's or Ajay's or anyone's house)? Why don't you all come here?'

'I don't feel like it,' he says. Or, 'Leave it, Ma.' I feel left out, miserable. As he grows up, he learns to slip away more unobtrusively, so that often I know he's gone out only when he returns.

'Where had you gone, Adit?'

'Oh, nowhere.'

'Whose phone was that?'

'Oh, just someone's.'

I think of Ketaki sobbing on my shoulders, telling me of the frenzy her girls drive her into by refusing to divulge anything, anything at all to her. 'And when I yell at Manasa, you know what she says? Pardon me for living, she says. I don't know where she picked that up. Pardon me for living.' She repeats the phrase as if it is the final nail in the coffin of her relationship with her daughter.

I laughed at her then, secure in the knowledge of my own relationship with Adit. Now it's I who cry and she who comforts me. 'They're all like that, Madhu,' she says soothingly. 'Heartless. Look at my two.'

But I see Ketaki's daughters hugging her, their faces close to hers, their cheeks against her cheek. Adit never does that, he doesn't allow me even to hold his hand.

'All children are like that, Madhu,' Som consoles me.

But Adit is not 'all children'. Ours is a special relationship, we've always done things together. Now I see a hard adamantine core in Adit that frightens me. He uses the voice he reserves for strangers when he speaks to me. I think of how his coldness with others had only accentuated his closeness to me. And now, to speak that way to me!

'Let him go, Madhu,' Som pleads. 'Let him go. Don't hold him so close, let him go.'

But I can't. I'm a mother, I can't let go, why doesn't he understand how I feel?

The door to his room is closed against us. 'He's growing up, what do you expect, this is natural,' Som tells me.

'Remember me, remember how I was?' Tony asks me when I complain to him.

I don't care about others. And Tony has no children, how can he understand? But Som too? It's natural, he says. How can it be natural to keep his mother out? I envy Som the ease with which he accepts Adit's closed door, the ease with which he opens it and goes in if he wants to. He isn't afraid like I am, he doesn't think like I do: what if he's angry with me? What if he stops speaking to me?

This frantic beating of my heart, this constant tumult within me, this ceaseless fear—is this mother love? Is this love? A small centre, a vast exclusion? No, there's only a centre, all else is a blank, a huge blank.

Moha—it was Som's father who used the word, speaking of someone's feelings for a child. 'That's not love,' he said. 'It's *moha, putra moha.*'

Obsession. If the word sometimes comes into my mind, I push it away. When I look into the mirror, I see only what I want to see: a mother, a loving mother. I blank out the eyes—possessive, frantic, frightened. *Moha.* I have to go a long way before I will know that Som's father was right, that it's this word, carrying a load of meanings—confusion, ignorance, illusion and pain—which is the right word, and not love. *Putra moha.* Yes, I am obsessed with my son.

Later, after it was all over, and Adit's room lay open, abandoned to our gaze, I went into the room. I nerved myself to enter, to look through his things, to search for what it was that he was hiding from me, the reason for his barring me from his room, for closing the door in my face. I went in, looking for traces of a secret life. What was in there that he didn't want me to see? Drugs? Porn magazines? Dirty books? Letters from girls? Pictures of girls?

But there was nothing in the room that was any reason for not letting me in. Nothing, except for a half-smoked packet of cigarettes.

It didn't reassure me. It told me something that went past all the defences I had erected round myself, a dagger that went straight into my heart.

Adit had had nothing to hide. It was his own self he had been guarding from me, his own self he had been protecting from my possessive, grasping hands.

I was fascinated the first time I saw Som's sister Akka perform

188

the *drishti* ceremony—the ritual to ward off the evil eye—for the children in the family. She did it at the end of each family gathering, during which the children had been much petted and admired by all of us. This, according to her, was sure to attract the evil eye. And therefore she would collect all the children, who sat in an untidy huddle on the mat, the boys disinterested, all elbows and knees, nudging one another, the girls giggling, pulling their skirts down over their legs. Once Akka began, all eyes were fixed on her, the children awed by the solemnity with which she performed the ritual. I watched too with great interest as Akka waved her clenched fists before the children's faces, muttered incantations no one could understand, and therefore awed the children even more. And then, when it was over, she would go out, warning the children not to move, and fling whatever it was she had in her two hands into the fire. There was a hiss, a splutter, the flame flew up in a slender waving sheet, then died down. Akka waited until it did, took some ash off the fire and dabbed the children's foreheads with it.

'There,' she said. 'Now they're safe.'

After Adit's birth, I was no longer a disinterested, distant observer. I was a participant, heaving a sigh of relief when the ritual was complete, picking Adit up from the lap of one of the older girls who'd been holding him, thinking—thank God.

Som was astonished and amused. 'Don't tell me you believe in Akka's mumbo jumbo?'

Why not? Babies are so frail, so vulnerable, anything that can keep Adit safe is welcome. I ask Akka to teach me, to tell me what I have to do, so that I can perform it at home for Adit. Rock salt, she says, in your hands. Or mustard seeds. Either will do. And the muttered incantations? She tells me what to say. After some meaningless rhyming words—*drishti mishti* and so on—you say 'protect the children, protect them from strangers, from neighbours, from friends, from family, from fathers, mothers. . .'

Mothers? Protect them from mothers?

I am surprised, but I repeat the chant Akka has taught me nevertheless, clutching the salt tightly in my fist, the rough hard edges cutting into my palm, hurting me, as I repeat, fervently: Protect my child, protect him from strangers, protect him from neighbours, from family, from friends, from his father, his mother . . .

Yes, I say mother too, I say it mechanically, without thinking. But now I know they were the right words to say, I know why they're needed. It is from those who love us that we need to be protected, it is with them that we put down our arms and become vulnerable and defenseless.

12

I have begun to dream again, the dark spaces of my sleep getting populated once more with people. Known people. Unknown faces. Anonymous, vague shapes. The dreams are only fragments, bits and pieces that refuse to connect when I wake up. I dream once of a large group of women, gathered, it seems, for a happy occasion—a wedding, a festival, or a puja; the saris and jewels indicate an auspicious occasion. Sunanda is there, wearing a nine-yard sari, like she always does for ceremonial occasions, and all her jewellery as well, including the 'nath' hanging from her nose, which gives her mouth such an odd shape. I can hear the buzz of conversation. A happy cloud of words seems to envelop the women. And then they see me, the faces turn to me in slow motion. In a moment, in the fraction of a moment, the sounds cease, the words are frozen, the sounds congeal about them and there is absolute silence.

This dream now, which I've just woken out of, was of my childhood home. Though the house in my dream had the shape and the look of this one, Hari and Lata's home, I knew it was my father's house. I knew too that Babu and he were in it somewhere, but I couldn't find them. I kept opening doors, one after another, so many doors, each one tightly closed, but none of the rooms revealed either my father or Babu to me. Did I call out their names? I think not. It was a dream without words, with no sound at all. A silent movie. Finally, I came upon a door that was locked, a huge lock, the same one that hung uselessly on our front door year after year. Yes, they were here, they had to be here. I pulled at the lock, I tugged at it, I knocked on the door, I began to push it with increasing anger, then despair . . .

I get out of bed in one abrupt movement. I don't want to lie in bed, going back to my dream, replaying it, trying to make sense of it. I hear Lata moving about and I see with relief that it's almost light. I get dressed and join her. We let ourselves out of the house, softly closing the door behind us, and step out into a world half-cloaked in darkness. People are nebulous shapes, still cocooned in their night selves, unable to break out, not ready to meet the world as yet.

This morning walk is now part of our daily routine, Lata's and mine. For her, it's the exercise. 'I'm getting fat,' she says. 'I'm putting on weight like anything.'

Which is not true. She is a healthy young woman, but measuring herself against some anorexic model, she considers herself bulky. For me, it is the movement, it's getting away from the night, from its dark dreams, from the spaces of sleeplessness and dark thoughts.

She is eager, all keyed up for her run, but she suits her pace to my walk until we get to the maidan. Then she breaks away from me and sets off at an energetic rapid pace, something she can never keep up for long. Just one lap around the ground and she has to stop, bent over from the waist, gasping for breath. And then, after a while, she sets off again.

The silence between Lata and me is intact until her run is over. On our way back home, she begins to talk, as if an unstated ban on conversation has been lifted. She bypasses small talk and plunges immediately into revelations and confidences. She tells me about her father's hobby of water-divining. Just a forked twig, she says, and he could spot the water underground. He would never tell them how he did it. 'I can feel it within me,' was all he would say. 'I can feel the water underneath waiting to be released, ready to gush out.' And yet, she says, he never sensed her mother's feelings, he never saw her fears.

'I wonder sometimes—why didn't his twig tell him what was happening inside her? What do you think, Kaku? After my mother's death, he gave up his water-divining, though. He never did it again and he never said a word about why he gave it up. People are strange, aren't they, Kaku?'

She speaks of her sisters, whose academic brilliance so overshadowed her that I see her as being constantly accompanied by them, measuring herself against them, finding herself wanting. 'I'm stupid,' she says, which she is not. She is sharp, quick to understand, and amazingly adept with figures.

She tells me she deliberately turned away from their path. They were, she says, so intent on their studies, that this single-minded pursuit left them no time for anything else. 'Just studies and exams and trying to get a rank. There was nothing else for them, only this ambition. But I decided very early I wouldn't be like them. I wanted to do lots of things, I wanted to have fun. I always took it easy. Only a few days studying before the exams was enough for me. What was I going to do with a rank? I'd already planned out my life. I was going to have an easy time—oh, I'd graduate, of course, because my father would be broken-hearted if I didn't do that much. But after that, I decided, I would enjoy myself for some time and then marry a rich man who would keep me in comfort.'

She chuckles at herself, at her own naïvety, perhaps. 'But where are all the rich men, Kaku? Where are they? Definitely not in Bhavanipur. Our only rich man is Ravi. Actually I did ask him to marry me, but he refused—he was quite rude. He told me to go back to my dolls.' She laughs again at the memory.

Nothing is held back. She even tells me of a 'love affair' she had when she was in college, long before she met Hari. An affair that, through vague hints and incomplete statements, she makes out to be a great romance, a doomed Romeo-Juliet, Laila-Majnu affair.

Her innocence is astonishing, her openness awes me.

Everything laid out before me, with no dark corners anywhere to be shielded from the light. I am confused, and bewildered as well. Is she this way with everyone? Or is this reserved for me because we share a house, because of our special relationship? Does she feel that since Hari and I are linked, even though distantly, through our mothers, intimacy between us is natural and right?

Whatever it is, it makes me a little uneasy. There are times when I don't know how to respond. I find myself ill at ease, acutely uncomfortable, like when she sobs in my presence, her face a soggy mass of misery. What can I do? What does she expect from me? Comforting words? *'It's only a spat, we all go through this, it'll soon be forgotten.'* Clichés, platitudes— they're so easy to say, but I am no longer able to offer them to anyone. I feel I've lost the key to making any gesture at all. I can only sit before her in silence.

In any case, she expects no more. She smiles gratefully when she has calmed down and goes off to wash her face. When she comes back, she seems refreshed by the bout of crying, comforted, to my surprise—for so she tells me—by my silent presence.

So, too, with these confidences. I listen, I say nothing. It seems to be enough for her. I'm beginning to understand that it's possible to go through life as a spectator, as a witness to other people's lives.

This is something I had not imagined, something I had not expected I would have to reckon with: the remorseless cruelty of the march of the calendar through the months. Birthdays, anniversaries, festivals proclaiming themselves, coming along as usual, as if nothing has changed, each one a handful of coarse salt rubbed into my raw wounds. Will I ever grow a skin thick enough to resist this constant, continuous invasion of pain? Will time ever become just a harmless agglomeration of days, like the calendars piled on the wall of Bai's room, one day like another, none differentiated by any significance?

I've thought of going away from here to avoid Divali. But where will I go? There's no place where I can escape from myself. And this is as good a place as any to be in; neither Hari nor Lata give me the impression of celebrating Divali in a big way. But today, I hear sounds that tell me they've woken up early, I can hear them moving about in the house, I hear them talking. It makes me think they're getting ready for the morning aarti, for the ritual oil bath. What if she asks me to be part of it, to join them in the aarti? I get out of the house quickly, quietly.

I'm walking so fast, I overtake almost everyone I meet. There are not many people out walking today, but the houses are awake and alive. Oil lamps are burning on thresholds and I see people moving about within, sleepy-eyed children coming out clutching their crackers. I walk faster, as if I'm trying to outpace my own self. Running now, like Lata does. But I'm twenty years older and unused to this kind of exercise. My breath goes in and out painfully, my intestines are twisted into a coil. By the time I reach the maidan, my heart is banging about in my chest as if it has got free from its moorings. Exhausted, gasping for breath, my legs giving way under me, I lean against a tree, wondering: is this a heart attack? But the heart is a tough muscle, Som says so, Joe used to say so. They're right. It goes back to its normal beat, my breath slows down, my legs stop trembling. I think fleetingly of my mother and her swift race towards death. With a husband and a baby to live for, surely she didn't go willingly, surely she resisted, surely she fought back?

The sun has risen, the mists have evaporated, a part of the maidan is bathed in sunlight. The sounds of the crackers are gradually fading out. I must go back, I've been here for too long. So long that, when I get to the house, I see that the lamps they'd placed on the doorstep after I left home, are already dying out, flickering, pale and uncertain in the daylight. They seem to have handed over the celebratory role to the marigold and mango leaf *toran* that's been put up above the door. Apart from these things, there's nothing else to mark the day as being special or unusual, except Lata's head swathed in a towel and her glowing skin, both of which speak of an oil bath. The two of them give me a quick look, which is followed by an imperceptible relaxation, and I realize they've been anxious about me. But they say nothing, apart from Lata's casual, 'Bath first, Kaku? Or breakfast?'

'A quick bath. I'll be with you in ten minutes.'

As always in the bathroom, I draw back from touching the copper boiler until I have switched it off, a habit that began the day it gave me a small shock. The irony of it strikes me: why, when I am not afraid of dying, when I would actually welcome it, do I dread getting an electric shock?

The phone rings constantly during breakfast—Lata's sisters, her father, Hari's friend, a cousin, his parents. I am glad there are no calls for me. The telephone is still an instrument that carries terror. Yet, there is a slight tinge of sadness at the isolation. The morning drags on, it seems endless. With all three of us at home, the house seems crowded. After lunch, I go to sleep, a heavy, drugged kind of sleep. I come out of it once to hear Lata's voice, I have a vague impression of her in my room, telling me something. I fall asleep again and wake up to darkness in the room and twilight outside. This kind of sleep is a mistake, I feel disoriented and sluggish. Lata has left a cup of tea for me on the table. It's cold, the dark brown surface crinkled, with minute oily specks floating on the surface. I pour it away and make myself a fresh cup. Lata is not at home—oh yes, that was what she was telling me, it comes back to me now. I take out a cup for Hari who's preparing the earthen oil lamps for lighting. I force myself to sit with him and watch him as he pours oil into the lamps, places the oil-soaked wicks into them and then lights

196

the lamps. He carries them out, carefully shading them from the breeze and comes back over and over again to light the ones that have gone out.

'I've never yet known a Divali that isn't breezy, that lets the lamps burn for a few minutes,' he says ruefully.

I see Adit's face in each light, Adit lighting crackers, Adit with his cousins, Adit fighting for his share of the crackers, Adit and Som standing over a cracker that hasn't gone off, Adit rushing back when it suddenly does, his face crowded with both terror and delight. I wonder where Som is and what he is doing, whether he is alone, or with Chandru or Tony. Or, is he with the family? Are they having the usual family gathering this year? Or is any celebration ruled out because of a death in the family? Each year the tradition of being together on the first day of Divali, each year the same things to eat, the same rituals. An unchanging pattern. But people change, the children specially. They grow up, they lose interest, they don't want to be part of these family occasions any more. Last year, Nisha's twins were absent, they had exams coming. Nisha said this over and over again, conscious of the reproach directed against her absent sons. And Akka said to Adit, the only young person with us, 'Next year I'm sure you won't be here, either.'

Will she remember she said that? Akka is a 'yesterday, last week, last month, last year' kind of person. Casually, randomly throwing a line into the past, willing to pull up anything that gets hooked on to the line, however trivial, however insignificant. Will she remember that she said to Adit, 'Next year you won't be here, either'? Is Som remembering this, thinking of it like I am?

I am sitting mending a sari when Hari joins me. 'I give up,' he says. 'I've left the lamps to their fate.'

'My mother used to do embroidery,' he says, suddenly interrupting our desultory talk. He speaks in Marathi for the first time, a reasonably good Marathi, lapsing into it, unconsciously I imagine, at the memory of his mother, the person with whom he spoke the language. It creates an atmosphere of intimacy which has evaded us until now. Or, is it something we've deliberately avoided?

'She was very good at it. The things she did were pieces of art, almost. She created her own designs—I remember her drawing them carefully out on a piece of paper. And when she began her embroidery, she put a frame around the part she was working on, like those presses you have for tennis racquets, you know. It held the cloth taut. Funny, I've never seen anyone else use that thing. After her illness she rarely went out, she worked at her embroidery every evening. Each time the needle went in, it made a kind of sound, because the cloth was so taut. I can still hear the sound sometimes in the evenings—a sort of plonk, plonk.'

He is silent for a while. 'I wonder,' and now he's back to English, 'I wonder where all the stuff she did has gone. It was beautiful.'

He goes on to speak to me of his mother's illness, a kidney problem. He tells me of his rage that a little thing like a kidney could cause so much suffering. Rage that men could find a way of reaching the moon, but couldn't do anything about an organ in their own bodies. She had a transplant, he tells me, it wasn't very common then, it was done in very few places. 'But it didn't help. She died anyway.'

He shakes off his thoughts and tries to go back to ordinary conversation, but it's difficult. And then, somehow, we've got to Leela and I'm telling Hari about her last days. Her disillusionment with trade unionism which had begun degenerating into violence and intimidation. Her heartache at what was happening to the workers with the continued mill strike, the mills closing down one by one. Her sadness at the changes around her. It was, though we didn't know it then, the end of an era, the city metamorphosing into something very different from the Bombay of mills, factories and workers, the

Bombay of middle-class dreams and hard work that she had known and loved.

The crackers have begun while we are speaking, but except once, when someone lights one of those long strips that go on for minutes, we ignore the sounds. I raise my voice a little each time there is a bang, that's all. Hari has closed the windows, but the sulphurous, acrid fumes snake into the room, winding around us and our words.

Leela went back to her room in Maruti Chawl after Joe's death, in fact, the day after his death. But it is no longer the same. Many of her neighbours have moved away, having come to the end of their resources. After pawning their little bits of jewellery, their brass and copper vessels, they sell their room and move away. Each time I visit Leela, there are different faces in the corridors, I pass different people on the stairs. The family in the room next to Leela's, old friends of hers, have gone. The new people keep their door closed all day, the only visible inmates being two brothers who look alike, dress exactly alike, and have, somehow, a menacing air about them. I can see the fear they evoke in the others, I see how they are avoided by everyone. Leela tells me they keep asking her why she doesn't go to live with her 'rich daughter', why she wants to stay in this wretched place. Shantabai, Leela's old companion who's come back to stay with Leela, tells me there are knocks on the door at night. When she opens the door, there's no one.

'They're trying to frighten Leelabai, they want to scare her into leaving the room,' she tells me. There are rumours that the chawls will be demolished, that enormous compensation will be paid to the tenants. 'Those people want this place, tai,' Shantabai whispers to me. 'Ask Leelabai to leave before they do something.'

But Leela pooh poohs our fears. No one will hurt me, she says.

I'm careful now not to come in my car when I visit Leela. I use the bus instead. Once, when the bus halts at the traffic light just before my stop, I see Leela at the grocer's shop, waiting patiently while he serves the others. I see her speak to him, but he ignores her while he attends to a pair of giggly young girls, to an impatient young man who wants a cigarette. The bus moves on. I get off at my stop and walk back to the shop. Leela has just got the attention of the grocer, she is counting out the money to pay him. I hear him speak rudely to her, 'Move aside, ajji, you're not my only customer.'

Leela sees me, she smiles, but I'm filled with rage. 'Why do you come yourself, why don't you send Shantabai?'

'So that he'll be rude to her instead of to me? What difference does it make? As long as my limbs are fit and I can move about, I'll do my own work.'

When she sees how upset I am, she tries to comfort me. 'Forget it, Madhu, it happens all the time.'

But I can't forget. I speak to Sunanda and Raghunath, I get Tony into it and together we mount a fresh assault on Leela, we urge her to get out of the place. Finally, when Shantabai is waylaid one evening by the brothers and warned, she agrees to leave. We get her a small place in Dadar, just a room and a kitchen, but with a balcony, which is a treat for her. Sunanda's daughter Rajani gifts her a TV set. Leela doesn't want it, but when it becomes the focal point for women and children who come to Leela's house just to watch the TV, she is reconciled. The women become part of her family. 'My women'—*majha bayka*—she calls them.

It is in this room that Leela dies.

The crackers are slowly fading out, the occasional silences as startling as the bursts were when they began. We can hear the sound of a scooter outside, the gate opening and closing, cheerful voices. Lata is back. She enters, bringing with her the festive fragrance of flowers, of sandalwood and attar. She's flushed and warm, as if she's come from a room full of people.

She looks vaguely at us, at the room, her mind still engaged with the people she's spent the evening with—her aunt's family, she tells me, her father's sister. She's wearing a Paithani sari, in a rich shot fig colour.

'It's beautiful,' I say to her.

'Isn't it? And so precious. It was Hari's mother's. I was given it at my wedding. I'm scared to wear it, I'm so afraid I'll damage it. But Hari says it's stupid not to use precious things.'

They smile at each other, some memory binding them together for a moment. Then Lata shakes herself and asks briskly, 'Have you two eaten anything? No? Good. Atya has sent you some stuff, there's enough food for ten people—so like her. I'll just change and come.'

As I set the plates on the table I think, I've got through this evening, I've got through the day. This day too has passed. But what am I congratulating myself for? What's it all for? What's the point of going on? And yet, I think of my involuntary recoil from the electrified copper boiler. Why am I afraid of it? Of dying? I thought that when you lost everything, there would no more fear. But when all is gone, there's still life itself, life pursuing its own ends of survival, of growth. Ultimately it's the body that dictates to us, coercing us into its purposes of living and growing. Survival is all, survival is what matters above everything.

I listen to Hari and Lata chatting while we're eating and I realize that Hari had been expected to go with Lata, to be part of the family gathering for Divali. But he stayed back for me. They planned this, they planned their evening, their entire day around me, around my needs and requirements.

Tony has always had the desire—and the ability—to periodically recreate himself, letting the different selves in him emerge. Earlier, it was his career through which he tried this out. First, he was to be a doctor, like his father. (I don't believe in this phase, I think it was an act he put on to please Joe.) Then he went to the J.J. School of Art—he would be a painter, an artist. No, he decided, changing his mind, it would be architecture for him. This fizzled out too, and he came back to the routine B.A. course and graduated in economics. Which quickly sent him off on the journalists' trail—yes, he would be one of those rooting-out-corruption journalists. And then it was advertising, which he slipped into by chance, when he joined a friend he admired to help out—only for a few days, the friend had said. By which time Joe was saying, yet once again, 'I wash my hands off you. You can ruin your life for all I care.'

Like all fathers. Amazing when I think of it, when I think of how unusual Joe was, his patience, his tolerance and his understanding—all of which failed him when it came to his son. The same way his vocabulary did. A man so sophisticated in his language, so finicky in his choice of words, he could do no better than mouth the usual 'good-for-nothing, loafer, waster' strictures to Tony, the 'you-disappoint-me' sermon all parents launch into to reprove their children. That Joe never used swear words possibly made it harder for him.

It's a pity Joe didn't live long enough to see Tony's success. He was sure the advertising phase would not last, that Tony would come home one day and announce, 'I've given it up, I'm on to the next thing.' But Tony didn't. He stuck to it. And it was then that he started altering his appearance. The long hair with those Clark Gable sideburns suddenly became a short forties' crew cut. There was a moustache for some time, a slim pencil line which burgeoned into a bushy squirrel's tail. A beard appeared, changed shape several times, then disappeared. There is a story, apocryphal of course, of Rekha coming home one day and going past Tony in the living room without recognizing him. I don't believe this myself. But, certainly, the way Tony changes his appearance is amazing. It helps that he has a naturally vacuous face which can take on any look he wills himself into adopting.

I saw this most clearly in Phillo's book, the scrapbook of Tony's pictures she's culled from different magazines. She's proud of it, she brought it home to show it to me one day. I turned the pages and saw the bewildering transformation, the various metamorphoses of Tony.

'Tony's Dashavatara,' I said to Rekha and Rekha, picking up my comment, went on to paint a classical Dashavatara panel, with Tony's face on each of the avataras. Tony as the tortoise, as the fish, as the boar—ending with Tony as Rama and Krishna.

Tony the Protean man. And yet in his personal relations, unflinching, loyal and steadfast. Constant to the people in his life. Above all, to four women: Leela, Paula, Rekha and I. Son, brother and husband. Not Paula's brother alone, but mine as well. Making himself my brother with a determination that was much at variance with his usual lackadaisical attitude. I remember the first Divali when he decided we would celebrate *bhau-bij*, when he said he wanted me to do the aarti for him. Leela, sensing his earnestness, appointed Sunanda our consultant. I can see Tony sitting a little awkwardly on the carpet, solemn-faced, cap on head, kumkum dot on his forehead, his normally vacant expression replaced by one of enormous interest in the proceedings. He followed Sunanda's instructions to the letter, Sunanda's sweet high Lata Mangeshkar voice accompanying the whole ceremony like an aarti song.

Your right hand, Tony. No, don't touch that. Be careful when you put in the money, take care of the light.

I had to be instructed as well, for I knew nothing. I was a savage—Paula was right—in the formal, stylized world of religious rituals. So there was Sunanda telling me:

The supari first, right to left, now the ring. No, no Madhu, left to right now. Three times, yes, now the aarti. Be careful with the light. Now put it down, here—here, child, where I've put the rice.

Tony made himself my brother that day; as far as he was concerned, we were now brother and sister. A relationship as newly minted as the one-rupee coin he put in the aarti plate on top of the ten-rupee note, his gift for me—and as light weight. We started off without the baggage of shared childhood, of shared memories, sibling rivalries, family jokes and stories. We missed out, too, on the coded language all siblings evolve for their communication through the years. But in time, our relationship has acquired the patina of age, the verdigris of shared memories. Above all, we've shared the death of Joe and Leela together. We were together during Joe's death. After he died, Leela became our joint responsibility and when she died, we mourned her together. Tony was with me, Raghunath and Sunanda at the lunch we had in Leela's room on the thirteenth day. He played host, along with us, to those whom we had invited—Leela's students, the people she had lived amongst, her colleagues, the women she had worked with, worked for.

And now here is Tony in Bhavanipur to be with me for *bhau-bij.*

'Lata can't believe you've come all the way from Bombay just for this,' I tell him when he wakes up, or rather when I wake him up for lunch.

'I can't believe it myself, I can't believe that I came all the way by bus. Remember, Madhu, how often I used to do these bus journeys—travelling all night, standing sometimes for hours. And now . . .'

He holds his head in his hands and tries to turn it both ways, wincing each time in pain. 'And now look at me! A wry neck, a painful back and a sore bottom.'

'Lata can't believe either, that you, a Catholic, care about *bhau-bij.*'

'Tell her to say it loudly, that I'm a Catholic, I mean. Father Francis has begun having doubts. Word has got around about my yoga and pranayama. And he's heard that I'm the host at

Rekha's Janmashtami puja. A Hindu wife, a Hindu sister—naturally, he thinks, I've finally succumbed and become a Hindu myself. I keep telling him you can't be converted to Hinduism, you've got to be born a Hindu—but he takes no note of that.'

After lunch, Tony introduces Som's name into the conversation. 'Has Som written to you at all, Madhu?'

'Two letters. Each with a cheque enclosed. Large amounts. What am I going to do with all that money? There's no way I can spend it here—not that I need anything, either.'

I tell him of my conflicts with Lata, of her obdurate refusal to let me pay for anything at all.

'You're family, Kaku. If I take money from you, Hari will throw me out of the house, he'll kill me. If I don't commit suicide first, out of shame, that is.'

'So I do a little shopping now and then, vegetables perhaps, or fruits, or I buy some magazines. And—and yes, that's all. I've bought myself a pair of walking shoes. That's it.'

'Why don't you buy her something?'

'Whom?'

'The kid. Lata. It's Divali, isn't it? And she has no mother. And you are, as she says, family.'

'Do you know, Tony, I'm ashamed to confess it, but I never thought of it at all.'

'Think of it now. Buy her a sari. Or a salwar kameez—or whatever she likes to wear.'

'Yes, I'll do that. Thanks for giving me the idea, Tony.' And then I say to him, 'You make me think of Joe. The same kind of . . .' I search for the right word, end up with 'generosity. No, large-heartedness.'

Tony is embarrassed. 'Not at all, Madhu, not at all. What are you saying? Papa's whole life was a giving. Imagine him giving up his flourishing practice to work in a public hospital for a salary! How many would have done that? He was a simple man. Whereas I, I don't mind confessing, I like my luxuries. No, no, don't compare me to Papa. Both Leela and he—you can't compare anyone with them. They're incomparable.'

I often tell Tony that Freud would turn in his grave if he heard Tony speaking of his father. No resentment, no anger, no grudges. Not for the constant carping, the ceaseless criticism that Joe subjected Tony to, not for Joe's unconcealed partiality for Paula, nor his preoccupation with her. In Joe's eyes, Paula could do no wrong, Tony could do nothing right.

But Tony, if he speaks of it at all, only says, 'I must have been a dreadful son for a man like Papa to have. I was a trial to him, I'm sure.'

So was Paula. And yet Joe gave her his uncritical, unflinching love. Yes, Tony is amazingly generous. Though sometimes I wonder whether his success, his drive, is not part of his desire to 'show' Joe he could do it, whether he doesn't sometimes, in the innermost recess of his heart, cock a snook at his father. And his affection for Leela, his adoption of me as a sister—don't they come out of some deep deprivation? But nothing about Tony hints at these things. These are only surmises, *my* surmises, based on nothing.

Now Tony goes back to Som, refusing to be diverted from his purpose. Som seems well, he says, as if I've asked him how he is. He keeps saying he's all right, Tony tells me. He's gone back to work, as before. But he's cut himself off from everyone. The family rarely sees him.

'I asked Nisha whether they meet him and she said Akka stayed with him for a while, but she had to go back home when her husband fell ill. Now he's alone. Chandru and I force ourselves on him occasionally, but he never comes to us. He wriggles out of all invitations.'

I know what Tony is trying to tell me. I want to tell Tony that I don't deny Som's grief or his suffering. Instead, I begin to tell him about my visit to Haworth.

It's one of the highlights of my short stay in England when I

SMALL REMEDIES

join Som during his six months in London. This visit to Haworth is a kind of pilgrimage for me, not just for myself, but for Joe as well. It was his 'think of the Brontes' that brought them into my life. Even after I read all their books, they continued to be 'Joe's Brontes' to me. Going to Haworth was like going to Kashi and doing the *pinda* ceremony for a parent. (Not that Joe was dead then; he was alive, and delighted that I was going to Haworth.) I wanted Tony to be with me for this visit, I wrote asking him to join me. He had an aunt in London, after all. But he didn't come. I can't afford it, he said. And I don't want to take Papa's money, he added.

And so it's Som and I who travel to Haworth. Som is no reader, but he knows about the Brontes too; all Joe's students do. Joe's first lecture begins with them. He gives his students the family story, he tells them of the deadly disease stalking the family until they are all dead, he gives the history of each death. After this, he speaks of their writing, of their books and of their genius, cut so tragically short. Only then does he go on to the disease itself. Som has not forgotten these things. This odd combination of literature and medicine was unusual, the students enjoyed these lectures, they were proud of them, of Joe. On our journey, Som tells me about it once again, he narrates the names of the family in the order of their death: Maria, Elizabeth, Emily, Anne, Charlotte. He counts off the names on his fingers, as if he's preparing for an examination. 'Right, Madhu?'

The place is a disappointment to me. The steep cobbled street seems the only genuine thing there, all the rest looks fake, like a stage set for a play. The tourists, the curio shops, the lunching, beer-drinking crowds alienate me from the women I've come to know through the books they wrote, the books Joe introduced me to. I can't find them even in the carefully recreated home. It is like a doll's house. Impossible to imagine the sisters pacing about the rooms, impossible to see their passion, their dreams, their tragedy in that claustro-

207

phobically tidy home.

It is among the graves that they suddenly become real. *'Think of the Brontes'*—it's when I'm standing in the midst of the dead that I suddenly know what Joe meant by the words. But strangely, for some reason, it is not the sisters or the brother that I think of, but the father who outlived all his children. How did he bear it? Do you finally get inured to death when it comes so often? Does it cease to matter finally, death, so frequent a guest, becoming a familiar presence, no longer able to awe or terrify? Is the tragedy redeemed because death means the end of suffering and pain?

'But Tony,' I assure him earnestly, 'I can tell you this—I never for a moment thought that it was easier for him because he was a man, or because he was a father. I don't do any father the injustice of thinking that his feelings are less deep or true. No, I can never belittle a father's feelings. I was brought up by my father, remember?'

Tony throws up his arms in mute surrender, a gesture that says, 'Okay, I get your point.' But there's a gleam in his eyes that tells me he's not given up, that he's going to pursue this—but later. For the moment, he's going to leave it alone.

In the afternoon, I take Tony to the market. He's fascinated, as always, by the shops, ready to buy things he knows he does not need, things he has no use for; Rekha calls him the Ultimate Consumer. I have a hard time dissuading him from buying something for me, and while I don't try to stop him from buying Lata and Hari a gift, I resist his attempts to make me get Lata a gift as well from these shops she knows so well.

'No, not here. *You've* never lived in a small town,' I tell him in exasperation when he goes on and on about it. '*I* know how it is. In Neemgaon, anything brought from Bombay or Pune was exciting. No, I refuse to buy Lata anything in Bhavanipur. It will have to be from Bombay.'

Lata and Hari are home when we get back. I see that Lata has made preparations for the aarti. We sit chatting, waiting for it to be dark, so that we can begin. I find myself longing for this twilight to go on. Fear—of what?—lies like a heavy weight on my chest, suffocating me. Finally, it's dark and the lights come on everywhere. Lata lights the lamps and then I do the aarti for Tony. My hands are cold, trembling so much that Tony has to steady the plate while he puts in his usual gift of money. I place the plate on the ground with enormous care, as if it weighs a ton.

'What about you, Lata?' Tony asks her.

'I?' She's surprised, embarrassed, pleased.

'Or am I too old to be considered a brother?'

As soon as Lata has finished, I go to my room and it's like an explosion of grief, a grief so thick, so clogging, that I can't breathe. Tony comes in.

'I can't go on, Tony, I can't, I can't . . .'

He puts his arms around me, holds me tightly encircled in them. 'Hold on, Madhu, hold on, I'm here, I'm with you, I won't let go, I'm here, Madhu, I'm here.'

He's crying too. I can feel his tears on my hands, my face, my shoulders.

'Come, let's go out,' he says, when we're both calmer.

'You go on. I'll have a wash and come.'

They avoid looking at me when I join them, they go on with their talk, which continues through dinner. It's Hari who is, unusually for him, cornering the conversation, speaking about his one year of travel through the country—from north to south, east to west.

'My own Discovery of India.'

The smile that underlines these words is, I guess, for his own younger self who thought of it that way.

'Though it was not Nehru who was my inspiration, it was Shankaracharya—one of our greatest men, I think, though they don't often mention him as one of the greats, do they? Look at the combination—scholar, visionary, poet, bhakta and practical man. Imagine travelling through the country in those times!'

I've been thinking how unusual it is for Hari to speak so much, to speak so much about himself. Then it strikes me that he's shielding me, like Leela and I did when we stood around Tony, protecting him when he began to sob after Joe died. They're all in it, Tony too, listening in an uncharacteristic silence—he's really interested, but the silence is unusual. Lata, her unwavering gaze fixed on Hari, her attention rapt, as if she's never heard this story before.

Dinner over, Lata collects the plates and goes out into the backyard. I follow her with the dirty vessels and find her lost in her thoughts. The clanging of the vessels when I put them down under the tap arouses her.

'I was thinking of the *tulsi lagna*,' she says. 'It's next week. It was my favourite festival.'

Her mother celebrated it with great eclat and enthusiasm, she tells me, like a real wedding almost. She speaks of how beautiful it had seemed to her, sitting under the stars and listening to the priest chant his mantras.

'As a girl, I also thought it very funny, this marriage between a plant and a tree. You know, making a bride of the tulsi plant—decorating it with bridal wear, green bangles, mangalsutra and all that stuff.'

'The best kind of marriage,' I say wryly. 'Nobody can get hurt.'

She looks at me in surprise. 'You're talking like Hari,' she says.

I've heard him too, speaking angrily about the rehabilitation plans for the *devadasi* women which seem to centre around marriage. As if there are only these two options for the women—marriage and prostitution—and to get away from one you need the other. As if happiness lies only in marriage, I've heard him say.

'Sometimes I wonder . . .' Lata begins, then abruptly slaps at

210

her arm. 'Mosquitoes! Let's go in, Kaku, or they'll eat us up alive.'

'So?' Tony asks me before leaving the next day. 'Anything I can tell Som? About your returning home, I mean?'

'I don't know as yet, Tony.'

'Why don't you ask Som to visit you here? It would do him good.'

'He won't come.'

'This is no good, Madhu.' He drops his fencing and becomes direct. 'You need to be together. You've lost Adit, but that's a loss you share. What's gone wrong between the two of you?'

'Not *between* us. *With* us. We . . .'

He waits for me to continue and then with a gesture of helplessness says, 'I can't force you to tell me anything, I can only say—come back to Som. Don't destroy everything because Adit has gone. It's not fair to either of you, not fair to Adit, either.'

Not fair to Adit? How can anything be fair to him now? Why do we speak of the dead as if they have any connection with us, with our lives, with life itself? It's all over for them. The finality of death makes nonsense of any idea of their responses.

Death is not an event, it's an end. It's like a nuclear devastation; there's nothing left. Som and I are moving through the rubble of our devastated lives, searching for something, for any bits and pieces of our past. But there's nothing.

13

Like an axe splitting through a log, Diwali has sliced into the seasons. Almost overnight, there's a sharp change in the weather, an abrupt shift into coolness. There's a cutting edge to the breeze when we go on our morning walks, a lightness of the air and a clarity of atmosphere in the evenings, so that distant sounds are clear and distinct. I notice the crinkling of the skin on my hands. Is it the weather, or is it part of the aging process, something I haven't noticed until now?

It's over a week since I visited Bai's house; the cook's smile, her murmured, 'long time', remind me of it. Hasina too, coming out of Bai's room gives me the nod and smile of a friend.

'She's sleeping,' she tells me. 'But it's almost time for her to wake up. Why don't you join us?'

I draw back at the threshold of the music room when I see they're all there, the twins, Abhay . . .

Hasina misunderstands my hesitation. 'It's all right,' she says. 'You can come in, it's not a class, there's no problem.'

I have to go in then, to listen to them, to watch Abhay. No problem? But there is and the problem is mine. I don't want to see Abhay, I've been avoiding him as much as possible. To see Abhay's face, the young boy moving into manhood, is to feel the searing brand of memory. He has grown even in these few months since I first saw him, he will continue to grow into manhood, he will change, his beard and moustache will get fuller, richer, his jaw more square, his shoulders broader. His parents will see this process, they will see the man Abhay, his mother will trace vestiges of the boy in him, sense the vulnerable child under the armour of manhood.

But Adit will never change. He has been frozen in time, sealed into his photographs as in a tomb. I will see only that Adit all my life, I will never see the adult, the man . . .

It's a relief when we hear the sound of Bai's voice calling out to Hasina. Bai has marked my absence as well, she knows Tony was here—news travels fast in Bhavanipur. She is full of questions—who is Tony? Why was he here? Is he really my brother as they say? Why then does he have a Christian name?

Her curiosity, which I'm seeing for the first time, doesn't please me, not because I have any problems answering her questions, but because I'm not sure I like her this way. I prefer her self-centred, uncaring, unaware of people. This makes her a little vulnerable, just a pathetic, nosy old woman. I notice that even a week has made some difference in her; she's slightly confused now about the day and time. She's conscious of her own confusion and uncertainty and it makes her uneasy. She slides over things, eager to get past her mistakes, trying to conceal them from me, pretending that she meant what she said.

Telling her about Tony, I have to speak of Joe. And she says, abruptly interrupting me, 'Yes, yes, I know him, he was my doctor.'

Joe, her doctor? My face reveals her mistake to her. Of course, she meant Chandru's father, it was he who was her doctor, she's getting mixed up between Joe and him. Then she begins speaking of Chandru's father, moving smoothly on to him, as if it was him she had meant to speak of, anyway. It suits me, because I find this interesting. The time when he was her doctor is one of those periods in her life that remains hazy. It's referred to as a 'difficult time' and passed over with the brief acknowledgement of her having been very ill. Bai acknowledges the illness, though she does not clarify what it was. 'I couldn't sing for nearly a year,' she says, making *this*

213

out to be the ailment, the disease. To lose one's voice is a kind of death for a singer, she says. But she was lucky she met Chandru's father. People kept telling her about miracles, about faith-healers, quacks, visits to temple and dargahs, but she put her faith in her doctor. And it worked. He was a real doctor, she says. A healer. If he hadn't helped me, if he hadn't looked after me then, I don't know what would have happened to me, she confesses.

Her career graph rose steeply after her recovery. This success has been linked to her friendship with Chandru's father, a doctor who had a great number of rich and influential patients. He used his influence on her behalf, it is said, and introduced her to the right people. There were others after that, patrons if the rumours are to be believed—a politician, an industrialist—who helped her rapid rise to the top.

But Bai herself demolishes this theory. It is one of those days when she speaks with great clarity and lucidity. (In any case, her confusion, whenever it manifests itself, is more about facts and dates, rarely about herself.)

'Those were hard times,' she says, 'when I was trying to get back. It doesn't take long for the world to forget you. I had to start from the beginning, to pick up my slate and start writing "*a aa ee*". All those years after my Guruji's death, when I had struggled to make a start, were wiped out. That was the time when I had to sell all my jewellery to survive.'

(And therefore no pearls? And therefore, once again the mangalsutra she had put away when she lived with Ghulam Saab? Is this the explanation then, not the desire to seem a respectable married woman once more?)

'It was hard, I can tell you. I could have taken the easy way out. I was young and good-looking—and in those days, it wouldn't have been considered very wrong if I had allowed a man to help me. It was done in my profession, it was often done by women. And, after all, people talked about you whatever you did. I could as well have done the things they said I was doing. But I didn't, I never took that road.'

This is a confession I never expected, it's a revelation, almost for the first time, of what there is behind the facade. It tells me what I've already noticed, that there is a quickening in our relationship, a change from its earlier static condition. She calls me Madhu, she speaks more familiarly to me, and gives me a feeling of being less guarded. I sense her reserve falling off.

'Not much time left for me,' she says once and I think of Leela in the last few months of her life, speaking to me of all the things she had left unspoken in our many years together. As if, in our final moments, we want a listener, a witness, before whom we can lay out our lives, as if we need the witness, the listener, for us to make sense of our own lives. Bai moves back and forth in time, she flits from memory to memory, she picks on events, occasions, people, at random. It seems utterly disconnected, but there is some connection in her mind, something that links these things together for her. A question, perhaps, that she's asking herself now, in these last days of her life.

Unlike our earlier sessions, these are more rambling. She's ceased to be businesslike. I know that when the time comes for me to transcribe these tapes, I will get scarcely a few pages out of them. It doesn't matter. I have no desire to do anything more now than to listen, to watch, to let the tapes run on. Yet, I can see that she has not let down her defences wholly. She has still not spoken of the time she lived next door. It is that period by which I orient myself in her life—'this must be before Neemgaon, this must have happened after Neemgaon'. That bit of her life is for me the tip of the iceberg, the only bit I saw. But she turns it upside down, submerges this portion and gives me a glimpse of the rest.

I give her a handle once when she complains about the fact that she's not allowed to eat ghee. 'The doctor says "don't"

SHASHI DESHPANDE

and that girl listens to him. She tries to cheat me, she says
there's ghee when there isn't any. I'm a Brahmin, does she
think my nose won't tell me the truth? My grandfather used to
drink a small bowl of ghee every day after his bath. He used to
say it gave him strength. And now they say it's bad for you.
Doctors!'

'You can't criticize doctors to me, Bai. I'm a doctor's
daughter, you know that. They tell you things for your own
good.'

She ignores my statement; to bring my father into the
picture is to unearth those two she so steadily refuses to speak
of. Old, sick, muddled though she is, she remains watchful,
alert, aware that this enterprise she has embarked on is a
perilous one, that she has to be on her guard all the time.

Her married home is, however, not taboo. It figures more
and more in her conversation now. She tells me of her
father-in-law's love of music and with this knowledge one
mystery is solved. It was her father-in-law, not her father, who
started her on music. This is unexpected, but it no longer
seems so astonishing when she tells me about him, about his
music mania.

His longing to be part of the world of music made him a
student all his life. There was always a teacher to teach
him—different instruments at different times. Vocal music,
however, was part of his learning programme throughout his
life. Sensitive as his ear was to good music, he must have been
aware he would never be good enough. Yet he kept on, more
to be in touch with music and musicians, to connect himself to
the world he so loved, than to become an expert singer. But it
was as a patron that he really found his place in this world, as
a patron that he moved from the periphery to the centre of it.
There were always musicians staying with him, he arranged
performances for them, both in his own home and outside.
Their huge house, the *wada*, was enlarged by the addition of
two large rooms on the first floor, with an exterior staircase

216

that led directly to these rooms from the street. This was where the visiting musicians stayed, the place where they gathered for informal *baithaks*, all-night sessions, friendly gatherings. These rooms were separated from the rest of the house and the door that opened into them was always locked. There was a window opening into the corridor, however, through which you could hear the music. Bai discovered this, a window to a mysterious, enchanting but forbidden world and she found that by keeping the window slightly open, she could listen to the music. She discovered that if she sat under the window, she was invisible, no one would know she was listening.

Once, however, her father-in-law, passing along the corridor, saw the open window. He was closing it when he saw the girl crouching on the floor, staring at him with terrified eyes. She was full of apprehension—what would he say? What would he do?

He did nothing, he said nothing. He moved on, leaving the window ajar the way it had been. She was still fearful; obviously he wouldn't speak to his daughter-in-law himself, he would leave it to his wife to deal with her.

But nothing happened. He's decided to let it go, she thought thankfully. Yet, there was a repercussion. A few days later there was a message for the women in the family: there was to be a performance that night. (They were not told who was going to sing. Clearly he thought that, their ignorance being what it was, it didn't matter.) The women could listen if they wanted to. The door would be opened, but of course, they would have to stay on their side of the house.

The excitement of the women was related more to the unusualness of the occasion, to the change from routine; music was only the excuse. Bai, however, was in a state of painful agitation. At first, it was wonderful. Then came dissatisfaction, irritation. The women's chatter, their stifled, excited laughter, their constant movements, the children's crying and talking and above all, her inability to see the musicians, made her miserable. She wanted to see the singer's hands accompanying the rise and fall of the notes, watch his face when his voice moved from an almost somnambulistic *alaap* to the vigorousness of the rhythmic part of the *bandish*, when he skilfully negotiated the *meends*, gliding from one scale to another. She wanted to see the accompanist: was it a sarangi? Or only the tanpura? She fidgeted, she fretted.

It was not that they observed any kind of purdah in their home. This was Pune after all, a town famous for reformist movements. There were schools for girls, there were even colleges where girls studied. Her own father-in-law, unlike her father, was a liberal. He believed in girls' education and all the young girls at home were going to school, despite much muttered criticism from the women themselves. Nevertheless, there was a clear line of demarcation between what females could do and what they couldn't. Associating with musicians definitely lay outside the Lakshman Rekha.

Knowing this, Bai must indeed have been desperate to do what she did. She *was* desperate. After that evening, she found it difficult to control her feelings, to pretend that the mundane domestic life she was leading satisfied her. She took a bold step. Part of her courage came from the way her father-in-law had walked on without closing the window, the fact that he had arranged for the women—for her, really, she knew that—to listen to the music. She wrote him a letter, pleading to be allowed to learn music. She went to his room, a room she'd never gone into, her legs trembling, her heart palpitating, and left the note on his table.

It is impossible to realize today what a radical step it was for a man of that class to let his daughter-in-law learn music. When a middle-aged woman came to the house saying she was there to teach Bai music, at first it seemed a miracle to Bai. Then she accepted it and didn't think any more about the whys and hows of it. This was how her lessons began. They sat in a small unused room on the first floor of the house, a room that looked down on to the back courtyard, where the vessels were cleaned and the clothes washed. All the sounds of these activities flowed into the room, as did the women's ceaseless talk, their arguments, their laughter. Not the ideal room for music, certainly. But in that musty smelling room, sitting on the frayed carpet she had spread herself, Bai entered another world far removed from the world of food, cooking, festivals, rituals, pregnancy and children that she had to inhabit as a daughter-in-law of the house.

Not that this teacher gave her much. Bai speaks of her with some contempt. The one good thing the woman did, Bai says, her lasting contribution, was to teach her breathing exercises. 'You need to use all the breath you have,' she told the frail looking girl. A month or two later, the teacher got permission to introduce a tabla player into the classes.

Bai makes this bald statement without any hesitation; she does not say any more. I know, however, that this is the point when Ghulam Saab entered her life. A tabla, therefore a tabalji. A man, since no woman played the tabla. A Muslim man, sitting a little distance from the two women, on a separate piece of carpet. The dim light in the room keeps them enfolded in a sort of shadowy duskiness. The man sees a girl awkwardly holding the tanpura, her childishly thin arms unable, it seems, to bear the weight of it for long, so that she lays it down every now and then. What else does he see? Or is it only the voice which registers with him, not her youth, nor her beauty, either? And when did he become something more than a pair of hands providing the rhythm, the taal for her music? She will never speak of these things. I have to imagine them, draw these pictures out of her silences. But I know, I am sure, that this is where their relationship began.

Bai's father-in-law had a mistress, a singer famous for her thumri singing. It was an openly known fact that he visited her regularly. The women of the family spoke of it among themselves, they gossiped about it, they giggled over it. None of them had seen her, but curiosity drove some of the more inquisitive among them to the servants for inquiries. She was not good-looking, they were told; she was plump, short and middling fair. Not as fair as the wife, either. What did he see in that woman? *This* was the point of discussion, of exclamation. That he had a mistress was accepted; a wife from one's own class, a mistress from another—this was normal. What made the women curious, what intrigued them, was this: what did a man who had a tall, fair, good-looking wife find in another woman?

For Bai to develop a relationship with another man, a tabla player, a Muslim—this must have been not only unimaginable, but the height of criminality. Did anyone blame the father-in-law for this? As the head of the family, a position that was indisputable then, he was not accountable to anyone. Nevertheless, there must have been comments and criticism. Did he blame himself? For a man, a wealthy man and the head of the family, to indulge in his love of music, even to have a singer as a mistress, was all right. But for a daughter-in-law to be learning music, and that seriously, as if she was going to be a professional! Surely there was outrage, surely there was anger in the family. Rules could be modified for the daughters, sometimes they were, purely out of affection, but daughters-in-law carry the weight of the honour of the family, its reputation, its *izzat*.

Bai had her father-in-law's support and his encouragement. But a man is not of much use to a woman. After all, she lives her life among women and with women. Anger, derision, contempt, ridicule—I can imagine that Bai had to face all these when she came out of the shadowy room back to her life among the women. I can imagine that it took enormous courage to face the jibes and the hostility. To be set apart from your own kind, not to be able to conform, to flout the rules laid down, is to lay yourself open to cruelty. Animals know this, they do it more openly, their cruelty towards the deviant is never concealed. But the subtle cruelty of persistent hostility leaves deeper wounds. There's always the temptation to succumb, to go back to the normal path and be accepted. To resist this temptation speaks of great courage.

Bai says none of these things. Her silence glosses over both her struggle and her endurance. She speaks as if her lessons took place in the midst of family approval. Only once does her guard slip. 'Sometimes I wished,' she says, 'that I had been born in one of those musicians' families, in which I would naturally have become a singer. In those families, you're born into the profession. There is never any problem even for women.'

But Bai has been in the music world long enough to know that these women didn't have it easy, either. They, unlike the men in the same families, were outside the circle of respectable society, their futures marked out for them, the ordinary life of ordinary women denied to them because of their birth. Nature is blind. It distributes qualities uncaring of social class, caste, gender. Bai was, in a sense, born into the wrong class. But so too perhaps, were many of the women who were born into professional families. If they had the freedom (was it freedom?) to be artists, they were denied the right to live the life most women do, the life Bai herself opted out of.

I remember a scene in *Devdas*, the movie I saw with Joe and Leela, a scene which, for some reason, I have never forgotten. The accidental, coincidental meeting between the two women in Devdas' life, one on her way to see the sick Devdas, the other coming from him, the two crossing each other, neither knowing who the other is. Paro, his love, the respectable woman married to another man, caged in her palki, shut off from the world; Chandramukhi, the dancer, walking through the fields, through puddles and slush. Each, perhaps, envying the other.

Freedom is always elsewhere. Did Bai, after leaving home, long for the life she had left behind? Did she suffer because she had sacrificed her reputation and status? Or did she enjoy the freedom she had gained, did she feel good to be able to do what she wanted? Once again I come upon the stumbling block of Bai's—what do I call it? Innocence? Caginess? A studied calculation? I don't know what it is that never allows her to speak of her own hardships. Perhaps it is nothing more than a reluctance to let in anything that will lead her—and me—to her flight from her married home, to her lover and her child born of that lover. Bai's statement, 'I didn't take the easy way out,' tells me nothing was easy. It tells me more—that she had no lovers. But does it also mean that she never used any of the men she was associated with? Do I believe her? Do I believe anything she says?

I was too young then to understand these things, but I can remember the Station Director of the radio station in Neemgaon, the man whose official car was often standing outside Bai's house, the car in which she went to the radio station for her programmes, for her recordings for other radio stations. This man's influence is supposed to have got her the contracts with the radio and given her the visibility which, as a young artist, she would otherwise have found hard, almost impossible, to obtain.

I remember the man very distinctly—his high forehead, his receding hairline, his clothes hanging on him as if they were made for a man larger than him, the slightly bewildered expression on his face. He looked, now that I think of it, like a taller, a less tramp-like Raj Kapoor. He was a kind of god in Neemgaon, the only government officer of that rank, the only one with a car and a driver of his own. He seemed unaware of his own importance though, and was always affable and anxious to please.

He was my father's friend, one of the Kakas who joined him in the evenings, more often than most of the other Kakas, because he was living alone in Neemgaon, his family having stayed back, since his posting in Neemgaon was to be a short stint. And with my father he could converse in Hindi—I imagine this was part of it too. To me, he was a familiar presence. But to Munni . . .

We were going to school, Munni and I, walking at the edge of the road as we always did, along the rain-water gutter, when the car went past us. And stopped.

'Going to school? Come on, I'll drop you.'

I got into the car promptly enough, but Munni didn't. In spite of the fact that he was holding the door open for her, she walked past as if she hadn't seen the car or heard him.

'Come, Munni,' he called out coaxingly.

'Munni, Munni,' I shouted, louder. I thought she hadn't heard him.

But she ignored both of us and walked on. I would have got out for her, but he held me back and banged the door. 'Go on,' he told the driver. 'We'll drop this baby at her school first.'

We drove past Munni walking in the dust, looking straight ahead, still giving the feeling of being unaware of the car, though the rigid set of her shoulders, the stiffness of her neck, the way she looked straight ahead, cried out her knowledge of it.

Munni believed the man was her mother's lover. I come to that conclusion now. I imagine they spoke of it in the town, that they sniggered and laughed. I do remember the girls calling him Munni's 'mama'—I took it as its literal meaning of uncle then, I didn't know it was a kind of euphemism for a mother's lover. I remember this now, I understand what it meant to Munni. Bai tells me she had no lovers. But to the town, it was very simple: why else would a man go out of his way to give her so many programmes? Why would he visit her so often? A woman who'd left her husband's home—what morals would she have, anyway! Bai was obviously damned by everyone. To the town she was one of 'those women' she

223

speaks of now, women who were only doing what was expected of them. Professional singers were expected to accept a man's protection. So why not Bai?

Women can never be free. Is that it?

No, knowing Leela and now Bai, I can't go along with this idea. Both these women got for themselves the measure of freedom they needed, they worked for it. And they both knew the price they had to pay for it. I know that Leela was, certainly, a person who accepted wholly the consequences of her actions. I remember how she put up with Paula, never showing any anger or hurt at Paula's atrocious behaviour towards her. When she married Joe, she knew she had taken on the problem of Paula. Therefore, no complaints. In her work, too, though she was sidelined after years of working for the party, though she never reached the top of the hierarchy, while men who'd worked under her got there, she never complained. Only once, when a woman was selected as a candidate for a by-election, this woman the widow of the sitting member who'd been killed, only then I remember Leela saying, 'It seems you've got to become a widow for them to remember that you exist.' Only that once, only that one comment about the chauvinism that ruled the party.

Bai too—she may not know the phrase 'gender discrimination', but she knows how much longer it takes for a woman to reach the top, how difficult it is for her to break through the barrier to get there. She gave me a hint of it once, when she said caustically, speaking of a young and swiftly rising instrumentalist, 'Nowadays they become Ustads and Pundits even before they have proper moustaches.' But this was not a complaint. In fact, I've rarely heard her complain about the problems she had to face in her professional life. To her, these were part of the road she had chosen, they just had to be endured.

But Munni wanted respectability. And therefore she rejected everything associated with her mother—music, genius, ambition, freedom. Was it Munni who denied her mother then, Munni who turned her back on her mother? I am confused. It's like turning the hourglass over; it's the same sand, but now running the other way.

What is it like to deny your mother? I was motherless, but she is still with me, the woman who gave me birth, the woman of whom I know so little, except that she was fleet of limb, short of patience and tall in aspirations. A woman who rushed with the same swiftness she brought to her races to her own death. And there is Leela, my other mother, resolute of purpose, straight and direct in all that she did in her life. To know that I am linked to these two women is to drink the draught of strength, the magic potion, the elixir of courage, it is to swallow the muscle-building spinach.

But Munni closed herself against her mother, against everything she was or stood for, and chose an ordinary life. I think of the girl I knew, the flash of her skinny white limbs as she flung up her skirt and rushed to the back of the house, behind a tree trunk or a bush, to relieve herself. Uninhibited, impulsive. And then Shailaja Joshi, the woman I met on the bus—another name, another person altogether. The result of Munni beating herself into shape with a savage determination, like dough being pounded into soft pliability, capable finally of taking any shape.

'Shailaja Joshi—only daughter of Savitribai Indorekar.' The notice of her death—giving her back the identity she had resisted all her life. I wonder who was responsible for that. Of course, now that Bai has reached the pinnacle of her profession, now that she is among the greats, her respectability, or her lack of it, no longer matters. She is above all these things. But did Munni herself ever regret her break from her mother once she saw the eminence she had reached? Or did she cling to her hatred and her anger, unable to let go of the emotions that had been the driving force of her life?

I will never know. In any case, it makes no difference what

225

Munni thought or felt, for it no longer matters. It is not the dead but the living who have to unravel the knots in a relationship, to tie up the loose ends, so that it is possible to live with the memory of that relationship. To live without guilt and remorse.

Bai reveals no sign of these. If guilt or remorse are troubling her, she very successfully conceals them. Only once I sensed something, when she said, not in the context of her daughter, yet linked, I felt, to Munni.

'If only I had known . . .'

Yes, if I had known. But we never do, not at that moment, anyway. Knowledge comes later, out of coping with the experience that follows your action. Knowledge is always the inseparable twin of pain and suffering.

'Birth and death,' Bai quoted her Guruji as saying, 'they're the two fixed points over which we have no control. The rest is all ours to play with, to make of it what we want.' He was speaking, she told me, of music, of the restraints of the rules of music, and comparing it to life. In both, he said, within the framework of the rules, everything is yours.

Is this true? Is it as simple as this? Given who we are, given the knowledge that we have, are not the choices that we make inevitable? Yet, we never cease to agonize, specially when the choice we make leads to disaster: could I have done something else? Only a saint can say—I made the right choice, there could have been no other, because *this* is the moral choice. If I have to suffer for it, so be it.

For the rest of us, the fact that we have taken the moral choice is no comfort, no consolation. What we wish for is the choice that saves us from unhappiness, what we want is to avoid suffering and pain.

Bai is dealing with the consequences of her choice in her own way. She has put it behind her, locked it within herself, refusing to let it out. Munni is there, I know it now, even if only at the edge of her consciousness. But, like the time she got into the car, seemingly unaware of the girl hovering near the house, she ignores the memory. She will not think of it, she will not speak of it. And perhaps she's right. Family secrets, blunders, tragedies, are safer locked into trunks, sealed into almirahs. Exhumation can only bring up hideous sights and ugly smells. Something stirs in the survivors, ancient memories and old wrongs send strange messages to the brain, driving humans berserk. The dead never give you the entire truth, anyway. Only partial truths will emerge.

No, the past is safer where it belongs, we don't need it to intrude into the present.

If I had known . . .

If I had not told Som . . .

But my silence would have been there nevertheless, a barrier between us, distancing me from him.

Yet Adit would have been safe, he would have been alive. Would he?

If I had not told Som . . .

But there was no way I could not have told him. Not at that point, anyway. Not with our relationship being what it was. For we were friends.

'Men and women can never be friends.' Chandru's words. He said it a few days before his marriage to Satee. (And how clearly it showed what their relationship was to be!) Men and women can never be friends, Chandru said. Matter-of-factly. Smiling as he spoke, as if it was nothing personal, as if it had nothing to do with his own feelings for the girl he was to marry. And Som and I, moving closer in those days, looked at each other and smiled. Pitying Chandru—for what else did that statement imply but a lack in his feelings for Satee? Som and I, content, smug in the pleasure of our slowly developing relationship, looked at each other triumphantly. Men and women can never be friends? Oh, how wrong you are Chandru, how unfortunate not to know how wrong you are, how unlucky not to have this, what we are enjoying.

Yes, we were friends, Som and I. I knew him first as Joe's student, then as Tony's friend Chandru's inseparable companion. And finally, he became my friend too. I was the one most sympathetic, the one who never laughed or joked about his feelings for Neelam, about the torments he said she put him through. I was the one who listened to him with

228

sympathy, the day he came to know Neelam was getting married, I was the one who comforted him then. After that, at some point, things changed, his feelings for me deepened and my own moved slowly from just friendship to love. And then to passion, to a joyous exploration of each other's bodies. When Adit was born, that fierce flame died down. But we were still friends, still lovers. And partners who shared much—above all, our child.

Aditya-ché Baba.

Aditya-chi Aai.

Our identities for the people we lived amongst, for our neighbours, for new friends, acquaintances, other parents. Aditya's father. Aditya's mother.

And then in a moment, it changed. It was madness, a madness that overtook Som; this is the only explanation I can give for what happened to him. But even that is not entirely true. There was a logic in his madness, a logic that his increasing frenzy never lost sight of. He was looking for the girl he had known, the girl he had married, the woman he had lived with for so many years.

If I want to know who it was Som thought he had married, I have only to recall his sisters' remarks. Ours was a strange courtship, with Som's family, the women in his family that is, wooing him for me. Or so it seemed. For it was they who made his feelings for me clear and obvious, even before he had declared them to me.

'Som says he's never met a girl as straightforward as you are,' Nisha, his youngest sister tells me.

Sandhya refers to my height, my dignity, my simplicity—Som is always speaking of these things, she says.

Som seems to think I'm so delicate, I'm made of glass, Akka tells me caustically.

Som's mother, who takes me into the folds of the family, says I'm a very brave girl. She says this not admiringly, but with pity. And I can see that this idea has come to her from

Som, who thinks of me as a waif, an orphaned waif.

Yes, Som does have these ideas about me. On the second night after our wedding, the first night for us, he asks me, 'Are you frightened?' and I know what he is speaking of.

'No.'

'Worried?'

'Not with you.'

He puts his arms about me, encircling me rather than holding me, making a point, it seems to me now, of my fragility, of *his* idea of my fragility.

'I won't hurt you, I promise.'

I smile at him. He takes my hand and starts kissing my fingers, one by one. His lips are cool, smooth, moist. He feels a quiver in me, I sense his response, but he controls his urgency.

'It's all right, Som, it's all right. I want it too.'

Startled, his eyes fly to my face. There's a puzzled look in them. And then he laughs and draws me close, he holds me tight. But for a moment before he does this, I see a look of regret on his face. It comes back to me now, when it's too late, telling me what I should have understood about Som: to him, I was chaste, I was untouched. I should have remembered that look, I should have kept it intact in my mind. But these things are lost in the trivia of daily living. And so, when I spoke to him, years later, on the night of my terrible dream, I was unconscious of anything but the need to unburden myself. Now I know that with my revelations I destroyed the girl he had married. Suddenly I became a stranger to Som, a woman he didn't know. And then it was he who changed. From a genial, easy-going man, he turned savage, destructive, hating me, hating himself.

Sometimes, trying to trace my way back to see where I went wrong, I stop here, at this point when I made the revelations of my past to Som. But in fact, the beginning lies even further in the past, it goes back to the day Leela told me about the family secret. Something that didn't seem to be a matter of great importance to me then, nor to her, though it was her family she was speaking of. Both of us unconscious of the impact this secret would have on me and Som.

Lata's mother is wrong. Disasters come without warning, without any omens to alert us to their coming, they give us no time to prepare, to arm ourselves. There were no owls crying, no bats flapping about, no dogs barking in the dark of the night to tell me what was coming. In spite of our knowledge of Leela's impending death, it was a time of peace and serenity for us.

She looks like a child, her scanty hair tied in a pigtail. Seeing her as regularly as I do, I don't notice how small she's become. It's only when her hand goes to her chest that I notice how little flesh there is on her.

'I've got something here,' she says, 'a lump.'

I put my own hand on hers and she moves her hand away, leaving mine on the spot. A lump. 'Gath' she called it, a word both of us, because of our association with Joe, are familiar with. But this is no tuberculous lump, we know that. I stare at her, feeling a heaviness inside me, as if her lump has travelled through my hand into my chest and is lying there now, large and ominously heavy.

I tell Som about it and Leela goes through the investigations, she undergoes the biopsy. When Som comes with the diagnosis, he knows her too well to give her anything but the truth. For a moment, she is silent. Her hand, which I'm holding, is unresponsive and lifeless. Then she smiles.

'Joe would have brought up those Brontes of his now, huh, Som?'

Later, when we are on our own, she says, 'Promise me something, Madhu. Promise me you'll do this one thing for me. I'll go through the surgery, it's not fair to all of you not to do it, but after that, enough! No more. I won't take any more treatment. You have to support me in this.'

I promise her. And I keep my word. She has a few good months after the surgery, then begins going downhill fast. It's a metastasis, the liver possibly, Som says. But it's only a surmise, since she won't allow any investigations. I go along with her in this decision, though it's hard. She has fever, she's in pain, she can't keep her food down. I think of Joe's words about cancer. The amazing, the magnificent whimsicality of life, the waywardness of it, he said. 'Vita mea, mors tua.' My life, your death. I remember the words and think of the cancer cells in Leela's body proliferating, flourishing, while her body shrinks.

We, Shantabai, Sunanda and I, work out a system so that one of us is always with her. One afternoon, when I go at my usual time, I find the door open, but Shantabai is not inside, and Leela's bed is empty. I can feel the flapping wings of panic in my chest. Where is she? Where could she have gone? And then I hear a sound from the bathroom. The door is ajar, I can see Leela on the toilet seat, her poor little face, almost skeletal now, screwed up in pain, concentrating on fighting an intense, internal pain. My throat tightens, tears spurt out of my eyes, a sob erupts from me taking me by surprise. I go out, put my face to the wall and begin to weep. When I hear the sound of flushing water, I compose myself and call out as if I'm just entering.

I help her back into bed. She looks peaceful when she's in bed, as if she's put her pain away. But my grief has not left me. I lose control and resting my head on the bed begin to sob, all the grief I've repressed through the months since I knew she was dying, pouring out of me. The tears are for her suffering, her impending death, for my helplessness and my terror at the thought of losing her. When finally I wipe my tears, and hers as well, we are both relieved. And lighter. We've crossed the hurdle of fear—the fear of death, of parting, of loss. We've accepted all these things. We are together after this, sharing the experience of her dying. I can come to terms with her death, because I am part of it. I know now that it helps.

It's after this that she begins to talk of her past to me. She is in bed, her body lost in the folds of the nightdress I have coaxed her into wearing. Her hair is now short. She made me cut it, gave herself to my hands with confidence, as if I was a professional hairstylist. I did it fearfully, but when it was over we were both pleased. Leela looked different, her small head elegantly poised on her neck, the bones of her face standing out clear and sharp. She was pleased too. It feels light now, she said. It's good to travel light, she says. I'm with her every afternoon now. And it is at this time that she tells me things, unseals the silences of her early life. She speaks of her childhood, of her sisters and her mother. These are gentle memories, there is no pain or anger in her, except when she tells me of her tyrannical grandmother and of her sway over her weak father.

'My grandmother thought she was punishing me when she got me married,' she says. 'She knew I wanted to study. And Vasant's family was not rich—everyone was surprised, they wondered why they couldn't find a better groom for me. But she did me a favour. I was happy, I got all the freedom I wanted in that house. Mai and Vasant were very good to me. Vasant let me go to school, I passed my matric. Mai was proud of me. So my grandmother's punishment turned out to be a blessing after all.'

She speaks to me of my parents, of my father. 'I don't know why he chose me to look after you,' she says. 'He had his brother—he was the right person, really. You know how angry your uncle was because he was ignored, he never took any notice of you after that. But your father was sure he wanted you to be with me, he wrote it down so that there would be no problem. And so I had you. I was the lucky one.'

She rarely speaks of Joe, except to say once, 'After Joe died, I knew loneliness for the first time. I still miss him, Madhu.

When Vaṣant died, I was very young and I was frightened. It was widowhood that frightened me, I saw what it was to be a widow, I'd seen it at home. But I was not lonely. There was Mai, there were the boys, we had to work.'

Her father came to take her back home after Vasant's death. She could have gone home and lived a life of reasonable comfort, at least as much comfort as a widow was allowed. But she knew she would have to toe the line, to live within the limits set for her by her grandmother. Besides, there was Mai, there were her two brothers-in-law; they were her family now. She had to help them, to earn a living for all of them until the boys were educated. She refused to go back home, perhaps she said things which caused a rift. There was no communication with her family after that. The next time Leela went home was nearly thirty years later.

When Leela speaks to me about this visit, she's very weak, but she wants to talk. I've stopped telling her not to exert herself, to talk less. 'Let me talk,' she says. 'The time will soon come when I won't be able to.'

And the truth is, whenever I am with her, she is lively. I sit by her, I listen to her, I give her the medicines she needs to take, I make tea for myself—she insists on that, she always has something for me to eat with my tea. When I listen to the story of her visit home, I have no idea that it is in any way significant, that it will change my life. I listen to her like always, my attention focussed less on her words and more on her body, trying to help her find a comfortable position, soothing her each time the pain begins. 'It's like a little dying, this pain,' she says. 'And then, slowly coming back to life again.'

Leela goes home when she gets a letter from her mother asking her to come. Her mother is living all by herself now, except for a distant family connection, a wordless man who occupies one room in that large house and an old woman who comes at night to keep her company. Otherwise she's alone.

She's changed immensely from the silent, crushed woman Leela remembers. It's not only that she's become a little peculiar, the way people who live by themselves for a long time invariably do; she's become assertive, combative almost, quarrelling with everyone she comes in close contact with. Once they move away, once they distance themselves, she gets over her hostility and forgets all the earlier acrimony, which is now reserved for others who are still in her circle. And, as if she's taken over her dead mother-in-law's place in all things, taken over her role in fact, she's turned excessively orthodox. She won't let Leela into the kitchen or the puja room. Leela is still a widow to her mother, her marriage to Joe not redeeming, but adding rather, to her pariah status.

If Leela has any illusions that her mother has asked her to come home so that they can be reconciled before her death, she is soon disillusioned. There is no word of regret for the thirty years' breach, no mention of it at all. She talks—and she does so constantly, making up it appears, for her earlier repressed silence—of irrelevant things, gossip about family, people Leela has forgotten, neighbours she doesn't know, has never met. So this is all there is to be! Leela relaxes, she decides to go through the week she has given herself, to make the best of it, listening to her mother, doing what she can for her.

But there's something she finds very odd. It's the way the old woman keeps following Leela about. Wherever she goes, she hears the patter of her feet behind her. At first she thinks her mother is making sure she's not touching anything, that she's not polluting the gods or the kitchen with her touch. Then it begins to dawn on her—she wants to tell Leela something. But nothing emerges, not until the last day.

Leela is getting ready to leave when her mother comes in with a cloth bag of amlas. From our tree, she says. You liked them. This is the first sign of affection, the first reference to this being Leela's childhood home. Leela is pleased. She puts the amlas into her small carry bag, and is ready to pick up her

SHASHI DESHPANDE

suitcase when her mother goes on, in the same tone, as if this is a remark as casual as that one, something she's just thought of.

'Your father had a son, you know that?'

A son? But there were just the six sisters, weren't there? One of the weapons in her grandmother's arsenal against her daughter-in-law. Or was there a son who died young, as an infant?

'No,' the old woman says, like a mind reader. 'Not my son. Your father's.'

Leela is still blank.

'He had him by that woman . . .' she uses the ugly word that means both widow and whore, 'your aunt's daughter, remember, she lived with us for a time when I was ill after Godu's birth?'

Now Leela does. Yes, a young widow, brought in to help. Leela waits for her mother to go on, but that's all. No more is said. It's time for Leela to leave and the mother lets her go with no sign of regret. All the way back, Leela thinks of it, wonders about it: was this why her mother called her home? To tell her, her first-born child, this secret, this wound she'd concealed, this hurt she'd lived with for so long? Was this what she had wanted—to unburden herself?

In any case, it no longer mattered. Within months after this, her mother died. And then it became a story that no longer concerned anyone, for they were all dead—Leela's parents, the woman, and her child too, the boy who Leela remembers lived with them for a while. When his mother died, he went away, he cut himself off from the family completely. He lived, they heard, a rather wild and dissipated life. Later, Leela says, he had some contact with my mother. A contact that my mother began, Leela smiles as she says this, mainly because she knew the family frowned on it, though she didn't know why. By that time he had changed, he was no longer living a reckless life, he had become some sort of an artist. A sculptor—or something

236

like that.

He died early, Leela tells me. 'Someone told me, I don't remember who it was, that he committed suicide; he hanged himself, actually.'

Leela was a woman who lived entirely in the present, she never clung to the past, never hankered for the future. And so, by the time she tells me this story, it's the distant past for her. If she felt anything when she heard it from her mother—sadness, anger, regret—it was all over.

And so I too forget it. I have many memories of Leela to live with, but the story she told me is not one of them. Until a few years later, when I see the painting and it comes back like a curse to destroy us.

It's at the opening of Rekha's gallery, the first exhibition she's holding in her own gallery. It is a great occasion for her. Her entire family is there, her parents from Kolhapur, her brother and sister from Pune. Rekha has built up a treasury of goodwill in her profession through the years, and a large number of artists have shown up. I see they are excited about the exhibition which is an unusual one, of the paintings of old, obscure artists which Rekha has been patiently collecting through the years. I know very little about painting, I'm there only because Rekha wants me, I'm there for Tony. I go through the motions of looking at the exhibits, standing for a certain amount of time (how much? Tony smiles knowingly, teasingly when he sees me hesitating) before each one.

And then suddenly I'm brought to a halt before one. I stand still, I can't move. There's something familiar about this painting. It's a woman, a tall statuesque woman in a nine-yard sari, faintly reminiscent of Ravi Varma's Damayanti. But unlike Ravi Varma's definiteness, a swirl of confused lines shape this woman—a sense of confusion about her that is finally concentrated in the woman's face. I've seen her, I've seen this woman: the tall figure, the filmy sari through which the tall columns of her legs are visible, they're familiar, as is the expression. I've seen her this way, wild, confused. But where? When? I look at the title. 'The Mistress'.

'Your father goes to a woman at night, he sleeps with her, you know that?'

Munni's words. But how . . . this painting can't have anything to do with my father . . . who could have . . .?

I go to the catalogue and look up the name of the painter, I read the words 'He died young, he committed suicide . . .' And in a second I make all the connections and I know who this man was and why he died.

Our lives changed in that moment.

15

It has been raining since morning, a persistent, soft rain that scarcely makes a sound. 'Ripi ripi rain,' Lata calls it, a phrase that carries the irritating monotony of the rain within it. When she returns home in the evening, with a film of dew-like moisture on her hair and face, she is in high spirits. 'I love this,' she says. 'Let's have ginger tea, Kaku. My father's favourite when it rains this way. It adds spice to the dullness, he says. But the truth is he loves the taste of it. You should see the way he drinks it. He takes a sip and goes—aha ha ha ha.'

When we're drinking the tea, I tell her I agree with her father entirely. Not about the spicing, though. To me there's something comforting about this drink, a kind of seductive cosiness about letting the ginger flavour go down your throat, while you hear the gentle drip drip of the moisture the trees have collected through the day. And then, as if to prove me wrong, to challenge our idea of the cosiness of the rain, it suddenly ceases to be a friendly presence. Without any warning, it turns into a downpour, drumming on the roof and beating at the windows, angry spasmodic outbursts that suddenly cease when the wind changes direction, before coming back in renewed fury.

'At this time of the year!' Lata grumbles as she flies about closing windows and doors. 'I never heard of such a thing.'

I collect the dry clothes from the backyard and rush to the back passage to place a bucket under the leaks. I've seen Hari doing this, his eyes on the roof, calculating the exact spot where the bucket has to be. The picture of the householder, I've thought him at such times.

'Kaku!' Lata exclaims in surprise when she finds me at it. 'You're really one of us now. You even know where the roof leaks.'

We go back to our interrupted tea drinking, making a fresh pot, but the tranquillity between us has been disturbed. I can sense her unspoken anxiety about Hari making his way home in such weather.

'It's the bike that worries me,' she says. 'And there's no place he can shelter on the way.'

Her ears are cocked to catch the sound of Hari's bike and, in spite of the sound of the storm, she hears it much before I do. I see her body perceptibly relaxing and I know that Hari is home.

He brings the wind and the rain with him. And something else that I, finely tuned now to disaster and bad news, recognize immediately. He does not keep me waiting.

'Savitribai has had a stroke,' he says. 'I met Abhay on the way, he was coming here to meet you. Hasina wants you to go to her. She's in the Mission Hospital.'

Hari says he will take me there. I protest, but how else do I plan to get there? they ask me. I have to give in.

I'm ready in a few moments. If in the house, with the doors and windows closed, the rain has been such a noisy monster, outside it's worse. It's frightening and intimidating, beating at our faces, on our backs. The buttons of Lata's raincoat which I'm wearing fly open, as if a magic hand has unbuttoned them.

'Hold tight,' Hari says. 'The roads are bad and with all this water I don't know what I'm getting into.'

There are no more words between us after this until we get to the hospital. My ears are so filled with the raging sound of the storm that I find it hard to adjust to the silence inside. This doesn't seem to be the kind of hospital in which sounds are kept out. The hush, I guess, is more of a lull between activities; it's silent only because nothing is happening here right now.

Hasina is sitting on a bench outside Bai's room, waiting for me, it seems, from the alacrity with which she gets up when she sees me. She scarcely notices Hari who, after a few words to me, goes away. Hasina, who held my hand the moment she saw me, clutches it even when we sit down, not letting go.

I've been wondering—why has she sent for me? We've scarcely spoken in the few months I've been a visitor to Bai's house, she's never shown any desire to be with me. And now, this! Why does she need me to be with her? But the hand that clasps mine, the hand that holds on tight, gives me the answer. I'm her ally in the fight against death. Death is the enemy we have to fight. To let any human die is to surrender to the enemy. Which is why we gather round the dying, we hold hands and say our prayers—as we did, Leela, Tony and I, when Joe was dying. And so Hasina now, holding my hand tight, the grip saying, 'Help me, help me to fight death, help me to defeat the enemy.' But only the two of us? Is there no one else?

'There's no one else,' she says between silences, as if answering my unasked question. 'They'll all come when she's dead, they'll send flowers and garlands and messages. They'll praise her, they'll write about her. What's the use? Look at her lying there, all alone, just the two of us for her.'

I can see that the hospital has already identified Bai as a somebody. The senior doctor, who has been called even in this storm, comes now in a flurry of rain. Suddenly the place is alive and bustling, with nurses and junior doctors racing up and down the passage. When the chief has gone—nothing to do but wait, he told Hasina—a nurse opens up a room for us at his orders. The rain has ceased and other sounds are now audible.

'She told me not to take her to the hospital if anything happened,' Hasina speaks abruptly, following some chain of thought of her own. 'But how could I take that chance? If she'd died then and there, it would have been all right. But that didn't happen. I had to call the doctor and when he asked me

241

to, I had to bring her here.' After a pause, she adds, 'Death doesn't come so easily.'

Hasina wants no response from me, she's talking to herself, really. I've never heard Bai speak kindly to Hasina; she's exacting, suspicious, often harsh. Why, then, does Hasina care so much? Or, is this an impersonal pity for a suffering human?

Hasina gives me the answer. 'I've been her student for fifteen years,' she says. 'These last two years I've been living with her. Now I have to be with her till the end. She and I are tied to each other.'

It's two o'clock, the time when human life is at its lowest ebb, the time, a police officer told me, when most crimes are committed. As if not just life but our humanity itself reaches its nadir at this time. 'He's a going out with the tide.' The first thing Joe said to me when I met him after his heart attack, quoting even at that moment, still taking pleasure in his beloved Dickens. 'Don't take me to the hospital if it happens again,' he said to us. Yes, Joe, who'd spent most of his life in hospitals as a healer, he said it too, the same thing that Bai did. But we couldn't just let him die, either. And so he died in hospital, in the ICU, alone, away from all of us, his beloved Paula coming too late, hours after his death.

Hasina has fallen asleep. Small snores escape her periodically, her head drops. She jerks awake, stares at me blankly, wipes her eyes and mouth, then asks me, 'What's the time?'

'Nearly four.'

My face tells her nothing has changed. She goes into Bai's room and comes out, wiping her wet face and hands with her sari. It's not tears, she's had a wash to wake herself up. Bai is the same, she says. 'If she lasts till morning . . .'

She does. As always, with the day, the possibility of life reasserts itself. As always, when I go out of the hospital there's amazement that people are going about untroubled by thoughts of sickness, suffering, death. These things have no place in their lives. Even for me, the waiting and fear recede and become distant, as distant as the storm of last night. There's nothing left of it, except the debris of branches, twigs and leaves under the trees and the plastic trash snarled together in the gutters instead of being strewn on the roads.

The bell wakes me out of the sleep I've fallen into after my bath. It's Hasina. Bai is conscious, she says, she's awake, she can't talk, but she seemed to recognize her, she says. Hasina is light-hearted with relief and sleeplessness. I persuade her to come in—one of the twins is in the hospital, she tells me—and urge her to have lunch with me. She sits stiffly in the chair outside while I make some extra chapattis. When I bring the food to the table, she says, as if explaining why she had not made any move to help me, 'Baiji wouldn't take any food from my hands. It began after her first stroke. Suddenly, overnight, she became an orthodox Brahmin.' She smiles. 'My grandfather once told me that she hated the rules and conventions of orthodoxy, that she never observed any of them herself.'

'Your grandfather?'

It's Ghulam Saab. She is Ghulam Saab's granddaughter. Of course. I wonder now how I hadn't guessed it earlier. Those eyes, how is it I didn't notice them—so like his and Munni's? I notice them now, looking at me openly, no longer veiled, no longer evading me.

We leave this alone; this is not the time for such things, both of us know that. But as if the confession has changed something, she helps me to clear up. When she brings the leftovers into the kitchen, she looks around her with frank curiosity, she asks me about Lata and Hari. 'I must go,' she says in a while. But comes back from the door to say, 'I forgot to ask you—it's what I came to say, really. Can you ring up the doctorsaab?'

For a moment I think she means Som. Then it occurs to me that it's Chandru she's talking of, Chandru, Bai's neurologist.

'Our phone isn't working, so I thought I'd ask you, he's your friend . . .'

Her voice trails away uncertainly at my silence and she goes on more hesitantly, 'He said he would come any time Baiji needed him. I know she is more comfortable with him.'

I'll ring him, of course I'll talk to him, I assure her. But when I call, Chandru is not at home. I can ask for Satee, but I don't want to speak to her. I leave my number with the servant instead. Chandru calls me at night.

'Madhu?' His voice is sharp with anxiety.

I'm fine, I reassure him. It's Bai. Yes, another stroke. Yes, she's recovering, but she wants him. Can he come?

'Okay, I'll be there. What day is it today? Friday, isn't it? I'll leave tomorrow, I'll be there on Sunday morning, tell them that. And I'll speak to the doctor there today.'

If Bai has been a special patient so far, Chandru's arrival turns her into a dignitary. I'm seeing Chandru in action for the first time; it's an impressive sight. He conveys confidence, knowledge, sympathy, assurance—the lot. The dignity and respect he's given by the local doctor, even by the chief here, is not only because of his seniority in the profession—a profession almost feudal in its hierarchical structure—it's the due given by small-town men to Chandru's personality, his success, his being an eminent Bombay consultant.

'They think I'm a Brihaspati,' he says with a grin when we're out of the hospital. 'And the truth is, there's nothing I've told them that they don't already know.'

'Will she be okay?'

'Until the next stroke—and God knows when that will be! If she's lucky, it will be a big one and she will be out of it. Otherwise, she'll go on this way, dying bit by bit. Terrible. Nothing like a heart attack. The royal road, my father used to call it. Well, where shall we go?'

244

Chandru has a car and a driver waiting for him, given to him by Ravi for his use as long as he's in Bhavanipur.

'Always the red carpet treatment,' I remark, when we get into the car.

'Ravi wanted me to stay with him. But I preferred a hotel. Shall we go there?'

I demur and so we go to my place, instead. Hari and Lata are out. Chandru is clearly relieved that we can be by ourselves.

'I came here as much to see you as for Bai,' he says bluntly, following me into the kitchen when I go in to make some tea for us.

'I guessed as much.'

'So, when are you returning?'

'Let's see, let Bai recover.'

'You can forget about getting anything out of her. She's not going to be able to tell you much now. I doubt if her speech will get back to normal and her mind will be even more muddled after. You'll have to manage with what you have. It should be enough, you've been here quite a long time. I never expected you to stay for so long. Maya says she thought the book would be ready by now. Come back to Bombay, Madhu, you can do the writing at home.'

I tell him I can't leave, not at this time anyway. There's Hasina, I've only just discovered that she's Ghulam Saab's granddaughter. I need to talk to her. Bai hasn't said a word about him, and he's important . . .

'Madhu, why don't you admit the truth? You're putting it off, you don't want to come back.'

'I need more time.'

'What for? Come on, Madhu, you've had enough. And some day you have to return. Surely, you can forgive Som now?'

'Forgive Som? What do I have to forgive him for?'

'For Adit's death.'

245

There is silence. Chandru steps into it with somewhat less than his usual bravado.

'You blame Som for it.'

'You're mad, Chandru. A bus blew up because someone had planted a bomb. Do you think I blame Som for that? Am I a fool to blame Som for the riots? For Babri Masjid? For Ayodhya? How can I blame anyone for these things?'

'You think Som was responsible for Adit's leaving home.'

Of course, Chandru knows all about it. How did I imagine that he wouldn't, that Som who tells him everything, wouldn't have told him this?

'Som said this to you? That I blame him for Adit's death?'

'No, he blames himself, he says it's his fault . . . Madhu . . . Madhu . . .'

His words are distant, fading away. And then there's darkness. I come out of it to see Chandru, his fingers on my pulse, his face, anxious and frightened, close to mine.

'All right?'

I nod. He continues to hold my wrist for a while before letting go.

'Don't get up,' he says. 'I'll be back.'

There's silence, broken by the parrot flapping its wings. Chandru comes back with a glass of water. 'You frightened me. What's wrong? Has this happened before?'

'No. I guess it's the lack of sleep. And no breakfast today.'

'Have your lunch now. Or will you come to the hotel and have it with me?'

'No, I'm fine. But let's not speak of—of all those things.'

'I know you're angry with me because I did. But tell me, Madhu, if I don't speak to you, who will? When I see Somya's face . . .'

Their friendship, which began when Chandru, a child of six, was sent to Som's father to learn Sanskrit, is a legend. They laugh at it themselves, they parody the friendship scenes in Hindi movies—the *'yeh dosti'* song from *Sholay*, sung by them, was a regular item at all picnics and parties when they were students. But despite their spoofing, the friendship is real.

He returns in the afternoon. 'I've sent the driver away,' he says. 'You can drive us, can't you? You know the place well enough now, I'm sure.'

I haven't been at the wheel of a car for months. I'm surprised how much I enjoy it, enjoy my own skill, the sense of freedom, of being in control. I took to driving easily and quickly—'like drinking water' the instructor said to me admiringly and approvingly. Whereas Som . . .

'Remember your first car?' Chandru asks, obviously thinking of Som's driving too.

Yes, I do. Chandru gave us his car—on 'long-term easy payments' as he said, trying to sound businesslike. He came with us on Som's first drive, sitting next to Som, while Adit and I sat at the back. I remember Adit's delight at being in our own car, the delight turning to fear when Chandru's voice rose, berating Som for his mistakes. Som was terrible, veering between a timorous crawling along the pavement and a sudden dash into the middle of the road, heedless of other vehicles.

'*Saala*, Somya couldn't drive. He still can't, though he gets angry if I say so. Where are you taking me?'

'Wherever you want to go.'

'Let's go round the town.'

But Chandru really wants to talk and we end up at his hotel, which is just outside Bhavanipur. He's on his best behaviour, he avoids speaking of Som and me, talks instead of Bai. He asks if she remembers me.

'I don't know. She hasn't said a word about our having been neighbours, or about my father, or Neemgaon. I think it's because she doesn't want to bring Munni—her daughter—into the picture. Or do you think she's forgotten that time entirely? Has the stroke erased it?'

247

'I doubt it. It can't be as selective as that. Words, yes, connections, yes, definitely they can go awry, but . . .'

'She does remember your father, though. Very clearly.'

'Papa? What does she say about him?'

'Oh, high praise. He gave her a new life, it was a rebirth, without him she would have died, etc., etc. She goes on and on. She wants me to put that in, she's keen that she gives him his due.'

'You're not going to do that, I hope?'

'Why, Chandru?'

'I don't want my father's name in the book.'

'But why, Chandru?'

This is a surprise, this is unexpected.

'I don't want him to be linked to her. People will put two and two together and make it five.'

'That five being?'

'That—well, that she was—you know . . .'

'That she was his mistress?'

'Yeah, what else?'

'But that was an important period in her life, she was going through a very bad time and your father brought her out of it. Her career really began after that. How can I leave that bit out? Or, should I say an unnamed doctor? That would be silly, it would make it even more fishy, as if there is something to hide. As her doctor, your father is important.'

'Write that and people will start talking.'

'Let them.'

'I have to think of my mother, I don't want her to be hurt.'

'And if I write about Ghulam Saab, his family will be hurt. If I bring Munni into the book, her family will be hurt. So what do I do?'

'But these are truths—that she had an affair with the man, that she had this child by him. These are known facts.'

'And that your father helped her is not the truth?'

'All right, all right, if you want to be a Harishchandra, go

248

ahead, write it, write about my father, write what you want. Yes, write the truth and damn everything and damn everybody else.'

'You know I can't do that. You're financing this book, I have to walk on the line you draw.'

Suddenly his anger is quenched. 'No, no, Madhu, that's not fair, it's not fair at all. Did I say that, did I say such a thing?'

'No, you didn't, you're very sensitive to my feelings. You don't need to be, Chandru. I—we—Som and I are used to taking favours from you.'

'Favours? What favours? Madhu, you must not talk like that, you're insulting me, you're insulting our friendship. Somya is my brother, you're my bhabhi, we're family, there can be no favours . . .'

As usual, when Chandru gets excited, his Marathi is spattered with Gujarati, English and Hindi words.

'Okay, I won't call them favours. But that doesn't change things. Our first car, my trip to England to be with Som, the flat—you know we got all these things because of you . . .'

'Come on, Madhu, stop it, you better stop it, you're making me really angry now. You know the one time I almost broke off with Som was when he tried to return the money for your trip to England. As if I had no right to do that for you.'

'Understand him, Chandru. It's not easy to be always on the taking side. It made him feel smaller.'

'Smaller? He's two inches taller than me, how can he feel small?'

Chandru laughs heartily at his own joke, his good humour restored, cheerful now that we've patched up.

'Let's have dinner here,' he says.

'I have to tell Lata and Hari.'

'Ring them up.'

But the phone keeps ringing. They're not at home, obviously.

'Join me in a drink,' Chandru pleads. 'You know I hate

drinking alone. Be a sport, Madhu, come on.'

Reluctant to imperil our amity, I give in.

'That's like a good girl.' And when he's taken his first sip, he looks at me and says, 'What a fool I was! If I'd had any sense, I'd have grabbed you instead of letting Som do it.'

'I thought you're Som's friend—sorry, Som's brother—and I'm your bhabhi?'

'I'm talking of the past, when Som had his Neelam.'

'And you had your Satee.'

His face darkens. 'Yes, I had Satee. I should have called it off then. But how does one know? Remember, Madhu, how she was then—so shy and gentle. And look at her now!'

'She's had a lot to put up with.'

I'm not very comfortable with Satee's sharp-tongued sarcasm myself. She's bitter and deeply resentful of Chandru's friendship with Som, which includes me. But I admire her for the openness with which she displays her hostility, scorning the subterfuges most women would resort to. And, unlike Som, I can see Chandru's faults.

'Put up with! What does she have to put up with? Tell me that, eh, tell me? She's got everything—she's mistress of her home, my poor mother doesn't say a word to her, she's got all the money she wants. But no, I have to be the villain and she the victim. It's all this feminism stuff you women have got into your heads. *Indian men*, she says all the time now. *Indian men*. What other men does she know, damn it!' He pauses after this outburst and goes back to his point. 'What does she have to put up with, tell me Madhu.'

'Well, your—affairs.'

'What affairs?'

'Shall I list them, those that I know of anyway?'

'I can't be friends with any female, can I, because I'm married? I can't speak to any female, that's it, is it? If Satee were more pleasant, I wouldn't have to, let me tell you that.'

After his second drink, Chandru's bellicosity vanishes, he

becomes sentimental, even maudlin, speaking of his daughters. 'My jewels, my flowers,' he keeps calling them. He soon goes back to Som and I sense a genuine bewildered grief behind the exaggerated reaction of a man who's drinking.

'Let's call up Som,' he says, 'let's talk to him.'

He dials the number and I can see from his face that the phone keeps ringing, that nobody is picking it up.

'God knows where he's gone, God knows where he goes. It's Sunday today, he should be home. I ask him where he's been and he won't tell me. Where does he go, what does he do? Madhu, don't you care any more? Madhu, he's so miserable, don't do this to him Madhu, how can you be so cruel, how can you . . .'

He puts his head on my lap and sobs. I sit silent, looking down at the greying head in my lap, until he recovers. He gets to his feet, suddenly sober, says, 'Sorry, Madhu,' and goes into the bathroom.

'I have to go,' I tell him when he returns.

'Okay. Just let me get my shoes on.'

I need to go to the bathroom too and when I return I find Chandru fast asleep, sprawled on the bed, his feet, one with a shoe on, hanging over the side. I try to wake him, but it's no use. I remove the one shoe, put his feet on the bed, cover him and sit by his side waiting for him to wake up. It's too late for me to go back by myself now.

I sit in the chair all night, dropping off and waking up and then going back to sleep again, perfectly aware each time of the two states of waking and sleeping, of my transition from one to another. When, in one of my waking moments, I see the dawning light in the window, I wash, re-drape my crumpled sari around myself, go out of the hotel and get into a waiting rickshaw.

Lata rushes out at the sound of the rickshaw. By the time I've paid him and got into the house, she's back inside. Hari is with her. I see accusation on both their faces.

251

'I'm sorry, I should have informed you, I did try to ring up, but you were not at home . . .'

'It's okay, you didn't need to. What does it matter if we worry? And it's our own stupidity, we're small-town people, we don't understand these things.'

I walk out of the room. When I come back after my bath, I see a cup of tea on the table. I wait until the sounds tell me they've both gone, take the cup into the kitchen and pour the tea down the sink. How dare she! How dare they presume, how dare they judge me!

'I've been stamped as an immoral woman who spent a night with you in your hotel room,' I tell Chandru, when he comes to me after his visit to Bai.

He laughs at first, then becomes remorseful.

'It's all my fault. I shouldn't drink so much, I must learn to stop. Somya's been telling me to slow down. It's okay, Madhu, I'll explain to them.'

'There's no need. I don't have to give any explanations to these people. Just because I'm staying with them, it doesn't make them the guardians of my morals.'

'I don't like anyone thinking such things about you.'

'Leave it, Chandru.'

When Lata returns, it's obvious she wants to make up. She comes straight to me.

'I'm sorry, Kaku, I was wrong, I shouldn't have spoken that way to you, it was wrong of me. Forgive me, Kaku, please, please . . .'

I look at her face, so confident of my succumbing, so certain I'll say it's all right. Spoilt brat, used to having her parents and sisters melt when she said she was sorry!

'What does it matter whether I forgive you or don't! Is it important?'

She draws back swiftly at that and goes into her room. Hari, who's just come in, says to me, 'She was worried, she was frightened sick when you didn't return. We went to the hospital, we went to Savitribai's house, then we rushed home, we thought you'd ring up.'

'I did, but you were not at home.'

'She wanted to ask Dr Shah to have dinner with us, we'd gone shopping to get a few things she needed.'

We sit in silence after that. I am filled with a cold anger, my heart is beating in a wild agitation. I don't need this, I don't need this at all. I don't want to be part of this, I don't want to be tangled up in anyone's emotions, not any more, not ever.

Lata comes in, her face soggy with tears, her eyes red.

'Kaku, I'm sorry, I mean it, really I do, I don't know what got into me. I'm ashamed of myself for speaking to you that way, I've been sick all day, I had no right to behave the way I did.'

This is real, not like the chest-beating drama of remorse she'd acted out earlier. She's sorry, not only about her words, but for hurting me, for damaging the relationship she's built with me. I know this, but I find it hard to respond. It's like re-entering a world I've walked out of, getting back into a distant past when I'd felt the tug of another human being's emotions.

'It's all right,' I say finally. 'And stop crying!'

'I can't. Once I start crying, I can't stop. And I cry so—so—too easily. I start sobbing even when singing the Jana Gana Mana.'

'So do I.'

She snaps out of her tears and looks at me in surprise. 'Kaku! You! I don't believe it!'

'It's true, I swear it.'

I put my hand to my throat and pinch it, holding a bit of skin between my fingers. It takes her a moment to realize I'm imitating her. She begins to laugh. And then suddenly stops to say, 'What a beautiful smile, Kaku! Do you know, this is the first time I'm seeing it? The first time I'm seeing you look happy?'

It's not joy, this is not *my* joy, in any event; it's her happiness that I'm echoing. We're like a pair of mirrors, endlessly reflecting her happiness.

In the evening, Chandru walks into an atmosphere entirely different from what he'd expected. Nevertheless, he goes through his prepared speech, he recites his *mea culpas*, he tells them it was all his fault, that I'm blameless and so on. He spends the few hours he has before it's time for his train with us, being his most charming self. To look at him, anyone would think that these two were his dearest friends, that nobody matters more to him than they do. I remember the joke about Chandru in Som's family, of how Chandru, asked to give the declension of 'Aham'—'I'—had said, 'Aham Aham Aham.'

'It's all *I* to Chandru, there's no *we*, no *us* in his language,' Som's father had joked.

Through dinner, which Chandru agrees to have at home with us, the conversation is carried on mainly by Lata and Chandru. Hari is quiet. I can see him watching his wife. Once I catch his reflective, pondering look resting on my face. He's not discomposed when I catch him. Is he thinking that Lata was right, that I did spend the night with Chandru—in the sense of having slept with him, that is? But at my age!

My age! What does it matter? I'm still a woman, Chandru a man. It does not matter that Chandru is Som's friend and that Chandru and I have been friends as well for nearly twenty-five years. I remember the waiter's look last night when he brought us our dinner, the gleam in his eyes when they rested on me.

Men and women can never be friends. Men can be brothers, fathers, lovers, husbands, but never friends—is that how it is? Is Chandru right?

If this is how it is, how did I expect Som to understand what I told him?

16

'Be a Harishchandra then,' Chandru said to me angrily, 'tell the truth and damn everything else.'

I go back to the Harishchandra story and think: what is this truth that Harishchandra clung to at the cost of so much suffering? I go over the story in my mind and realize that it's not what *we* call the truth that the story is about, that it has nothing to do with a truth that emerges through words. What the story tells us is this: you can't tell the truth, you can only live it. It tells me how little the idea of truth is connected with words, how much of it lies in our connections to the unseen world which, whether we know it or not, we are always conscious of.

'Tell me the truth,' Som says, over and over again. He dismisses the truth of our life together, of our love, our friendship, our life as parents of a beloved son. What he wants is something separate and distinct from these things, something which really is, though he refuses to recognize this, a minute part of a whole. To him, that part is the whole.

Tell me the truth.

But Som wanted the truth in words, he wanted me to tell him something that he thought was the truth. I could not give him this, I could not speak the words he wanted to hear. And so it began, the change in Som, the struggle between us. He believes that the truth is somewhere with me, he imagines me to be the enemy obstructing him, preventing him from getting at it. He flings away all the words I offer him as being untrue, he goes on doggedly, savagely, after what he wants. Which, for him, lies in my life before I married him, in all the unspoken areas of my early life, and for the first time I understand that I should have offered him my entire life as a starter to our matrimonial meal. He traces his way through my past, picking his way through it with precise care, bringing up the names of all those he imagines could have been my lovers. My friends in college, Venkat, Ketaki's brothers, her cousin who was often with us, Hamidbhai's nephews, who for a few months lived with Hamidbhai. When he speaks of them, I know he's thinking of my room, just along the passage, so conveniently close, and of the bed in my room, the narrow bed on which he and I had let our erotic imaginations come alive.

(How strange it is that he never brings up Dalvi's name, Dalvi, the man whose eyes and hands had made me so unpleasantly aware that I was a female, a female with breasts, hips, thighs and something else I didn't have the word for then.)

It's when he adds, in desperation I now think, Tony's name to the list, that I retreat into silence. I will no longer answer him, I will say nothing, I will deny nothing. But my silence makes things worse, it's a bigger barrier between us than my words had been. If my denials could contain untruths, how many more lies did my silences conceal? I sense an enormous grief under his suspicion and his anger, I can feel the weight of his grief, I even share the burden of it with him. At times, I pity him, at other times I'm filled with a helpless rage. I turn on him in fury then. *What* does he want? *What* is it that he wants from me?

In my despair I think of tearing off my clothes and saying to him: look, look at me, look at this. This is the woman you pursued and married, this is the body you slept with and enjoyed all these years. If you think the truth lies in this body, if you imagine that the truth is what this body has done, look carefully at it. It has changed from what it was when you married me, the breasts are sagging a little, there's some more flesh on the hips, the thighs and the waist than there was, there are folds on the abdomen, wrinkles on the neck. But these are aging changes, a process your body shares with mine. Nothing else has changed. Why then does it seem so changed to you? I sit at the dressing table—the table that was the gift of his rising prosperity to me—and look at myself in the mirror, trying to see myself with his eyes. Have I changed? Why is it that something that happened so many years ago makes me a different person in his eyes?

I know it is Som who has changed. I can't recognize this sad and angry man, distraught, possessed by a madness that seems to have no end. This is not the genial, generous, affectionate man I knew, not the man I married! From where has this man emerged? It's like the mobs that appear in the streets at the same time, mobs that come it seems from nowhere, to loot and kill, sowing seeds of hatred and revenge. And then, their work done, they disappear, dissolving into the mass in which there are no looters, no killers, only fathers and husbands, sons and brothers.

For a while he continues to sleep with me, though there is something savage in his love making. He throws himself at me in a kind of desperation and I sense a concealed violence that both frightens and infuriates me. I resist, but our bodies are so used to each other, they settle down, in spite of us, into a rhythm, a shadow of our earlier love making. Soon this stops and he ceases even to touch me, he is careful to make no physical contact with me. One night, his arm falls across my body. I wake up feeling the weight of the arm, I lie still, wanting to move away from under it, but afraid to wake him up. He wakes up himself, becomes aware of my body under his arm and draws it back with a sharp sudden jerk, as if my touch sears him. I lie awake, conscious that the body beside mine is rigid and taut, like one huge muscle gone into spasm.

When will this end, oh God, how will it end? I think of leaving him and going away, but where will I go? And there's Adit. Som and I are locked in a silent, fearful struggle that exhausts us. We are like two travellers embarked on a terrible journey, rocketing at a dangerous speed, on the verge of going out of control, yet unable to stop, unable to help ourselves. My only comfort is that Adit is out of it, that Adit knows nothing. For we keep our routine going, we somehow manage to keep the surface of our life intact during the day. Only at night, with Adit safely ensconced in his room, does the nightmare begin.

Tell me the truth, tell me the truth.

Adit safe? What a fool I am to imagine that by keeping him in ignorance he's out of it all! He's with us, part of our disastrous journey, the three of us travelling together.

'What's wrong, Mama? What's happening? What's going on? What's wrong with Papa?'

He's frightened, he's appealing to me for reassurance, he wants me to tell him all is well. And all I can offer him are lies.

'It's all right Adit, it's nothing. Som is a bit under stress, you know how these riots are affecting his work. You know most of his patients are Muslims, they're staying away, it's making him anxious. He'll be okay, don't worry, it'll be okay.'

'You're not telling me the truth, you think I'm a fool, you think I'm still a child.'

What do I tell you, Adit? That I slept with a man when I was a girl, a child really, and your father can't take it? That your father is tearing himself apart, and me too, because of something that happened—and only once—years ago?

The irony of it is that when this happens, we have reached a plateau of better understanding, the three of us. Adit is in his 12th, the crucial year for him. He's decided he wants to be an architect, he's working hard for his exams. Som is happy with Adit's hard work, with his spurt of ambition, he's reconciled to his rejecting medicine. I'm easier with Adit too, more able to accept his growing self, the almost adult self he presents me with. I manage to conceal my hurt, my chagrin at being kept out of his life, more successfully. I go out often with Som, with

Ketaki, with Tony and Rekha. Sunday evenings we go out, Som and I, for a play usually. We're always a crowd, for Som can never buy only two tickets. There's Nisha and her husband, sometimes Rekha, sometimes Sunanda and Raghunath, or Rajani and her husband. We're a cheerful crowd, we go out for dinner after the show, there's much talk and laughter. And suddenly I see Adit's face, cheerful at the thought of our going out, at being on his own, I think of his reassuring—or so he thinks—'Go on, Ma, I'm fine, I have to work', and I feel a pang. But I crush it, I join the others in speaking of how wonderful it is to be free of the children, to have these pleasures after so many years of planning every outing around the children's needs.

On the day of the opening of Rekha's gallery, a Sunday, we have dinner together after it's over. There's a crowd of us, all friends. Som and I come home in the uplifted mood that good food, company and drink bring on. And at night I have the nightmare, the nightmare that is the beginning of the nightmare of our own lives.

'If you could keep such a thing from me, how can I believe anything you say, how can I ever believe you again?' Som asks me appealingly, almost humbly, in one of his better moments.

I know he can't. Trust has gone. Without trust there can be no truth, without it our relationship has no chance of survival. Nothing can survive without trust. But what does he mean by the truth? Does he mean revealing everything? It's true that Som shares everything with me—his day, his friends, his family, his ideas, his thoughts. It's part of him, part of his family, who are always sharing things with one another—whether it's a headache, an upset tummy, or just a bad day, it is immediately announced to anyone who's around. It's physical too; they're touching, patting, hugging one another all the time. Som's hands constantly seek mine, his fingers clasp my fingers, his palms slide up and down mine. There are no barriers, no partitions between us. He leaves the bathroom door open when he bathes and comes out after his shower, leaving his wet towel in a heap on the bathroom floor, his bare body offered to my gaze.

'I told you everything about Neelam, I kept nothing from you. If you can keep such a thing from me . . .'

I can understand what he's saying, I know how he feels. Why can't he understand me? Doesn't he know that I am not like him, that constant revelation is not part of me, that I cannot open out my self to others, even to him, the way he can? Soon, my anger and helplessness give way to a sliver of greater understanding. I know what the truth is that Som wants from me: that it has not happened, that I was a virgin when he married me. I begin to understand the truth that he could, perhaps, have borne: that I had been raped, forced into the act, that I was a victim, not a participant.

But I could not give him any of these things, they were not true.

I have thought a great deal since then of the different ways in which I could have told him, of how I could have rephrased it, of the most innocuous way I could have put it. But there was no way of telling that could have taken the lethal quality out of the words. The catalyst that turned my words into poison lay within him, it was he who made the words what they became—destroyers of our life together, destroyers of our son's life. Yet I go back to the moment over and over again, I ask myself—why did I tell him? Why did I speak of it to him? I knew the moment I spoke that I had done wrong, his face told me the enormity of my wrong. But it was already too late, I'd taken the plunge and there was no parachute I could open, nothing on the ground to soften my fall.

I know this too, that my speaking to him was something I had no control over. I was not *telling* Som, I was sharing something with him, a thing I'd just discovered myself. The ·

knowledge came to me even as I was speaking to him. I was still in the nightmare when Som woke me up, still grappling with the horror of it. Disoriented too, yes, but with the clarity that waking out of a nightmare suddenly confers on you. The world is hazy, but the dream is suddenly clear, more coherent.

'Madhu, Madhu, wake up, wake up, what is it . . .?'

I can hear Som speaking to me. At the same time I can see the nightmare as well, making all the sense it never did when I saw it in my sleep. I begin to speak to Som about it.

There was this sack, a gunny sack, its mouth fastened with jute string, like a bag of grains. I opened the sack, it took me some time, but I untied the knot and opened it. And there was a face looking at me, a man's face, his mouth open, tongue hanging out, weals round the neck. Marks of a rope. And even as I stared in horror at the face, the face came alive, the eyes opened, they looked at me, they saw me . . .

I am shivering, a violent shivering like the beginning of malaria. Som holds me close, he makes soothing sounds. He's listening to me the way we listen to other people's stories, with the touch of condescending understanding we confer on people's dreams, even on their nightmares. His interest in the dream is feigned, but his concern about my state is real. He's sleepy too, he wants to go back to his interrupted sleep. He pats me sympathetically, yet briskly. 'It's over,' he says soothingly. 'It's over now, don't worry, just try to sleep.' He is yawning, stretching, preparing to get back under his blanket. Yes, it is over for him.

But I can't stop, I am still in that dream, looking now at the man's face, recognizing him, and I have to go on, following the course of my discovery, sharing this with Som.

'I know him, I know the man, Som. He was my father's friend, he committed suicide, he hanged himself.'

I hear Som's exclamation of horror, of pity. But he's still distant from it, the pity a momentary emotion, to be forgotten the instant we get back to sleep. Which is what he wants us to do.

261

But I can't stop, I have to go on and I do, rollercoasting to disaster.

'He killed himself, he killed himself because of me. He hanged himself because of me.'

'What!'

'He slept with me, I was only fifteen then. He—I don't think he meant it, but it—it happened. And that's why he—that's why he died. He killed himself because of what he did to me.'

Words cannot bear the weight of the truth, they cannot contain the vastness of it; they can only give a partial picture, a distortion, often, of the truth.

It is the man's death that I'm speaking of to Som, the suicide, the horror of his hanging himself, of the body suspended from the roof, twirling in space, undiscovered perhaps, for days. These are the things that crowd my mind, filling me with terror and pity. And trailing on these comes the memory of the man's face, the look on it the last time I saw him, a look so full of self-loathing and anguish that, years later, when I remember it, I know without any doubt why he died.

This is what I'm speaking of to Som, this is what I'm sharing with him. But it's the single act of sex that Som holds on to, it's this fact that he can't let go of, as if it's been welded into his palm. Purity, chastity, an intact hymen—these are the things Som is thinking of, these are the truths that matter. I know this when I see his face, when I feel the hurting grip of his hand, when he says, 'Tell me, go on, go on.'

Go on with what? There's nothing else as far as I'm concerned. The memories are vague, confused, they come to me in insubstantial wisps—the smell of the man's clothes, the roughness of his hand, of his cheek . . .

But Som wants facts, hard facts. How often had this happened, how long had it gone on? Tell me, tell me.

262

Only once. No, never again. No, never before, either.

Som cannot believe me. He won't believe there is nothing more to tell. He thinks I'm holding back. When I say it's all very vague, he thinks I'm evading him, when I tell him I'd forgotten about it, he goes rigid with disbelief and anger.

But it is true. Even now, when it is more possible for me to unravel the sequence of events, when it is possible to think of them with greater clarity, it is hard to untangle this one event from the many things that happened then. It remains part of a confusing blur of events—my father's illness, his going away to Bombay for surgery, his death. All the other happenings whirled round this central fact of my father's death, this was the column that stood out clear and tall, dwarfing the rest.

My father is ill. He has been unwell for some time now. How long? Weeks? Months? For a while, he keeps it from me; or, perhaps, it is I who don't notice. Then I begin to see things. I notice how often he is at home when I return from school, how many times I find him in bed, resting, he says. One day I have to wake him, his patients have been waiting so long, they're getting impatient. I call out to him and he wakes up instantly, startled, his eyes blank, staring at me but not recognizing me. He recovers quickly and asks me to tell the patients he'll be out soon. I hear him coughing when I leave the room, the same painful, racking cough I hear from his room at nights. His deep, bronchial cough has always been part of our home, but this is different, there's something ominous about it.

I begin to look furtively at him now, and I see how exhausted he seems, even in the mornings. I notice the way his clothes hang on him. I hear a friend, one of the Kakas, arguing with him one day. A few days later there's a visitor—an old classmate of my father's, now a well-known doctor in Pune. I hear them talking of their student days, I hear them laughing and I'm reassured—my father is all right, there's nothing

wrong with him. But the next day he has to go to the hospital
for tests. His friend comes to take him, the 'Car Kaka' I call
him, because he's one of the few people in Neemgaon with his
own car, a tiny two-door car. He always announces himself
and his car to me by calling out, 'Chalo Dilli'. This time there
are no jokes, he is silent and grave. And my father, walking out
to the car, looks like an old man.

'What is it? What did they say?' I want to ask him when he
returns, but his face stops me. Neither of us speaks. That
evening he tells me he has to go to Bombay for an operation.
They think—they hope, he carefully corrects himself—he will
be all right after that. He himself is sure he will be all right. I
am not to worry, he says.

I want to go with him, I tell him. But he says, no, I can't.
He'll write to me, he'll be back soon. I'm not to worry, he says
again. I can sense his apprehension—will I cry? Will I create a
scene?

I'm nearly fifteen, and I'm no child. I have never been a child
in the sense of indulging in tantrums or tears. I don't do so
now. He looks too exhausted to argue with, anyway. I sit
quietly by him and he seems comforted by my presence, he
falls asleep. When he wakes up, he speaks to me of Leela. I
hear the name for the first time. She's my aunt, he tells me. My
mother's eldest sister. Her husband, Joe, is a doctor, a famous
doctor in Bombay. It's he who is making the arrangements for
my father's surgery. Leela is a very good person, he tells me. I
can trust her, I should trust her. He wants me to remember
that.

Why is he telling me this? Why is he saying these things? I go
to my room and sit staring at my books, blinded and choked
by terror.

I get one letter from my father after he reaches Bombay.
After that, nothing. It's holiday time and I have nothing to do
but brood. I move about restlessly, waiting for the postman,
for my father's letter. I seem to be cut off from my friends and

their activities by this fear, this sense of something impending. My father's absence is dense and heavy like a thick fog about me. Without his messages telling me when he is returning, my life seems to have gone adrift; there is nothing I can moor myself to. His friends, the Kakas and their wives, keep coming home, they try to persuade me to go to their homes, to stay with them until my father returns. But I have been firm about this, and I continue to be determined—I want to be in my own house. Babu's silence is better than the wanting-to-comfort-me chatter of the Kakis. And it is here, to our home, that his letter will come.

It is not a letter, but a telegram that comes—one of those bits of brown, misspelt messages, harbingers at that time of bad news, of doom. I don't know that it has come, it is a neighbour who asks me, What is the news? What did the telegram say?

A telegram? I rush home, I race from room to room, calling out to Babu. He is nowhere. I find him finally in his own room, a place neither my father nor I ever enter.

Babu is not alone, there is a woman with him. I see her first, a woman I've never seen before, standing against the wall, her face against it. She is tall—I first notice the long columns of her legs, visible under the filmy stuff of her sari, and then the neat knot of hair tied at the nape of her neck. I can't see her face, I can only hear the muffled sounds that come from her. It's not like anyone crying, it's a wail, 'Ai-ga . . . Ai-ga,' that goes through me like a knife.

I make some sound myself perhaps, for Babu, who's had his back to me, turns around. His face—he's crying too, the tears are running down his cheeks, his surly face is almost unrecognizable. Babu crying! My body goes cold. He's dead, my father is dead. Even as Babu opens his mouth to speak to me—the woman has not yet seen me, her keening goes on—I rush out of the room, bolt the door and throw myself on the bed, my whole body going into shuddering, convulsive movements. My father is dead, it's all over.

'Madhu, Madhu . . .'

I can hear Babu's voice, I hear him knocking on the door, asking me to open it. I don't want to hear his words, I don't want to listen to what he's going to tell me. I put the pillow over my head, my fingers in my ears and give myself up to a frenzy of grief. In a while the passion of grief runs down out of sheer exhaustion. Babu's voice, the knocking on the door, has ceased; it's silent outside. I don't know how long I lie there, staring at the ceiling, my mind a total blank—it's as if I'm dead myself—when I hear a knock on my door again, a voice calling my name. This is not Babu's voice.

'Open the door, Madhu.'

I unbolt the door and return to the bed. He enters, hesitant, unsure. It's one of my father's friends, but not one of the 'Kakas'. This man is different. A taciturn man who lives alone in a single room, he's a rare visitor. I don't know him as well as I do my father's other friends, but I know he's a welcome visitor, that my father likes him, he admires him. He's a painter, he did a picture of me as a child which still hangs in my father's bedroom.

'Madhu? What is it?'

'My father—my father is dead. Baba, Baba, Baba . . .'

Grief overcomes me once more and I give myself up to it.

'Madhu, that's not true, he's not dead, listen to me, will you listen? I won't tell you anything until you stop crying, stop it now. Now, listen to what I'm saying. Your father's operation is over, you can go to Bombay now, he's asked Babu and you to go there. You're going today, do you hear me? Babu has gone to get the tickets, you have to get up. Get up, stop crying and get your things ready.'

His words penetrate, they make me sit up. Somehow, this man's words carry conviction. I know he won't tell me lies, he won't fool me.

'Come on, pack your bag. The train is at nine, you don't

have much time. Come on, get up.'

'Was the operation . . . did they . . .?' I can't go on.

'No,' he says after a little hesitation. 'They couldn't do much.'

I know, doctor's daughter that I am, what this means. They can't do anything for him, he's going to die. Baba, Baba . . .

'You have to go to Bombay, Madhu, you're going to be with him. What good will you do him if you behave like this?'

It's no use, there's nothing he can say that will help me. Realizing this, he stops speaking, he begins to pat my back, the pats too hard, hurting, the hands of a man unused to doing this kind of thing.

'Do you think he'll die?' I ask finally.

He is silent.

'Is he already dead?'

'No! No, he's not dead.'

'But he will die, yes, he will, and I'll be alone. I want my father, I want Baba.'

The sobs erupt out of me with such force that my body seems to explode with them. He puts an arm about me, holding me tight, trying to stop the desperate, convulsive movements of my body.

'Ssh,' he says, holding me within his arms. 'Ssh, stop that.'

I am not used to being touched. My father is not a demonstrative man, nor am I. And since I grew up, he has been even more chary of any physical contact. Now this man is holding me close, tight, I can smell his body, his clothes with their distinctive smell—of turpentine?—I can feel the texture of his shirt, the rough scraping of his unshaven cheek. All these things penetrate through my grief. And almost at the same moment, his hands fall away from my body, he moves away from me. I suddenly feel cold and blank. I want it back, the closeness, the comfort that the closeness brought me. His body seems to be the one centre in my disintegrating world, the one solid thing I can hold on to in the maelstrom whirling about me. I want more—I want to feel his skin on mine, to feel his breath on my face. Do I know this? Do I admit this to myself? Is there still an innocence in my feelings, my responses?

He has moved away, he has gone to the door where he stands and looks back at me. Is it something he sees on my face, or some movement that I make which brings him back? Or has he gone to the door only to bolt it, as he now does? I don't know. I will never know. But he comes back to me and things are now different. His hands, his touch, his breath—I am conscious of these things, I feel intoxicated, a little heady with them, so that I stop thinking. There is a moment of strangeness, of fear, when I realize he is fumbling at my clothes, at his own, but at the contact of bare skin, the fear is immediately overlaid by a sense of shock, like plunging into cold water. There's the joy of feeling the cool water against my bare skin, its ripples teasing my body, caressing my skin. Pleasure runs swiftly along my nerves, through my body. I am conscious of my body, of the rich sap within it, rushing to meet and mingle with him. Nothing is unknown, nothing is strange. An ancient memory, waiting to be released all these years, is directing my body's responses, making me aware of the pleasure, the pleasure that reaches a climax despite the pain, the agonizing pain, when my body accepts him, when it mingles with his.

Then it's over and he's leaving. He pauses again at the door, his hand on the bolt, on the point of opening it, and looks at me as he did that first time before he bolted the door and came to me. But his face and his eyes frighten me now. He sees the fear on my face, he comes back to me and touches me on my head, a gentle reassuring touch that I scarcely feel, a touch that makes me a child again. He goes away then and I fall asleep until Babu comes to wake me up, to tell me we're going to Bombay, we have to leave in an hour, I have to get ready.

We get on to the train and I move away from Neemgaon, I move on to Bombay and my father's death, to a new beginning. The past, this man, what happened between us, has no place in this life, it's irrelevant. My father's death has blotted out everything else, like a huge cloud it covers the entire sky. And this incident is lost, forgotten—until the day I see the painting in Rekha's gallery. In a single moment, the facts come together, there is a spark, a flash of fire that illuminates everything for me, so that I know that the woman in the painting is the woman I saw in Babu's room that day, I know the painter is the man who was my father's friend. I also know that he was the child Leela spoke of, the child her father had had by another woman. 'He was a sculptor or something like that,' Leela had said, 'he died young, he committed suicide, he hanged himself.'

Later, much later, when it is all over and we are on our own, Som and I, with nothing to break the silence, the deadness between us, I speak to Som, I tell him the things I'd left unsaid earlier. Even then it is not easy. It is hard to speak of something that happened without words, there are no words to frame it in. I see it in my mind like a silent, wordless play unfolding itself, an almost ascetic union of two bodies, the eroticism played out not in lush arabesques, but in spare, straight lines.

Nevertheless, I speak to Som. I tell him that I did not speak of this incident to him, not because I wanted to conceal it from him, but because I had lost it, I had misplaced it in the chaos of my life after my father's death. Memory denied it, put it away.

Som listens to me silently until I am done. He says nothing even after that. Both of us know it is too late for these revelations, for any explanations.

I've had much time since then to think of these things, I can see the past more clearly now than I did then. And I know that even if I had forgotten what happened to me as a child, it came back to me in occasional dreams, light, like wisps of cotton floss, scarcely touching me. It was there, a feather-touch on my skin, when Som and I made love, manifesting itself like a ghostly twin that almost, but not quite, replicated the present moment. But it was never real, it was always like a dream, always like some memory of a past life.

In any case, even if I had remembered, it would have made no difference. After Adit died none of it mattered, neither what I told Som or what I didn't. Nevertheless, I had to speak, to close the door that had been left ajar, so that we could be free to deal with the fact of our son's death.

17

Bai is back home and the household has reverted to its routine as if nothing has happened. The only visible signs of change are the two nurses. The only one I meet, the day nurse, has been so quickly absorbed by the household, it is as if she has always been here. She's sitting by her patient when I go to see Bai, reading a book—murder stories, I imagine, from the lurid covers of terrified women and bloodstained knives. When she sees me, she smiles, and putting away her book, a marker neatly marking her page, she goes away. I hear her speaking to the cook, the soft murmurs of their conversation occasionally interrupted by the child's high voice, which is quickly hushed.

Lying in bed, Bai's wasted frame reveals no other handicap than her age. But when she wakes up, when she opens her eyes and tries to speak, when she tries to make herself understood, this illusion is shattered. This woman, struggling to make herself understood, is in pain—not a physical pain like Leela's was, but the pain of helplessness, of losing a part of oneself.

I have to wonder again: is there no one else for Bai but these paid employees? Are they the only people left for her? I think of Leela in her shabby little room and of how we were all with her in those last days—Shantabai, Sunanda, Rajani, Som, Tony, Rekha. I remember the group that gathered on the thirteenth day after her death, not only her students, her protégés, her colleagues and her neighbours, but even people like Phillo's sister and nephew—all of us united by the memory of Leela. For Bai it will be, as Hasina said, condolence messages (to whom will they be addressed?), journalists and glowing obituaries.

But I am wronging Hasina by thinking of her as a paid employee. She's in charge of the household now, openly so, dealing with the doctors, the nurse, the physiotherapist, seeing that Bai has her medicines, helping the nurse and the physiotherapist with Bai. I hear her speaking to Bai in a low comforting tone when she is struggling to say something and I think: why are you doing this? And slowly, through the days, I begin to understand the complex ties that bind these two women together. 'She's a great musician,' Hasina said to me. 'I've been her student for fifteen years.' But this is not the whole answer. It's the past that links them together, it is their history which includes the same man.

It seems odd to be able to speak to Hasina without fear of interruption. It's Hasina who initiated these conversations. 'I want to talk,' she said. 'I can't leave the house, can you come here in the afternoons? I'm a little free at that time.'

So I do. The house is quiet then, the nurse dozing by Bai's side, the cook and her child somewhere at the back. Hasina has cast aside her reserve, the night of vigil when we shared the fear of Bai's death has opened the door between us and she speaks freely to me—of her grandfather, most of the time. She knows that Bai has not spoken of him to me at all, she is aware that even in that silence some information has been given, which she wants to correct.

'I know you will have heard stories about him,' she tells me. 'There are so many stories and most of them are false. I know him better than anyone else, I can give you the truth about him.'

She, his favourite granddaughter, was the one closest to him in the last years of his life, he spoke to her of much that he never did to anyone else. These are the things she wants to talk to me about. It soon becomes obvious that she's not trying to put Bai in the wrong, nor has she any intention of maligning her. She only wants to set the record straight. So she says.

If I have thought of him at all, it has been as Munni's father, as Bai's lover, as the kind man who lived next door. Hasina sketches out the artist to me, Ghulam Saab the tabla player, who was the best in his time, according to her. He was incomparable, '*lajawab*' she calls him, there was no one with his skill or knowledge, she says. His fingers were magical, they could weave complex taal patterns with ease and fluency. Nevertheless, he held his own art in rein, kept it tethered to the singer's needs, never impinging on the singer's right to lead. He did not play the game of one-upmanship so many tabla players do now, Hasina says. He was always the support, the prop.

'Without heartbeats, there's no life,' Hasina quotes him as saying. 'But you don't need to be conscious of the heartbeats.'

Enormous as her pride is in her grandfather's stature as a tabla player, however eager she is to share this with me, it's more important for her to correct the idea that I have of his role in Bai's life. It upsets her that Bai has been silent about him, it hurts her to think that I may know him only as Bai's lover.

He's the one who helped her to get where she did, Hasina says, he's the one who made her what she became. Bai speaks as if her Guruji was the only one who shaped her, but Ghulam Saab did more, much more. There's the famous story of Bai selling her gold bangles to pay her Guruji when he took her on as a pupil. Hasina smiles as she speaks of this and tells me that this is only part of the story. Bai's bangles may have paid Guruji's fees, but it was Ghulam Saab who earned the money for their survival, for their living. He worked as an accompanist, he worked for a while in a professional drama troupe, he worked with a music director for films, he gave music lessons.

'You know Shivji was his student?' she asks me.

Shivji? Oh, yes, the tabla-playing twin.

'He was one of the students my grandfather taught when he

lived here.'

There's more, according to Hasina. Ghulam Saab was the one who made Bai known. He met people on her behalf, he arranged her programmes, he made the contacts for her. It was not easy for a woman to do these things then; it's not easy even now, Hasina adds after a pause. Without Ghulaam Saab, Bai would never have been able to manage this part of her professional life.

Hasina does not tell me why they parted. When I ask her, she says she does not really know. He never spoke of it to her. All that she knows is that one day he returned home, to the family he had deserted.

And his wife took him back?

'What choice did she have?' Hasina asks simply.

Obviously, there was no question of forgiveness or reconciliation. He came back to his place in the family, that's all. But the family had changed by then. The girls were married, the sons too were men with their own families. Ghulam Saab was a changed man as well. There were stories being circulated that he had become a drunkard; these rumours had reached his family. But when he came home, they found that he had given up drink entirely. He had always been a devout Muslim, now his entire life seemed to be governed by the religious code.

His wife, an orthodox woman herself, should have been pleased, but Hasina says she wasn't. It was his vegetarianism—which began when he started living with Bai—that enraged her. She could have put up with drinking, but this—this linked him to that woman, his mistress, it was a constant reminder of the place she had had in his life.

'My grandmother was a very angry woman,' Hasina says. 'My mother used to say she had not always been that way.'

But years of living the life of an abandoned wife, of living on the charity of others, of bringing up children on her own, had embittered her.

'Even my mother hated Baiji,' Hasina tells me. 'That woman squeezed my father's heart like an orange, she used to say.'

Between Hasina and her grandfather there was a special relationship. Hasina's mother and her children visited the family home every vacation. These holidays were very special to Hasina because of her grandfather. There was something more powerful than the blood tie that bound these two, something apart from her being the only granddaughter that made the child precious to him. It was their common obsession with music that brought them close.

Ghulam Saab had given up the tabla when he left Bai and came home. But music was in the family, it was an intrinsic part of it; there had been musicians in every generation. Ghulam Saab's younger brother was a vocalist, one uncle had been a famous singer too, while Ghulam Saab's second son was a tabla player. It was the brother who coaxed Ghulam Saab into accompanying him when he sang, it was he who induced him to start teaching children.

Hasina was fascinated by these classes. The high, childish voices of the boys calling out the 'bols' of the taal enchanted her. She sat by her grandfather, a silent presence, watching him lead the children into the heart of the rhythm. She saw him clapping his hands as he counted the beats. She saw him guiding the children's fingers, gently massaging them when the children were tired. They took no notice of her presence, she was ignored, until the day her grandfather, needing the harmonium to be played on a note the boys could follow, told her to do it. Just put your finger on this key, he said, and this one.

She did it with ease. She became part of the group after that. She longed to learn the tabla herself, but her grandfather told her it was not for girls. Women can't play the tabla, he said. You need strength in your fingers, in your arms and your shoulders, he told her. Instead, he began to teach her vocal music.

He was a very good singer, do you know that? Hasina asks me. In fact, for some time, it was he who taught Bai.

And so the child begins. Music enters her soul, she longs for the vacations when she can go back to it. But both her mother and grandmother disapprove. The grandmother, after her husband's desertion, had turned away from music; she put her faith in education. Her children would be educated, they would become doctors, engineers, teachers, lawyers—even the girls would graduate. One son, however, disappointed her, taking up his father's profession. And now Hasina. But Hasina is adamant and, with her father's support, she gets her way. She starts classes in Bombay where they live. Later, when Ghulam Saab, after his wife's death, comes to Bombay to live with his son, he takes her to an old colleague, now a very respected singer, and asks him to take Hasina on as a student. It is clear by now that Hasina is good, that this will be her career.

It is in the last year of his life that Ghulam Saab breaks his silence and speaks to Hasina of Bai. The old man and the girl listen to her records and cassettes together. It's part of Hasina's education, he says, but she knows it's something more than that for him, it's an escape into his past. She's the best, he says. (He almost never uses Bai's name.) Listen, just listen, he says, holding up his finger when it comes to the point when she arrives at the 'sam'—the climactic point of the tala. 'Listen to that! Nobody can do it the way she does.'

And it's different each time—'Sometimes like thunder and a flash of lightning, sometimes like the tender meeting of two lovers.' Ghulam Saab's words.

'Listen to that control. That voice is pure metal, not alloy. You can draw it out like gold, to any length, any fineness.' Again Ghulam Saabs's words.

She also hears him playing the tabla for Bai in these records, though he never refers to it himself. She notices the ease and comfort with which they move together, the seamless union between the voice and the instrument.

It's much later that she brings Munni's name into our conversations. For so long has Munni been an unspoken shadow, that in my mind she has taken on the insubstantiality of a ghost, as if she never was a real person. Now, when Hasina speaks of her, the words bestow life on her and an excitement fills me. Yes, Munni did exist, Munni was real.

Ghulam Saab never ceased to mourn Munni, the daughter he lost. He often called Hasina 'Munni', angering his wife. 'Her parents have given her such a beautiful name, why can't you remember it?' she asked. It was after his wife's death that he unburdened himself to his granddaughter.

Hasina and I converse in Marathi, a language with which she's as comfortable as I am. But when she speaks of her grandfather's feelings for Munni, her Marathi takes on a different tinge, it seems to echo the Urdu in which the old man spoke to Hasina, and the emotions she speaks of are imbued with a more flamboyant colour. They're spoken of in terms of the body—the liver, the heart, the guts, the blood. I can understand this language very well, I know these are the right words to use. It is your heart, your guts, the blood coursing through your body, that speak of love. I sometimes think it is a disease that rages in your body, a disease that some of us lack the antibodies to fight.

I've seen Ghulam Saab's feelings for Munni. Now Hasina tells me of his grief at having lost her. He could not have spoken of this to anyone else in his family. His love for the child of his adulterous affair was a kind of betrayal of his wife, of the children of his marriage. But Hasina listened with sympathy, she understood him. It was after Munni went away, back to Pune, that he started drinking.

Remembering Munni's obsession with her 'father' in Pune, I am not surprised she went back there. What I'd really like to know is: did she go on her own, or was it her mother who sent her away? And again, why did Bai's in-laws accept the girl?

Actually, what arouses my curiosity even more is, why did they keep her with them at all for those first few years? Was it because they thought the child was the husband's? But if that was so, why did they send her away at all?

Hasina has no answers to these questions. Nor is she much interested in such things. Her interest in Munni is minimal; it does not go beyond her grandfather's love for her, his grief at having lost her. What she is offering me now is her memory of her grandfather, the man she loved and revered. 'I want you to know the truth about him,' she says over and over again. 'I want you to write the truth.'

Hasina is offering me her truths about her grandfather, but she calls it 'the truth', she wants me to accept it as *the* truth. I think of the seven blind men trying to describe the elephant, each one making a different discovery about the animal, each convinced that his knowledge about the elephant is the entire truth.

It's not a matter of making choices as I had thought. I have to discover my own truth which will encompass all the different bits of knowledge offered to me, which will make some sense of them. The tail, the trunk, the ears, the legs—yes, I have to put them together, I have to create an elephant out of these disparate bits.

I see now that it is possible that it was Ghulam Saab who left Bai and went away, that without his daughter there was nothing left for him in the relationship, and that, therefore, it was he who abandoned her. In any case, they never married, so it was not difficult for him to walk away. Why didn't they marry? If they had been married, they could have acknowledged their child openly. And he was a Muslim, it was possible for him to marry Bai, even though he had another wife living. For Bai, too, marriage would have been a boon, it would have given her the status of a married woman, saved

278

her from malicious gossip. And more—given her looks and her ambiguous marital status, it's not hard to imagine that she had to put up with a great deal of unwanted attention from men. When I think of women who, even today, speak of a relationship as a marriage, knowing very well it's not, who wear a mangalsutra to prove it, I am surprised Bai didn't succumb. Certainly, it would have made her life easier.

But I don't think they married, not even in secret. Nowhere in all the gossip about them, in all that is written about her, is there any hint of a marriage. Bai continued to remain a woman who was living separate from her husband, a woman living with a man she was not married to. Was it Bai herself who didn't press for it, Bai who didn't want it? After all, marriage was not so important for the man, his reputation would not suffer much from the fact of their living together without it. But if Bai had wanted marriage, if she had insisted on it, would Ghulam Saab have held back? So, was it Bai who didn't want to commit herself to yet another man, to yet another relationship, knowing she could not give much of herself to him? Was there more honesty in this?

Honesty—this is the second time I find myself stumbling on the word when I think of Bai. It came to me first when I thought of Bai's refusal to sing bhajans, to sing any devotional songs at all, despite her Guruji being a man to whom music was, above all, a means of devotion to God. She set her face against it, even when it became the fashion to include bhajans in a programme, when the audience expected and clamoured for devotional songs. Was it because Bai knew she did not have the faith and devotion she had seen in her Guruji that she refused, even at the cost of losing some popularity, to fall in with these demands?

'You plan out your programme—this raaga, this bandish—oh, so many things, then you find the right pitch and begin, but after that you never know where you will go,' Bai said to me once, speaking of her performances. 'All kinds of unexpected things can happen. You yourself are surprised.'

Yes, this is how it is when you're writing a book as well. I'm beginning to understand that it's not a question of planning, of deciding on the kind of book you're going to write, it's not a matter of making choices as I had thought. Plans go awry, rules are scattered, new discoveries lie in wait. But I think I've found the right pitch. Bai's honesty—yes, this gives me the note on which I can begin.

I wonder whether it's something that Chandru said or hinted at, but it seems to be taken for granted that I will be leaving Bhavanipur soon now.

'We'll miss you, Kaku,' Lata says. And then to Hari, 'We haven't taken Kaku out anywhere, we haven't shown her any of the places around. Let's plan something.'

Hasina too speaks as if my time here is coming to an end. 'I wish you didn't have to go, but I suppose there's nothing more to keep you here now.'

It's true, my work here is almost done. There's nothing more I can get out of Bai. And in any case, I have most of the information I need. Between Bai's scrapbooks and albums and my tapes of our conversation, I have enough material to construct Bai's life. These are the pieces of the jigsaw puzzle I can now start putting together. Yet, there is a sense of something lacking, of dealing with a story whose end I will never be able to offer. It's only with death that a life is complete; relationships then cease to be inchoate, they take on a definite shape. As long as even one of the parties to a relationship is alive, it can still change, take a different shape and form.

Am I waiting for Bai's death to begin writing about her? I draw back from the thought. It seems like treachery, not the idea of wanting her dead, but of wanting her to die for *my* purposes. For Bai herself, death can never be unwelcome. She is improving, she sits up a bit—Hasina has got her a wheelchair in which she sits for short periods—she looks more alert. This improvement is more than what the doctors expected. But her life is confined to the purely physical. Unable to speak, at least not coherently and clearly, her communication with the world has become minimal.

Much can be communicated without words, much can be said even in mime. So I have thought, so I have said to Tony. And it's true. Yesterday, Lata and I were suddenly halted at a cross road by another scooterist, who came unexpectedly at us out of a side road. Both Lata and he came to a screeching stop at almost the same moment. Then the man made a gesture that said, 'I'm going first'. And Lata, knowing he was wrong, knowing that she had the right of way, yet waved both her hands in a flowing gesture that said, 'Go ahead, it's all yours.' There was contempt and sarcasm in that gesture, all of which the man understood, so that when he started he was shamefaced, he waved his hands backwards in a kind of apology. I laughed in delight at the wordless spectacle which conveyed so much, and Lata, simmering with anger, asked me grumpily, 'What's so funny, Kaku?'

But even this is not possible for Bai. With her damaged brain, there's nothing left in her but the basic needs of the body. No, I'm wrong, there's still a spark that makes her go on, trying everything that the tireless Hasina and the nurse make her do. 'Gutsy old woman,' the young doctor says. And for some reason I find it offensive; there's something patronising about it, like a pat on a child's head. Why should he be surprised to find courage in an old person? Do people lose their human qualities, the traits that made them what they are, in the process of aging? Can't the aging body contain vestiges of an unchanged self? I see that self often in Bai. Disoriented, aphasic she may be, but she knows that these things are happening to her, she's sensitive about it, frightened at the way things are slipping away from her.

281

I'm with Bai almost every day now. She likes me to be with her. Hasina says she looks forward to my visits, she gets restless and impatient if I'm late. I can see the pleasure on her face when I arrive. My visit is not just part of her daily routine, like the doctor's visit or the physiotherapist's session, it means something more to her. She seems content when I'm with her. I go to her in the afternoons. When I get there, she's just woken out of her sleep and, washed and spruced, like a child being taken on an outing, she's settled in her wheelchair in the little veranda outside her room. She has a shawl wrapped round her shoulders, prepared for the slight nip in the air that will come on a little later. From where we sit, we can see the mango trees, covered now with tiny blossoms. I can feel the leaves a little sticky under my feet when I walk under the trees, as if the burgeoning sap is oozing out of these fallen leaves. Bai wants her share of this process of regrowth, of flowering. It takes me a while to understand what she is saying. Finally I get it. She wants '*panha*'—the raw mango sherbet.

'You'll have to wait, Bai. The mangoes are still to come. There are only the flowers as yet.'

'I can't wait, no time left for me.'

Yes, I can understand this too. 'No time left for me.' Even if she has lost words, she hasn't lost touch with the reality of her impending end.

I see her struggling for my name one day. It takes her a while. I don't help her, I know she doesn't like it. She gets it finally.

'Madhu.'

Impossible not to share her pleasure, her triumph.

'You're writing a book on me.'

'Yes.'

'Don't write about this old woman. No. No.'

The emphasis seems to exhaust her. After a moment she says something which I understand as 'This old woman, this is not me.'

No? Then which is the real Bai? The pampered child? The young girl who discovered what her life was going to be? The young woman who abandoned her child and eloped with her lover? The great musician, the successful Savitribai Indorekar?

All of them, of course. It's always a palimpsest, so many layers, one superimposed on another, none erased, all of them still there. I came here to see Munni's mother, the woman who lost her daughter, like I did my son. I thought that woman no longer existed. I thought Bai had successfully got rid of that person, Munni's mother, that she had cut the umbilical cord, severed it wholly, leaving no scar behind. Now I know better. I know that Bai lost her daughter long before she was blown to pieces. Hasina, searching for something, found Munni's wedding card and, knowing I would be interested, brought it to me. A showy red, frayed at the edges now, the letters in ornate gilt, almost undecipherable—a card like many others, but different in one thing: the bride was identified only by her father and grandfather. The mother's name nowhere. I thought there was something cruel about it, about the rejection of Bai as a mother, this erasing of her from her daughter's life.

'If I were you,' Hari said to me, 'if I were you, I'd write about Leela.'

But I can't. She's much too close to me, she's too much a part of me. And I find it hard to see Leela the trade unionist, Leela the activist, the rebel. Instead I see her, feet drawn up under her on her chair, peering through her glasses at her Marathi newspaper, I see her face when we heard Joe was dead, I see her in bed, her hair in a little pigtail, her hand in mine, talking to me of her past.

Bai should be easier, she's distant and remote enough, someone I can look at with detachment and indifference. But I've begun thinking that in writing about Bai, I'm writing about Leela as well. And my mother and all those women who reached beyond their grasp. Bai moving out of her class in search of her destiny as a singer, Leela breaking out of the conventions of widowhood, reaching out from her small room to the world, looking for justice for the weak, my mother running in her bare feet, using her body as an instrument for speed, to break out of the shackles, finally triumphantly breasting the tape—yes, they're in it together. But they paid the price for their attempts to break out. Munni's rejection was the price Bai paid, Munni who yearned for the commonplace, the ordinary, and stifled everything that connected her to her parents. I know now that Munni is with Bai still—at the edge of her consciousness, maybe, but she is there. Bai put her grief away like my father did his after my mother's death, storing it in the cupboard with the cups she won, while he went on with his life. Bai lost her daughter, but her life moved on. Even today, sick, old, dying, childless, when everything seems to have ended for her, she's not wholly bereft.

I find her in the music room one afternoon, her chair placed in the archway that divides the room, listening to Hasina. It's not one of the student's classes, nor is it her *riaz*. It sounds like the preparation for a programme. Abhay is there with the tanpura, as are the twins at their instruments. Just as I get there Hasina comes to the end of the alaap, the tabla enters into it, rhythm joins the music and its pace quickens. There's something tentative about all of them, as if they're unsure, as if they're trying out something. There are interruptions during which Hasina speaks to the twins and Abhay listens with concentration. Bai is watching this in rapt attention. All the music I've been listening to in the last few months encourages me to ask Bai, 'Yaman?'

She nods, pleased that I've got the raaga right. I'm pleased too. I go back to listening. The next time I steal a look at Bai, she is crying. Silent tears, the face crumpled like a child's, nose running. I wipe her face but the tears keep flowing, the nose drips. The easy tears of the old and the sick. Is she remembering herself doing this, remembering when she was part of it, bound in a tight group as these four are?

When Hasina comes to the end, she gets up and comes to Bai. Bai has recovered, there's no trace of her tears. She says something to Hasina, something I can't understand. But Hasina does, she calls the twins and tells them what Bai has said. Appreciative words, I imagine, for they bend down and touch her feet. Hasina wheels Bai away to her room and comes back to me, her face alive with excitement. She tells me her news. She's going to sing for Guruji's death anniversary this year. Bai had suggested her name and last night it was finalized.

'My first big performance,' she says. 'My first chance to prove myself, to show the world what Baiji has given me.'

'Now you can't go until my programme is over, you have to hear me sing.'

Hasina is sprouting shoots of excitement, radiating flashes of happiness, words and emotions pouring out of her. I could never have imagined her this way. This is her first big chance, she tells me. Fifteen years she's been with Bai as her student, occasionally, and only in the last three or four years, accompanying her as her *saathi*. She's sung by herself too, but only at a few small programmes.

'Baiji kept saying—wait a little, you're not ready, not yet. I wondered if my time would ever come. And now this—to sing for Guruji's *punyatithi*! Baiji did this for me, it was she who asked them to invite me this year.'

Hasina's presumption that I know what this event is, that I know how significant it is, leaves dots and dashes which are filled in by Lata. It's an all-night performance at the Bhavani temple, a tradition that began the first year after Guruji's death as a homage by his students to their teacher. Guruji's most famous student, Rashid Mian, sang that year; since then, each year one of his disciples has given a performance. Lata tells me she has attended the performances since she was a child, she's rarely missed a year. Everyone in Bhavanipur is there, she says. It's a great occasion for the town, she tells me, musicians from all over India come to attend it.

Bai's house now throbs with music all day. And, like in Neemgaon, the doors are open throughout the day, with people walking in and out all the time and piles of footwear in the hall. I become part of it, taking phone calls, sitting by Bai, making tea when there is a sudden call for it and the cook is busy.

'You shouldn't,' Hasina murmurs when I take the tea to them, but it is an absent-minded, polite demur. She's too caught up in planning the programme, in choosing her pieces and preparing them with her accompanists to think of anything else. She's found an old book of Bai's with Guruji's song-texts in it. I see them exclaiming over the book, trying out some lines, the harmonium twin's fingers flying nimbly over the keys, trying out the notes.

Hasina is using the same team. 'We've worked together for over a year,' she says. 'My grandfather used to say he would play the tabla for my first performance. And see how lucky I am! Here is Shivji who was his student.'

Hasina's total focus on her music puts everything else in the shade; even Bai takes a back seat. But when Bai wakes up one morning, unable to move, her eyes terrified, her bed foul-smelling, Hasina is distraught.

'Don't die, Baiji, don't die,' she pleads. 'I want you to live, I want you to be here when I sing. I want you to know I'm singing where you did, where your Guruji did.'

It's another stroke, there's nothing that can be done, the local doctor tells Hasina. Don't hospitalize her, Chandru advises her on the phone. She may be better in a day or two—if she doesn't die, that is. This last, Chandru says to me, not to Hasina, but the words hang in the air between us, they hover around Bai's bed. And Bai does improve, though she's marginally worse than what she was before this stroke. For Hasina, it's enough that she's alive. She rings Chandru up every evening, to her it's this connection with Chandru that's working the miracle, keeping Bai alive.

A miracle? If it were not for Hasina, I would pray for Bai's death, for her to be relieved from this degradation. I'm amazed at the strength of her life, at the perversity of nature that keeps her going.

'I'd rather die than live helpless, dependent, unable to do anything for myself.'

I'm sure Bai, like most humans, has had this thought. But now that death is near, I can see fear in her eyes. I see her clutching at life, afraid to let go, struggling to come out of the corner her illness has pushed her into. Her agitation drives her into trying to speak, but no words emerge, they're just sounds. Her eyes keep moving to the music room; is she trying to say something about Hasina?

'Hasina is preparing for her programme, for Guruji's *punyatithi*, you know, you arranged that yourself,' I tell Bai. I make an attempt to speak to her as I would to a normal adult, sure that she can hear, that she can understand.

No, that's not it, it's something else that's troubling her. The eyes are agonized, appealing.

'Don't worry, Bai, it'll be all right. Don't worry.'

Can anyone sick and dying accept these facile words of comfort? What's all right? I remember my own anger when they said it to me after Adit's death, when they assured me it would soon be all right.

'What do you think it is that's worrying her?' I ask Hasina when she comes in, as she does every now and then, to check on her.

But Hasina can't help. In fact, she's unable to take interest in anything but her own preparations. She's in a highly tensile state, moving between trepidation and eagerness. Looking forward to the day, but frightened of facing the audience. Gratified at the number of musicians who're coming, yet terrified of failing, of being judged harshly by them.

Hasina has been preparing for this moment for a long time, she's ready for it, and in spite of her fears, her professionalism asserts itself. I realize this when Ravi Patil, who's also the Chief Trustee of the temple, comes to me with a proposal. Maya's idea, really, he says. They want me to write an article about the event, about Bai and Hasina. Maya thinks it could be a curtain-raiser for the book, Ravi himself thinks it's good publicity for the event. It has been losing its importance, he tells us, not many people from outside Bhavanipur come for the programme. This year, in Bai's final days, Ravi wants to revive its old glory.

I'm surprised by Hasina's enthusiasm. I've regarded her as a reticent, a very private person. But now she's ready to tell me whatever I want to know—about Bai, about herself. She gets me two pictures of herself to go with the article. I can scarcely recognize her in the pictures, a woman with shaped eyebrows, make up, Benaras sari and jewels. But this is the woman she's going to present to the world, this is the singer who's been waiting in the wings for her cue to emerge.

I will do the article, won't I, she asks anxiously. Maya is going to see that it is published in a national paper, all that I have to do is to write it.

Yes, I tell her, I will do it. But I need to visit the temple once, I've never seen it as yet.

'We'll take you, Kaku,' Lata offers. 'I'm ashamed we haven't done it as yet. Let's go on Sunday.'

But on Sunday Lata wakes up a little feverish. So it's only Hari and I who set out on his motorbike for the Bhavani temple.

It comes out of the blue. We've turned off the main road on to a narrow one, asphalted once, but worn down in places to its foundations now, so that the surface is pocked with pits of all sizes and shapes.

'Hold tight,' Hari tells me. 'This is a tricky patch, but it gets better in a while.'

He keeps swerving to avoid the potholes, saying 'sorry' after each one of these manoeuvres. The road is so narrow that the oncoming traffic—bullock carts and motorcycles like Hari's mostly—pushes us almost into the fields that edge this road. Whatever it is that's growing here—I can't guess, all the plants look alike to me—is waist high. It's quiet, we've left the buses and trucks behind us on the highway and the sound of Hari's motorbike is like a small part of the silence. Once or twice we meet men on bicycles who smile at him. He raises his hand slightly from the handlebar in return. His work takes him into these villages, he tells me, people around here know him.

When Hari slows down, at first I think it's because of the slight inclination. Then I see that there's a branch fallen across the road. Right across, so that there's no way we can go on. It does not strike me as odd, the way it's fallen, completely barring our passage.

'Damn,' Hari says and gets off. So do I. He cuts off the engine and there is a sudden silence. The birds are suddenly audible—and the rustling in the fields. Even as I take this sound in, figures rush out of the field and we are surrounded by men. It takes us so much by surprise that I don't realize for a moment that they're after us. But Hari does. At once. He climbs back on his bike. 'Get on, Madhu,' he shouts. But it's too late. They're on us. Someone pushes me away, pushes me down, I feel a blow on my back, I'm down on the ground, I can see only feet, I can hear sounds of blows, grunts. I can't get up, there's something lying on me, something on my foot, I hear a scream—who is it?

And then there's silence. The men have gone. I can feel an

agonizing pain in my foot; it takes me a moment to understand what has happened, that my foot is lying under the wheel of Hari's bike. I try to get up, I pull my foot out from under it with a jerk that sends pain hammering through me. But I'm free. I can see Hari lying a little distance away, his arm flung out at an odd angle from his body.

'Hari . . .?'

He opens his eyes. Thank God! Oh, thank God, he's alive. My body breaks out into a sweat, the breeze dries it in an instant, I find myself shivering.

'I think they've hurt . . . they've broken my arm,' he says, still not making any attempt to get up.

When I try to help him up, a small moan escapes him.

'No, no, don't, I'll manage myself.'

It's a struggle for him to stand up, but he does so, and with my support moves to the side of the road, leans against a neem tree and then, sliding down, collapses at its foot. I can see huge globules of sweat breaking out on his face as he tries to contend with the pain. For the first time I see the bone pushing through his shirt sleeve. I feel a little sick at the sight, but I've got to help him, I can't afford the luxury of fear.

I go back to his bike. I can't pick it up, it's too heavy, but luckily the water container is intact. I give him a glass to drink, wet the end of my dupatta and wipe his face with it.

'Is it very bad?'

What kind of a question is that, his look seems to ask me. I look around for help. We are in the middle of fields with no sign of human habitation. I can't leave him alone and go, I have to wait, hoping someone will arrive soon. I can hear voices, but they're obviously at a great distance, for the entire landscape, as I see it, is without any humans.

When I come back to Hari, I see his head has dropped on his chest. He's fainted. I'm glad for him: let him escape the pain for a while. But when the stillness continues, I'm frightened.

'Hari? Hari? Hari!'

I sprinkle water on his face, dab at it again with my dupatta. His eyes open, vague, disoriented for a moment, then clear.

'I'm sorry. Just the pain. Don't be frightened.' He looks at his arm. 'Can you put it back inside?' He speaks as if his bone is an object like a watch or a purse that's fallen out of his pocket.

'What?'

'Push it back in.'

'But Hari, I think it's a fracture, not a dislocation.'

'What?'

'Best leave it alone. We'll get help soon, we'll get you to a doctor.'

He closes his eyes again, he begins to moan. No, he's mumbling. It's the Surya-namaskar. '*Om Suryaya namaha,*' he begins and goes on in perfect order. I find myself saying it along with him, mechanically, unthinkingly.

'*Om Adityaya namaha.*'

Adit, doing the Surya-namaskar, grinning at me when he comes to his name. Adit swooping down on the floor, his hands held before him in an absolute straight line . . .

I move away. Behind me, Hari's murmurs trail away. There's such a silence around us, it's as if we're cut off from all humanity. Where is everyone? Why doesn't someone come?

'Hari,' I whisper, just to break the silence, merely to hear his voice.

'I'm okay.'

And then I hear the sounds of a motorbike. Thank God. I'm getting up when he calls me. 'Madhu.' His voice is urgent, like a hand gripping mine tightly. 'Madhu, don't tell anyone what happened. Say it was an accident.'

I can see the bike approaching me, there are two men on it. Suddenly, when they're near, there's a moment of fear. What if they're the same men come back to make sure? But it's too late. They've seen me, they get off, they take in the fallen bike, the branch, Hari lying under the tree. And thank God, they're not the same men.

'What happened?' one of them asks me in Kannada. 'Accident?'

'Yes, an accident.'

Both of us use the English word 'accident'. In any case, I couldn't have said anything else. I don't know enough Kannada to say anything more.

It's late evening. I've only just switched on the lights when Lata comes home. They've operated on Hari's arm, he'll be all right, she says. Right now he's sleeping, sedated. Her uncle is there, as also two of Hari's friends. She'll be going back there to stay the night, she's come home merely to tell me about Hari, to see how I am.

'How are you, Kaku? How is the foot?'

'Better. They tell me there's no serious damage. The swelling should go down by tomorrow. I'm quite all right.'

But she's not reassured. She won't let me get up, she won't let me do anything. She's full of guilt.

'I didn't even ask you how you were, I was thinking only of Hari, I was so selfish. It was Ravi who told me you were hurt as well and I was so ashamed of myself, Kaku.'

Ravi took good care of me, I tell her. He did everything that was necessary, he brought me home, he made me comfortable. But she refuses to accept my reassurance, she's determined to make up for her selfishness, as she calls it. I have to sit and watch her cook a quick meal for the two of us, rice and *pithla*. Leela's crisis meal, the only thing she could cook. And Joe's joke, that she went so often to her room in Maruti Chawl so that she could eat her own *pithla* and rice.

'Come, Kaku, let's have dinner.'

There's something calming about sitting down to a meal as if nothing has happened. The tumult in my mind dies down, the darkness that had surrounded me since the men pushed me down, lifts a little. But when we've finished dinner, Lata goes back to the incident, she wants to know what happened.

Don't tell anyone, Hari said, and I haven't. An accident, I said. Hari was trying to avoid the branch when he lost his balance and . . .

But Lata is Hari's wife, she has to know. I tell her all of it, including Hari's insistence that I say it was an accident.

'But everybody knows what happened, Kaku. That's why Ravi came rushing to the hospital almost immediately after I got there. There's a police officer waiting to question you. Ravi told them you were hurt, he asked them to put it off till tomorrow.'

I'm surprised by her composure. When she came to the hospital, she had been frantic with terror, her face wild, her body declaring its agitation in a million movements.

'But that was because I didn't know what was wrong; it's not knowing that's terrible,' she says. 'Now that I know, I can cope. When they told me there was an accident, I thought Hari was dead. I'm always scared of his dying, Kaku. I wake up in the middle of the night sometimes, thinking he's dead. Then I hear his breathing and I think—thank God. This is no way to live, is it, Kaku?'

'No, it isn't.'

'When I was a girl, I swore to myself that I wouldn't get caught in this . . . this *chakkar*. Then Hari came.' She pauses for a moment. 'I've never spoken of this, of my fears, to anyone, not even to my father, I'm so ashamed of myself. I know I'm foolish and unreasonable.'

Her fear, she tells me, began when she knew that Hari was living on only one kidney. He had donated one to his mother.

'She refused, she said she wouldn't take it, she wouldn't allow him to do it, but he threatened to donate it to the worst human being he could find.' Lata smiles as she says this. 'Hari was only twenty then, he told me about it before we got married. I had a right to know, but I shouldn't worry about it, he said; a person can live just as well with one kidney. I know that now, I read about it, I asked my sister about it. And yet, since then, I'm always scared. Thank God you were with him, Kaku. What if he'd been alone?'

But if he had been alone, maybe it wouldn't have happened. Or would it? We don't know. We do know, however, that Hari was not the real target, his body was only the instrument the men used to send out a message: Hasina can't sing in the temple. This was the anonymous message Ravi received that sent him rushing to the hospital.

Lata's cousin is coming to stay the night so that I won't be alone. To protect me—the words are not said, but they are understood. I protest, I'm all right, I tell her, but Lata is serious. She checks all the doors and windows before she leaves. I wait then for her cousin who, when he comes, turns out to be a scrawny teenaged boy, so nervous with me—what has Lata told him?—that I have to smile at the thought of him being my protector.

When I go to bed, I think of Lata's words, 'Then Hari came . . .' Three words which, to me, have the poignance, the force, of a line of poetry. Three words in which she has revealed to me the core of her existence, something that all the torrent of words between us has not been able to do.

18

Hari's arm, set in plaster and supported by a sling, proclaims his handicap, which he tries to play down. 'I'm all right,' he says to me. 'Nothing to worry.'

Nevertheless, he is irritable, more I imagine because of the dependence, the inability to do things for himself, than because of any residual pain. I admire Lata for the way she deals with him and the situation. I'd have thought she would get into a flap, but she refrains from fussing and leaves him, for the greater part, to manage himself, though clearly it calls for an effort on her part. She even goes back to work the day after he comes home from the hospital. I can see she's reluctant to go, but she conceals it from him, only her fervent 'Thank God you're here, Kaku' revealing it.

But there's little I can do for him. In fact, there's nothing that he will allow me to do. I tell him about Leela's panacea for any pain or illness—a glass of Horlicks. 'I don't know where she got the idea, but you know how these things are sometimes, it got fixed in her mind: a glass of Horlicks will make you well. When she brought it to you, you knew she was really worried about you.'

Hari laughs. 'I'm okay. No Horlicks for me. If there's something I'd like, it's a cigarette. I'd give anything for a smoke at this moment.'

It's three years now since he gave up smoking, he tells me, but even now, at certain times, at certain moments, the longing for a smoke returns, the smell haunts him; like a phantom it accompanies him wherever it goes.

'Just one, I tell myself, but I know it won't stop at one. So I resist.'

He's more relaxed after this confession and so am I, now that I know his irritation is not connected to pain, but to this itch to smoke. We speak of the accident for the first time since it happened.

'At first it seemed to me that they were coming for you,' he says.

We wonder then whether they thought I was Hasina. I was wearing a salwar kameez that day, perhaps it was this that misguided them?

'But Hasina wears saris!'

'Oh well, you know the stereotypes we live with. She's a Muslim, therefore she would be wearing a salwar kameez.' And then he asks me, hesitantly, did he faint? He has a vague memory of a blackout . . .

'Yes, you did.'

'It must have scared you.'

I confess to him my shame that I could not help him, that I could not even look at the bone sticking out of his sleeve.

'You kept telling me to push it back inside . . .'

'I know. The doctor tells me I said the same thing to him. I had a strange feeling that the bone was not part of me, that once it disappeared from view, I would be fine.'

We're now interrupted by a visitor. There has been a constant stream of visitors for Hari since the news of the attack on him spread. The threat, that Hasina would not be allowed to sing in the temple, is now openly known. The police have tried to persuade Ravi to change the programme, but he is adamant. No, he will *not* cancel the programme, he will *not* get someone else instead of Hasina, he will *not* convert a public performance into a small closed-room one. It's going to be like it always was, he insists.

It's Hasina who has been unhappy at the thought of causing trouble, she's been dithering. She's here now to speak to Hari, to apologize to him, she says.

'What for?'

The parrot, which had set up a squawking when Hasina entered, suddenly falls silent.

'It's because of me that you were attacked. Those blows were meant for me. They must have thought Madhu was me.'

I find it hard to extract a single thread from the tangled skein of memories of that day. The only clear memory that comes to me is that of anger—anger at being forced to crouch on the ground, at the ignominy of my position, down there among all those trampling feet. But there's nothing that tells me I was the focus, the target of the attack. In fact, they pushed me aside—or was it Hari who did that? He can't remember, either.

'But what does it matter now? It's over. And in no way are you responsible for what happened.'

'I've told Patil saheb I'm not going to sing.'

'And he's accepted your decision?'

'N—n—no. But once he understands that I'm not going to change my mind, I think he will . . .'

Hari tells her of Lata's theory that this is the work of outsiders, he tells her of Lata's faith in Bhavanipur. He agrees with her, he says. This is the work of politicians who're trying to extract some advantage for themselves out of this. The elections are in a few months . . .

'What does it matter who's behind these things? The results are the same. I'm scared, Haribhai. My parents live in Bombay, my mother was so shocked after the riots, she fell ill. It's always the innocent who suffer, I don't want anyone to die, I don't want people to suffer because of me . . .'

Abruptly I go to my room. I can hear Hasina's voice, Hari's, the parrot's deep guttural croaks that sound like snores. The murmurs cease, the door bangs. The parrot starts again, stops. There is complete silence in the house. Hari comes to my room.

'Madhu?'

I see from his face that he knows, he knows why I left the room.

'Do you want to speak of it?'

I look dumbly at him.

'I remember, very vaguely, reciting the Surya-namaskar that day. It's like a dream, but I can remember that you got up and walked away when I said '*Adityaya namaha*'. Is it so hard even to hear your son's name?'

After all these days, after so many months, suddenly it's time for me to confront the chaos, to make sense of it, to speak of it, to convert the fractured images, the vague shapes and sounds into a coherent word pattern. Certain images still escape me, they whirl around in a dark, chaotic maelstrom. The final moments of madness between Som and me, when I, driven to desperation by the wildness of a man I could no longer recognize, cried out loudly. The pain and darkness in my head, the thudding sound—was it Som banging my head against the wall, or was I doing it to myself? And then Adit's face, his anguished face, his panicked cries. And who was it who cried out, 'Go away, Adit'? Was it Som, or was it I? Whose voice was it that drove him away, that sent him to his death? At times—more often—it is my own voice I hear shouting at Adit, telling him to go away, at other times, it's Som's voice that says those words. Did Adit come to us, did he come between us, did he try to stop the senseless violence? I don't know. I can only remember the sudden silence, the cessation of all sound, the emptiness in my head that only moments ago had been full of pain and darkness. And Som's blank face, the rage that had suffused him for so long, spent, leaving behind a hollow man.

These are the things I can't speak of, these are the things I don't speak of to Hari. I begin with the waiting, the two days and two nights of waiting for Adit to return, the two days and two nights of sitting by the phone, waiting for it to ring, waiting for Adit's voice to speak. But after that first night, when it rang four times, and I heard Adit's voice once, it was never Adit.

'He's a going out with the tide . . .'

We no longer believe that there are any links between our lives and the ebb and flow of the sea, the movements and conjunctions of the planets, the phases of the moon. Yet, at times, an ancient belief struggles through the layers of reason and reason itself wonders: placed as we are in the midst of all these phenomena, knowing how they are all connected, how can we alone not be linked to the rhythms of the universe? Why do we imagine that we humans are set apart from the rest of creation which is linked in so many mysterious ways we can never hope to decipher? Why is the unseen and the unknown the impossible to us?

December, January, February—mobs running amok in the city. These things have never happened before, not this way. I have heard Leela speak of what happened after Independence—in '47, '48. But this time there is a difference. There's a sense of an efficient malignant force at work, working out its plans through these mobs. Even we, who live in our safe middle-class apartments, way above the ground, can feel the subterranean rumblings. Even I, caught up in my conflict with Som, can see the difference when I go out on the streets. For thirty years I've moved about in this city and never once known fear. But now, it lies like a pall above us. The streets are almost deserted at night, and those who have to be out look nervously over their shoulders and walk at a rapid pace. Hostility, suspicion and anger, which have become a part of my life at home with Som, are waiting for me when I go out of the house as well. There's a miasma, the smell of disaster in the air, but we are still free of it, still immune to it. Or so we think.

It is the third day of our waiting for Adit. We have lived through two days and nights of his absence, of not knowing where he is, nights choked with fear and grief. But there's hope, too; he will come back, surely he will return home, any moment he will be here with us. Som has gone out, I don't know where, and I am alone at home. It is so silent that I can hear the two clocks ticking, two separate sounds, the time in the two never merging. For me, it is like two different racks on which I am stretched, each moment, each ticking second, one more since Adit left, one more without his return.

I am sitting by the phone, as I have been since that first night. The first time I picked up the phone that night, I heard Adit's voice, I knew it was Adit, though I could not get a word of what he was saying. It rang again, three times after that, but each time there was only silence. Nevertheless, I knew that each time it was Adit on the line. I spoke to the silence, I pleaded with it. 'Come home, Adit, come home, Adit, please come home.' I cried out the same words over and over again. What else was there that I could say to him, what more did I want to say, anyway? The final, the fourth time it rang, Som took the phone from my hand, he pulled it out of my tightly grasping hand and held it to his ear.

'There's no one,' he said. 'It's dead.'

He didn't understand, it *was* Adit, I could identify even the silence as Adit's. It didn't matter to me that he did not speak; he could hear me, he could hear my voice, that was enough. And I had to speak, I knew I could convince him to come back home.

All day I sat by the phone. Each time it rang, I picked it up on the instant. And when it was neither Adit, nor his silence, I put it back, keeping my hand tightly pressed on it, shutting off all those voices clogging the phone, preventing Adit from reaching us. And then, remembering that, perhaps, even at that moment, Adit was trying to get through, I took my hand off the phone and waited for it to ring, for Adit's voice to come to me.

Now all that has ended. I have almost given up hope of hearing Adit's voice on the phone. It rings repeatedly, but it's always for Som, patients each time, asking me where Som is. And repeatedly, a voice that gives no name, saying, 'Tell doctor-saab not to go out today, tell doctor-saab to stay at home.'

For the first time I begin to notice something odd, the silence not only in our flat, but outside. An eerie lack of sound. The world has changed for us, we no longer have any routine left. These two days have distanced us from it so much that it lies at an immeasurable distance. And so, at first it does not sink in, the fact that the silence has given way to sounds, sounds of cars driving in, doors slamming, the lift moving up and down, children's feet running along the corridors, children's voices calling out—children who should have been at school at this time. All these sounds, unusual for the time of the day, are like the untimely flight of birds frightened by something.

The door of our flat opens and the phone rings at almost the same time as Som enters. He picks it up and listens. Something in his expression startles me, I get up in one wild flurried movement. Adit! He sees me, he makes a gesture that says 'no, it isn't Adit'. He listens, he nods, he says no more than 'Thik hai, thik hai'. When he puts it down he tells me it was someone asking him not to go out. To stay at home. He tells me then what has happened in the city, what is happening to it. He tells me of the bombs that have gone off across the city, a series of macabre bonfires lighting it up. The Stock Exchange Building, he says. Air India . . .

I listen to him, not really interested in what he is saying. What has this to do with Adit? It's Adit I'm waiting for, it's news of him I want. I say so to Som and he listens without a word. We sit across each other at the table, both of us silent, both of us waiting. A little later, he puts his head down on the table. Is he crying? Is there something he hasn't told me? I shake him, I rouse him out of it, but there are no tears on his face. Just blankness. Some time in the evening, the bell rings. Som opens the door and comes back to tell me he is going out, he will be back in a while. I wait, I don't know for how long. Time has ceased ticking, I can no longer hear the sounds, as if both the clocks have stopped. I can hear only the pounding in my head, the blood singing in my ears—these are the clocks counting the minutes for me now.

Later—how much later?—they come in. Chandru, Tony and Som. Yes, Som is with them, it is his face I look at. And in an instant I know what they have come to tell me, I know what they are going to say. I don't want to know, I don't want to hear the words. I can't remember what I say or do, I can only remember a voice calling out my name over and over again, someone sobbing. And then silence again.

They say your identity is stamped on every cell of your body, your signature is all over it. Did they see Adit's name when they collected the limbs and gave them my son's name? They say you can't be identified by your possessions. But they identified my son by his—his watch, his clothes, his ring . . .

The flat is crowded. I'm surrounded by people, people crying, sitting silently, speaking to me, putting their arms about me. None of it reaches me. Somewhere, in the labyrinthine tunnels of my mind, I can hear the phone ringing, I can hear the silence that is Adit. I'm still sitting by the phone, I allow no one else to pick it up. But each time I take it, there are different voices, all of them saying the same things: *I heard the news. Is it true? I'm sorry . . . we are sorry . . . we're so sorry . . .*

What are they sorry about? What are all these people doing in our house? I want them to go away, to leave us alone. Adit won't come home until they've gone, I know that. And finally, thankfully, Som and I are left to ourselves.

'He's dead, Madhu. Our son is dead. Listen to me, just listen, he's dead. I cremated him myself. Adit is dead, Madhu, he's gone, stop waiting for him.'

I won't listen, I refuse to hear these words. They keep coming, Chandru, Tony, Rekha, Nisha, Rajani—even Phillo comes, her face, wet with tears, as swollen as her feet in her too-tight shoes. Ketaki holds me close, she cries, but it's like meeting an acquaintance from a past life. At last, tired of meeting my intransigence, understanding it's no use, they stop coming. Tony is the only one who won't give up.

'You must accept it, Madhu. Adit's gone. He won't come back. Cry for him, mourn him, but don't wait for him.'

I understand now what I have to do. It's not enough to believe he's alive, to say that the body they cremated was not Adit's. I have to do more, I have to go out and find him. I start going out every day, I begin looking for him. And one day I am rewarded, I see him. He's part of a crowd waiting at the traffic light to cross the road. Even as I move towards him, the lights change, the throng races across. I run after them, narrowly escaping collision with a taxi—the lights have changed again, the traffic comes roaring down the road, the taxi driver mouths curses at me. I am uncaring of everything but Adit. I must get to him, I must catch him. But he's disappeared.

It doesn't matter. I've seen him, he's alive. I say this to Som. I'll find him and bring him home tomorrow, I promise him. His face changes, I can gauge his disbelief, I can see pity for me on his face. But I go out the next day buoyed by hope. This time I'll get to him, I'll speak to him, I'll bring him back home. Som will see I am right, he'll realize I was always right. And yes, the next day I see Adit again, but once more it's only a glimpse. I see him board a bus, a bus that moves away before I can get near. It doesn't matter, I've noted the number of the bus. I take the next one, I go all the way to the terminus, but it's no use.

I'm not unhappy. The glimpse I had was reward enough. Now each morning I wake up with the hope, with the thought—I'll see Adit today. And I do. Flashing glimpses, but they keep me alive, they keep me going. I roam the streets till evening and then hurry back home, along with all those men and women returning at the end of a day's work. I sleep a sound dreamless sleep at night now—it's like a death almost—and in the morning, I join the army of workers once again. I am scarcely at home. I don't know who cooks, but there is food on the table when I return.

'Stop this,' Som pleads with me. 'Stop it, Madhu, it's madness.'

Tony begs me to go out for a holiday with him and Rekha. 'Just for a few days,' he says. 'It'll do you good,' he says. As if I'm ill, as if I'm a convalescent. Som and Chandru want me to take some pills, they want me to stay home, they beg me not to go out any more.

These people are shadows, their words only meaningless sounds. The only reality is my son, the sight of my son.

Then one day, all of a sudden, the sightings cease. I go to all the places where I've seen him, but there's nothing, nobody. It's the third day of my fruitless wandering. It's evening and I'm on the beach. How did I get here? I don't know how long I've been here, either. But I've been sitting here for so long that my back has become anaesthetized against the sharp hurting rock I'm leaning on, my body has hollowed out a home in the sand under me. I sit and watch the feet go past me. In a while it gets dark. I can feel, rather than see, the darkness. The voices become whispery strands flung about by the breeze, the sea is louder, the foreground to all the noises now, not the background. Occasionally a pair of feet pause before me, then move on. One pair does not go, it stands before me. I can hear a voice saying things, soft murmurs loaded with filth, obscenities. I feel a hand on my shoulder. I look up and in an instant the hands drop, the feet move on. Once again there's someone who won't go, another pair of feet, a different voice. But there are no obscenities this time. Instead, the voice is gentle, persuasive, saying, 'Go home, Bai, don't sit here, it's not safe.' This voice, this pair of feet, too, move on in a while.

Much later, I hear a voice and I look up instantly. For a moment I think it is my father, the face is like his in those last days when he struggled for each breath. But it's Som, his face as spent and exhausted as my dying father's. He does not speak. He puts out his hand. I get up and go home with him.

'Have a bath,' he says. When I come out of the bathroom, he's waiting at the dining table. There's only one plate—mine. Silently he watches me eat. 'Now go to bed,' he says. For some reason, I go to Adit's room, the room I've avoided all these days. And it is there, at the sight of the room I haven't entered for so long, a room tidied by someone, everything in its place—it's in this dead room that the madness ends for me. I know Adit is dead, I know he will never return.

If Som hears me sobbing, he doesn't come to me, he leaves me alone, like I left him to himself when I heard him sobbing the first night after Adit's death. I face the grief of our son's death alone as he did.

I can't go on, I have to stop. Hari has listened to me in silence. When I pause, he waits patiently. When the silence stretches, he makes a small movement. I restrain him with a gesture and continue with what I have to say. I tell him about how they haunt me, those last three days of his life. I can't come to terms with my ignorance of those days, I am obsessed by the need to reclaim them from the darkness. Sometimes I think I could have borne his death if I had been able to be with him, to see him die. We have a right to share it, the most profound human experience of death, with those we love, we have a right to be with them, to travel part of the way, even if we cannot go all the way. But I was denied that right, I was deprived of it. I don't know, I will never know how he faced the moment.

Once again I pause, and this time he remains still. He knows that there's something more I have to say.

They say, they all say that I've changed, that Som and I have changed. How can you not change after meeting death? Death changes you, how can it not? But nobody knows, except those who have gone through it, what that change is. You cross a threshold and enter a region of utter hopelessness. I've got into it, I'm trapped in it, I can't get out. I try, but it's impossible. How can I live like this? How long will I live this way? And what for, oh God, what for?

Words have scooped out a great hole inside me and grief pours out of this with the force of a tidal wave. I am sobbing, I can hear my own sobs, I can feel hands patting me on the back, I feel an arm going about me . . .

I draw back fiercely, thrusting the arm, the person, away, crying, 'No! No!'

And then I see it's Hari, his face twisted in pain, holding his injured arm, the arm I've pushed away with such violence . . .

He looks at me for a moment, on the verge of speech, then goes away without speaking, leaving me to myself.

'Are you all right, Kaku?' Lata asks me. Has she done something to hurt me? Has Hari? If they have done anything wrong—unintentionally, of course—I should scold them, I have the right to do that, I can shout at them, I can be angry. But I must forgive them, they have the right to ask for that, haven't they?

Lata's anxiety and her concern about me push their way through these light, trying-to-be-casual words. I understand her distress, but there's no way I can respond, except with the meaningless patter of 'I'm okay, there's no problem, no, really, there isn't, don't worry, it has nothing to do with Hari and you . . .'

I can see from her face that she's hurt. She thinks my words are a distancing, a rejection of her. But what else can I say? And it is true that this has nothing to do with Hari or with her. The problem lies in me. It's my own self I hate, my own face I can't bear to see in the mirror. It's not only that I imagined something that wasn't there—Hari's touch was the touch of compassion, no more than that—it's my own response that has shaken me. My body's almost Pavlovian response to his touch. I try to be reasonable, to tell myself that it was merely the body reminding me of its existence, like it does when I draw back from touching the copper boiler. I ask myself, am I not making the same mistake Som did, am I not giving the body's actions more importance than I should? I know I should put this response away, where it belongs, among all those other spurts of desire for anonymous male bodies. Men do this better, they're better at dealing with the needs of their bodies, they accept it as natural, as part of our human identity.

But it's hard to convince myself and even harder to say these things to Lata. I retreat into myself instead, I spend more time out of the house. I prefer to be with Bai, her room has become a kind of refuge for me. She's the one person who won't ask me any questions, who won't be hurt by my words, or my silences, either. She sleeps most of the time, short naps into which she keeps dropping, conceding, it seems to me, these little bits to that final great sleep, keeping it at bay with these morsels. She moves almost imperceptibly from one state to another, drifting between sleep and waking so lightly, so easily, that they seem the same. Yet, there are times when she comes out of the blankness to an agitation, a wild burbling that makes no sense. I wonder then whether there's something she is trying to say, or whether it's just a frantic panicking, a wild flailing of wings at being trapped in a cage of non-understanding, of helplessness. Anything is possible in that mind where words finally have lost their place and only images, formless images, are left.

One day she makes a small gesture, a slight raising of a hand, an uplifted look, the eyes coming back then to rest on her own wasted body, her own dying self. Is she asking—where is God? Where is that God who has done this to me?

'There must be Heaven or we must despair, for life seems bitter, brief, blank.'

Charlotte Bronte's words, which I came upon, not through Joe, but on my own. And when I did, I remembered all those graves and thought: what choice did she have but to cling on desperately to a belief in God? A God in Heaven looking after us, God, that last resort of humankind. But that comfort is not for me, I've never had it. I've believed in people—how could I not, living as I did with Leela and Joe? But I lost this faith when I saw the cruelty of the mobs, all those faceless men who cold-bloodedly planned the death of innocents. Bai didn't believe in God, either—she has never said this, she doesn't have to, her refusal to sing bhajans tells me this as clearly as if she has confessed it to me. But Bai believed in herself. And she has her music. Unresponsive as she seems now to almost everything, she responds, even if minimally, to the music that drifts into the room. Once, it is Abhay's voice that brings on an agitation in her. It seems to me that she is asking, 'Who is that?'

'It's Abhay, Bai. Abhay, Hasina's student.'

It means nothing to her. Another day, when we hear Hasina's voice, I see tears in Bai's eyes. She makes a small sideways movement of her head and the tears run down the sides of her face into her hair.

What are those tears for? Is she remembering something from her past? Are there some memories still intact inside that damaged brain? Or is it just the beauty of Hasina's voice, the music itself?

There is no regeneration in the brain and the heart—these are the two seats of death. The cells once dead are dead forever.

Joe's words which Som and Chandru recalled with laughter, laughing at themselves for having chosen these two 'hopeless' specialities. No regeneration in the heart and the mind? But here's Bai moved to tears by music. How do we know in what hidden crevices they lurk, our dreams, our thoughts, our loves, our fears? How do we know that they don't continue to exist, concealing themselves, guarding themselves from the blows that come, from the blood vessels that burst? How do we know?

Naada Brahma Swara Ishwara.

Hasina's voice, Hasina teaching her students, the children repeating the words after her, their voices following the trajectory of hers.

Naada Brahma Swara Ishwara.

The sound is Brahma, the note is God. The sound and the note—the beginning of the world. And the word? What about it?

'You must sing, Hasina, you must do it for Bai,' I have been saying to Hasina like all the others. But Hasina is unrelenting. And Lata is certain the solution lies with me. 'Write the article, Kaku,' she says. 'Once people know what this programme means to us in Bhavanipur, once people read about how many Muslims have sung in this temple, it'll be different. Just you see!'

The word is important, the word matters. Lata's belief.

If we think we can influence people for the worse, why can't we believe they can be influenced for good?

Tony's belief, which Lata is echoing.

To both of them, the word is the flashing sword, the flaming torch, the disperser of darkness and ignorance, the bestower of knowledge.

Do I believe this? I don't know. But I want Hasina to have her chance. I want her to sing in the temple where Bai once sang in her Guruji's memory, where Bai's Guruji himself sang the glory of the goddess every evening and where his disciples gathered every year to remember him. Hasina, Bai's disciple—keeping her name alive, continuing Bai's musical existence. Hasina must sing there. If there is the smallest chance that I can help, I must do it.

Lata and I leave home early in the morning. In a kind of unspoken agreement we haven't told anyone, except Hari, about our going. Nor do we speak on the way of my last aborted visit. Lata asks no questions about the accident, but obviously she knows where it happened, for once we're past the spot, she relaxes, she begins to point out the sights to me. There's the railway station where Bai got off and walked through the fields to Guruji's house. No fields now, of course. A cotton ginning factory, instead, which explains the bits of white fluff on the electric wires overhead and on the bushes, giving them a kind of bedraggled Christmas tree effect. We enter the railway station, deserted now since the little railway line was abandoned. The stone exterior still has some dignity, as also the softened beauty of aging stone. The British bestowed dignity on whatever they built, they built things to last. I say this aloud to Lata, but Lata, a child of independent India, is not interested. To her, the British and their rule are a part of history books, as distant as the Mughals and the Marathas. However intact it seems from the outside, inside the place is encrusted with bird droppings—we can hear the frenzied flutter of wings the moment we enter—and strewn with rags and plastic bags left behind by homeless people who've spent the night here.

The road curves along a lake and once past it the hills appear before us. 'There was gold in those hills once,' Lata says. 'It was only a small—what do you call it? Vein? Anyway, there was not much and it was soon over. But the boys used to come here searching for gold, they used to boast they'd found it. As kids we were stupid enough to believe them. We thought . . . Look! There's the temple, Kaku.'

It's a small building, looking even smaller against the backdrop of the hills. Lata parks her scooter under the peepul tree, we wash our feet at the tap outside and walking through the narrow doorway, step down into the courtyard. The branches of the peepul tree cover the courtyard and loom over the temple, as the hills seemed to do when we saw it from a distance. The main shrine is right in the centre of the courtyard. It's significant, I've been told, not for its architectural beauty or its antiquity, but because it has been a place of uninterrupted worship for nearly a hundred years. Built by Ravi's great-grandfather, it has, since the beginning, been the family's responsibility and pride.

It's quiet inside, the cooing of the birds mingling in a muted harmony with the murmur of human voices. Lata is silent, confronting, I imagine, her memories. But it's impossible for her to contain them within herself for long; she begins to speak, to share her memories with me. As a child, she used to come here with her mother, who visited the place every Friday. 'My mother never missed a visit and until I got into a proper school, nor did I.' I think of her running about the courtyard, circumambulating the shrine, like some children are now doing. But Lata's links to the temple go back to even before her birth. Her mother came here when she was pregnant for the third time, praying to Bhavani for a son after two daughters. Instead, there was Lata. Lata smiles cheekily as she tells me this.

The priest comes out of the shrine when he sees us. Lata greets him, she speaks to him with the intimacy of an old friend. 'We were in school together,' she tells me when I join them. 'We were in the same class. He was a brilliant scholar, he got a rank in his S.S.C., but instead of going to college like all of us, he went off to Benaras, to the Sanskrit University, and came back to become a priest. Now, he's a saint and he doesn't want to talk to sinners like me. Isn't that so,

Shrinivasacharya?' She pronounces the name with a deliberate, verging-on the-impertinent formality.

The priest, a grave, unsmiling man gives her a reproving look and says something to her in Kannada, remonstrating with her, I think. She laughs. He turns to me and speaking in chaste Hindi, says, 'This girl still hasn't grown up. She's just like she was in school.'

She offers him our bag of offerings and he goes away. I can hear the crack of the coconut. He returns, lights the lamp and begins the aarti.

Like all dark stone goddesses, Bhavani is beautiful. Each time the lamp lights up her face and focuses on the kumkum on the forehead, on the gleaming jewels and the eyes, I think of the goddess riding triumphantly in her palki on the shoulders of men, I see the flickering lights and shadows on her face, I imagine Guruji's voice raised in adoring devotion. The aarti over, Lata goes off with the priest—she has to meet his mother, she tells me—and I go round the temple. There are very few people inside. Only one large group, actually, who are now on the pillared veranda that runs along the outer wall. They've just performed a puja and are getting ready for breakfast. Or is it lunch? I see that the banana leaves being laid down are the large-sized ones. But only a few leaves are being placed, certainly not enough for the whole group. And then I notice, with a heart-stopping pang, a mother and child sitting down before one of the leaves and I know it's an *upanayanam*. This is the *matru-bhojan*. I don't want to watch, I can't see this, but I seem rooted to the spot. The boy—he's just about eight or nine—looks self-conscious and awkward in his dhoti and bare chest, unhappy about something—maybe, the head-shaving that is soon to follow. He's sitting next to his mother, a few other children clustered round them. I'm a little surprised by their seriousness, their solemnity. There's no joking, no teasing of the boy. They're trying to persuade the boy to sit on his mother's lap. He's reluctant, but he does so finally, perching himself on the very edge of her silky lap. Mother and son. The son being babied for the last time, being fed by his mother for the last time before he enters the world of men. The last time the mother can claim him as her child before letting him go.

But I didn't, I never let go, I held on, until he was taken away from me.

'Shall we go, Kaku?'

Lata takes me round the place. There was once a mango orchard behind the temple, she says. Now there is a row of houses, built for those who are working in the temple. The aura of sanctity and the murmur of mantras gives way to a cosy domesticity, to the mundane sounds of vessels being scrubbed and clothes being washed. Guruji's house was beyond the orchard, but like the orchard, it too no longer exists. We go up to the lake. Beyond it is the highway, and we can see the traffic rushing along. The sounds come to us from across the lake like the sounds in a dream, an illusion of activity we're shut out of.

'It's a pity we can't stay till evening. That's when it's most beautiful. The evening aarti is somehow magical. It's so peaceful and quiet and when they ring the bell, the echoes come back from the hills. They light lamps all along the wall and around the shrine; it looks really wonderful.'

When we get back to the temple after visiting the priest's home—his mother asked Lata to take me there—the *upanayanam* group is still there. They're getting ready for lunch, the real meal this time, not the ritual one. Lata goes to the priest to get our prasad and I see him introduce Lata to one of the women. They converse for a few moments, then come up to me.

'They want us to have lunch with them—if it's all right with you, Kaku?'

The woman seconds the invitation with a smile; she's been told, obviously, that I can't speak Kannada. I nod and she goes

313

back to arrange our plates. Lata gets into conversation with the woman next to her during lunch, and I marvel again at the ease with which she is able to reach even a stranger. I guess that they're discovering links between their families and I'm right. Lata, who turns to me every now and then, sharing the information she has, tells me they are distantly related. As I listen to Lata speaking to the other women, to me, I'm filled with wonder and pleasure at the ease with which she negotiates her way through the network of links. Once I hear Lata clucking her tongue sympathetically and she tells me, at the first opportunity she gets, that there has been a death in the family. Therefore the small, unostentatious ceremony, therefore the sombre mood.

The moment lunch is over, the child who's had his *upanayanam* races to the place where they've piled their bags and picking up one, pulls out some clothes. He's eager, I can see, to change out of his dhoti, to get back into the clothes which will allow him to run about, to be a child again. A woman goes to him and begins to remonstrate with him, she tries to take the bag from him. He holds on to it obstinately, his body and his face speaking the language of obstinacy and resistance. Suddenly it comes to me: *this* is the boy's mother, not the one on whose lap he'd sat during the *matru-bhojan*. I realize now what was wrong with that earlier mother-and-child picture, how stiff and formal it was, with none of the curlicues that add life to a picture. This woman's face has the tinge of melancholy that hints at a recent sorrow, and this, as well as the simplicity of her sari and lack of jewels, tells me whose death it is they're mourning. She senses my look on her, she says something to the boy who listens, forgetting his tussle for the bag. He gives me a wary, under-his-lashes look, but obediently follows his mother when she comes to me.

'Give him your blessings,' she says to me. And to him, 'Do your namaskar and ask for her blessings.'

I can understand what she's saying, even if I don't know all the words. Obediently the boy lets himself down in a namaskar at my feet, the skinny body straight as an arrow, the scapular bones, like two wings on either side, slanted like those of a bird in flight, the newly-shaven head giving him the look of a fledgling bird. He gets up swiftly in almost the same movement. I touch him on the head.

What do I say? *Ayushman bhava? Chirayu bhava?*

May you live long. But what blessing can contend against our mortality? Mustard seeds to protect us from evil, blessings to confer long life—nothing works. And yet we go on. Simple remedies? No, they're desperate remedies and we go on with them because, in truth, there is nothing else.

'*Sukhi bhava,*' I say finally to the child.

Som's father's usual words of blessing. 'Be happy'. That's possible, that's something we can hope to have some control over.

'What's your name?'

'Bhaskar.'

He gives his mother an appealing look; with a smile she relinquishes the bag to him. He flees with it and in a few moments is a child like the rest, racing about, climbing the tree, holding his cap firmly on his head to protect his bare skull.

'You know Kannada?' she asks me in Hindi.

'A little. I'm learning it from Lata.' I reply in Kannada.

'We were very happy you shared our lunch,' she says with a smile—she has a beautiful smile—a smile that takes the cold formality off the words, and goes away.

I watch her retreating back and think: so many of us walking this earth with our pain, our sorrow concealed within ourselves, so many of us hiding our suffering, going about as if all is well, so many of us surviving our loss, our grief. It's a miracle, nothing less than a miracle.

315

19

Rekha is with us. Tony was to come as well, 'but as usual, something turned up,' Rekha says with a smile. 'And so, here I am on my own.' Her arrival adds the necessary edge of excitement that guests give an occasion. I felt a slight tinge of it in Bai's house too when I was there in the morning, in spite of the subduing influence of Bai's condition.

We leave home nearly an hour before the music is to begin since Rekha wants to see the temple and to spend some time there. While Rekha goes around the temple, gives her offerings for her puja and stands for a while absorbed in prayer, Lata and I watch the lamps being lit around the temple. 'It's very beautiful,' Lata had said and so it is. Not the lights alone, but the musical ringing of the bell during the aarti, the Devi stotra that Shrinivas, Lata's friend, chants while the aarti is being done. It's the Shankaracharya shlokas in praise of Annapurna that he recites, a tradition in this temple, Lata tells me.

When we go into the courtyard, a makeshift auditorium today, almost all the chairs are occupied. Hari has kept our seats for us. Shrinivas joins us in a while, nearly unrecognizable now that he has changed out of his priestly attire into a pyjama-kurta. After all the fears and the threats, it seems peaceful, just an ordinary audience waiting to enjoy an evening of music.

'There won't be any trouble,' Ravi has been saying confidently, and it looks like he's right. 'Thanks to your article,' he said to me, but that's not true, he's just being polite. Possibly, Hasina changed her mind because of what I wrote, but as for the rest, everyone knows that Ravi has been working in many ways, using both his influence and money. And of course, there is his knowledge of this town and its people. It was for this that he came back home, I think now, as I watch him look over the audience. It was for this control and power that he gave up a successful career in a prosperous country; gave up his marriage too, as Lata tells me he had to, his wife being reluctant to live in Bhavanipur.

The function begins without any fuss—just Ravi introducing Hasina and her team. They're grouped on the dais, the way I've often seen them at home, Hasina sitting cross-legged, almost in Padmasana, her eyes fixed on her hands in her lap, as if she's meditating or praying. After Ravi's introduction, there's absolute silence for a moment; when it stretches, the audience shifts restlessly and there's the usual burst of muted coughing and throat clearing. And then Hasina, drawing the mike to herself, speaks. Briefly, she speaks of her Guru, Savitribai, and of her grandfather, Ghulam Saab, her first Guru. The way she brings their names together, publicly, it's like an answer to the question I asked her when my article appeared in the paper: 'You don't mind my having referred to your grandfather's relationship with Bai?'

'Why should I? It happened, it's true.'

Again a moment of silence, then Hasina, with a glance at her accompanists, begins and the audience sits up with a start. For she is beginning with a prayer, the same Devi stotra we'd heard Shrinivas recite earlier. Hasina sings it on her own, without any instruments accompanying her, and I remember Bai telling me how different the Ramraksha had seemed to her when her mother sang it. Hasina's voice rises with that strange haunting quality the unaccompanied human voice has. When she reaches the words '*bhiksham dehi*'—give me alms—at the end of every stanza, it is taut, like a silver string, and my hair stands on end.

The slight nervousness with which Hasina began slowly

gives way to confidence a little while after she embarks on her first raaga. This composed woman—is she the same woman whose ice-cold hands had grasped mine convulsively when we were parting in the morning? Her ease communicates itself to the entire group and in a while they are in it together, relaxed now, speaking their own language of nods, smiles and gestures, communicating with each other, scarcely aware, it seems, of the audience before them. Yet essentially they are performing for us, it is to us that they are speaking, it is our attention they want, our responses that they are calling for. Hasina lets Abhay take over a number of times and as always, his voice, mature and confident, so much at variance with his innocent startled-bird look, takes me by surprise. By the time she comes to the end of the raaga, the crowd has been converted by some alchemy into an intimate group, we are part of the conversation they are carrying on. The hills give us the music back in an eerie lingering echo, which, without being a distraction, merges into the original sound. The stars are out and the sky is the midnight blue of Rekha's sari. It is getting chilly. Lata, her feet up, is snuggling in Hari's arms, she makes a slight movement when I look at her. Hari tightens his hold, I laugh, and she puts out her tongue at me.

As Hasina sings the Malkauns, which she does in a meditative, reflective mood, I remember her at her namaaz. She is giving this the same intense concentration that she gives the physical motions of prayer, she brings the same total absorption to this raaga that she brings to her prayers. I think of Ketaki on the evening of her wedding, looking at herself in the mirror, looking beyond the image to a distant future. Ketaki, I know it now, weighed down with the knowledge of her own destiny, seeing it, moving towards it. So it is for Hasina now; this is the beginning of a journey for her. These decisive moments don't happen often, they don't come to everyone, but for Hasina it is here, the moment that is going to change her life. Abhay, sitting a little in the shadows, watching her intently, knows this, as do the twins.

It is well past midnight when one of the twins announces in Kannada that Hasina will sing a bhajan. An Akka Mahadevi *vachana.*

Bai never sang bhajans. 'I'm not a tamasha woman trying to seduce my customers by dancing the way they want me to,' she said. Now her student Hasina, a Muslim woman, sings this poem, composed centuries ago by a woman, a Hindu woman, whose entire life was a statement of her faith. The anxious proprietary looks of the twins tell me that it is they who have given her this song, they are wondering how she will handle it. There has been a murmur from the crowd when the announcement was made. These people know this song, it is in their language, the poet and her words are a part of their lives. There is a kind of ruffled movement amidst the crowd when she begins that tells me of their familiarity with the words, of their response to them. Hasina has prepared well, her pronunciation is perfect, and so too, I see, is her understanding of the words. 'I saw a dream, I saw a dream,' she sings, affirming the vision over and over again. Each time Hasina utters the words, she brings out a different emotion through the changing combination of notes—ecstasy, wonder, awe, quiet acceptance, revelation. It seems to me that it's not the dead poet's dream alone that Hasina is singing of, but her own as well, the dream for which she has given up so much, including, she hinted once, a marriage. She's speaking of my dreams too, so many of them, all woven about Adit. And Som's dreams for his son. It's all over now, there are no more dreams left for me, for either of us. Rekha senses my agitation, she puts her arm about me, she holds my hand tight.

It's nearly dawn when Hasina comes to the end. Already the sky shows the pearly luminosity of the coming daylight in a corner. 'That was beautiful,' Rekha says repeatedly on our way home. She uses the word 'surekh'—Leela's favourite word, the word she used so often, Leela, who lived most of her life in a chawl among sooty mills and shit-pocked roads, among men and women who had little beauty in their lives.

We are drooping with weariness when we get home. Rekha's face, so lively when we left, is heavy and dark. But it seems impossible to separate, to break the thread that has linked us for the last few hours. We sit at the dining table, yawning loudly and repeatedly, dragging the words out of ourselves. Lata's head droops on the table. Hari gives up trying to persuade her to go to bed. 'I'll make some tea for us,' he says and goes in. As if a spell has been broken, Rekha gets up and disappears into her room. I'm trying to make the effort to stir myself, when I hear the sound of a car stopping, of a door banging. Hasina enters in a flurry of silk, her body as taut as an arrow. She doesn't seem to be touching the earth.

She comes directly to me. 'I couldn't go home without seeing you,' she says and puts her arms about me. We embrace, not cheek to cheek, but looking over each other's shoulders, an ancient salutation that came from those lands, perhaps, where you looked for concealed weapons. But Hasina and I have nothing to conceal. She draws away, murmuring, 'I must go, Baiji is alone,' and walks swiftly out. Lata, who's woken up, is looking in bewilderment at the vanishing figure, Rekha in her wrapper comes out at the same moment, as does Hari with the tea. Suddenly we are awake, animated. We drink our tea and discuss Hasina's performance. The tarana—wasn't it great? So joyous. And the twins—did anyone know they were so good? And Abhay—what a voice! He's got a great future. And thank God there was no trouble, thank God it was peaceful. While we speak of these things, we are in reality speaking of the experience we've shared, a night of music that may never happen again.

'Breakfast anyone?' Lata asks. Yes, everyone is hungry. The aroma of hot oil and of curry leaves roasting in it, the splutter of mustard seeds—these things float out to me with the promise of food. Sleeplessness has honed my receptivity to a fine point and all the smells and sounds come to my heightened sense of awareness loaded with significance, with memories.

When we finally part, going to our rooms to get a little sleep, Rekha gives me a letter. 'From Som,' she says.

I take it to my room and put it on the table without opening it. This is not the time, I think, and fall asleep instantly.

20

B ai has gone into a coma. She's been cheated of the 'big one', which, it now seems, will no longer come to her. She is crawling to her death. It could happen any time, the doctor says; on the other hand, she could go on for some more time like this, she could continue to live in the shadowy land between life and death. I can no longer wait for it to happen, stay on and share Bai's final moments with Hasina. Bai's death is almost a non-event anyway—a happening of no importance, a by-the-way. It is her life which is important and that is more with me—in the papers, tapes and photographs I am taking back with me—than in her near-moribund body.

This is my last day in Bhavanipur. Lying in bed, waiting for the day to break, I remember my first morning here when I woke up in a strange house to the thought of living with two absolute strangers. I think of the voices I heard that morning, voices raised in a choric harmony that woke me out of my uneasy, troubled sleep. I never heard them again, I don't know who they were, why they went past this road and what they were singing. I will never know now and I am no longer curious, either. Some mysteries have to remain unsolved, some answers will never come.

I can hear the sounds of Hari and Lata moving about, speaking to each other in low tones. I know they are awake too, as restless as I am, troubled by the thought of my leaving. Lata broke down at dinner last night, suddenly bursting into tears and then shamefacedly recovering.

'I'm sorry, Kaku. I told you, I can't help it, tears just come— it's the thought that—you won't be here with us tomorrow . . .

the house will feel so empty.'

I hold her hand and wipe her tears while Hari watches her silently, a look of brooding tenderness on his face. I will always remember this moment, I will think of Hari, remember this look on his face—the thought slips into my mind. And I know I have moved on, this is already becoming the past.

'It will be a year now'—Som's letter begins with this stark statement. He does not have to specify what he is speaking of. And for the first time, Som has said, 'Come home. We need to be together at this time.'

Som is not a great believer in rituals, though his family is scrupulous about them. I don't know whether they will have any ritual for this first anniversary of Adit's death, whether it needs to be done at all for a boy of Adit's age. But I know that Som is not referring to these things, I know what he means.

We need to be together, we need to mourn him together, we need to face the fact of his death and our continuing life together. Only in this is healing possible. I think of how Tony and I, when we speak of Joe and Leela, bring them back into our lives for a while. Som and I will have to do this for Adit, *only* Som and I can do it for him; between the two of us, we can recreate him, we can invoke his presence and make his existence real. And then, maybe, we can have our own ceremony, Som and I, we can wash away the darkness and ugliness, not only of Adit's death, but of what happened before, with our own oblations of sesame seeds and water.

I've often wondered at parents who write of their dead children, of their illness, their suffering and death, making, I've thought, a sob story of it for public consumption. It has seemed distasteful to me, a kind of exhibitionism, this public display of a private sorrow. Now I am beginning to understand. It's not just living children who need to be free, the dead clamour for release as well.

'May this life enter into the immortal breath, may this body end in ashes. Remember, O Intelligence, remember.'

The ancient prayer comes back to me and I think, *yes, remember, remember.*

'It hasn't gone anywhere, your life with your father is still there, it'll never go away.'

Joe's words. It was just a few days after my father's death. 'Come,' Joe said to me, coming home unexpectedly in the middle of the day. He took me out for a drive and he drove on until we came to the sea. He stopped the car then and we stood in silence, watching the monsoon waves swell and surge towards us in an unending rhythm of thunderous sound. The rain had let up for a while, but the sky was brooding, heavy with more rain, and the sea, its thirst unappeased as yet, seemed to be reaching up for it. A silent figure was walking along the shore, looking steadily down, as if searching intently for something, uncaring of the waves which dashed against his legs and climbed up to his knees. All three of us, inhabiting the same solitude, linked by the same silence. Joe suddenly spoke then, saying to me, 'It hasn't gone anywhere, your life with your father. It's all still there.'

Some kind of an understanding came to me then, an understanding that came to me from the glory of the sea and the clouds, from Joe's presence beside me, even from the silent man absorbed in his own solitude. And I, sore with the pain of my father's death, with the disruption of my entire life, had felt a kind of healing in the words.

How could I have ever longed for amnesia? Memory, capricious and unreliable though it is, ultimately carries its own truth within it. As long as there is memory, there's always the possibility of retrieval, as long as there is memory, loss is never total.